ALSO BY THE AUTHOR

Untouchable

Among Wolves

HALF
WORLD

A NOVEL

To Sharon —

SCOTT O'CONNOR

Simon & Schuster
New York   London   Toronto   Sydney   New Delhi

90

Simon & Schuster
1230 Avenue of the Americas
New York, NY 10020

First Simon & Schuster hardcover edition February 2014

SIMON & SCHUSTER and colophon are registered trademarks of Simon & Schuster, Inc.

For information about special discounts for bulk purchases, please contact Simon & Schuster Special Sales at 1-866-506-1949 or business@simonandschuster.com.

The Simon & Schuster Speakers Bureau can bring authors to your live event. For more information or to book an event contact the Simon & Schuster Speakers Bureau at 1-866-248-3049 or visit our website at www.simonspeakers.com.

Interior design by Jill Putorti

Jacket design by Christopher Lin

Manufactured in the United States of America

10 9 8 7 6 5 4 3 2 1

Library of Congress Cataloging-in-Publication Data

O'Connor, Scott.
 Half World : A Novel / Scott O'Connor.
   pages cm
 1. Psychological fiction. I. Title.
 PS3615.C595H35 2014
 813'.6—dc23
 2013024016

ISBN 978-1-4767-1659-6
ISBN 978-1-4767-1661-9 (ebook)

For my father

And ye shall know the truth, and the truth shall make you free.

—JOHN 8:32

And ye shall know the truth, and the truth shall make you free.

—INSCRIPTION AT THE ENTRANCE TO CENTRAL INTELLIGENCE AGENCY
HEADQUARTERS, LANGLEY, VIRGINIA

HALF
WORLD

The way the Devil Reads the Bible
[Interprets]

ACROSS COUNTRY

They drove west. Arlington to Charleston, West Virginia. Charleston to Lexington, Kentucky. Henry had purchased a new leather-bound ledger and in it he wrote the dates and distances traveled, what he and Ginnie spent on gas, meals, motel rooms. Seventy-six miles to Louisville. Eighty-one miles to Jasper, Indiana. Seven dollars at the Pine Needles Motel. Six dollars at the Apple Tree Lodge in Carmi, Illinois.

The station wagon jostled along the imperfectly paved county routes, the local thoroughfares. A brown Chevrolet, their first new car in ten years, since just after Hannah was born. A pair of suitcases strapped to the top, the back filled to the ceiling with crates and boxes, all of the clothes and silverware and china that Ginnie hadn't wanted to leave for the movers.

In the rearview mirror Henry checked on Hannah and Thomas in the backseat. Thomas seemed content, for the most part; Hannah less so. She was unhappy about the move, having to leave school before the end of sixth grade, abandoning her friends, the house in Arlington, the high-ceilinged bedroom she loved. She sulked, watching her reflection in the windows, the landscape pulling across the length of the car, the ticking away of each town that took her farther from home.

Carmi to St. Louis, St. Louis to Joplin. They celebrated Thomas's seventh birthday in a roadside diner. Thomas moved along his invisible train tracks to a corner booth where they had hamburgers and milk shakes and a slice of chocolate cake with a line of striped flickering candles. Ginnie had warned the waitresses, but once the cake was presented it was as if they couldn't help themselves, and they burst into a loud, wailing recital of "Happy Birthday." Thomas's hands flew to his ears, he shut his eyes tight, but the waitresses took this as a joke of some kind, a cue to sing louder, and then Thomas was flailing in the booth, swinging his arms, kicking, scattering plates and glasses, sending knives and forks sailing, tines out. Henry and Ginnie were able to grab his wrists and ankles, hold his hands away from the window, keep him immobile. Hannah pulled napkins from the dispenser and cleared glass from the table, out of Thomas's reach. Ginnie whispered in his ear, singing softly. Henry held his son down in the booth, the boy so big, so strong for his age. Sweat from Henry's hands sliding down to Thomas's jackknifing wrists. Pressing into him until it passed, until Thomas had exhausted himself and they were able to carry him to the car and start out on the road again.

In a camera shop in Fort Smith, Arkansas, Henry purchased a used Kodak Signet. He'd never owned a camera before. He told Ginnie it was to document their trip, so they could look back when they were old and forgetful. He took pictures of the scenery, the children in front of the scenery. Hannah pouting or sticking out her tongue. Thomas standing rigid, wary of his father's new device, his hands at his sides, his face without expression, staring at the camera lens, through the camera lens.

The surprise of this seeming indulgence delighted Ginnie. That Henry had finally found a hobby. It had only taken him forty years. It seemed to promise a more relaxed existence the farther they got from Washington. She watched him frame a shot, smiled at the way he approached his new interest, applying to this personal pursuit the same rigid precision he'd always brought to his work. Lifting the camera, leaning in, the lens of his glasses tapping the viewfinder. Taking half a breath, holding it in his chest. She wanted to tell him how happy this made her, but she was careful not to speak while the camera was in front of his face. He startled so easily these days.

Henry recorded the specifics of each shot he took in the ledger, the type of film, the shutter speed and aperture, the lighting conditions. He kept the ledger in the glove box and every evening in the motel Ginnie read the page aloud, an account of their day in numbers and lists, clipped phrases.

April 2, 1956. Monday. 96 miles. Partly sunny. No wind. Aperture, F3.5. Dinner, $1.90. Motel room, $6.49.

When Henry had come home with the news of his reassignment, Ginnie had taken it upon herself to devise the route west. She'd sat at the kitchen table in Arlington with the *Rand McNally* and a sharpened pencil, plotting points, connecting dots. She'd found the major cities first, then the smaller towns in between, what looked like a good day's drive. Stretches of highway that a vacation guidebook said were particularly beautiful that time of year. Three weeks, coast to coast.

Henry wasn't convinced of the need for a family trip. He would have preferred to accomplish the move quickly and cleanly, driving alone, setting up their new lives in California before Ginnie and the children arrived. But Ginnie did not want him to travel by himself. A year ago, she might have considered it, but after the incident in Washington, she couldn't let him go. She pictured him lost, adrift in the mountains, in the desert, and so she set about to convince him to decide otherwise.

When she was finished with the route, she left the map out for him on the kitchen table, where he would find it in the morning. She knew he could be persuaded by a well-made plan.

There was a small identification tag hanging from the neck strap of the Signet, and while changing film in the car outside Baton Rouge, Hannah pointed out that she had written his name on the paper inside. *Mr. Henry March.* On the address line she had written *Arlington, Virginia,* then had crossed that out and written *Oakland, California* in smaller letters above. Henry thanked her, and then quietly, at their next stop, slipped the paper from the tag and flushed it in the filling-station restroom.

Shreveport to Opelousas. Opelousas to Oklahoma City. Ginnie with the ledger on one of the twin beds in the motel room. Hannah in the other bed, Thomas on the floor with a sheet and a pillow, finally asleep after another bath-time breakdown. Henry with his coffee and cigarettes in the chair by the window. *Kodak Tri-X, 400 speed.* Ginnie's voice in the room, her soft, southern lilt. *Cloudy skies. Slight northwesterly breeze.*

They called him the Mutual Man, younger officers, older officers, after the featureless Mutual of Omaha adjusters who came to Washington periodically to investigate claims or explain benefits. Right-angled and exact in his manner, his movements. Nondescript in appearance, his suit the color of the sidewalk outside.

Their jokes masked their uncertainty. Henry's colleagues found him inscrutable. He was a grudging socializer, a rare participant in after-hours drinks or weekend cocktail parties. He had only a handful of friends in the organization, most kept at arm's length. He did not have the same background, the social connections, the family money. He was a foreigner in class terms.

He had never tried to be liked. The nature of his department's work made this impossible. Finding leaks and weaknesses. Finding the unfaithful, the untrue. Finding those whose loyalty had lapsed, or was never there to begin with. His job was to distrust his colleagues, and so they distrusted him in return. There was only one man Henry had been allowed to trust, whom he had trusted for almost fifteen years, and that man had turned out to be the most faithless of them all.

They were sending him west to keep him away from the agency's vital organs. Moving him to the periphery, the fingertip of the country. He had seen this happen before, to others. He had been the man to send others away. He knew the danger in keeping a damaged individual so close to the company's heart.

What had happened was not something they could look past. With another officer, possibly, but not with him. For Henry to be of value to the organization, his integrity had to be beyond reproach. If that was no longer the case, then all that was left was his sense of duty, his willingness to follow orders.

Gallup, New Mexico, to Williams, Arizona. Henry used three rolls of film at the Grand Canyon. Shots of Hannah, annoyed and impatient, standing against a guardrail. Shots of Thomas, oblivious to the magnificent sight around him, more interested in the tourist train pulling into the station on the other side of the parking lot. Shots of Ginnie beside the Chevrolet with a demure smile, hands on her hips, her auburn curls standing in the wind.

Ginnie held Henry's hand while she slept, while he lay on his back and stared at what he could see of the ceiling, the dark room around him. He had never slept more than a few hours a night and now he slept even less. Back in Arlington he would have walked the house, the yard, smoked, fixed himself a cup of coffee, the day's work still in his head, trying to untangle a personality, a web of connections. All of the documentation would be back in the safe in his office, but he never needed the paperwork once he'd read through it an initial time. He kept the facts in his head. The facts, the half facts, the outright deceptions. He walked the yard, he sat in the living room, assembling pieces, solving a riddle. Here though, in a motel room in Williams, in Oklahoma City, in Alamagordo, he stayed in bed, looked at the ceilings, the small dark rings of water damage, the bare patches where the paint came away in tiny chips. There was only one riddle now, but he did not know where to begin to untangle it.

At the end of the third week they reached Oakland, the house on the hill that had been rented for them. Three bedrooms and a small den where Ginnie could paint. Henry parked the Chevrolet in the driveway, and they all stepped out and stretched. Thomas chugged into the house along his imagined tracks. Hannah walked in the front door and burst into tears. Henry cleared out what remained in the car: sheaves of paper the children had filled with backseat drawings, the ledger, the Signet's instruction manual, the box of exposed film. He set the drawings on the floor in the dining room, where the table would eventually sit. He placed the ledger and the box of film in his briefcase and set the locks.

That first night, after Hannah and Thomas were in their sleeping bags in their new rooms, Henry looked for Ginnie in the dark, unfamiliar house. He finally found her outside, standing on the front lawn, looking down the hill to the bay and the bridge. Breathing deeply, her eyes heavy. The salt air was warm and light. She whispered his name, calling him to her. She took his hand and they stood and watched the black water, the lights of the city beyond.

"This is where we begin," she said. She squeezed his hand. "This is where we begin again."

PART ONE

Telegraph Hill

1

San Francisco, Spring 1956

The landlady opened the door and led him into the apartment he'd tele-phoned about, the rooms above the mechanics' garage on Telegraph Hill. She stood to the side while Henry walked to the far end of the liv-ing room and looked out the windows through the last of the morning fog. Alcatraz to the north, the bridge and the bay and the black hills to the east. A beautiful corner view. He would need to cover it.

He held his hat in one hand, his briefcase in the other. The bright-ness through the windows showed every imperfection in the room, the scuffed wood, the scratched baseboards. There was a nearly matching sofa and armchair, a vase of dusty plastic flowers on the coffee table, a wooden crate of LPs by the bedroom door. The landlady said that a pair of young women had lived there most recently, working girls, secretaries down-town, and that they had left the furniture when they vacated the apart-ment two months before. Henry asked if there was any chance that they would return for their belongings and the landlady assured him that there was none. The girls had sailed off to Asia with a pair of merchant marines.

The landlady's name was Mrs. Barberis. A widow, she said, God rest her husband's soul. Henry asked her about the mechanics, and she told him that they had been renting the garage for as long as she'd owned the building. They kept to themselves, and so did she. She had moved out of the city after her husband passed and she rarely came back, preferring

the rent be sent by mail, that the tenant handle any necessary maintenance or repair. She asked Henry if this was acceptable, that she would
be an absentee landlord, and he told her that it was.

The kitchen was to his left. There was a Formica-topped table with
three vinyl-padded chairs, a stove and a white refrigerator that looked like
the model Ginnie had bought for the house in Arlington. There was a pair
of small windows above the sink and a larger, lower window that led out
to a fire escape. Henry leaned out, looked down three floors to the alley.
A Negro mechanic in a blue jumpsuit stood there, smoking a cigarette, the
bald oval at the crown of his head shining in the midmorning sun.

He had spent his first week walking the streets of the city. Every morning after breakfast, he left the house and drove across the bridge into
San Francisco. He walked in loops around the financial district, gradually widening his radius until he could form an accurate picture of each
street, the connections between them. Ten, twenty blocks a day. Only
then would he move farther. He had a map, but he rarely used it. He
needed to know the place in his own way. He had been taught not to
work within a landscape that he didn't understand.

He opened a bank account with the two letters of recommendation
he'd been given before he left Washington. He had never heard of either
of the recommending businessmen whose signatures closed the letters.
He wasn't sure if the men existed or if they existed only enough to open
a bank account. Once it was open, he deposited the check he'd brought
with him and sent the account number back east.

His new name was printed at the top of the bank letters. He wrote the
name in his ledger. He repeated the name to himself while he walked the
city. He repeated it at night in the house in Oakland as he circled sleep,
knowing that the last thing on his mind at the end of the day would be
the first thought he woke to in the morning. Sitting up in bed with the
name on his lips, surrounding himself with the name while he shaved and
washed and dressed, while he kissed Ginnie and Hannah and Thomas
good-bye, while he drove into the city and walked the unfamiliar streets.

*   *   *

The bedroom was small, dimly lit. There was a single window above the alleyway, two twin beds, a dresser standing against the south wall. Mrs. Barberis pulled the chain for the overhead light, the cord for the ceiling fan. The walls were painted mustard yellow, except for one which was covered with dark-patterned paper, tightly wound floral swirls framing the bathroom doorway.

The toilet flushed and Mrs. Barberis gave a proud nod. She turned the taps over the sink to demonstrate the water pressure. Henry opened the medicine cabinet, empty except for a bottle of aspirin sitting alone on one of the glass shelves.

He knew no one in the city. Most days he didn't speak to another person except for a brief exchange at a newsstand or a market. He could drive home in the evenings and count the number of words he'd spoken throughout the day.

He repeated the new name as he walked, as he looked for apartments, drank coffee in an automat. He repeated it at the dinner table, silently, while asking Ginnie and Hannah about their days, while helping Thomas cut his meat. He practiced writing the name in the ledger. He let it enter his body, so that after a few days when he stepped onto the bustle of Market Street and passed his reflection in car windows, shop windows, the new name was the only one that identified the man he saw there.

They crossed the small vestibule and Mrs. Barberis showed him the south apartment, which was also available. The two apartments were mirror images of each other, she said, the only difference being that the southern rooms had views of the city, and the northern rooms had views of the bay. He could take his pick, whichever he preferred. She told him that the north apartment was two hundred dollars a month. He asked about the rent for the south apartment and she said that it was the same.

They stepped into the south bedroom. Henry looked up at the molding along the ceiling, down at the baseboards. The rent was due on the first of the month, Mrs. Barberis said. No exceptions. All utilities were paid. He could make alterations to the apartment, within reason. New paint, new drapes, carpet, whatever he liked.

He stood at the wall that was shared with the bedroom in the north apartment. He touched the paint with a fingertip, as if determining a place to hang a picture, and when Mrs. Barberis turned her head to clear her throat, he tapped the wall once, twice, to test its thickness.

At the end of that first week of walking he reached the Embarcadero. Sea level, suddenly. The fisherman's wharves, rows of sailor's bars and flophouses. He turned and looked at the city rising behind him. Off to the side, a concrete tower protruded from a thick grove of trees. He consulted his map. This was Telegraph Hill, high above the waterfront, standing apart, seemingly, from the rest of town. An isolated, private perch.

The next morning he began looking for rooms to rent.

They stood in the vestibule between the two apartments, at the top of the stairs that led down to the front entrance. Henry opened his wallet and began unfolding the bills for the first month's rent. He had two phone numbers on a slip of paper in his wallet. The first number belonged to an electrician and the second, he had been told, belonged to a cop. They had given him the new name and the letters for the bank and the paper with the phone numbers, with the instruction to call the numbers, in the order they were written, once he had secured a location.

Mrs. Barberis produced a small note pad and asked his name and Henry told her and she wrote that on the page, *Mr. Henry Gladwell*. Then she asked him which apartment he would prefer, the north or the south. He passed her the money and told her that he would take both.

2

They were a small unit at the start of the war, a handpicked group of officers working under Arthur Weir, who was only five years Henry's senior but had already established a near-mystical reputation as a genius of counterintelligence. The idea of an organized espionage unit was new to the military, so the group had been sent to London to learn tradecraft from the experts, before being dispatched to Rome to disrupt Mussolini's homeland apparatus and encourage the small but committed underground.

Henry had felt at home in that world immediately. He was surprised by how easily he moved through it. His natural stillness served him well. He could hear amid the noise of war. He could see. He could discern small gestures, whispers and glances, deciphering meaning, piecing together motives and personalities. The way people spoke and didn't speak, this made sense to him. The things they did in secret, the ways in which those secrets could be uncovered and used.

Weir took a special interest in Henry. They spent long evenings discussing their work, and the work yet to come. Weir was an evangelist. He did not see the war as the final word, merely as the end of one era and the beginning of the next. Already there was evidence of movement by the Russians, positioning for the future. Most of Henry's colleagues couldn't wait to get back to the States and resume their interrupted lives, but through Weir, Henry began to see what they were doing as the first clash in a much bigger battle.

They discovered that they had poetry in common, both having studied it in college. To Weir, reading poetry was another way of looking for secrets, of deciphering code. It was proof that their work could be beautiful, an art in and of itself. Eventually, Henry showed Weir some of his own poems, verses no one but Ginnie had seen. For a few days he lived in fear of Weir's judgment, until one morning Weir returned Henry's pages, saying only that it seemed both men were wasting their talents on the U.S. government.

When the war ended, the intelligence services were dissolved, despite Weir's protestations. A few high-level officers were scattered to various military departments and the rest were sent home. Henry and Ginnie married and moved to Chicago, where Hannah was born, and Henry took an accounting job at a firm downtown. He rode the train every morning, feeling incompatible, a man out of place. Ill at ease, now, in civilian life. He kept in contact with Weir, who was still making the rounds in Washington, trying to convince politicians of what was happening on the other side of the world while their country slept. But there was no appetite for more conflict, and eventually Henry lost touch, resigned himself to tax codes and actuary tables in the West Loop.

Five years later, Henry looked up from his newspaper on the morning train to see Weir standing at the opposite end of the car, a slight, sly smile pulling at his lips. They had coffee at a bar on Madison, only a few blocks from the office where Henry should have been at his desk. It was an entirely uncharacteristic shirking of responsibility, wholly thrilling to Henry, there with Weir while the workaday world went on as usual around them.

Weir made his pitch, though it was really little more than a formality. People in power had finally listened, and they were creating the skeleton of a new organization. Henry would be Weir's number two in a legitimate counterintelligence division. They would be late to the war, but, Weir said, still smiling, better late than never.

They shook hands across the table. That afternoon Henry tendered his resignation at the accounting firm. By the middle of the week Ginnie was packed and Hannah was out of kindergarten and they were on a train to Arlington.

It felt to Henry as if he was coming home.

3

There was a knock at the door of the north apartment. Henry opened it to find an adolescent boy standing at a lopsided attention, his head cocked to one side and most of his weight shifted to the other. He wore a cap with earflaps that reached almost to his chin, carried a small stepladder and a large leather tool bag. Without speaking, the boy set down his bag and rummaged in the pockets of his work pants, then in the pockets of his jacket and shirt, until he finally produced a business card and presented it to Henry. On the card was the name *Salo Perelman,* the electrician Henry had called from a pay phone, the first number on his slip of paper.

The boy's hand was still out, waiting to retrieve the card. Henry handed it back and the boy stepped through the doorway into the living room and unzipped his bag, pulling out a pair of work gloves and various sizes of pliers.

Henry said, "Where's Mr. Perelman?"

The boy dug deeper into the bag, coming out with spools of electrical wire which he stacked beside his tools. Henry repeated himself, louder this time, and the boy finally turned.

"Isaac," the boy said. His voice was strangely bloated, the vowels over-full, the consonants imprecise. Henry realized he was deaf or close to it even before the boy pushed the flaps of his cap back, revealing large twin hearing aides.

"Your name is Isaac?"

The boy watched Henry's mouth as he spoke, nodded.

"Isaac Perelman?"

The boy nodded again.

"Is your father coming?"

Isaac shook his head and returned to his work.

Henry showed him the places where he wanted the wiring, beneath the molding and the baseboards, under the couch and beds, behind the toilet, alongside the ceiling fans. Isaac stood on his stepladder and drilled tiny holes in the walls, cut small compartments into the ceiling. He ran the wires, the strands eventually converging in the south wall of the bedroom, and then he drilled a larger, deeper hole and ran the wires into the adjacent bedroom in the south apartment. He worked in silence. The only sounds in the rooms throughout the day were that of the drill or some small grunts he made while guiding a wire through a wall.

Later in the afternoon, Isaac pulled cans of paint from his bag and selected those with colors closest to the walls and ceilings, carefully masking his work. When the boy was finished, Henry walked through the apartment, looking from room to room, hard-pressed, with the day's light almost gone, to see where anything had been done at all.

Henry sent a letter back east informing them that he had procured an appropriate location and requesting funds for what he thought he would need. He had the locks to the apartments changed, making certain that he had the only keys. He had the office furniture delivered and carried up the stairs to the vestibule. Once the deliverymen were gone, he dragged it all into the south bedroom. It was beginning to look like a proper office. He placed two desks side by side, facing the shared wall between the two apartments.

He took a streetcar to a bookstore on Nob Hill and purchased books on photograph developing, the mechanics and chemistry involved. The Lazarushian mystery, raising an image from a glossy white square. He installed a blackout curtain over the window in the south apartment's bathroom, changed the overhead bulb to a safelight he'd painted red. At a photographic supply shop he bought an enlarger and developing equipment, jars of the liquids and packets of the powders listed in the books.

He read the books cover to cover before he attempted to develop a single frame. He kept notes in the ledger, important points he would need to reference. There had been a time when the ledger wouldn't have been necessary, but he could no longer trust his memory.

He practiced mixing, heating, cooling the chemicals. He trained himself to work without light. Placing the developing tank in the bathtub, pouring developer into the tank. Agitating the tank until it was time to remove the developer and pour in the stop bath. Agitating again until it was time to remove the stop bath and pour in the fixer. Reaching for jars without seeing them. When he dropped or bumped a jar, he cleaned up and started again. Working with the strips of film from the cross-country trip, St. Louis, Opelousas, the Grand Canyon. Working until he was able to move confidently, silently, until there were no accidents. Days of repetition, until he had mastered the room in the dark.

1 Bell recorder, with headphones
4 wood card files
1 metal equipment rack
1 Monroe calculator
1 combination file
1 safe
2 office desks
2 swivel chairs
1 bookcase
1 lot of electrical small parts including microphones, etc.
2 Diebold cameras
1 studio couch
2 desk lamps
2 Royal typewriters
1 York air conditioner
1 radio

1 voice compressor

1 polygraph

A few days later, Isaac Perelman returned, this time with his father, to install the mirror between the two apartments. Henry stood outside in the vestibule, smoking while they worked, watching down the stairwell for Mrs. Barberis or a curious mechanic, anyone who might be drawn to the noise of the Perelmans cutting through the wall.

When they were finished, Henry stood with them in the office and looked through the new window into the darkened north bedroom. Then he stood in the north bedroom and looked at the new mirror that hung above the dresser. His own dim reflection. He cupped his hands and peered into the glass. He could just barely make out the shapes of the father and son standing on the other side. He motioned for them to turn out the overhead light and Salo Perelman reached up and pulled the chain and the room disappeared.

The paper rose to the top of the pan, breaking the surface of the developing liquid. A fuzzy image of a woman in the Grand Canyon parking lot, standing by the car next to their station wagon, a cigarette held between her lips while she stretched her arms behind her back. Henry had focused the camera on Ginnie, but at the last instant he'd moved and activated the shutter, photographing the stranger behind his wife.

He lifted the picture from the pan, clothespinned it to dry on the line he'd strung overhead. His first successful print. An image he alone had witnessed and captured and documented. The woman unaware of being photographed, the negative and print seen only by him. An airtight process. A perfect secret.

He placed the next square in the solution and let it sink.

A box with the cameras and audio equipment arrived. Henry spent a morning attaching it all to the wiring Isaac had threaded through the walls of the north apartment, positioning the microphones, placing the cameras into the small compartments the boy had cut into the ceiling.

When he was finished, he stood in the south apartment office, looking through the new window, wearing the headphones and listening to the empty-room hiss of the north bedroom. He could hear the faint sound of honking horns from a few streets beyond the open window, and then, just barely, the ticking of his watch, which he had placed under one of the beds. He stopped the recorder, rewound the tape, listened again to the previous few seconds. The just-passed car honks, the old air in the room, the ticking of his watch. He replayed it again, to be sure. The captured moment.

He gave each of the children a photograph from the trip, which he told them he'd had developed and framed at a shop in the city. Thomas on the banks of the Mississippi with a riverboat paddling in the distance; Hannah blowing a gum bubble at a filling station in New Mexico. Hannah was particularly moved by her picture. She hung it on the wall beside her bed, fascinated with the photo, not so much because of the image but because she couldn't remember Henry taking it. A recovered instant she hadn't known she'd lost.

He gave Ginnie a photo from the Grand Canyon, the image he'd taken after he'd snapped the picture of the other woman. Ginnie standing by the station wagon, hair blowing in the wind, hands clasped at her waist. She placed it on the mantel in the living room, proud of both how poised she looked in the photo and Henry's skill in taking it. She jokingly called it her fashion shoot. Hannah asked her to re-create the pose and Ginnie obliged, lowering her hands to her waist and tossing her hair, eliciting an admiring smile from Hannah, much overly loud whooping and clapping from Thomas.

And my photographer, she said, nodding to acknowledge Henry, who shook his head and raised his hands, waving off the renewed round of applause.

*   *   *

After dinner in the evenings, while Ginnie washed the dishes and Hannah retreated to her room and her homework, he sat at the table with Thomas and his transit maps and rail schedules. Henry removed his watch and set it on the table and called off times and Thomas pointed to the spot on the map where the train would be at that moment. Twelve-fifteen on the B Geary line and Thomas tracing a finger along the route, bringing it to rest at the correct station. Always the correct station.

Most nights were like this, the two of them at the table until the fraught, complicated bath-time process, Thomas unclamping himself from his invisible railroad tracks and getting into the tub, Ginnie rushing to get him soaped and rinsed before he felt his fuel was completely depleted. If she spent too much time washing his hair or scrubbing his nails, Thomas flew into a frenzy, splashing and kicking, screaming, Henry running in to pull him from the tub, pin his arms to his sides, holding Thomas to his chest, both of their bodies straining, the tight embrace in the small room. Finally Thomas would grow tired enough that they could get him dry and dressed, get him back on his tracks to his room, where he plugged himself into the imagined outlet in his wall and lay down on the floor beside his bed.

They would stand in the doorway, Henry and Ginnie, feeling the new bruises surfacing on their arms and chests, listening to Thomas's deepening breath, so peaceful so suddenly. Ginnie's weight leaning into Henry, her hand on his shoulder, on the back of his neck, squeezing, holding on.

The office was nearly dark but he'd left a light on in the north bedroom. He could see it glowing on the other side of the new window. Something caught his eye, some movement beyond the glass, a figure crossing the space.

Henry looked up. The bedroom was empty. He could see the beds, the dresser, the lamp. He walked to the window, his face close, his breath fogging the glass. No one there. Just the room, waiting.

He finished his cigarette and returned to his desk. He removed the slip of paper from his pocket, the two numbers. He drew a line through the first, the number belonging to the Perelmans. He looked again at the window, then lifted the receiver of the new phone.

4

Thomas on his tracks, moving through the front door, his head straight, his arms pumping, feet shuffling, the sound of his engine, the low, rhythmic rumble coming from deep within his chest. He continued into the living room, then down the hall, making a sharp turn into his bedroom. Ginnie followed to his doorway and watched him in the far corner. He expertly pantomimed the unclipping of an invisible electrical plug from his belt, then stretched the imaginary cord down to the power outlet at the base of the wall. He stood straight again, his eyes closing, his arms and hands relaxing. The machine at rest.

She was careful as she left the doorway, stepping over the places in the hall where Thomas believed his tracks lay, mindful that he could be watching her leave, one eye open. She was back in the living room before she stopped walking on her toes, looking for rails to avoid. Sometimes she understood how easy it would be to slip into his world, to decide that if she couldn't guide him back to this place then she could join him in his.

She poured herself another cup of coffee and stood at the front windows, morning light warming her face, her hands. The roofs of the neighboring houses stretched down to the bay. Across the water, the top of the skyline was starting to surface through the rising fog. Henry was down in there, somewhere. Setting up his new office space, he'd told her. Trying to get the lay of the land.

Hannah's school was at the bottom of the hill, and once Henry had left for work, they'd made the walk, Ginnie holding Thomas's hand and Hannah a few steps ahead, books under her arm, her gaze fixed forward, blocking out her mother and brother, refusing to acknowledge the surrounding houses of the new neighborhood, walking as if she were alone again on the route to her old school back in Arlington. They reached the front doors and Hannah disappeared inside without so much as a look back. Ginnie and Thomas made the return trip then, stopping at the train station to watch the departures and pick up some new schedules and maps. Thomas stood at the display of timetables, unfolding the pages quickly, absorbing new information, a change in an arrival time or a temporarily closed station. They had stayed until his excitement had turned to fatigue and then they had hurried home before an overtired breakdown.

She unpacked while Thomas slept. The movers had come a few days after their arrival, and the furniture was in place, but the rooms were still ringed with boxes. She opened one and found the record player, a smaller box of LPs. She unwrapped picture frames, wiped the glass, arranged them on the mantel next to the photos Henry had taken on the trip, Thomas at the river and her own glamour shot. There were more in the box, wedding photos, Hannah's school pictures, a photograph that a friend in Washington, Roy Pritchard, had taken of Thomas as a baby. In the picture, Thomas's eyes were blue and clear as he looked up at the lens, smiling. Then another picture from Roy, taken just a year later. This one with the now-familiar closed book of Thomas's expressionless face.

She set the two pictures together on the mantel as she had in Arlington, though she knew it bothered Henry and Hannah. It was painful to be reminded of the Thomas they'd known in that first year. But Ginnie needed to see those pictures together, what the distance between them made plain. That she'd missed something, she'd let something slip past. He had gone somewhere, just like that. Somewhere in that space she had lost him.

There was a box with the books she was using for Thomas's lessons, as well as the books the doctors in Washington had given her. Folded within the pages of a behavioral journal she found the self-portrait Thomas had made during one of his sessions, the crayon drawing of how he saw himself: a small metal figure, with a silver head and arms and legs, wheels connected by rods where his feet should be, chugging along on tracks that stretched from one end of the page to the other.

The Locomotive Boy. This was what one of the doctors in Washington had called him. This after all of the psychiatry sessions, the tests, the disastrous attempts at the special school. Ginnie sitting in the doctor's office and the man telling her this as if it were a diagnosis of some kind, as if he'd solved the mystery. The Locomotive Boy. Ginnie kept her mouth shut and listened. She'd spent years keeping her mouth shut and listening. She imagined standing, pounding the arm of her chair, clearing the doctor's desk with a sweep of her arm. She imagined shouting until she was heard by this man, by all of these men. Shaming them into silence. How dare you. This is my son.

When the doctor had finished, Ginnie thanked him and rose from her seat and picked Thomas up from the playroom down the hall, knowing that this would be their last appointment.

She did not want him pitied, treated as if he was sick. She was tired of being accused, blamed by specialists who spent as much time trying to analyze her as they did Thomas. She would teach her son at home. She would find ways in, subjects that interested him, that sparked something, inevitably becoming unshakable obsessions, but openings nonetheless. She would use these openings to help him learn about the world, even in the smallest terms. How to read a transit map, a train schedule. How to talk about these things. The doctors, the teachers at his school had seen his long, loud monologues as symptoms, further proof of his illness. Ginnie saw them as successes. Thomas able, finally, to communicate. She didn't care how loud or for how long he spoke. He could shout about transit schedules until Kingdom Come as far as she was concerned.

There was a door at the back of the kitchen, a staircase leading to the unfinished basement. She'd had the movers put Henry's desk down there, his bookcases. She'd arranged his poetry books on the shelves in what she remembered as their order on the shelves of his study in Arlington, though only Henry would know for sure. Some of the books had been with him since college, coming along into their marriage. Springtime in Chicago, she remembered, those early months after the war, soft evenings, sitting in their apartment and Henry reading verses of past friends, schoolmates, and then some of the masters, Yeats, Eliot, Williams. Henry's voice deep and rich, wondering at the lines, the beauty and the mystery. Ginnie sitting on the window seat in the living room, pregnant with Hannah, watching Henry smoke, watching him read, an accountant by day, his head full of mathematics, but this beautiful man at night, his mind buzzing with words, with lines that found voice only with her.

Things had changed with the move to Washington, and Henry's new position. He came home late in the evenings, his dinner waiting for him in the oven, the children in bed, and when Henry read it was the newspapers. After the incident, he had returned to his poetry books, but then he read them almost secretively, certain volumes over and over, making notes in the margins, marking pages, returning to the same passages as if he was looking for some clue. It seemed like work, now. A burden more than a joy.

The incident. This was how she thought of what had happened, that day in December. Henry's incident. She didn't know how he thought of it, what word he used. It wasn't something he wanted to discuss.

There was a noise from Thomas's room, the low hum of his engine warming up. She opened his door to find him in his sleeping spot, on the floor beside the bed, looking out the window at the cerulean sky. After a moment he sat up and crossed to the electrical outlet, where he unplugged his imagined cord and clipped it back onto his belt.

She reminded herself to be careful again, where she walked. Thomas stood in his doorway, looking out into the rest of the house, studying his rails. Sometimes he believed that his tracks had been disturbed, kicked or moved by Hannah, by the postman coming up the front walk. Altering some part of his apparatus was the easiest way to send him into a tantrum. It took a half hour sometimes to calm him down, holding him while he wailed, a strange, alien threnody, a single note of deep frustration. A sound so lonely that Ginnie could hardly bear it. There was a sense in that noise that no one understood, including Thomas himself. It was something she heard long after the tantrum was over, while Thomas splashed in the bathtub or Henry read him a storybook beside his bed.

She emptied another box in the living room while Thomas played with his toy trains on the sofa, pushing the cars over the cushions, making engine and bell noises. In the den, she set her easels and rolls of unstretched canvas against the wall. She hadn't brought any of her paintings from Washington. She hadn't painted since Henry's incident, months ago now, but it may as well have been years. She unpacked the rest of her supplies. The brushes felt unfamiliar in her hands.

The house began to dim. An orange afternoon. In the foyer she helped Thomas into his jacket, put on her own. They would go to the market, then pick Hannah up at school. Hopefully, Henry would be home soon after.

It would take time to get used to this place, this house, the progress of sunlight across the walls, the way the day moved through the rooms. It would take time, but she was patient. She had learned to be patient.

She opened the door and stepped outside, waiting for Thomas to see his tracks, to take her hand with a coupling click. Then they started down the hill in the cooling air, the whistle of the train in the distance, her heels clicking on the sidewalk and the sound of her boy's engine thrumming along beside.

5

Weir had been unreachable for only a few hours before panic set in. The man had never missed a day of work, so when there was still no word from him by lunchtime, Security sealed Weir's office and began a search.

Henry stayed at his desk, close to the phone. Rumors twisted through the hallways, so he kept his door closed, waiting, hoping for some kind of misunderstanding, some miscommunication. Weir ice fishing at his favorite lake in West Virginia; Weir visiting his elderly mother in Bethesda. Unlikely scenarios, Henry knew, but he clung to them as he watched the phone, the clock. Every hour Roy Pritchard knocked and leaned in the doorway and shook his head. No word. The afternoon waned. Henry sat at his desk with the incomprehensible possibility. Almost hoping, despite himself, that they would find a body rather than the alternative.

Rain began to fall, then freeze, tapping on the glass, coating the sidewalks, the leafless trees. The windows in Henry's office went dark. He pictured Ginnie and the children at the dinner table, the light and warmth of the house in Arlington. He tried to imagine moving from this spot, moving in the world again, but it was unthinkable, the idea of being anywhere but behind his desk, waiting.

Another knock. Henry started to speak but found that he had no voice. Roy opened the door, stood in the hallway staring at Henry's desk, the windows behind.

"He's gone," Roy said.

They were brought to Weir's house to view the wreckage. There was an FBI man sitting in a car in the driveway, a few others still poking around in the living room, though the house had been turned numerous times by then. Paul Marist from Security led Henry and Roy into the familiar kitchen, then through a door and down a flight of stairs to the basement. Henry had never been below the house before. A line of bare bulbs were fixed to the joists in the low ceiling, burning away into the distance. A long, large space, empty except for a congregation of boxes at the far end.

They walked across the basement in silence. Marist opened the lids on a few of the boxes. Memoranda and project files, personnel files, accounting sheets. Henry recognized his own signature on many of them, Weir's on many more. There was a box of undeveloped microfilm, a box of audiotape spools. They turned to a small desk and some wireless encoding equipment that sat on top, still plugged into the electrical outlet on the wall. Marist flipped a switch on one of the machines. There was a low, rich hum as it warmed up.

"We've already tested it," Marist said. "Moscow on the other end."

Henry looked back the way they had come, the line of lights leading to the stairs and the doorway. Innumerable times, he had shared coffee in Weir's den ten feet above, dinner in the dining room. Over drinks once at the kitchen table, Weir had nodded to the basement door and complained about the useless enormity of the space, how he was too intimidated to even attempt finishing it into usable rooms. Henry had repeated the remark to Ginnie in bed that night, and she had rolled her eyes and offered to trade houses with Henry's childless, bachelor boss with too much space on his hands.

Footsteps creaking above. The FBI men moving through rooms. Marist left Henry and Roy alone with the boxes and equipment, walked back across the basement toward the stairs. Roy seemed on the verge of saying something a number of times, but stopped himself, running his fingertips along the edges of the box lids. Henry stood motionless, looking at the keys of the encoder.

Everything they had worked on, everything they had discussed, it had all been sent east into the mouth of the enemy. He wanted to set fire to the room, to the house. Even though the damage was done, even though what had been left behind was simply a message, a preening show of accomplishment. Henry pictured it all in flames, the papers, the boxes, the encoder, the house above. He wanted to burn the whole thing to the ground.

Roy was speaking to him.

"You should go home, Henry. Get some sleep. They'll want to talk to you soon."

It took an hour to drive to Arlington, through the aftermath of the ice storm, the streets in sheets, lawns and roofs glistening in the moonlight, tree branches sagged and creaking. Not quite alone. He knew there'd be an FBI man in a car following somewhere behind. He was a suspect now.

He sat in his driveway with the car lights off. In the living room window, he could see Hannah reading to Thomas on the sofa, Ginnie clearing the table in the kitchen beyond. This feeling was impossible to define. As if the structure on which he was made had been taken away, the armature pulled from his body. He had been trained to distrust everyone except Weir. Weir was the control. Weir was the truth against which all else was measured.

He sat in the driveway and watched his house, his children. He pictured Weir loose in the world, a new man now, or something other than a man, intangible, flying east, his old clothes discarded, his name, his old face shed. A ghost in the night.

6

San Francisco, Spring 1956

He introduced himself as Jimmy Dorn, the name as he said it sounding like a single word. He spoke in a distracted headlong rush, his eyes settling briefly on Henry before moving to the details in the background, the layout of the north apartment, the sight lines out the windows. A veteran cop's sizing up of the premises.

"Heyhowareya. Gladwell? Jimmydorn."

He was a great grappler of a man, possibly ten years Henry's senior, thick in the neck and chest, his head bare and pink as a thumb. His brow was wet, the collar of his shirt dark with sweat from the climb up the stairs. He was breathing hard but that didn't slow his forward momentum as he walked past Henry, immediately filling the space. His voice was low and loud, with the cigarette-and-booze roughness Henry had first heard during their brief phone conversation the day before.

Dorn cracked a cough into his fist, pounded himself on the chest to jar something loose.

"So show me around. This the bedroom in here?"

Henry watched him, silent. Dorn wore a sharp blue suit, custom-cut. Not the kind of outfit easily afforded on a detective's salary alone. He kept moving, briskly inspecting the kitchen, the closets, asking questions without waiting for answers.

"Where's the head? In here?"

Henry waited in the living room. The toilet flushed once, twice.

"Henry? Hank?"

Dorn said the second name as if he had already decided on it. He returned to the living room, lifted the curtains away from the walls, poked the couch cushions with the toe of a wing tip.

"Who did your decorating? The place looks like a Catholic girls' dorm."

He stopped in the center of the room, finally catching his breath, then turned to look at Henry.

"All right. Enough bullshit. Show me your setup, Hank. Let me see all the secret stuff."

They had lunch at an automat on Powell. Henry sat at a table by the window with a cup of coffee, watching Dorn make his way down the line of lit compartments. With every plate he pulled, Dorn lowered his head and sniffed, recoiled and replaced the item. He finally settled on what looked like tuna salad and toast, sat down across from Henry.

"Let's not make a habit of coming here. I know a million great places where you don't pull your lunch from a hole." Dorn looked at his tuna salad without enthusiasm, then at Henry's coffee. "Did you already eat or are you not eating?"

"I'm fine with coffee."

"This is all I can have." Dorn indicated the limp sandwich. "Half this. I'm trying to get back down to my fighting weight. Two-ten. Two-fifteen. My wife is on my back." He took a bite. "Where you from, Hank? Originally."

"The Midwest."

"The Midwest."

"Chicago," Henry said.

Dorn flipped his tie back over his shoulder, tucked his napkin into his collar and spread it across the front of his shirt. "You married? Any kids?" On Henry's look he waved off his own question, took another mouthful of tuna salad. "Forget I asked. Too personal. Won't happen again."

"What do we need to get started?"

Dorn wiped his mouth on his napkin. "We'll need two girls. Maybe three, but no more than that. They chirp like housewives. I'm thinking a white girl and a Negro. A Negro would widen the net. That way you're going to get Negro males, and white males who are into Negroes. We could have a Chinese, too. That could be number three. Then you've pretty much got the whole city open to you, except for the queers. The queers are a different story. I don't know if you want to go that route or not."

"Let's start with two."

"Two it is. No problem. You got any preference, Hank? Blondes, brunettes? I'm just joking. You look like a family man. I'm just pulling your leg."

"How are they paid?"

"Cash at the end of the night. And a few favors. I can keep them out of trouble. The protection is what instills loyalty. It'll keep them quiet. You look a little queasy, Hank. You sure you don't want something to eat?" Dorn produced a pen and a small black datebook from his breast pocket. He touched the tip of the pen to his tongue and jotted a note on a fresh page.

"All discussion of this type is off the record," Henry said.

"What record? There is no record." Dorn finished his note, closed the book, and returned it to his pocket. "Don't worry about any of this, Hank. I'll take care of everything."

7

Fifteen workdays in a windowless room with Paul Marist and Marist's subordinates from the Office of Security. Questioned without rest, eight hours a day, except for a brief lunch when one of the officers brought in sandwiches. Marist and his men devouring the food while Henry consumed only coffee and cigarettes and thought back through the morning, what he had been asked, the answers he had given.

He knew of Paul Marist. He knew of everyone. Marist was a veteran of the gung ho operations wing of the company, an energetic figure who strode the halls, smiling and shaking hands. Something in him that Henry distrusted, that Weir had distrusted. That clear-cut sense of confidence.

Fifteen days. Henry knew that there was an element of revenge to this. These men had spent years in fear of Weir, of Henry, and now Henry was alone, stripped of his patron. They had been correct to distrust him, to distrust Weir, they had been proven right, and now they would take full advantage of the redistribution of power. He had no argument. He understood their anger, their sense of betrayal. He understood their fear, the savage uncertainty. He was trying to discover the answer to the same basic question they were asking. What he knew when.

They recorded the interviews, took copious notes. They gave Henry a polygraph test every day for a week. They never told him the results, but they implied that he'd failed, which was common practice in these situations. He didn't argue. Henry stated his story and answered their questions and corrected Marist when he tried to lead Henry down another path. This was Henry's job. They were good, but this was Henry's job. They tried every technique they knew. They questioned him one at a time, two at a time, a roomful of officers at a time, a Greek chorus of accusation. They made promises and threats, insinuations. Some of these men he had trained. Some of his very techniques turned against him. Like being interrogated by his own children.

He said nothing to Ginnie for the first two weeks. The shock was too great, the shame. What he had unwittingly helped Weir accomplish. It was something he needed to contain within himself. When he was home, he moved as if sleepwalking, his head still in the room with Marist while he and Ginnie and the children ate dinner, shoveled the driveway and the walk.

Finally, during the third week, he sat at the breakfast table and told her that Weir was gone, that he was being questioned. Ginnie stood at the counter with a stunned look, an oven mitt on her hand. What does that mean, she'd asked, and Henry had said that he didn't know.

On the fifteenth day, he sat alone with Marist in the conference room. No polygraph, no notebooks, no papers on the table. Marist was relaxed, sitting back in his chair, looking at Henry as if they were two friends sharing a drink.

Marist said that they had reached a conclusion. They were confident that Henry hadn't been involved in the deception in any way. He would be returned to his normal duties. His office would be open to him again. Everything would be as it was.

Marist stood and Henry stood. As Henry left the room, Marist stopped him, said that he had some good news for a change. That he, Marist, had been promoted. He was moving to Henry's department. Starting that Monday, he said, he would be taking Arthur Weir's place.

8

San Francisco, Spring 1956

Henry thought that he had entered the wrong apartment. He stood in the living room, disoriented, almost dizzy. Heavy burgundy drapes covered the windows. A chenille sofa and chair sat where the secretaries' furniture had been. Paintings hung on the walls, nude women reclining and bathing, white and Negro, Oriental couples in various sexual positions and combinations, all lit with small electric pin lights clipped to the wood of the overly ornate frames. The walls were still wet with paint, a dark, nearly blood red. Drop cloths covered the floor, color-stippled along the edges.

In the bedroom, the twin beds had been replaced by a large four-poster covered in a gold spread, with an assortment of fringed velveteen pillows. The utilitarian dresser under the mirror had been replaced with something massive and baroque.

"Don't worry, I didn't screw up any of your stuff." Dorn stood in the doorway, dressed in spattered painter's overalls, holding a paint roller in one hand and a martini glass in the other. "You should give me a key, it'll make it easier to get in."

"Who else was here?"

"You don't think I'm capable of doing this? I have an eye for this stuff."

"Who else was here?"

"I already told you, Hank. Nobody."

Henry walked back through the living room, crossed the vestibule, and unlocked the south door.

Dorn followed at a distance. "You don't trust me?"

"I don't know you."

Henry went through the office. All seemed to be in order. The recorder, the shutter controls for the cameras. He unlocked the top drawer of his desk. The ledger was still in its place.

"Nothing else changes," Henry said. "Nothing else comes into the apartments without my approval."

Dorn raised an eyebrow, nodded.

Henry said, "Understood?"

"Aye-aye, Captain."

Henry backed out of the south apartment, locked the door, brushed past Dorn on his way to the stairs.

"Don't start worrying already." Dorn sipped his drink, called down over the railing. "We haven't done anything yet."

9

On her way home, Hannah tried to remember the same walk in Arlington, the long stands of birch and ash trees, the familiar houses, the neighbors' cars in welcoming colors, but all she could see was the new town, its paint-peeling weathered ugliness, and then back over her shoulder the imagined crash and glow, the city in flames across the bay.

They'd shown a civil defense film at school, footage of atomic bomb tests cut together with a projected aftermath, images from the San Francisco earthquake standing in for the next great destruction. Hollow shells of buildings, piles of brick and glass, smoke rising to the sky. A narrator warned of the dangers in the city after the bomb: radiation in the air, in the water; desperate criminal activity; still-falling masonry.

She couldn't get the movie out of her head. She could picture her father at work in the city, the building in which he sat crumbling from under him, his desk and chair tipping, other desks tipping, men in suits grabbing for their hats as they fell. She reached the house, their new house, tried to imagine it as the house in Arlington, but the light from the explosions across the bay flickered in the windows.

She didn't want to talk to her mother. Her mother wouldn't understand. Her mother would say what she always said, that it wasn't worth thinking about the bad things. As if that made them go away. She wouldn't let Hannah walk to school alone again after a scene like this, coming home in tears. Hannah would be forced back into the ridiculous parade of those first weeks here, she and her mother and Thomas ambling down the hill.

She would wait for her father. He had always been the one to take her fears seriously. He was different now, she knew this, something had happened that had made them move, something had happened to him, he was further away somehow, but he was still the one she went to when she was afraid.

Inside the house she marched straight to her room, ignoring her mother's questions, closing the door and crying until the light outside dimmed and she heard the front door open, her father's footsteps in the hall. It was the only thing she had really learned about this new place. She could tell the sound of him in the house.

When he opened her door she ran to him, clinging to his waist, blubbering about the movie, embarrassing herself but unable to stop, tears and snot on the belly of his shirt, the tail of his tie, gulping air from hiccuping sobs, pleading with him not to go back into the city. He sat with her on the bed, listened to her recount the story of the film. He didn't try to convince her that what she had seen wasn't real. He considered everything she said. She could see him working it over in his head, so when he told her, finally, that she didn't need to be afraid of this, she knew she could believe him, that there was some truth there, something to hold on to. Exhausted, she lay back onto the bed and he covered her with the blanket, her hand in his, her breathing slowing, deepening.

When she woke it was dark in the house. She was still in her school clothes, though her shoes were off and her hair was down, had been brushed. She sat up and thought she could see explosions again out the black window, fire across the water, but then her father's hand squeezed hers and she lay back down beside him, closing her eyes in the safety of his arms.

10

The girl leaned across the bed, tapped her cigarette against the wall to pack the tobacco. She found a box of matches in her purse and lit the tip, inhaling, blowing smoke in a long steady stream. It was part of some kind of show, Henry knew. She was establishing her character for him. A hard-edged woman of the world.

She was twenty, maybe, skinny and pale and angular. Her hair was blond, showing dark at the roots. She wore a thin blue dress that matched her eyes. There were bruises on her knees, and one on her thigh that Henry could see when she crossed her legs.

She said her name was Elizabeth. The first time she had buzzed at the front door he had turned her away. She'd had his name wrong, had asked for Mr. Stonewell. An hour later she returned with the correct name and he let her in, followed her up the stairs to the north apartment.

"What has he told you?" Henry passed her an ashtray, stood back by the dresser while she sat back on the bed.

"About what?"

"About this."

She looked around the room, caught her reflection in the mirror, pushed her hair behind her ears. "That I'll be bringing men here a couple times a week."

"And then what?"

"Slipping them something, maybe. In their drink."

"How long have you known him?"

"Jimmy?"

"Yes."

"A couple of years."

"How long have you been doing this?"

"A couple of years." She looked to the mirror again, then back at Henry. "There's going to be someone else? Another girl?"

"Possibly."

"Will we be working together?"

"How do you mean?"

"I mean will we be working together."

"That's yet to be determined," Henry said. "What did he tell you about me?"

"He didn't tell me anything. Just your name: Mr. Gladwell." She gave a smart-aleck smile, getting the name right.

"Nothing else?" Henry said.

Elizabeth leaned across the bed again, tapped the end of her cigarette into the ashtray. She looked back at Henry. "He said that you're someone who likes to watch."

11

At night, he sat at his desk in the basement of the house in Oakland and worked on the biography. He believed he had been away from Washington long enough to think clearly, that there had been enough time since Weir's betrayal and what happened after.

During the interrogation he was so unsettled that he couldn't remember everything. What he could remember, he didn't want to give to them until he'd had time to go through it himself. If it were anyone else involved, he would have been the one asking questions, and he saw no reason why things should be different in this case. During the weeks of questioning he came home every night and spent hours writing, making sense of the memories their questions had triggered. Then there was the thing that happened, the indiscretion at the Christmas party, and after the indiscretion he went back to those notes and realized that they made no sense. Some of the memories were obviously false; some were confused amalgamations of unrelated events and discussions. It wasn't until he was away from Washington that he was able to try again.

There were nearly ten years to recount—the years during the war and then the years in Washington, with Chicago in between. He started to tell the story in chronological order, but found himself remembering things in no particular sequence. He wrote on loose paper so that he could physically move memories around, changing the shape of the

whole. He asked himself questions, letting the answers lead to other recollections. Hours spent this way at the desk in the basement. The small
window high on the cement wall, ground level outside, moonlight on
the grass. The quiet house a soft weight above.

They had discussed everything. Weir was a voracious consumer of
gossip, eager to hear what was said at the rare cocktail party he missed,
what was whispered out in the secretarial pool. His favorite spectator
sport. Henry learned early on that there was more than a prurient interest, that even the most mundane-seeming quarrel or liaison was information to be filed away, whether true or not. Rumor carried its own
currency, had its own uses.

Weir had given him many books over the years, poetry and poetry
journals, most with Weir's comments and opinions scrawled along the
perimeters of the pages. Henry read through the books again at the
desk in the basement. Auden, Pound, Cummings. Lesser-known poets
in hand-sewn chapbooks. Student work from university journals that
Weir found promising or laughably pretentious. Clippings from poems
that surfaced in popular magazines. Weir's notes often longer than the
poems themselves. Smudges of cigarette ash on the pages, coffee drips
and rings. His own or Weir's, impossible to tell.

He'd thought that he had known Weir's thinking inside and out, but
he had been wrong, so he spent hours with the books, reading and rereading poems he had memorized long ago, forcing himself to see them
stripped of his long-held interpretations. Reading Weir's comments as if
the man was sitting beside him, as if they had resumed their daily conversations, but this time with Henry aware of the truth, or part of the truth,
Weir's double life, and looking for clues to the deception.

Weir pored over Eastern Bloc poetry, Soviet poetry. Much of it was
by-the-numbers propaganda, but there was almost always something
deeper to find. It's hard to write a poem and not include some truth,
Weir would say. Look for what slips through. Weir with his cigarettes and
coffee and stack of Russian verse, saying, I'll take a bad poem over a good
newspaper any day.

First light at the window. A thin, golden glow. Henry reshuffled the papers. Conversations from six years ago, eight years ago. Weir's words and then Henry's words. He heard footsteps from above, the creaking of floorboards. Ginnie waking, the house coming to life. There was no telling how long this would take. Weeks, months. No one back east was waiting for this, no one was expecting it. It was his alone, a project of one.

He reshuffled the papers. There were ten years to analyze, looking for what he had missed.

12

There were three or four bars in the neighborhood where girls hooked johns, Dorn said. He gave his briefing in the north living room, walking a slow perimeter as he spoke. Elizabeth watched from the window seat, smoking. Henry sat on the burgundy sofa, looking at the heavy matching drapes, the boudoir paintings. The apartment looked like the movie set of a low-rent Parisian bordello.

The girls also met men on the street, Dorn said, but these encounters were less desirable than the bar meetings. There was more danger on the street. The possibility of being pushed into an alley, pulled into a doorway.

Elizabeth finished her cigarette, stood and crossed the room. She was wearing another short, loose cotton dress. She walked barefoot across the rug, arching up on her toes with each step, betraying a dancer's grace, maybe, somewhere years ago, a previous life.

Some of the girls were skilled at slipping mickeys into johns' drinks, Dorn said. It was a lucrative side business, almost foolproof. Most johns wouldn't go running to the cops when they came to and found they'd been rolled.

Elizabeth stood in front of the couch and Henry handed her a cigarette. She leaned in for a light, giving him a clear look down her dress, the absence of undergarments, and then she straightened and walked to the record player by the bedroom doorway. She began flipping through the secretaries' abandoned crate of LPs, Glenn Miller and Lester Brown and Frank Sinatra.

Dorn lit his own cigarette, watched Elizabeth's behind as she bent over the crate.

"You ever see a magician?" Dorn said. "Whadotheycallem? Street magicians. Close-up magicians." He smiled at the retrieval of the proper term. "They can find a canary in your pocket or a nickel behind your ear. That kind of shit. Prestidigitation. Some of these girls are like magicians."

Henry lifted his cup to his lips. He stopped, just shy of a sip, looked at his coffee, now shot through with a faint white swirl, the new liquid rapidly disappearing into the old.

Henry looked up. Dorn was watching him with a smile. An old Benny Goodman tune began from the record player. Elizabeth began to hum along.

"I've always loved magic," Dorn said.

They crossed the Embarcadero in Dorn's big blue Lincoln. Dorn drove slowly, close to the curb, his arm hanging out the open window. The stretches between streetlights were dark; the smell was strong: salt, fish, cigars, urine, garbage. Spilled beer when they passed a bar with an open door. Every few blocks Dorn lifted his hand and pulled on his Lucky Strike. The thing looked tiny in his beefy mitt, like a child's candy cigarette. He had the radio on, a late-night classical music program playing low.

"Prostitutes, pimps, vagrants, queers," Dorn said. "There's nobody else down here. Let me know if you see anybody different. You won't."

Most of the bars were full, men spilling out onto the sidewalk to laugh and smoke and argue. A few girls walked alone or in pairs, stopping to talk with groups of men or to lean into the open windows of cars that pulled to the curb.

The people on the street eyed them warily. Henry couldn't tell whether they recognized the car, if they saw Dorn's big bald head in the red dashboard light, or if they were just in a constant state of vigilance.

"Every guy down here is carrying something," Dorn said. "A knife, a gun, a bottle he can't wait to crack over your head. The girls, too, most of them. This is another place entirely. The rules are different. The rules are pretty much the opposite of the rules where you're from. Remember that and you'll be fine."

Dorn brought his cigarette to his mouth, left it burning between his lips. He took a hard turn onto a pier access road, cut his headlights, and let the Lincoln coast. Men and women moved in the shadows. Some lay on the sidewalk, passed out or sleeping something off. Small groups huddled around trash-can fires, passing bottles. After about a hundred feet the pavement ended at the pier. The water beyond rolling and purple-black, striped with thin veins of moonlight.

"These people aren't like us," Dorn said. "You can talk to them and sometimes they sound like human beings, but don't get fooled. They don't have families. They don't have mortgages, kids in school. They're drunks or dope fiends. Nut cases. I spend all day with these people and none of them is worth a damn."

The Lincoln slowed to a stop. More movement in the shadows ahead.

Dorn turned to Henry. "You don't believe me yet," he said. "I can see that. But you'll come around."

Dorn switched on the headlights. Men scattered in every direction, half dressed some of them, wild-eyed and flailing for cover.

"These people are barely even here," Dorn said. "Nobody'll miss them when they're gone."

13

Sometimes she woke and found herself alone. Dawn an hour away, Henry down at his desk in the basement. Ginnie didn't know if he'd slept, or for how long if he had. An impression from his body on the other side of the bed, cool to her touch.

She cleaned the basement when he was in the city. She was careful not to disturb anything. She knew that he was writing a history of his time with Weir, their relationship. He kept the pages he had written locked in a drawer in the desk. The sensitive nature of his work. The things the two men knew. This was what she reminded herself while she was cleaning, that the lock had nothing to do with her.

In Washington, he had been questioned for close to a month, and she could only imagine how difficult it had been. Every evening when he came home during those weeks, he'd seemed a little thinner, a little smaller. The exhaustion stretched across his face. But she knew that this self-interrogation was even harsher. He had no sympathy for himself. He would be relentless in his questioning, ruthless in his assessments. She had been worried for him during the weeks in Washington but she was far more worried now. She had seen Henry driven, she had seen him obsessed, but she had never before seen him like this, filled with anger and fear.

She'd thought that the move west would give them the space to talk, but Henry was back to another inflexible schedule. He was avoiding her concern, postponing time together while he worked in the city, or in the basement. She saw him now mostly at dinner, or playing with Thomas, and even then he seemed distracted, as if his head was still in one of those other places.

She wondered if she should force the issue, press him to talk, but that is what they had done, his colleagues in Washington, and she did not want Henry to see her on that side of this, against him somehow. She would give it time. They had time out here, she could feel that.

Some nights she woke alone with his impression beside her. He'd been there and gone, drawn back to his basement interrogation. On those nights she moved closer to that space, the imprint he'd left, and tried to sleep with at least the thought of him, the memory of his body beside hers.

What this man had done to him. Ginnie wondered if even she could betray Henry any deeper than Weir had.

14

A cold night, a harsh wind coming in off the bay, whipping around the streets on the hill. Henry sat in the darkened office, just his desk lamp burning, looking at the page in his ledger marked with the date and a time he kept erasing and rewriting every few minutes. Through the two-way mirror he could see the empty bedroom, dark except for the lamp on the bedside table.

He heard footsteps on the stairs, then a key in the lock. Dorn came into the office with a burst of cold air, lit a cigarette, sat in his chair beside Henry.

"They're a block away."

Henry switched off the light. He handed Dorn a pair of headphones, settled his own over his ears, started the recorder.

They listened to the air hiss of the empty apartment, long enough that Henry began to wonder if Dorn had been mistaken about whom he'd seen on the street. But then there was more noise on the stairs, Elizabeth's high heels and a heavier, looser gait, a man climbing drunkenly. Then they heard her key in the door of the north apartment and voices in the living room.

Nice place.

Let me take your coat.

Cold in here.

It won't be.

Henry could see Dorn's smile in the light from the bedroom. He marked the time in the ledger.

The Benny Goodman record started, the volume low. They could hear a kitchen cabinet open and close, glasses clinking. Henry stared through the mirror at the empty bedroom, trying to picture the rest of the apartment. The john sitting on the couch, or standing in the kitchen doorway, watching Elizabeth pour drinks.

Dorn had run her through some basic lines, getting her comfortable with something the girls never did, which was to ask questions. Nothing too personal yet, nothing that would arouse suspicion. Just name, rank, serial number.

There was a loud, scraping squeak, weight settling on uncooperative springs. Dorn winced. The sound of the sofa amplified through the microphone beneath. Henry lowered the gain on the headphones. Elizabeth's heels returned to the living room. Some low-volume, unintelligible conversation. A sly, murmured laugh from Elizabeth. More squeaking from the sofa springs, added weight. A few minutes of movement on the couch, heavy breathing, Elizabeth cooing.

You haven't told me your name.

You haven't told me yours.

Elizabeth.

My name's Clyde.

Dorn removed a flask from his breast pocket, held it out. Henry shook his head. Dorn shrugged, tipped the flask back to his lips.

Is that your real name?

A moment of silence, then Clyde's voice returning, confused.

What else would it be?

Don't get mad. I was just wondering.

Clyde is my real name.

That's fine, honey. I believe you. Don't get excited.

You sound like the cops.

Do I look like the cops?

No. A pause, then Clyde gave a hoarse laugh. Not like any cops I've ever seen.

Come, she said. Follow me.

Footsteps across the living room, and then they were there, Elizabeth and Clyde, visible through the mirror. A shock ran through Henry when Clyde looked into the glass, but then the man's eyes moved on, surveying the rest of the room. He was tall and sinewy, with concave cheeks and deep-socketed eyes that held the shadows. His hair was thinning and unwashed, his clothes loose and untucked. He hadn't shaved in a few days.

Clyde set his glass on the dresser, what looked like scotch with ice. Half empty. The spiked drink. Henry wrote the man's name in the ledger, *Clyde,* under the date and time.

Elizabeth turned Clyde so his back was to the mirror, began unbuttoning his shirt. Henry lifted the small control box for the camera above the ceiling fan and squeezed the shutter. The camera made no sound that they could hear, or that Clyde seemed to notice, preoccupied with his hands under Elizabeth's dress.

You haven't told me where you're from.

Who cares? His voice muffled, his face buried in Elizabeth's neck.

I'm a curious kitty.

Buffalo, Clyde said. And then St. Louis. And then Tucson.

You're a world traveler.

I go where the work is. And the pretty girls.

Awwwwww. Elizabeth took a step back, pulled her dress up over her head and let it fall to the floor. She unclasped her bra, letting it drop slowly, then slid her thumbs into the waist of her underwear and pulled down. Clyde's breathing got faster. He took a step toward her, stumbled, righted himself. Shook his head, trying to clear the cobwebs. He pulled his belt loose and dropped his pants. Pulled off his shorts, almost falling again as he tried to step free. Henry squeezed the shutter again.

Elizabeth reached into her purse and held out a packet.

You'll need to put this on.

Come on, honey.

Them's the rules.

Can't we just—

Them's the rules.

A whispered curse. Clyde breathing hard, looking down, hunched over himself, concentrating, adjusting.

There. Happy?

Very.

Jesus, this really—

Come here. She sat back on the bed, legs crossed, her arms back, holding herself up.

If I'd known I'd have to—

Come here. She uncrossed her legs. Clyde moved toward her, then climbed on top, losing his balance, righting himself, then thrusting and grunting, stopping every few seconds and shaking his head as if trying to refocus, then back to his business. Henry squeezed the shutter on the camera above the fan, the camera hidden in the dresser. All he could see of Elizabeth were the bottoms of her feet.

Clyde's thrusting slowed, stopped again. He pushed himself up, then lost the strength in his arms and collapsed onto Elizabeth. They lay like that for a moment, and then she rolled him off, sat up on the bed. Henry could hear snoring in his headphones. Elizabeth bent and pulled Clyde's wallet from the heap of his pants. She removed a couple of bills, lit a cigarette, stepped into her underwear. Picked her bra off the floor and refastened it over her shoulders. She combed her hair with her fingers, turned to Clyde, splayed across the bed, then back to the mirror, looking directly through.

She gave a little rolling flourish with her hand, then bent at the waist for a bow.

They stood in the vestibule between the closed doors of the apartments. Elizabeth held her hand out to Dorn, who laughed, too loudly. Henry worried that he would wake the sleeping man in the other room.

"You've already been paid tonight," Dorn said.

"Funny." Elizabeth left her hand out and Dorn dug his wallet from his jacket pocket, handed her a few bills.

She said, "Cigarette, too."

"Nobody taught you to say please?"

"Please."

Dorn handed her a cigarette, gave her a light. Elizabeth disappeared down the stairs, the sound of her heels receding, the front door opening and closing behind her.

The bedroom smelled like smoke and sweat. Clyde was still passed out on the bed. Dorn lifted him under the arms, propped him up into a sitting position.

"Are you, or have you ever been, a member of the Communist Party?"

"Dorn."

Dorn slapped Clyde across the face. "Speak up, boy. I didn't hear an answer."

"Dorn, enough."

"You think he cares? He's not going to remember any of this."

Dorn held Clyde upright while Henry pulled on his clothes. They carried him down the stairs, Henry waiting while Dorn checked that the street was clear. They walked with Clyde propped between them, two men helping a drunken friend home, taking side streets down the hill until they reached the Embarcadero.

They sat Clyde against an alley wall. Dorn straightened his jacket, put the man's hat back on his head, patted him on the shoulder as they left.

Henry let the tape play back in the office, Elizabeth's voice, Clyde's voice, the early conversation and then the breathing and grunts and the slumped silence.

Dorn straightened up the north apartment while Henry shut himself in the darkroom and developed the film. When he was finished, Dorn stood behind him in the office, drinking a martini he'd made in the kitchen, looking over Henry's shoulder at the wet prints.

Dorn said, "I can't see a goddamn thing."

"I'll have to adjust the cameras."

"There's this gray smear fucking this gray smear."

They left the building as the sun was rising, the fog settling low on the hill. Standing in a cloud. Dorn walked away down the street toward where he'd parked the Lincoln. As he disappeared into the fog, he stopped and turned, called back.

"Congratulations, Hank. Looks like we're in business."

15

Washington, D.C., Winter 1955

Henry sits at his desk. His office door is closed. He has just finished lunch at his desk. He always eats lunch at his desk. It is early afternoon, nearly a month since the interrogation.

The light through the window behind him is bright white. Clear, cold December light, seemingly from no single source, simply from the winter world itself: the half inch of snow on the ground, the frozen reflecting pool in the mall. There is a neat stack of papers on his desk, another neat stack of file folders. He lights a cigarette, sets it in the glass ashtray. Replaces one folder, retrieves another from the stack.

What Weir knew. What Weir had whispered into the ear of the enemy. How many had suffered for Henry's mistake? Agents in the field, assets, sympathizers. Operations had been rolled up by the Russians, the Chinese. Brave men would spend the rest of their lives in prisons, torture chambers. Brave men would be killed. Had been killed. How many had already been killed?

They were right to have accused him. It was not all for show. Marist had stood in the conference room and called Henry a traitor and Henry could feel his hands around Marist's throat, his thumbs pressing the windpipe, fingertips on skin. He had wanted to kill the man from anger and shame.

The papers slide from the folder, off the edge of the desk to the floor. Henry kneels beside his chair, gathering the pages.

There is a knock at the door. Henry ignores it, continues to pick up the papers. The door opens. Marist is there. His suit coat is gone, his tie is loosened, there is a drink in his hand. Henry can hear laughter from down the hall, a shout, some applause. It is the afternoon of the office Christmas party.

Henry stands. More papers fall to the floor.

Marist looks at the spilled folder. "Why don't you come down?" he says. "Close up in here. Take a break." He places the drink on Henry's desk. "I poured that for you. Bourbon, neat, correct? Your wife is from Kentucky. I've never met your wife." He pauses, considering something. "We're having a get-together at our place tomorrow night, Angela and I. We'd like you to come. You and your wife. But first, I want you to close up in here, come down the hall. You've missed the worst of it, I assure you. Everyone's drunk now, so it's easier to navigate."

Marist waits, looks again at the bourbon in the desk. "Are you going to drink that or am I?"

Henry gathers the last paper, stands. "Be my guest."

"It's not a request, Henry. I don't like the idea of you holed up in here alone. There's nothing to work on this afternoon."

"There's always something to work on."

Marist starts for the door. "Close up and come down. That's a direct order." He turns the corner and disappears.

Henry looks at the drink. A tumbler from the bar set in Marist's office. Weir's old office. The bourbon was Weir's as well, a rich single-barrel. Henry takes a drink.

The sound of an off-key Christmas carol from down the hall. Marist had insisted the party go on as planned. Weir's betrayal had shaken everyone, but Marist believed the party would help to release some of the tension and frustration. Would prove that the world turned, the show must go on.

Henry couldn't fathom what it would take to walk down into the party. Everyone there assumed he was guilty in some way. This was the organizing principle that he had instilled in the company, that Weir had instilled. Proximity to guilt is still guilt. It is a communicable disease. He would bear it always, by his own design. A skin he could never shed.

He takes another drink, places the folders into the appropriate drawers and file cabinets, locks the locks. He unbuttons his suit coat, carrying his cigarette and the drink with him as he leaves the office, locking the door behind him.

An older secretary noticed first, her eyes widening at the sight as Henry emerged into the large, open space. The party was in full swing. Recognition spread quickly, voices quieting as other secretaries and officers noticed him, conversations stumbling and then ceasing altogether as they realized who the naked man was. The shock of the most improbable sight, Henry March, standing pale and bare, holding an empty whiskey tumbler.

He had stripped himself on the walk down the hall, following the sounds of the party, leaving his clothes behind in a trail stretching back to his office door. Shirt, undershirt, slacks, underpants, socks, shoes. Even his glasses. The world before him a soft blurred whirl.

Roy Pritchard approached, looked Henry in the eye, and when he saw no one there that he recognized, led Henry by the elbow back up the hall. A few titters from some of the tipsier secretaries, openmouthed surprise from the others. Similar reactions from the officers. Henry March standing naked before them, a pale ghost, there and then gone. Marist stood in the farthest corner of the room, stopped in midconversation, watching without an immediately readable expression.

Roy took Henry back to the office, collecting clothes as they went. Once inside, he closed the door and turned Henry to look at him again.

"I have nothing to hide," Henry said. His voice all the more disturbing to Roy for its measured tone. Henry's normal, everyday voice, calm and even.

"You see?" he said, looking at Roy, his face steady, his eyes steady. "I have nothing."

16

The second girl arrived. She was tall and strongly built, a few years older than Elizabeth. She said her name was Emma. Dorn rolled his eyes at this. They gave her the briefing in the living room. She sat alone on the sofa with her legs crossed and her hands in her lap, listening with her face set as if she didn't quite believe them either. She had many of the same questions as Elizabeth: how she would be paid, if she would be working alone or with another girl. She had a low, deep voice, a southern accent, country rather than city. Henry was surprised that Dorn quoted her the same rate as Elizabeth. He had assumed Dorn would pay her less because she was a Negro.

She walked through the apartment, inspecting the bedroom, the bathroom, the kitchen. She flipped through the crate of records, unimpressed, and Dorn gave her some money to buy new ones, anything but Benny Goodman. She looked at him like he was speaking a foreign language, like she had no idea who Benny Goodman was.

"You can drink in here," Dorn said. "But no drugs. Not in the apartment."

Emma smoothed the front of her dress. "I don't know what you're talking about."

"Not in the apartment. Understood?"

She turned to Henry. "Is he a cop, too?"

"He's not a cop," Dorn said.

"He doesn't look like a cop."

Dorn lit a cigarette, passed it to Emma. "What does he look like?"

She stared at Henry through the smoke. "He looks like a teacher or something. A professor."

Dorn laughed.

"I don't know what he looks like." Emma took a pull on her cigarette. "He just looks like a regular guy."

17

Arlington, Winter 1955

Henry was unwell, that was what the voice on the phone said. It was a day not long after Henry's official questioning had ended. Thomas was napping, Ginnie was finishing her lunch when the phone rang. The man on the other end of the line spoke with a smooth timbre, a hint of the affected Brahmin tone she heard from many of Henry's colleagues. He introduced himself as Paul Marist.

Henry is unwell, Marist said. He'll be coming home soon.

A half hour later she heard a car door closing, the sharp bark of metal in the cold. She looked out the kitchen window to see Roy Pritchard's beetle-black Ford idling at the curb, exhaust billowing in the December air. Linebacker Roy, seemingly Henry's only friend left in Washington. Roy came around to the passenger side and opened the door, hunched by the raw wind, holding his gloved hands at the buttons of his coat. Henry stepped out onto the sidewalk, head down, coat open, his face obscured by the brim of his hat. Ginnie stood in the doorway, trying to see Henry's face as he made his way up the walk. She was one of the only people who could read his expressions. If she could see his face, then she could gauge the seriousness of the situation.

They reached the door. Roy took off his hat. It looked like he was about to say something, but then he set his hat back on his head and turned and walked to the car.

Henry didn't lift his head. Ginnie was afraid to touch him. She had never seen him like this, unsteady, uncertain. She asked if he would like to lie down. He nodded and she stepped aside to let him pass. She didn't lay a hand on him until he was in bed, still fully dressed, the sheets pulled up to his neck. Sent home like a sick child. She tried to undress him, but he wouldn't let her take his clothes off. He gripped the front of his shirt like he was afraid it would be ripped from his body.

She set her hand on his forehead. His skin was cool. His eyes were squeezed shut as if he was trying to force something away.

Later, he would tell her that he had become ill at work, that something he had eaten at the Christmas party hadn't agreed with him. This was not the truth. If she couldn't get the whole story from him, then she could still tell when she wasn't getting the truth. The man she had opened the front door to was not a man who had simply become sick at the office. Something deeper had happened.

Who he had looked like was Thomas. She tried to banish the thought, but it stayed with her, the rightness of the comparison making it impossible to send away. In that moment on the bed he had looked like Thomas after coming through a tantrum. Thomas reborn, bewildered. A new boy emerging into a frightening world.

18

Oakland, Spring 1956

They stood on the Sullivans' front step, waiting for the door to open. Ginnie made one last attempt to smooth Hannah's hair, but Hannah pulled away, took Thomas's hand. Thomas stared straight ahead at the door, adjusted his earmuffs.

The sound of footsteps from inside. Ginnie leaned into Henry. "Doris and Dick," she whispered. "He's a lawyer for a firm downtown. She was a beauty queen years ago. Miss Golden Gate Bridge or something."

Doris Sullivan welcomed them effusively, the guests of honor, then led them through the house to the back patio doors. She weaved a little as she walked, her hands out to her sides in a half dance step, seemingly more than a little drunk.

It was a larger party than Henry had expected. The yard was full of neighborhood families. There was a line at the barbecue, another at a bar in a corner by the fence. The noise was considerable, but Thomas seemed all right as long as his earmuffs were on and Hannah was by his side. She was happier than Henry had seen her since the move, the protective big sister, guiding Thomas along the hors d'oeuvre table, over to the sidelines to watch a badminton match between some of the other children.

Ginnie was at ease here. She had a poise and confidence in social situations that had always seemed effortless to Henry. She moved across the lawn, touching elbows, throwing her head back to laugh at one of Dick Sullivan's jokes. Henry followed a step behind, smiling mildly, concentrating on his drink.

"And what do you do, Mr. March?"

Doris Sullivan had cornered him by the edge of the patio. He'd become separated from Ginnie, somehow. It shouldn't have been so hard to give his standard answer, that he was an accountant, but he found himself tripped up here, still off balance from the unexpected crowd, stuck in Doris's close, unblinking gaze. He forced a smile, cleared his throat.

"Henry is a photographer."

Ginnie was there, suddenly, sweeping in beside him, a hand on his arm.

"How fascinating," Doris said. "Portraits or landscapes?"

"Portraits, mostly," Henry said.

"You'll have to show us your work," Doris said. "Dick is a shutterbug himself. Nothing at your level, I'm sure, but he loves talking about cameras. Would you do that sometime? Show us your work?"

"Of course," Ginnie said. "That sounds wonderful. Doesn't it, Henry?"

"Wonderful," Henry said. "Yes, it does."

Doris beamed.

19

The girls went out with their lists of names and came back with johns that Dorn wanted questioned, open cases in his department that had grown cold utilizing standard methods.

Dorn procured the drugs. Cannabis, mescaline, morphine, scopolamine. They tested the efficiency of various delivery systems. Whether a drug was smoked in a tainted cigarette or consumed in a spiked drink. They measured onset times, the degree to which the drug softened resistance, loosened tongues.

The results were different with every john. The men talked, or slept, or wanted nothing but sex for hours. They found that it was better for the girls to ask questions after sex, lying in bed with johns who expected them to dress and take their money and leave. The flattery of the extra attention, the unexpected intimacy. This was far more effective than asking questions earlier in the encounter, while teasing or withholding, which tended only to make the johns angry.

They watched things Henry would have preferred not to. His eyes on the window and then down to the ledger, reading what he'd written in the spilled-over light from the other room. Taking his attention off the scene when he could. Trying not to think about the fact that these girls were daughters, that they might have brothers and sisters, may have once been part of a family. The girls slapped or pushed or held down. The first few times this happened, Henry rose from his chair but Dorn told him to stay put, that one of them running in would do nothing but blow the project and put the girls in further danger down the road. So Henry sat and looked at the ledger when he could no longer watch the window.

He checked the post office boxes, sent paperwork back east. He typed up brief memos, the barest outlines of the operation, dates and times, the relative success or failure of a particular night. Funds arrived in the bank account and Henry withdrew enough for the rent and the liquor cabinet, the film and reels of audiotape.

They used the apartment three or four nights a week. Henry was home during the mornings, working on the biography of his time with Weir, or sleeping when he could, the sounds of Ginnie and Thomas reading or playing in the living room weaving in and out of his dreams. Hannah would already be at school. He seldom saw her during the week. After lunch and maybe a trip to the park with Thomas, he was back in the city, getting to the apartments no later than sundown. The end of the workday on the streets around him, men walking to the train, loosening their ties, heading home. Henry walking against the flow, crossing from one place to another.

He had told Ginnie that he would be working nights now, mostly. He didn't give her any more information and she didn't ask, though he could tell she wanted to. It wouldn't be for long, he said. Things would be back to normal soon.

Dorn arrived after his detective's shift, and they ate the sandwiches Henry had picked up from the deli on Powell. Sometimes Dorn insisted that they go out for a real meal, and then they took the Lincoln to one of Dorn's favorite spots, a restaurant in Chinatown or North Beach where the maître d's had booths waiting and the bartenders kept Dorn's martini glass full.

My name is Clarence. My name is Heath. My name is Stan. I'm a longshoreman, a truck driver, a shoe salesman in town on business. They all had different wants and needs, different things they told the girls to do. Some of the white men wanted to be rough with Emma; some wanted her to be rough with them. Some wanted to be tied to the bedposts with their belts, burned with cigarettes. Some wanted to be coddled, caressed, held.

The range and depth of need didn't surprise him. He had been trained to seek out the weaknesses in others. He'd seen photos, read private letters, heard recorded conversations. What surprised him was watching it play out just a few feet away. Human bodies in motion. There was nothing more intimate or frightening than two people alone in a room. It was difficult not to consider what his own need would be, what could be drawn out of him if he were on the other side of the window. What he would be willing to risk everything for.

He listened in the headphones, snapped pictures. He leaned forward at his desk, peering into the glass before the drugs knocked the johns completely out, straining to hear if their answers to the girls' questions were any more revealing in that brief moment before the men lost control. Dorn sitting beside him with a cigarette and a drink, chuckling or clucking his tongue or whistling low, whispering to Henry that this was the best goddamn television show he had ever seen.

20

They had him visit an agency-approved physician in Washington. The doctor asked questions, ran tests, told Henry that he was suffering from nervous exhaustion, that his senses had been overrun by the stress of the last few months. Henry left the office with a small bottle of sedatives, a smaller bottle of sleeping pills.

When he returned to work there were days of nothing, anesthetized days. Henry sitting in his office, moving paper. Roy Pritchard came to visit. Henry's secretary brought him coffee, avoided eye contact. Everyone avoided eye contact. Doors closed when he approached, conversations ceased in midsentence when he entered the room. Henry taking his pills, moving through the hallways, immaterial, an invisible man.

One morning he was summoned to a conference room by a couple of Marist's men. There was no explanation for the call. When he was seated, they pulled down a projection screen and turned off the lights. A film came to life in front of him. Faces of American soldiers, one after another, skinny teenagers, sunken-eyed and gaunt. Unshaven, if they were old enough to grow beards. POWs in a cement room. They stared blankly at the camera. They recited long, rambling lists of grievances against the United States, denigrating their homes and families, telling their fellow soldiers to turn their arms against their commanders. Each

of them speaking in the same emotionless monotone, with the same lus-
terless look in their eyes.

The North Koreans were using brainwashing techniques they'd
learned from the Chinese, maybe the Soviets. The voice came from
the back of the conference room. Henry turned but the man who had
spoken was standing in shadow. He introduced himself as a staff psychiatrist. Henry turned back to the screen. Sleep deprivation, torture,
possibly drugs, the psychiatrist said. Drugs that create an overwhelming
sense of paranoia, that sow doubt. Drugs that empty a man's mind so it
can be filled with something new.

*I would like to say that the United States is an imperial, racist nation,
bent on domination of the Asiatic countries and their benevolent people.*
Words the boy on-screen would never have found in his own head. *I
would like to say to my fellow soldiers that the enemy is behind you, the
enemy is beside you.*

Marist's voice came from the back of the room. He said the boy's
name and rank, his hometown. He said that these soldiers were part of
a mission that now appeared to have been compromised by Weir. Information passed to the Soviets and then on to the North Koreans.

The boy extended a shaking hand out of the frame and brought it
back with a lit cigarette. His stare into the camera was direct, as if he was
speaking to Henry, to the other men in the conference room.

Henry sat forward in his seat. He could feel his own mind working
again, despite the sedatives. He could feel himself coming back, drawn
through the fog toward the boys on-screen.

He asked how much film they had like this, how many POWs, and
Marist asked how much Henry wanted to see.

He began watching every day, sitting alone in the conference room, looking at the films and the list of names and hometowns in the file folder.
Private Milt Whitman, Private John Stone. Somebody's fiancé, somebody's son. He needed to watch these boys, to listen to them. He felt that
he owed them this. They had been captured because of him, because

of Weir. There was no information on their current status but he felt in some irrational way he was keeping them alive by replaying their films. That if he stopped watching, if he took his eyes off the screen, then they would truly be lost.

One evening he entered the conference room to find a film already playing. Private Jacob Weiner projected against the far wall, the only soundless clip of the batch, the boy's mouth moving mechanically, looking in his silence like a ventriloquist's dummy.

Marist sat in a chair at the front of the conference table, the back of his head silhouetted against the screen. It was the moment in the film where Private Weiner cups his hands over his mouth and coughs. A lost boy from Camden, New Jersey, whom someone had brought up well, his politeness reflexive, his manners persevering despite war and captivity and torture. Somebody's fiancé, somebody's son.

"We need to find out how they did this," Marist said. He did not turn from the screen. "Most officers would shrink from what we'll need to do, what I'm asking you to do, but they haven't seen this, they haven't sat in this room. You understand the severity of what we're dealing with better than anyone. What's at stake. He taught you that. Weir."

Marist lit a cigarette, still watching the screen. A close-up on Jacob Weiner's face, the boy's features four feet high, dominating the room.

"I listen to politicians tell me that the enemy is not real or that the threat is not as dire as we think and then I come back here and watch this to remind myself that they are fools. Or that they are the enemy themselves, possibly. How can we be sure? We know how patient they are, how deeply they have penetrated."

Marist smoked, watching the next soldier, the next.

"I have nightmares of my wife and daughters speaking this way," he said. "I have nightmares where they are on film, in a room like that, staring at a camera. Do you have those nightmares, Henry? After watching these boys? I'd imagine you do."

Henry could imagine Ginnie on that screen, in that room. He could imagine Hannah. He watched Private Milt Whitman, Private John Stone. The boys' eyes in the conference room, lightless, emptied. Their minds broken like plates.

"You are alone here, Henry," Marist said. "They all wanted to cut you off, cast you out. But I told them that I needed you. And that is the truth. I need someone who knows what is at stake."

Private Weiner was back on the screen. Henry watched the boy cup his hands over his mouth again, cough.

Marist said, "We need to know how this is done."

21

Oakland, Spring 1956

Ginnie sat on the floor beside Thomas's bed and read to him from a children's book about San Francisco. The pages were full of local landmarks, the wharf and the hills and the streetcars imagined as playfully askew renderings in charcoal and watercolor.

She could hear the sound of audience laughter from the living room, where Hannah was watching *You Bet Your Life*. Ginnie pointed to the characters in the book. She asked Thomas to identify them, but he sat passively, staring at the pages as he so often stared at her, at anyone, looking through rather than engaging in any way. She found the page with the streetcars, and he sat up, leaned forward, focusing on the drawings, and she asked him questions about the lines and types of cars, the B Geary and J Church, the Baby Tens and Iron Monsters. He was with her now, answering each inquiry in his metallic monotone, then standing to retrieve his timetables from the desk on the other side of his room.

Another night without Henry. He was working late now, sometimes very late, even spending the night in the city. She hadn't asked for an explanation. They didn't talk about his work. She knew that it made him uncomfortable to lie.

There had been plenty of talk at some of the parties in Washington, what the Russians were up to, the Chinese, headlines and generalities, but as the nights grew later and drinks were refilled, the men retired to the living rooms and the women moved into the kitchens and voices lowered, talk loosened. What their husbands were really up to. Dropping leaflets over the Ukraine, dropping paratroopers into Albania, toppling Mosaddegh in Iran. The women intoxicated by their husbands' roles in shaping history and by their own proximity to those roles, what they felt they contributed in the way of advice, a female perspective, whispers across pillows in the dark.

Ginnie had little to add to these conversations. It seemed reckless to her, as she knew it did to Henry, discussing these things openly after too many cocktails at someone's country home. To add a layer of inebriated innuendo and speculation onto an already opaque subject. Even when they were alone, she and Henry didn't discuss his work. They talked about the parties instead, marveling at the money and servants and silverware, leaving the more sensitive subjects where they belonged, in Henry's office, in Henry's head.

This was the third night in a row he'd been away. She'd told herself that she wasn't going to keep track, but she was. Three nights this week, three nights the week before. She slept fitfully when he was away, waiting for him to return safe from what still seemed like a foreign city.

They all slept fitfully. Hannah still woke in the night from dreams of the bomb. Ginnie tried to comfort her, but there was nothing she could say. Hannah only wanted Henry. Only Henry could reassure her.

More TV laughter from the living room. Ginnie stood and replaced the book on Thomas's shelf. Thomas plugged himself into the wall, lay back on the floor beside his bed. She turned out the light, covered him with a sheet and a blanket.

Thomas was shouting, suddenly. *The B Geary line runs continuously from six a.m. to eight p.m. and on an intermittent overnight schedule. Streetcars running every ten minutes during the workday, every half hour thereafter.*

Ginnie knelt beside him, held her finger to her lips.

The Geary Street rail service will close at the end of the year, he shouted, *with buses replacing the streetcars. Thereafter streetcar service will permanently cease operation.*

"Switch," she whispered. "Switch." She could see Thomas struggling for the meaning of the word, his eyes circling the room, then it came to him and he pressed the imagined button on his chest, closed his mouth, his eyes, the power draining from his engine.

Ginnie could hear a big-band theme from the living room, the quiz show signing off. She leaned in and kissed Thomas on the forehead. She stood and watched him flinch, recoiling, as if wishing away the simple feeling of contact.

22

Henry's visions began not long after they'd started with the johns. Fleeting things, in windows, mirrors. The moments in the north bedroom that Henry turned away from, brought back to him later, as if trapped in the glass. The car windshield, the television in the living room of the house in Oakland, its screen dark in the early morning, Ginnie and the children asleep.

A john with Elizabeth, a john with Emma. A john holding Elizabeth's wrists and Henry looks away, down from the glowing window to his ledger. A john pulling Emma's hair, slapping her across the face. A john holding Elizabeth by the neck, shouting into her open mouth.

At a movie theater with Hannah and the images on-screen twist into a nightmare memory. At the breakfast table, cutting Thomas's toast and a movement in the window catches Henry's eye. A john's arm swinging and a girl falling and the first body climbing onto the second.

He looks at Hannah, at Thomas. He looks at Ginnie in the passenger seat beside him and can see the north bedroom in the car's window beyond.

That is Henry Gladwell. Henry March would not allow these things. He needs to remind himself of the distinction. This is something Weir taught him. Every operation has casualties. There are always compromises made for a larger good. This was why other names were necessary. There were practical reasons and then there were deeper concerns.

A girl in a window with a man who means her harm.

Henry Gladwell, Henry March. He excuses himself from the dinner table and looks in the bathroom mirror, the face reflected there. Repeating the name. You have to go home at night, Weir had said. Don't forget this. You have to remind yourself of who you really are.

23

The man from Washington arrived on the first afternoon of the summer. He seemed like an extension of the day, bright and blond and blue-eyed, tan from his time on the road in the rented convertible he'd parked half-way down the block.

His sleeves were rolled to his elbows, his shirt open at the collar. He approached Henry with a matinee-idol smile.

"Let me guess. They didn't tell you I was coming."

Henry shook his head.

"Dr. Cameron Clarke," he said, offering his hand. "You can call me Chip. Paul Marist says hello."

Clarke walked through the north living room, taking in the furnishings, the artwork.

"This is really something."

Henry poured Clarke a scotch in the kitchen. The man was familiar somehow. Henry tried to place the face. The name didn't register, but the name could have been invented two weeks ago, could have been created in the convertible on his drive west.

"Where's the other man?" Clarke said. He sat on the sofa, sipping his scotch.

"Dorn."

Clarke lifted a packet out of his shirt pocket, set a cigarette on his lower lip. "I've been told he's quite a character."

"That would be an accurate description."

"How many"—Clarke lit a match, looking for the word—"*ladies* do you have working?"

"Two."

That Saturday-afternoon smile again. "Ever thought you'd be doing something like this, Mr. March?"

"Gladwell."

"Gladwell, right. Mind if I call you Henry?"

"That's fine."

Clarke shook his head, delighted by the entire thing.

Henry said, "Did we meet in Washington?"

"I don't believe so. Do I look familiar?"

"No."

"Well, there you go." Clarke sipped his drink. "I have a delivery for you, down in the car. Locked in the glove box, don't worry. I meant to bring it up, but I was so eager to see the place." He leaned back on the couch, smiling at the prints on the walls. "This is really something else."

"We should go down."

"Of course." Clarke rose from the sofa, swallowed the last of his scotch, shaking a sliver of ice into his mouth. "You'll want to meet Stormy." He looked at Henry. "That's what we call it. I have no idea who came up with the name, but it fits. Just wait until you see Stormy in action."

They sat around Henry's desk in the office. Clarke opened the box and unrolled a sheet of newspaper. He removed a glass vial and held it between his thumb and index finger. The vial was half full with a clear liquid. He turned it to catch the light from the desk lamp.

He talked about dosage. He talked about onset period and duration of effects. He talked about precautionary measures to take when handling, not to let the liquid touch their clothes, their skin.

"What's a microgram?" Dorn said.

Clarke set the vial on the desk. They all stared, as if waiting for it to do something on its own.

"One millionth of a gram," Clarke said.

"That means nothing to me."

"One-tenth the size of a grain of sand."

"And how much is in there with the water?"

"Five hundred micrograms. One dose."

"How much is too much?" Henry said.

Clarke shook his head. "You can't overdose. Not that we've seen."

"Have you tried it?" Dorn said.

"Yes."

"And?"

Clarke smiled. "And everything changes."

He said that everyone back east used the pet name for the drug. Small caps when written, whispered when spoken. STORMY. They even used the name in official correspondence, though official correspondence on the subject was rare and discouraged. STORMY was a more accurate description, Clarke said, more elegant than its full Christian name.

"Which would be what?" Dorn said.

Clarke lit a cigarette, shook his match out into the ashtray on Henry's desk. "Lysergic acid diethylamide."

Dorn stared at the vial, tapping his teeth with his fingernail.

"How many doses did you bring?" Henry said.

"Enough."

"Where are they?"

"They're secure."

"They're not secure unless they're with me."

"I'll hang on to them," Clarke said.

"That's not acceptable."

"I've been instructed to hang on to them." Clarke pulled on his cigarette, set it to rest in the ashtray. He looked across the desk at Henry. "Do you want to try it? You could consider it hands-on research."

"No."

Clarke looked at Dorn. "How about you?"

"No." Henry answered before Dorn could open his mouth.

"Have it your way." Clarke sat back, lifted his cigarette. "But you have no idea what you're missing."

24

They left the house early on Saturday mornings, dressing quietly and meeting in the kitchen. Henry drank his coffee and Hannah rushed through her cereal, anxious to leave before her mother and brother awoke. Standing in the doorway, arms folded, foot tapping, gestures she'd learned from impatient television wives.

They approached the bay through the surrounding neighborhoods, the sky beginning to lighten as they made their way down the hill, and then the bridge appeared, rising to fill the windshield, the long spans revealed, steel arms glinting in the sun.

They drove the lower deck, in the lane beside the trains. Every week Henry asked if Hannah wanted to drive all the way over, into the city, and every week she said no.

The bridge itself fascinated her. She rattled off information as they drove, things she'd learned in school, the height of the towers and length of the span and the time it had taken to build. It seemed like an ancient structure to her, something that had stood since an unimaginable past, but Henry was always struck by the facts, how quickly something so colossal had been constructed and its relative youth, only twice as old as Hannah.

She talked while he drove. This was more like the Hannah he knew. She had always been genial and outgoing, a member of the Brownie

Scouts, leader of a Polly Pigtail Club she had founded with a group of friends in Arlington. She had her mother's self-assurance, making her a mystery to Henry in the same way that Ginnie was a mystery to him. Their ease in the world. But the move and the film had changed her, had made her wary and uncertain in ways that Henry understood.

She still woke two or three times a week, crying from nightmares about the bomb and the devastated city. On the nights that he was home he tried to reassure her, but it was becoming clear that there were no words convincing enough. So he tried something else, bringing her post-cards from drugstores and newsstands, photos of Chinatown storefronts and Union Square hotels, seals sunning themselves on the piers. Evidence of normalcy in the city. Proof of life.

She preferred black-and-white postcards, which surprised him. He would have thought she'd find the color comforting, more like real life, but she felt the black-and-white images had an authenticity the others lacked. She studied the pictures in her bedroom, holding them for long silent moments, eyes moving slowly across the thin cardboard. She looked for the most mundane of images, rows of tidy houses, street signs, men loading a milk truck curbside. Moments so commonplace that they'd be impossible to fabricate, wouldn't be worth constructing a lie around. When she found one, she thumbtacked the postcard to the wall with the others she'd selected. Then she stepped back and looked at the images, at the larger image the smaller ones created.

Into the tunnel, the sun and sky gone, suddenly. Hannah pointed across the tracks to the doorway-size openings in the far wall. Those are dead-man holes, she said. They're for the gandy dancers. So rail workers can step in and disappear if a train is coming.

They never drove farther than Yerba Buena. Henry parked the car on the island so that it faced the bridge and they watched the sparse week-end traffic crossing between cities. Ginnie and Thomas would be up by now, having breakfast in the kitchen. Ginnie watching the clock on the stove, worrying. She had lost some of her confidence, too, since those last months in Washington. His uncertainty had made them all unsure.

Henry suggested that they take the train the following week, have lunch on Market Street, ride a streetcar up the hill to see Oakland from the other side of the bay. He always suggested this, and Hannah always responded in the same way. Looking out at the towers in the fog, nodding, noncommittal, still unconvinced.

They drove home, back across the bridge. Hannah was quieter now. She looked out her window, pointing to dead-man holes, watching the railmen working on the sides of the tracks and then looking for a train. Wanting to see the system work, the safe escape. Waiting for the noise and the engine lights, for one of the men to step into a doorway and disappear.

25

Dorn is late and when he finally arrives at the south apartment he's drunk.

"I don't want to see that look, Hank. It's been a bitch of a day." He crosses to the breakfront bar, grabs the scotch. "I spent all afternoon in the hospital."

"What happened?"

"Nothing happened." Dorn pours a drink, tosses it back. "My wife needed some tests."

Henry's ledger is open to a blank page. He checks his watch, writes the date and time. He almost writes the full name of the drug and then stops himself, inscribing the nickname instead.

Dorn says, "Any word from Emma?"

"Not yet."

Dorn fills his flask, spilling scotch, cursing under his breath.

Henry says, "What kind of tests?"

Dorn takes a drink, screws the cap back onto his flask. "Not the good kind."

He goes back outside to wait.

Henry checks his watch, looks up from the ledger to see Clarke on the other side of the mirror. Clarke is standing in the bedroom, almost perfectly still, except for a slight turn at the waist. His eyes moving, trying to spot the equipment, the cameras and spike mics. Trying to see the room as the john will see it. Looking at the walls, the ceiling. He doesn't look into the mirror because the mirror is obvious.

Clarke speaks softly, *Hello, hello.* Henry hears his voice in the headphones and knows who Clarke is, finally. He recognizes the voice, the psychiatrist at the back of the conference room in Washington, the man standing in shadow while the films of the captured soldiers played against the wall.

Noise on the stairs and then Dorn comes into the office, Clarke following close behind. They pull their chairs alongside Henry's, facing the glass. They put on their headphones. Dorn starts to cough, pounds his chest. Henry and Clarke watch him as if they're at a theater and the performance won't begin until the noise subsides. Dorn passes his flask to Clarke and Clarke takes a long drink.

Front door, shoes in the living room. The sound of Emma pouring drinks in the kitchen. Henry pictures the eyedropper in her purse, now in her hand, the dropper uncapped, the liquid squeezed into the drink.

STORMY.

Henry marks the time in his ledger.

Voices in the headphones.

This ain't your apartment.

Me and a friend, Emma says.

Where's your friend?

Out.

She coming back?

Not tonight.

Dorn sucks an antacid. The slight squeak of the circling tape reels is the only other sound in the office.

Emma says, I know you. Your name's Lonnie, right? I've heard you play.

Where?

That club on Post Street.

Never played there.

I've heard you play. I remember your face.

You can't see my face when I'm playing.

I remember it from when you lowered your horn. Another man playing. You were standing there waiting, watching him, bobbing your head. Holding your horn at your side. I remember your face.

You want money or dope?

We can talk about that later.

We can talk about that later. Who you trying to kid?

I want to hear you play.

I ain't playing tonight.

You've got your horn.

I've always got my horn. But I haven't played in a month.

I'll just sit and listen.

Put on a record. We'll listen to that.

I don't want a record. I want to dance while you play.

I don't play fast.

I don't dance fast.

The sound of the horn in the headphones. Henry lowers the gain, looks to Dorn, worried about the noise. The neighbors across the alley calling the police, someone coming out to knock at the door.

Clarke takes off his headphones and cocks his head, listens to the music through the walls. "Body and Soul," he whispers, and for some reason Henry writes this in the ledger.

Lonnie's naked back to the mirror. Long, thick scars crossing his shoulder blades. Emma on her knees in front of him, invisible to the men in the office. Lonnie's head back, looking up at the ceiling fan, and Henry takes a picture.

Emma stops. Her face appears beside Lonnie's waist.

What's the matter, baby?

She stands and takes a step back and looks at Lonnie.

I can see the sky, he says.

How's that?

The roof has curled back and I can see the sky. There. He points to the ceiling.

Maybe you should sit down.

Where's my horn? He sits on the bed, still looking up.

Baby?

Where's my horn? I have to play this.

The sound of Dorn clearing his throat and then he steps into frame, the view through the mirror. Lonnie still sitting on the bed looking up at the ceiling. The rest of the room of no interest to him. Emma stands from the bed, her long limbs, like a crane dipping when she bends to pick her dress off the floor. She backs out of the room.

Lonnie looks right at the camera hidden behind the ceiling fan and Henry takes a picture. The captured moment: Lonnie on the bed, Dorn inside the door, standing slightly hunched, some great beast arrived at the heart of the thing.

Lonnie.

No response.

Lonnie.

Who's that?

Look over here.

Who's that?

Over here.

Oh, Jesus.

Do you know who I am?

Oh, Jesus.

You know who I am?

I know. I know. I can see your eyes.

Henry removes his headphones, sets them on his desk during the screaming.

Many questions. Names, dates, who knows who, where can I find this man, who does this man know. Lonnie's answers are meaningless. Bears, green, green, "St. James Infirmary." As if he's hearing different questions. As if he's having another conversation somewhere else.

The two men circle the room, Lonnie stumbling backward, crawling over the bed, Dorn following, deliberate, until Lonnie has run out of corners and stands with his arms spread, his hands flat against the wall.

Lonnie touches every place on his skin where he's struck and lifts his fingers to his nose, smiling as if smelling a flower.

The night passes. Lonnie and Dorn stand almost nose to nose, a half inch of air between them. Dorn frustrated, asking the same questions, and Lonnie only smiling in return, lips pulled back, his face stretched almost to a death mask. Henry takes a picture just before Lonnie touches Dorn's nose with the tip of his own and Dorn rears back and brings his forehead down, cracking Lonnie open and sending him back to the wall.

"Found out nothing."

"You're wrong."

"Found out a lot of fucking bullshit. How his name smells." Dorn's forehead open, knuckles open, blood on his unbuttoned shirt.

"You're wrong." Clarke standing in the bathroom doorframe holding a Dictaphone case, nearly manic with what he's seen.

Henry and Dorn are cleaning Lonnie in the sink. His lips and nose are swollen. He's asleep or unconscious or just quiet with his eyes closed.

"We need to keep him longer," Clarke says.

"No." Henry wiping blood from Lonnie's split lips. Water running red in the sink.

"I need to observe him coming out of it," Clarke says.

"He can't be here when he comes out of it."

"I want to talk to him."

"No."

"I have orders," Clarke says.

"We're cleaning him up and getting him out," Henry says. "We don't know what we have here."

"I know what we have." Clarke staring hard at Henry, then deciding something, switching focus to the recorder and microphone in his hands. "I need a place to talk."

"The room beside the office," Henry says.

"The bathroom?"

"The other room."

"Can anyone hear me in there?"

"No one can hear you."

Clarke leaves with his Dictaphone. Dorn pulls a towel from the back of the door, runs it over the top of his head, mopping sweat. Henry holds Lonnie alone, his face in the mirror beside Lonnie's ruined reflection.

They leave Lonnie in an alley a few streets up from the wharves. Dorn has refilled his flask and is drinking hard while he steers the Lincoln, his nerves scraped raw from the night. When they return to Telegraph Hill, Clarke gets out of the car without a word, still clutching his Dictaphone. He walks toward his convertible, somewhere back in the fog. Henry watches him in the rearview mirror, disappearing into the mist.

"I'm sure you've followed him, too," Dorn says.

Henry nods.

"He's a risk," Dorn says.

"He's who we've been sent."

"They're problematic, queers. Easily compromised."

"I'm aware."

"They talk."

"So do cops."

Dorn takes another long pull from his flask, holding the metal lip between his front teeth. Henry steps out of the car, shuts the door behind him. Dorn pulls the Lincoln away from the curb.

He found Emma sitting on the sofa in the north living room, her knees up under her chin, her arms around her shins.

Henry said, "How long have you been here?"

"The whole time. You walked right by me when you dragged him out." Emma rocking a little on the sofa, hugging her legs to her body. "What did I give him?"

"Nothing."

"Is he dead?"

"No."

"Where is he?"

"He won't remember any of it."

Henry stood in front of her, took out his wallet.

"Can I stay here?" she said.

"No."

"Use the shower?"

"No."

She took the money, folded it into her purse. Wiped her nose with the back of her hand. "What if I don't come back?"

"Then Dorn will find you."

Emma picked up her purse, stood.

Henry looked at his watch, crossed back to the front door.

"You can use the shower," he said. "But don't touch anything else."

26

Henry parked in the driveway, but found himself unable to enter the house. He backed out and left the car on an adjacent street and now stood up the hill, the warm day rising around him as if it was growing out of the ground.

Blood on the cuffs of his shirt, dried and brown. Dorn's or the musician's or both. Dorn had stripped off his own shirt and tossed it, disgusted, into the brush down the hill toward the Embarcadero. He had seemed pained by this, losing the shirt. It had seemed to bother him more than anything else that had happened that night.

Lonnie. The man had a name. The musician. Henry had written it in the ledger.

He had the ledger in the pocket of his overcoat. It was too warm for the overcoat, but he needed to keep the ledger close to his body, needed to remind himself of who had done this, who was responsible. The name in neat columns across the first few pages of the book.

Henry Gladwell Henry Gladwell Henry Gladwell.

He had cleaned up the bedroom with the sound of Emma in the shower and by the time he was finished she was gone. He put the tape reels into the safe. He went back into the bedroom and stood on the bed and opened the slots in the ceiling, removed the film from the cameras.

In the darkroom, the images rising. His fingertips dry, flaking from the chemicals in the pans. Lonnie and Emma. Lonnie and Emma. Lonnie sitting alone on the bed, looking up at the ceiling. Lonnie crying, Lonnie shielding his face from Dorn.

Henry stood at the worktable, cropping the extraneous information from the frame. Dorn, the furniture in the room. Then at the enlarger, focusing on one section, the central fact of the image. Lonnie's face rising through the liquid in the pan. Then at the enlarger again, going closer. Just the man's eyes this time, blurred from the imprecision of the lens and the effects of the drug. The look of horror there, and then nothing, his eyes lightless and flat.

There were compromises to be made for a larger good. Amends for mistakes. He thought of Private Milt Whitman, Private John Stone. Boys locked in rooms far from home. Others out there, possibly, betrayed by Weir, by Henry's ignorance, his blindness. Those men or the musician. It was reasonable, logical to trade one man for many. To trade two men, ten men. What they had done in that room, to that man, what they would do, could be distilled from the blood and noise, could be stripped down to pure mathematics, to accounting.

Lonnie. The man had a name.

Henry stood up the street from the house, the sweat drying on his back, his neck. The ledger in his coat pocket. He watched the front door. Ginnie and the children would be inside, starting their day.

Henry Gladwell. He tried to expel the name, force it through his mouth, his fingertips. He would not move until the name had left him completely, until it was safely contained within the covers of the ledger.

He watched the door. He waited for the name. He would not enter the house until he was sure he was the man they could trust.

27

Observation took place on night of 15 July. Observation took place on night of 18 July. Subject is Negro male in late thirties. Subject is Chinese male, approx. early fifties. Subject is Caucasian male, indeterminate age.

Initial cannabis dose occurs in Powell Street bar. In Beach Street bar. Subsequent STORMY dose occurs in apartment. Approx. 350 micrograms. Approx. 500 micrograms. Onset period of twenty minutes. Onset period of thirty-five minutes.

Subject loses interest in female companion. Subject begins to speak to walls of room. Subject begins to experience auditory hallucinations. Voices of ex-wife, deceased parents. Subject appears distraught, frightened. Subject becomes violently ill. Subject becomes agitated and accusatory. Subject becomes physically hostile, sexually aggressive.

D enters the room. D enters the room. When D suggests Subject discuss certain aspects of business dealings, Subject spits in D's face. Confrontation with D leaves Subject with minor bruises and contusions.

Subject refuses to speak. Subject speaking rapidly in unidentified language. Subject believes self to be invisible. Believes self to be physical component of the room, an extension of the walls and floor. Subject frustrated by D's lack of comprehension.

C enters the room. Subject doesn't appear to find C's arrival unusual. Subject and C have lengthy conversation regarding Subject's childhood and biography. Subject given additional STORMY dose. Approx. 150 micrograms. Approx. 200 micrograms. Subject uneasy. Subject agitated, requires restraint.

Subject has forgotten name. Subject has forgotten biography. Subject disoriented, uncomfortable. Subject given name and biography of famous film actor by C. Subject quiet, considering. C speaks with Subject as if Subject is said actor. Subject considering. Subject answers to new name. Subject repeats new biography in its entirety numerous times as if it was his own. Subject able to answer questions about new biography, elaborate on details. Subject at ease in conversation. Subject calm. Subject calm.

Subject addressed by C with Subject's real name. No response from Subject. No recognition of that name.

Subject cleaned and dressed and removed from apartment, deposited suitable distance from premises.

Observation ended at 4:35 A.M. Observation ended at 5 A.M. Photographs developed. Recording reviewed.

Now on nights when there was no observation, Henry still drove into the city. He went to the apartments and opened the panel in the wall of the unused room in the south apartment where Clarke believed he spoke privately to his Dictaphone. Henry removed the small recorder he had hidden there and listened to Clarke's observations.

On the tapes, Clarke talked about how the project had gone far beyond what he had predicted. He spoke in an impassioned rush, describing the look in the johns' eyes after they were drugged and questioned, or, more importantly, the lack, the absence of a look. The men removed of all history, all motivation. The drug had emptied them, left nothing but clothes, skin, bone.

Ego-death. Ego-death. Clarke's voice on the recording repeating the term, as if sounding an alarm.

Henry erased the tapes after listening to them. He went to a coffee shop or an automat or a newsstand. He walked down to the Embarcadero and looked for men he recognized, men from the other room, not sure what he would do if he saw one. Imagining himself pulled into an alley and beaten with a bottle, sliced with a knife. Walking the streets by the wharf with the waves battering the docks and waiting for this to happen.

He sat in coffee shops and listened to conversations, the waitresses behind the counter and the one or two other occupied booths. His teeth had begun bothering him, sensitive on the upper right, so he let his coffee cool in the cup before he took a sip and then only on the other side of his mouth. He waited for a man he would recognize to walk in the door. He imagined sitting in a booth across from one of those men and calling the man by his real name, the name they had taken from him. He imagined the man's response, all the possible responses, the endless potentialities. The man grabbing the ketchup bottle, cracking it on the edge of table, jabbing the ragged remains into Henry's chest. He imagined sitting in a booth across from Private John Stone, Private Jacob Weiner. He imagined asking for their forgiveness and the soldiers giving no response, reaching across the table for cigarettes, covering their mouths as they coughed.

One morning he came home to find that Hannah had removed all of the postcards from her bedroom wall. At breakfast he asked her about this and she said that she no longer wanted the information secondhand. She didn't know who had taken those pictures. Even the most basic of images, trees standing in a park, players at a baseball game, were suspect. They still harbored a sliver of doubt. She wanted Henry to take photographs. She wanted to see what he saw when he was in the city. Something he had seen that he brought to her, she knew she could believe.

At a newsstand he stood under the awning, out of the midnight drizzle. Steam rising from the sidewalks, worms uncurling on the cement. Long racks, stag magazines, detective and science-fiction paperbacks. The newsstand attendant sat on a stool at the far end, picking his teeth with a match. Henry looked at the covers. *Climax* magazine. *Frolic. Fury. True Photo-rama.* He opened the magazines and looked at the photographs, the staging, the posed bodies. Seeing nothing real, nothing that shocked or frightened him.

A noise from the side, a pulsing hum, the sound Thomas made when he was observing something from his tracks. Henry turned and a man was there, a few feet away, holding a magazine at arm's length, making the humming sound, his whole body rocking with it. The man replaced the magazine and lifted another from the rack. The man slightly younger than Henry, tall and broad, bent at the shoulders. Thomas in thirty years, possibly, here through one of the time machines on the covers of the science-fiction paperbacks. A man, possibly, whom Henry would see soon enough, in the bedroom, on the other side of the glass.

The man rocked and hummed until the attendant called down to him. The man smiled at this, or at something else, some private stimulation that just happened to coincide with the attendant's voice.

Henry watched the man until the attendant called out again. The man's smile widened and Henry stepped away from the newsstand, back out onto the street.

28

Waiting in the darkened office, the three men, headphones on, cigarettes lit, cameras and recorders loaded, listening for footsteps on the stairs, watching the black window, the invisible room.

They heard the front door open, then the sound of running, stumbling, someone topping the stairs and then pounding on the outer office door. Headphones off, all three men up. Dorn motioned for them to stay put. He moved alone into the outer room. Someone still pounding on the door. Dorn looked through the security eyelet, turned the locks. He opened the door and Elizabeth was leaning against the frame, breathless. There was blood on the shoulder of her dress, cuts under her eye, along her ear. Dorn ushered her across the vestibule, into the north apartment, Clarke following, Henry heading down the stairs to check the front door, the street.

She sat on the sofa, looking thin and cold. They surrounded her, Clarke standing by the armchair, Dorn back by the windows, leaning with his face to the glass to see down the street. Henry was the only one in motion, pulling a pillowcase free in the bedroom, filling it with ice in the kitchen.

Dorn lit a cigarette, shook the match. "Did they say anything?"

Henry handed Elizabeth the rolled pillowcase and she pressed the ice to her eye, winced.

"They told me they'd heard things," she said.

"What things?"

"Things I was doing to men."

"And you came back here," Clarke said.

"Where else was I gonna go?"

Henry stood by the record player, watching her. They were all watching her.

Dorn said, "How many?"

"Two, I think."

Clarke fumbled in his pockets for his own cigarettes. "You think?"

"It was dark."

"What else did they say?" Henry said.

"Nothing." She shifted the ice to her ear. "Just that they'd heard things."

"What did they look like?" Dorn said.

"It was dark, I couldn't see right. They were behind me."

"And you didn't tell them anything?" Clarke said.

Elizabeth looked up at him. "I didn't tell them shit."

Dorn stepped toward Elizabeth, gestured with his cigarette. "This is it? The eye and the ear?"

"And the back of my head," Elizabeth said. "They hit me in the back of my head to start."

"You're lucky." Dorn turned back to the window. "You're really goddamn lucky."

"I feel lucky," she said. She shifted the ice back to her eye. "I feel like I won the fucking jackpot."

An hour later, Dorn came through the apartment door, shook off his coat, hung it on the rack.

"I gave her some money and told her to stay home for a while."

"Did you find Emma?" Henry said.

"No."

"We need to."

"I will."

"Soon."

"I said I will, Hank." Dorn stepped into the kitchen, poured a tumbler of vodka, added a handful of ice from Elizabeth's melting pillowcase, slopping liquid over the sides of the glass, onto his fingers.

Clarke was sitting on the sofa. He looked at Henry. "I know what you're thinking."

"What am I thinking?"

"You want to shut us down."

"There are men out there who know," Henry said.

"Who know what?"

"Enough."

"Who are they going to tell?" Clarke said. "The police?"

"The fact that they know is sufficient."

"What do you think, Jimmy?"

Henry said, "I'm telling you what I think."

"And I'm asking Jimmy."

Dorn took a drink, stared into his glass. "It's a problem, but not a big problem."

Clarke nodded. "We're not stopping now. We're close."

Dorn said, "Close to what?"

Clarke sucked his teeth, forced a yawn.

Henry lifted a cigarette from his pack, lit a match. His hands weren't steady. He struggled with the light. Clarke was watching. Henry could see his face reflected in the glass.

"Any further objections?" Clarke said.

Henry finally lit his cigarette, shook out the match.

"Good." Clarke stood from the couch, stretched. "Then meeting adjourned."

29

He began complicating his route home in the early morning, often driving a half hour around the city before crossing into Oakland. Watching his mirrors, the cars in front and behind, men passing in train windows. Looking for a face he recognized. Lonnie, Clarence, Clyde from Buffalo. A john waiting somewhere outside the apartment and following Henry to the station wagon and then following him home. A man on the street, on the sidewalk. Henry sitting in the car, the ledger on the seat beside him. Ginnie and the children sleeping and a man standing in their driveway, staring at the dark windows of the house.

The museum was housed in a boat shed on one of the wharf's piers, a long, high-ceilinged space filled with old mechanical carnival games, telegraphs and early telephones, antique cars with exposed engines. There was a decommissioned railway passenger car at the back of the museum and Thomas headed for it immediately, unlatching his hand from Henry's, ignoring the machines and display cases he passed along the way.

The museum was nearly empty, just a few mothers with young children, boys, mostly, working the levers of boxing and baseball games. Henry took a seat in the passenger car and watched Thomas move down the aisle, taking tickets from invisible passengers and depositing them into an imagined slot in his own chest.

Beyond Thomas, Henry could see some movement in the windows. He lit a cigarette, tried to ignore it, but there was nowhere else to look. They weren't the usual violent scenes of the girls and johns. Instead, there were men in suits, smoking, listening through headphones, photographing through the windows, taking notes. Henry tried to ignore them, but their movement kept drawing his attention. Their faces, their camera lenses. Finally, he looked straight at the glass, intending to meet their eyes, hoping to dispel the visions with direct confrontation. But he could see now that they weren't watching him. They were watching Thomas, listening, observing, photographing.

Henry couldn't catch his breath. There were more figures in the windows now, so he took his glasses off, blurring his vision. His hands were shaking. The passenger car floating, it felt like, loosed from the pull of the earth, up through the top of the shed, spinning into the open sky.

He could hear the sound of Thomas's engine hum. Henry looked away, afraid of what he was showing, what Thomas could see. Thomas stood before him, made another sound, a high teakettle whistle, two long blasts. Henry kept his head down, the muscles in his hands and face jerking. Silence then, except for the sound of the cameras clicking, the men in the windows murmuring. Henry wanting to scream them away, wanting to stand and put his hands through the glass until he felt Thomas on the bench beside him, his son's weight at his side, Thomas's hand around his own, squeezing with a coupling click.

30

Alone in the office, he listens to the recording, a tape made after Elizabeth had been attacked. Dorn and Clarke talking in the Dictaphone room, thinking they were alone, unheard.

So I come to you with these types of concerns? Dorn's voice is low. Both men are smoking, their inhalations audible on the tape.

That's correct, Clarke says.

Because I'm thinking of a catastrophe. The potential for catastrophe. Something going wrong to that degree.

It's unlikely.

But not impossible, Dorn says.

No.

And then what? Dorn sucking on his cigarette, holding the smoke in his lungs, exhaling.

You're a police officer, Clarke says. You start making arrests.

Dorn coughs, swears, pounds his chest.

March is eminently deniable, Clarke says. He's an unstable personality. What he's doing out here will come as a complete surprise, officially.

What about his stuff?

Those things disappear. Paper is easy.

His book.

Easy.

Not that I'm thinking this is going to happen.

No.

But in the event.

In the event. Yes.

A scream of hinges on the recording as Clarke opens the door. His voice fading as he exits the room.

It's always better to be prepared, he says.

31

They sat in the living room, Dorn on one end of the of the sofa, Henry on the other, listening as Clarke told them that he had received orders from back east. It was time to move into a new phase of the operation. It was time for the project to evolve. A few hours, a single night with the subjects wasn't enough. He needed to observe them over a longer duration.

Clarke told them that they'd have the building to themselves in a matter of days. Mrs. Barberis and the mechanics would be taken care of. Henry was to call the Perelmans to reinforce the bedroom's windows and doors, to soundproof the walls.

Henry asked where, specifically, these orders had originated, and Clarke declined to answer.

Marist?

Clarke declined to answer.

Dorn told them that it would be difficult to keep junkies for that long a span, that they'd be dealing with medical issues, withdrawal. Clarke said that they were moving on from junkies, from drunks, lunatics. They needed to observe someone from straight society, an upstanding citizen, a man like any of them. A traveling businessman, maybe, someone whose wife wouldn't get too nervous if he didn't call for a few days.

A few days, Henry said. And then what?

Clarke declined to answer.

He develops the pictures that he takes for Hannah. The line at a bus stop, a cook filling the wall of slots at an automat. He uses only black-and-white film for these photographs. A woman walking her dog across Union Square Park. A boy climbing onto a streetcar. Henry stands in the darkroom and waits for the images to materialize.

He listens often to the recording of Dorn and Clarke. He knows every moment, but he still listens. He is like Hannah in this way. He can't trust the voices he remembers. He needs to hear the documentary evidence, the sounds on tape, the inhalation of cigarette smoke, the pauses between words.

March is an unstable personality, Clarke says. What he's doing out here will come as a complete surprise.

More images. The steeple of a church in North Beach. An old salesman cleaning the windows of the photographic supply shop. A young woman sitting at a table outside a café sipping espresso.

The idea of Hannah without him, of Ginnie and Thomas alone. Henry lifts a print from the liquid, hangs it on the line above.

Something going wrong to that degree. Dorn's voice on the tape.

It's unlikely, Clarke says, and Dorn says, But not impossible.

32

They stood at the bottom of the hill, watching the water, the setting sun turning the bay gold and black. They were waiting for the train. When it finally came, Thomas let go of Henry's hand and covered his ears, opened his mouth. Like the sound of the freight cars was coming from inside him. The wind blowing their coats and hair.

As they returned home, Henry noticed a car parked at the top of the hill, half a dozen houses past their own. A small sedan, an older model. A man in the driver's seat, the figure indeterminate in the last of the day's light. They continued up, the car blocked by trees at certain steps, disappearing behind branches, and when it appeared again Henry could see the bulk of the man in the front seat, his bald head.

He told Thomas to stay where he was, then continued up the hill alone. The man in the car didn't move. Henry heard something behind him, Thomas's engine, and he turned to find Thomas following, chugging up the hill. He shouted for Thomas to stay put. The sedan's engine started, so Henry continued back up, faster now. The car appearing and then disappearing behind branches. He heard Thomas again and turned and yelled for Thomas to stay where he was. The noise of the engine and the noise of his voice on the street. Thomas started to yell, a confused and frustrated howl, and Henry called out, telling him to go back to the house. Thomas still approaching and Henry walking backward, turning, almost to the top, where the sedan was nowhere to be found.

He walked out into the street, looked one way, another. Thomas still howling from below. Henry turned and Ginnie was there, Hannah was there, they were standing with Thomas, trying to calm him. The sun sinking into the water. Ginnie was looking up the hill at Henry, and Henry called out, Get back in the house. Shouting in the street. Neighbors' faces in windows, in doorways.

Henry shouting, Get the children back in the house.

33

She folded the laundry, Thomas's shirts and pants laid out across the sofa, Hannah's dresses over the armchair. She had just put a record on the player, something to break the silence in the house, a Bach recording by a young Canadian pianist she'd purchased earlier in the week. The music sounded clean to her, cleansing, the clear run of notes, the telephonic trill.

They'd come in from the scene on the street and she'd calmed the children down and put them to bed while Henry descended into the basement, to his desk and papers. She'd just started with the laundry when he reemerged and told her that he would be gone for a few days, maybe longer. Standing drained and hollow-cheeked in the entrance to the living room. She kept wondering why she didn't say something, why she didn't act, and then she took a breath and heard her own voice in the room.

"No, Henry. You are not well."

She saw his eyes move up to the mirror on the fireplace mantel, then shift quickly to the wall, negative space.

"I didn't do anything before," she said. "I kept quiet and let it happen. I won't do that again."

"Ginnie, please."

"I never ask, Henry. I never ask you about any of it."

"We can't talk about this."

"We have to talk about this."

He shook his head, his mouth flattening to a tight line. He looked so hurt, so angry, as if she had broken faith with him, crossing the last boundary they had agreed on long ago.

"You need to come home, Henry."

"I am home."

"No, you're not," she said. "I don't know who this is."

He looked like he was fighting against something, the muscles in his face straining, his hands stiff and open. Then he'd taken his coat and walked out the door.

In all their years together, he had never removed himself from her in that way. Fleeing the scene. Ginnie felt sick from the feeling that remained. Fear of Henry in that moment and then relief that he was gone. Feeling safer, somehow, alone.

She checked on the children, listening in their doorways, the sounds of their breathing, the sound of the piano, the record in the living room. She finished the laundry, standing by the front window, watching the street for headlights, not sure if she was waiting for their arrival or hoping that they wouldn't appear.

34

By the end of the week the mechanics' garage was empty, the doors locked, the windows covered from inside with brown butcher's paper.

The Perelmans returned and began work on the north bedroom, soundproofing the walls, the floor, sealing the window, the transom above the door. They installed an electric bell in the wall with a wire that ran to a switch in the office. Salo Perelman showed Henry a schematic of a bedroom door he would construct, a great metal box congested with tumblers and gears. The interior side of the door was flat, without a handle or knob, without purchase of any kind. The exterior side had a long lever that was pushed down to lock the door, pulled up again to open it.

Clarke said that they would need to increase the amounts Elizabeth and Emma were paid. Dorn had bumped the rate up after Elizabeth was attacked, but they'd need even more. The new room would spook the girls, Clarke said, and he couldn't afford to lose them now.

Henry stood at the kitchen window and watched the boy, Isaac, in the alley below, smoking his father's cigarettes. Two a day: the first after lunch and the second in the late afternoon before they packed up for the night. The low autumn sun slanting into the alleyway, the boy walking in slow curves with his hands clasped behind his back, kicking stones and bottle caps and chunks of plaster with an easy agility that evinced long hours of practice. He played only as long as the cigarette lasted, and then he was back into the apartment with his father, assembling the door from parts they brought from their shop every morning.

When they were gone, Dorn tested their work, standing in the bedroom and yelling at the top of his lungs while Henry listened from the stairs, out in the alley. He could hear nothing. There was nothing to hear. He watched through the office window while Dorn shouted, pounding the smooth face of the new door. Then Dorn standing silent, waiting, the first red flashes of fear on his face and neck. Staring into the mirror, breathing hard. Dorn's eyes searching the room, looking for an exit he knew no longer existed, sweat beading in the accordion-fold wrinkles of his forehead, sliding down his temples to his cheeks. Henry watching until Dorn started to shout again, the tendons in his neck straining, his veins purpling in animal terror. Only then did Henry leave the office, crossing back into the north apartment to unlock the door.

Clarke spent a couple of nights in the hotel bars down in the financial district until he found their man.

A real loudmouth, Clarke said. Some kind of frustrated writer. Sells phones for a living, here for a week for the Western States Telephony Convention. He'd introduced himself as "Denver Dan, the Telephone Man." Wife and kids back home in Colorado. Very interested in finding a date, some female company after a long day on the convention floor.

He seems, Clarke said, like the kind of guy everybody knows, but nobody will miss.

35

Denver Dan sitting on the edge of the bed in the bright room. His prodigious stomach hangs over the waistband of his undershorts. Long red stretch marks radiate out from his navel, wheel spokes reaching into the dark hair on his breasts. Garters still hold his socks halfway up his calves. He'd broken his glasses hours before, but at some point since had stopped squinting, ceased trying to discern details in the exterior world.

First dose at 11 P.M. Second dose at 3:30 A.M. A few hours of galloping around the room, singing loudly, pounding on the walls and door. His hair soaked with sweat, dripping from his nose, his mustache. Henry sending Dorn in to hold him down while Clarke checked his pulse, made sure he wasn't on the verge of a heart attack.

Finally, the calm, the slow crash. Denver Dan sitting on the edge of the bed. Henry watched him from the office, the other side of the glass. Dan nearly motionless, just the rise and fall of his chest, an idle scratch of one calf with the other stockinged foot. Every few minutes, his tongue slid out from between his lips, lizardlike, finding the underside of his mustache before retreating back into its hole.

Henry sat with the contents of the man's wallet spread across his desk. Business cards, driver's license, membership badges for the Rotarians and Loyal Order of Moose. *Daniel Davis.* Height, weight, date of birth. There was a laminated card with a color painting of an American flag on one side and the Pledge of Allegiance printed on the other. Folded behind the card was a handwritten note with the times of his flights to and from San Francisco, a phone number for a taxicab service, the address of his hotel. The handwriting was a woman's, neat and round. Dan's wife, most likely, the woman in one of the photos from the wallet. The other two photos were of his children, two young girls, twins, smiling in school pictures.

Henry checked his watch, marked the time in the ledger. He stood, nudged Dorn from his snoring heap on the couch, nudged Clarke from his dozing nod at the other desk, sending them into the room.

One day into the next. No light in the office, only Henry's watch for news of the hour, occasional confirmation from Clarke or Dorn stepping outside to buy food or cigarettes. It's day, it's night. Time is nonexistent in the rooms. They strap Denver Dan to a chair, dose him, question him relentlessly, trying to empty him of all memory and experience. Once he answers a question it is as if that fact disappears from his body, as if the answer leaves his mouth and drifts up to disappear in the gray cirrus of cigarette smoke clinging to the ceiling.

What is your name?

Where are you from?

Are you married?

Do you have any children?

Why are you here?

Henry says, "He has a wife."

"He's told us," Clarke says. "Wife, two kids."

"He hasn't called her in days."

"What's today? Wednesday?"

"Thursday."

"Thursday. Jesus."

"Three days," Henry says. "She's worried. He missed his flight home. She's making calls."

"Let her worry."

"Hospitals. The police. Who saw him last. His colleagues asking around."

"Let them ask," Clarke says. "There's nowhere to look. He's disappeared."

What is your name?

Where are you from?

Are you married?

Do you have any children?

Why are you here?

What is your purpose here?

Henry watches from the office. At some point he stops taking pictures. There is no longer any need. They do not capture what is happening. Denver Dan getting lighter, smaller, leaner. His cheeks growing sallow; his eyes sinking, darkening. The man hasn't eaten in what must be a few days, but it is more than that. He is being reduced. Each fact, each memory that they take from him shaves more flesh from the bone. Transforming him, one man into another.

They are creating someone new.

"We need to know what he'll do," Clarke says. "What instructions he'll take."

Dorn says, "That's a big step."

"He just has to go in, wave the thing around."

Dorn says, "Loaded?"

"Jesus, no."

Henry listens to the conversation as if it were happening without him, as if it were not occurring in the same room.

"And then what?" Dorn says.

"Then we bring him back here," Clarke says. "Ease him out of it. Send him on his way."

Clarke and Dorn look over at Henry, as if waiting for him to interject, to argue. This is a performance of sorts, Henry knows this. He watches, keeps quiet. This is information that he is simply supposed to absorb in advance of future events.

What is your name?

Where are you from?

Why are you here?

What is your purpose here?

Where did you get the gun?

Dorn says, "Will he do it?"

"I don't know." Clarke pushes the heels of his hands into his eyes, arches his back. Through the window, they can see Denver Dan sitting, restrained in his chair. Henry glances at the ledger to remind himself what day it is.

Clarke says, "We won't know until we know."

My name is Lawrence Tarhammer.

I am unmarried.

I have no children.

I came here for the money.

I am in need of money.

The gun is my own.

36

Halloween night. Ginnie loved the holiday, the costume making, the decorations. Henry can imagine her setting the large serving bowl on the front step, filling it with candy. Checking the sky, gauging the weather. Helping the children into their outfits. Thomas pushing his fists through the straw-packed sleeves of his scarecrow costume, Hannah affixing the pipe-cleaner butterfly antennae into her hair. The porch light burning in the gloom, the first neighborhood children coming up the hill, masked and garbed, bags and pillowcases at the ready.

Through the mirror, he watches Dorn dress Denver Dan in a black sweater and slacks. Denver Dan silent, nearly motionless. Lifting a leg so Dorn can force on a shoe, one hand resting lightly on Dorn's shoulder for balance. Staring at a point just over the door. Henry checks his watch, sets and winds Dorn and Clarke's watches, returning them when the men come back into the office.

Ginnie looks at the clock on the mantel, handing Thomas and Hannah their pillowcases. Out the door, into the sidewalk parade. A drizzly, slate-gray evening. Falling into step with the neighbors' wives, the women chatting while the children run up each walkway and ring the bell, waiting impatiently for the men of the house to open the door and feign fear or surprise, drop candy into each openmouthed bag.

"What's this?" Clarke is holding a plastic Halloween mask he found on Dorn's desk, a wide-eyed panda with black half-moon ears, a comically expansive smile.

"Peter Panda," Dorn says, sliding his watch over his wrist, checking the time.

"Where did you get it?"

"I never disclose my methods."

Dorn pulls a gun out of his waistband.

"Let me carry it," Clarke says.

"Why?"

"I've never held one before."

Dorn turns the gun in his hand, holding the barrel, hands it to Clarke.

Hannah has joined a group of girls from her school. They run a few houses ahead, as far from their mothers as they can without being called back. Across the street at the Sullivans', Ginnie and Thomas wait behind a pair of children, headhunters with broom-handle spears and slashes of face paint. Doris Sullivan smiles when she sees Ginnie, claps her hands to her cheeks at the sight of Thomas the scarecrow.

"And where's Mr. March this evening?" she says, kneeling to drop an apple into Thomas's pillowcase.

"He had to work," Ginnie says.

"What a shame." Doris looks up at Ginnie, smiles sympathetically. "He's missing all the fun."

Dorn checks to make sure the street is clear. They usher Denver Dan out to the Lincoln, collars up, hat brims down. Henry hasn't been outside the apartments since they brought Dan in. Three days, four days.

He puts his hands in his coat pocket and his fingertips find the corners of the ledger.

They pull from the curb, hook around on the street, back down the hill.

"What's your name?" Dorn's eyes up in the rearview mirror, finding Dan in the backseat between Henry and Clarke.

Dan seems not to have registered the change in location. He stares at a point just above the windshield, lips pursed, head bobbing slightly.

He says, "My name is Lawrence Tarhammer."

They cross into Chinatown and Clarke slides the panda mask over Dan's face. Adjusts the eyeholes, rests the thin elastic band atop Dan's ears. Clarke hands Dan the gun. They continue south, deeper, the streets narrowing.

"Why are you here?" Dorn says.

"I heard a voice that told me where I could get the money I need." Dan's words muffled behind the mask.

"Whose voice?"

"The voice comes from my television. You've heard the voice. It's in your television, too."

"Where did you get the gun?" Dorn says.

"The gun."

"Yes."

"The gun is my own."

Dorn guides the car into an alley, kills the headlights, the engine, lets the car drift before coming to a stop. The close-pressed walls are lined with garbage cans, service-entrance doors, fire escapes. The men sit and listen, watch for movement. Dorn exits first, adjusting his pants as he stands. He opens Henry's door as Clarke steps out the other side. They stand in the alley, steam rising from the Lincoln's hood, mingling with the fog. Denver Dan is still sitting in the backseat, staring at the same point above the windshield.

"Lawrence." Clarke's voice low, carrying no farther than the car. He says the name again and Dan turns, looks at Clarke through the eyes of the panda mask, slides across the seat and out into the alley.

*   *   *

From the other side of the street, Ginnie watches as the neighbors' children knock on her door, ring the bell, waiting impatiently before giving up on an answer, running from the house without noticing the bowl of candy on the front step.

Thomas knocks at a neighbor's house, the Bixbys', freezes when the door opens. Ginnie whispers to him, *Trick or treat,* and Thomas repeats this, shouting his greeting into Mr. Bixby's face.

Henry takes his position across the street, a few doors down from the liquor store. He can see through the front window, an oblique angle to the cashier's counter. A man's arm moving in and out of his field of vision, handing change to a customer who turns and exits the store, his bottle wrapped in a brown paper bag. The customer walks down the street past Clarke in a dark doorway, past Dorn just inside the mouth of the alley.

Henry watches the storefront, waiting to be sure there are no other customers. He lights a match and drops it into a puddle on the curb, the flame hissing and dying in the water. The signal flare. He shifts his eyes to the alleyway, the dark opening between the buildings. He sees nothing and then Denver Dan emerges, walking slowly, the eyes and mouth of his mask as dark as his clothes, black holes, only the white cheeks and forehead of the bear visible, glowing in the street's low watery light.

Dan walks in a perfectly straight line, no attempt to avoid the puddles in his path. Shoes wet, pant cuffs wet. His hands at his sides, swinging in time with his footfalls, like a man approximating an idea of normal human movement.

He reaches the front of the store and curls his hand around the handle and pulls.

Henry walks down his side of the street, a greater angle of the liquor store coming into view through the window as he closes the gap. Dan stands in the center of the store's main aisle, facing the front counter. The man behind the counter is old, with thin, graying hair, a slight hunchbacked curl to his shoulders. His back is to Denver Dan. There is a radio mounted high on the wall behind him, and the man is reaching up with a broom handle affixed with a coat hanger to change the station.

Denver Dan stands motionless, arms at his sides.

Lawrence Tarhammer. Henry needs to think of him as Lawrence Tarhammer.

Clarke crosses the street, coming up a few doorways behind Henry. He is moving too quickly, too conspicuously, afraid that he'll miss something. Henry watches the man in the liquor store turn the radio knob with his stick and coat hanger. A delicate, practiced movement. The broom handle trembling a little, the longer it stays aloft. Tarhammer standing, waiting for the man to turn.

The children empty their pillowcases onto the living room floor. They spread the candy across the carpet and Hannah begins taking inventory, dividing their spoils into disproportionate piles. Ginnie carries the serving bowl in from the front step. The street is nearly empty, just a few shadows at the doors of the farthest houses, stragglers, older kids. The fog lowering and the drizzle increasing until they are impossible to separate. A single gray thing. She turns out the porch light, closes the door.

The old man lowers his broomstick, sets it in a corner behind the counter. He turns and notices Tarhammer for the first time. Clarke is nearly at Henry's side. There is some sort of exchange in the store, the old man saying something and then listening as Tarhammer says something through the mask. The rain has picked up and Henry struggles to see, the windows of the liquor store fogging from within. Tarhammer still in the same spot, rooted in the center of the store. Henry needs to check the rest of the street, to keep watch for someone coming, but he cannot take his eyes from the graying window. The old man says something else and tilts his head, waiting for a reply. Tarhammer reaches into his coat and his gloved hand comes away holding the gun. Henry hears Clarke take a sharp breath. He listens for the exhalation, but the sound doesn't come. Tarhammer raises his arm. There is no hesitation. The old man yells something and starts to lift a hand and then there is a muzzle flash in the store and the sound of the gunshot and then Clarke's exhaled breath. A red flash and the old man drops behind the counter. Tarhammer's arm straight out in front of him, unwavering. Jesus Christ, Clarke says, and Henry is already in the street, has already closed half the distance to the liquor store. Tarhammer's shape in the window shaking in his vision as he runs, the whole scene blurred by the fog and rain, the pavement hard under his shoes, and then he hears Dorn shouting from the alley, *Leave him,* and it takes a second time, *Leave him,* for that voice to pull Henry away, changing his trajectory so he is up on the sidewalk and running into the alley. Dorn ahead, Clarke coming up behind, all three sprinting to the Lincoln, Dorn gunning the car forward, then through a bewildering series of turns into deeper alleys, the sides of the car almost scraping the walls, bouncing over potholes and pavement humps, Henry and Clarke in the backseat with no one in between.

Dorn finds Clarke in the rearview mirror. "Where was he shot?"

"It looked like the shoulder."

"It looked like the shoulder or it was the shoulder?"

"It looked like the shoulder."

Dorn says, "It looked like the head to me."

"Find a pay phone," Henry says.

"You want me to pull over?" Dorn incredulous.

"We can't stop," Clarke says.

Henry says, "Find one and pull over."

"For what?"

"I'm calling an ambulance."

"Someone heard that shot, Hank," Dorn says. "Someone will call."

"Pull the car over," Henry says.

Dorn's eyes up in the rearview mirror, looking for Clarke again.

"Fine," Clarke says, meeting Dorn's eyes and then looking away, out to the street. "Find a phone somewhere and drop him."

*   *   *

They were in the north apartment when Henry came through the door, trailing water, rain dripping from the sleeves of his coat. Dorn stood in the kitchen doorway with his half-drained glass. He looked up when Henry entered the room.

"Jesus, Hank, where have you been?"

Henry crossed the floor. Clarke sat with a drink, the back of his head visible over the top of the sofa, his hair wet, newly combed.

Dorn said, "Did you walk all the way up here?"

Henry grabbed Clarke by the collar of his shirt, pulled him up and over the back of the sofa, Clarke's drink falling to the floor, the glass breaking, his cigarette hitting the rug in a tiny burst of sparks. Clarke struggling, letting out a strangled cry of protest.

Dorn stayed in the kitchen doorway, drinking, watching.

"Hank." Clarke squeaking. Henry with his hands around Clarke's neck, pushing him into the floor. Clarke's eyes wide, feet kicking, trying to get free, knocking over a lamp, spreading the broken glass from his drink, tearing the fabric of his slacks, the skin of his legs. Henry's thumbs at his windpipe, pushing harder.

"Hank, are you going to kill him, or what?" Dorn's voice from the kitchen doorway. "Because if you're not going to kill him, then you're just making a mess."

Henry opened his hands. A dark necklace of finger marks forming across Clarke's skin. Both men breathing hard, both wet, blood from Clarke's leg smeared across the rug. Clarke coughing, rubbing his throat.

Dorn took another drink. "I think you'd better go, Chip."

Clarke staggered to his feet, looked at Dorn, Henry, looked at his leg, his torn trousers. He moved past Henry to the coat tree, limping. They could hear his footfalls on the stairs, then the front door closing behind him.

Henry was still standing behind the couch, the water from his hat dripping into the streaks of blood on the floor.

Dorn set his glass in the sink. He walked into the living room, took in the scene. The broken glass, the blood, the toppled lamp. The open bedroom, the monstrous metal door, the shattered furniture within, the torn and strewn bedclothes, the chair with the straps where they'd kept Denver Dan.

"Look at this fucking place," he said.

He crossed to the coat-tree, took his coat, his hat. Stepped over the stippled trail of Clarke's blood and out the door.

Henry sat alone at his desk in the office, the contents of Denver Dan's wallet spread out before him. The driver's license, the Pledge of Allegiance card, the photographs of Dan's wife and children.

He had found a pay phone at the northern boundary of Chinatown and called for an ambulance. An operator had asked him what the emergency was.

Henry wrote the address from Dan's driver's license into the ledger, then pushed the contents of the wallet into the trash can. He lit a match, dropped it in. A slip of paper caught first, the note where Dan's wife had written his flight information, the name and address of his hotel. The paper curled in spasms, burning white to brown.

The operator had asked Henry what the emergency was and Henry had said that a man had been shot. A shopkeeper. A shopkeeper had been shot in the head.

He waited until everything from the wallet had burned, the cards and photos, the license. He watched them shrink and curl and powder, until there was nothing in the can but ash.

There was noise from the next motel room, muffled through the wall. A man and a couple of women laughing, beer bottles clinking, music on a radio. Henry sat on the edge of the tub in the bathroom, washing his pants, his shirt, Clarke's blood on the cuffs. A bar of soap from the tub, a shoe brush he'd found in the closet. A cigarette burning, perched on the porcelain beside him.

He had gone home, had walked in the front door and stood in the hallway, and then he had turned away, back into the city. He had left a note, that he'd be away a few more days. He could not be there, in the house. Not with what he carried. What was still with him, on his clothes, in his head.

At a bus station in the Mission District he had paid for a locker, placed the ledger inside. The key now sat beside his cigarette on the edge of the motel bathtub while he washed his slacks.

More laughter from the next room. Someone's body banging against the shared wall. He scrubbed his clothes until the color was gone. His hands shaking so badly that when he wanted to smoke he had to kneel beside the bathtub, lower his head to the edge of the tub and take the cigarette in his lips. Inhaling while his hands flopped, his knuckles drumming wildly on the floor.

Henry Gladwell. Trying to get the name out of his head, his body. Unable to do so. Weir would know how. This is what he would ask Weir, now, if he could ask him anything. Not about the deception, the lies, the treason. He would ask how to remove this name, this person he'd created. How to return to the man he was before.

37

Roy Pritchard arrived half an hour late, coming through the rain into the automat, setting his umbrella and briefcase on the floor beside Henry's table.

"I can get this weather back in D.C." Roy took off his overcoat, hung it across the back of his chair. He sat, noticed the slice of pie Henry had set on his side of the table. "Key lime," he said. "You remembered." He sliced a bite of pie with his fork, lifted it. "How's Ginnie? How are the kids?"

Henry nodded.

"Adjusting?"

"Yes."

Roy set his fork back down on the plate. "You look terrible, Henry."

"I want to be relieved."

Roy speared the pie again, looked back down at his plate. "I'm afraid that's not possible."

"I want to take my family and go." Henry's voice rose, enough to pull Roy forward. Roy lowered his voice to a harsh whisper.

"Where, Henry? Back to Washington? There's nothing there for you anymore. Believe me." He sat back in his chair, resumed his normal tone. "We need you here."

"I need to be relieved."

"Hear me out first."

Henry stood, tried to button his coat, unable to keep his fingers steady.

"You'll want to hear this," Roy said.

Henry shook his head, fumbled with the buttons.

Roy said, "There's been a change of plans."

Henry finally dropped his hands. Went to his shirt pocket for his ciga-rettes. Went to his coat, his pants. Roy produced his own pack, slid it across the table. Henry sat.

"Do you remember a man named Grigori Valerov?" Roy said. "He made contact in Helsinki a few years ago. Fairly high in Soviet counterin-telligence. Maybe not as high as he said he was, but fairly high."

Henry slid a cigarette out of Roy's pack, set it on his lip. He could taste the tobacco, the paper. He waited for the drug the paper might hold to flood his system. Waited to go mad, madder.

"Valerov came to us because he felt his talents were unappreciated," Roy said. "He thought his bosses were jealous, sabotaging his career. He was working in Helsinki and got in contact with our man there."

"Jameson," Henry said. "We told Jameson to keep him in place."

"And things were going fine," Roy said. "Then about a year and a half ago, he shows up on Jameson's doorstep. He thinks his superiors are onto him, that his life is in danger. He wants to come to the States, bring his wife and kids, his mistress. Jameson tries to convince him to stay in place, that he's overreacting, and this is when Valerov brings up Weir."

Henry said, "A year and a half ago."

"Let me finish."

Roy lit a match, held it across the table. Henry inhaled, felt his body fill with smoke.

"Valerov told Jameson that Weir was a double. Said he was Weir's man in Moscow. *Monarch* was the handle they used. He put all these cards on the table for Jameson. He was desperate to get out. So Jameson made a few calls, and the decision was made to bring them all in. We flew them to the States, put them up in a safe house in Chillum, started the questioning. The mistress, obviously, stayed somewhere else." Roy pulled his own cigarette from the pack.

"Who was handling this?" Henry said.

"Marist, myself, a few others. We couldn't bring you in. We didn't know if Valerov was full of shit or what. At the time we believed that Weir knew nothing about it, that we'd kept it from him."

Two older women passed by, sat at the table directly behind Henry, speaking in Italian, what sounded like the civilized, public version of a long-running argument.

"Monarch was not the only handle Valerov gave us," Roy said. "He alluded to a much larger penetration. Weir was the tip of the iceberg. We worked him for months, but he was impossible to pin down. One day he seemed reliable, it seemed like we were building a case. The next day it seemed like he was making the whole thing up. He became increasingly difficult. His list of demands grew. We were about to shut the whole thing down when Weir disappeared."

The argument at the table behind Henry increased in volume, the surrounding tables growing louder to compensate.

"Valerov shut up tight after Weir flew," Roy said. "We've been unable to get anything else out of him. It's possible that his larger penetration story was bullshit, that he's dry and now he's trying to justify his expense. Or it's possible that the story is true and he's holding out for something else."

"Or he's a double," Henry said.

"Or he's a double. Yes. Maybe he was sent because they no longer had any use for Weir. They had gotten everything from him. Or Weir was no longer cooperating, and so blowing him would turn everything upside down, would lead to a witch-hunt. Which it has. This is like McCarthy times ten. We're eating ourselves alive back there. The polygraphs are running nonstop. You wouldn't believe who we're looking into." Roy took a pull on his cigarette, exhaled. "Well, maybe you would."

The rain had tapered. A white morning sun glowed above the tops of the neighboring buildings. Roy sat back in his chair, stretched his shoulders, looked out the window. "Valerov has something or he has nothing or what he has is bad. Whatever way it is, we have to know."

"And then what?"

"And then we need him to forget," Roy said.

Henry lifted his glasses from his ears, removed his handkerchief from his coat pocket.

Roy lowered his voice again. "What did you think I was going to say?"

Henry slid the cloth across his lenses, erasing the smudges and dust. "That you wanted him removed from the equation."

"Jesus." Roy tried a shocked laugh. "We're not that far gone yet, are we?"

Henry returned the handkerchief to his coat. "When would he arrive?"

"Soon. We're sending him on a vacation to calm his nerves a little, clear his head. No wife, no mistress. He's always wanted to see the Golden Gate Bridge."

"Who'll be handling him?"

"Someone from Security will be on his flight, get him into his hotel. But once he's here, he's all yours." Roy checked his watch, looked back to Henry. "This will be it. We finish this, and I'll make sure you're out. You have my word."

Henry set his glasses over his ears. The room sharpened back into focus.

Roy stood, put on his coat, his hat, extended a hand. Henry took it. Roy turned from the table and walked to the door. He hustled across the street and continued down the sidewalk, out of Henry's line of sight.

Henry finished his cigarette, his coffee. He paid the bill and stood from the table, taking Roy's abandoned briefcase with him as he left.

Shouting from the next motel room, a man and a woman, the woman's voice rising to a shriek, the words unintelligible through the wall.

Henry couldn't remember the last time he had slept. He no longer even attempted. He sat in the chair by the bed and watched the wall, the scene beyond. He could see through things now. There were windows everywhere.

He would keep himself here. This would be his room. There was a home across the bay, but it was another man's home.

Another shout, another shriek. Henry stared at the wall, watching. There were windows everywhere.

38

Valerov exited the elevator, crossed the hotel lobby into the bar, passing a few feet from where Henry sat looking at a newspaper. Valerov was not quite as heavy as he had appeared in the photographs. He looked healthy, vigorous. He was dressed for a vacation, loose wool trousers, a plaid shirt, collar open, exposing a thatch of curly black hair.

The file said that he began drinking alone nearly first thing in the morning, but as the day progressed he sought company. He was particularly adept at talking to women. He had a charm the authors of the file found impressive and preposterous for a man with his limited physical gifts. He preferred women of a high social standing, but he also had a predilection for prostitutes.

Henry switched sections of his newspaper, changed seats so he could see into the bar. Valerov had found a stool between two stewardesses and was already ordering drinks for the three of them. Henry watched him around the edges of the paper. He pictured Valerov's life as an almost perfect inverse of his own. Weir and Henry; Weir and Valerov. That this man may have known everything that Henry did not. Information passing from Henry to Weir and then eventually, on a trip to Amsterdam or Berlin, to Valerov. Valerov a link in the relationship Henry had never known was missing.

The stewardess sitting farthest from Valerov checked her watch and stood. There was a whispered conversation between the two women and then the first stewardess gathered her purse and kissed her friend on the cheek. Valerov stood and kissed her hand and she left the bar, passing Henry on her way out of the lobby to the street. Valerov bought more drinks.

Henry followed them to an Italian restaurant two blocks away, watched their window table from across the street. Then back to the hotel, Valerov and the stewardess swaying drunkenly as they walked, his arm around her waist to keep her on her feet.

This was reckless and unnecessary, following the man for an entire evening. Henry only needed to confirm Valerov's presence in the city, but he couldn't take his eyes off him. The revelation of the man, the disbelief that this was the answer, the thing he had been looking for. The looseness of the man's bearing, his attire. The exposed chest, the arm around the woman he barely knew. This was the man Weir had trusted. A drunk, a philanderer. This was the man Weir had given everything to, the man who knew everything Henry did not.

By the time the elevator door closed, Henry had interrogated him countless times, in countless ways. By the time he had lost sight of the man, Henry could already see him, contained, on the other side of the glass.

It took him three hours to get home. Doubling back and doubling back and doubling back. Struggling to get the right name in his head. Henry March. Certain that he was being followed but unable to confirm. Lonnie, Clarence, Clyde from Buffalo. Tarhammer and his mask and his gun.

He moved slowly through the house, trying not to wake Ginnie and the children, making his way through the kitchen to the basement door at the back.

He read through his summary of his time with Weir, returning again to the blank areas, the gaps in the story that Valerov might be able to fill. Henry's handwritten pages beside the photographs in Pritchard's file. Valerov in Berlin, Valerov in Maryland. The florid, bearded face, the laughter-crinkled skin around the eyes. What this man might know.

He gathered the pages of his biography, of the Valerov file, and slid them into the trash can beside his desk. He no longer needed the paperwork. He had it all in his head again, finally. He pushed his chair to the wall and climbed on top, opened the window. He lit a cigarette and stood on the chair for a moment, inhaling the smoke and the cool night air. Then he lit another match and set the paper in the trash can alight, watching the flames lick for oxygen, the bright orange glow in the dark basement.

39

She heard him come in, so she got out of bed and stood in the moonlit kitchen and poured a glass of wine and waited. Smelling smoke from the basement. Henry's cigarettes and something else. Burning paper. She fought the urge to knock on the door and ask if everything was all right. She already knew the answer.

He finally came up through the doorway and took a sharp breath when he saw her. He looked startled, exhausted, thin, the muscles in his face twitching.

"Where have you been?" The question sounded ridiculous to her, her tone of voice, indifferent, almost, casual, as if she was merely curious.

"I can't, Ginnie."

She nodded, looked down at her wine, turning the glass in her fingers.

"I'm going to be away for a while," he said. He didn't look at her. He looked past her, to the kitchen doorway, the front door beyond.

"Thank you for not leaving a note this time."

It was as if he didn't hear her. "It will be another week," he said. "Longer, possibly."

She wanted to say no. She wanted to grab him, shake him, hold him to her until this passed, whatever this was, whatever had burned itself into him. His face in her neck and her hands in his hair. Holding him until it was gone. She wanted to say no, but she had already said no and that had pushed him further. She felt the delicate line of the moment, the taut thread. Henry at the far end.

She said, "Back to Washington?" She knew he wouldn't answer but she needed to hear a name this time, needed to imagine him safe, in a place she could picture, a known city with noise and people and light.

"Los Angeles," he said, and she ignored the lack of conviction in his voice and pictured what she knew of the city, sunshine and palm trees and the Hollywood Hills, gated celebrity homes from movie magazines.

"Los Angeles," she said.

"Yes."

She had to believe him. There was no other choice. She had to trust that he would return from this. She had asked him to lie and he had lied and now she had to go along with the fiction.

Los Angeles. She smiled at the thought. Henry in shorts and sandals and a flower-print shirt, walking along the beach in the warm sea breeze.

"Maybe after you're back we can all go," she said. "We can drive down the coast. Just for a week or so, when Hannah's out of school."

"That sounds nice."

"When you're back you can tell me all about it," she said. "And then I'll know if the real place is anything like the place I'm imagining."

He was on his way out the door when he heard Hannah calling. Ginnie had gone back to the bedroom but Henry had been unable to leave, standing by the door in his coat and hat. He'd left the car keys on the table in the hallway. He would take the train now. He didn't like the idea of leaving Ginnie and the children without means of escape.

Hannah was sitting up in bed when he opened her door. She saw him and began to cry harder, saying, *It's gone, they did it, it's gone.* He didn't want to touch her, he was afraid to touch her, he couldn't get the other name out of his head, but she wouldn't stop crying and Ginnie hadn't appeared, so Henry took Hannah's hand, led her out into the hall to the front door. He covered her with his coat and took her outside, kneeling beside her, the knees of his pants soaking in the dew. He put his arm around her shoulders and she shook and he pointed down the hill, across the bay to the lights of the city, white points in the fog.

"See?" he said. "It's still there. It was only a dream."

She was shaking her head, as if she couldn't believe her own eyes, as if the dream had more power.

"It won't happen," Henry said. He pulled her closer, their breath revealed, white puffs in the chill air. "I won't let anything happen."

40

Valerov's handlers had given him a list of sights to see, tourist spots, along with a map of a neighborhood that he might find more interesting. He had been told of the Embarcadero, the north end of Powell, a particular bar, the types of women he could meet there. The night that Valerov arrived in the city, Dorn made an appearance, a couple of arrests, knowing that word would spread quickly and the place would be clear of competition for a while. So two days into his trip, on the night Valerov entered the bar, Elizabeth was the only girl working the room.

It was after midnight when they stumbled out, Valerov appearing so intoxicated that Elizabeth's drunk act seemed unnecessary. They started up the street, haltingly, Henry following a block behind. When they reached the top of the hill, Henry stayed at the corner, watched Valerov and Elizabeth make their way to the apartment and turn inside. He waited a few minutes and then followed. Easing the front door open, taking the stairs quickly, then into the office, where Dorn and Clarke sat in the dark, headphones over their ears. When Henry slid on his own, he was stunned by the noise, Dizzy Gillespie at a high volume and Valerov's roaring laughter.

Henry took off the headphones. The office was quiet. He looked away from the window. He wouldn't miss anything he hadn't seen or heard before. Valerov and Elizabeth drinking, having sex; Valerov passing out somewhere in the room. Henry sat in the silence. He was anxious, eager to get started, but he was willing to be patient, to wait through the formalities, the hours or even days before the man had been turned inside out enough that the first real question could be asked.

It was almost like he had slept, dozing off for some indeterminate length of time. When he looked back up to the window, the bedroom was there, floating beyond the office wall. The lamp on the table was lit and Valerov was lying naked on the bed, the rise of his stomach obscuring any view of his face. The picture above the headboard was hanging crooked and the bedclothes were strewn across the room. Elizabeth was nowhere to be seen. Dorn appeared in the mirror, then Clarke, carrying a black physician's bag. Clarke removed a stethoscope from the bag and stood over Valerov and listened to his chest. He removed a sphygmomanometer from the bag and fastened the cuff around Valerov's arm and inflated the pressure, watching the gauge, listening through the stethoscope. Dorn said something and Clarke nodded, still watching the gauge. Clarke removed the cuff from Valerov's arm and then removed a syringe from the bag, affixed a needle to the end. He ran his thumb across the crook in Valerov's arm, strumming the vein, then inserted the needle and slowly pressed the plunger. He removed the syringe and looked at his watch and wrote in a small notepad. Dorn said something else and Clarke nodded. They walked toward the door, disappearing from the frame.

Valerov sat on the edge of the bed, still naked, staring at the mirror. Henry was at his desk, watching. Valerov's limbs and torso covered in hair, his hands limp at his sides. Like an ape, like watching an ape in a cage. There was a fat purple bruise in the bend of his arm where Clarke had inserted the needle.

Valerov was sweating profusely. His eyes were glassy and dull. He was breathing heavily through his mouth. Clarke had given him a sedative so that when he woke he would be calm. He was calm. Henry watched. Without the ledger, all he could do was watch. No recordings, no photographs. There would be no record, no history. There would be the thing as it was, what would happen in the room, and then there would be nothing.

Do you know why you're here?

Valerov sat motionless on the edge of the bed, staring at the mirror. It seemed that he was ignoring Dorn, or that he hadn't registered Dorn in the room, but then he began to shake his head, slowly, once to the left, once to the right.

You're here because you're a liar. You've been lying to the people who are trying to help you.

Henry could only see Dorn's left arm hanging into the right side of the mirror's frame. The rest was just a disembodied voice in the headphones.

No response, again, and then that same torpid head turn, Valerov still looking straight ahead at the mirror.

Henry had told Dorn about Weir, what Valerov might know. Dorn had already heard it all from Clarke, Henry had listened to their discussions on the tapes, but he wanted Dorn to hear it from him, wanted to be clear so that there would be no mistakes.

If you admit that you're lying, Dorn said, this will be a lot easier. We can go from there, no problem. Do you understand what I'm saying? No problem?

Dorn's arm disappeared from the frame and he clapped sharply once, twice.

Do you understand what I'm saying?

After the sedative wore off, they left Valerov alone, let him test the new door, the metal slab over the window. Let him pound on the walls, the ceiling.

Dorn questioned him for the remainder of the afternoon. Valerov obstinate, defiant, demanding to be released. Threatening Dorn, Dorn's family. Refusing to speak. Speaking only in obscenities and insults. There were a few brief struggles, but by and large Dorn stood in nearly the same position for hours, arms folded, watching Valerov move around the room, getting close, nose to nose, then receding into the corners, onto the bed. Dorn repeating the questions Henry had given him, the endless repetition, regardless of the answers. The circular interrogation designed to break down even the simplest responses, the bedrock of personality, core facts questioned so many times that the answers became meaningless, became less than words, just knots of sound, animal utterances. It went on, seemingly without structure or goal. Any hesitation, any inconsistency in an answer forcing the questioning to begin again.

What is your name. What was your father's name. Your mother's name, your wife's name. How many children do you have. What are their ages, their names.

Each answer from Valerov receiving no response from Dorn. As if the answers were unimportant; as if only the questions mattered. Clarke quickly grew bored watching this, but Henry gained focus as the hours passed, attuned to the smallest details, the unconscious cues from Valerov, the sweat, the slowed speech. The man had been interrogated before, would know the tactics and techniques. He would believe he could outlast them. This would be the professional's response. Henry let the questioning continue past the point of his own distraction, to where he began to feel the numbness coming from the other room. Hours more, until he saw Dorn's knees giving a little, his weight pulling down, and then Henry sent the signal, a single ring of the electric bell in the wall, and Clarke went out into the north apartment to unseal the door.

They fastened him to the chair with the leather restraints. When he was secure, Dorn stood back by the door and Clarke sat on the edge of the bed asking the same questions. Valerov irate, straining against the straps, his face red, then purple, veins surfacing on his forehead and neck.

Kept like an animal, he said, spitting the words in English and Russian. Kept like an animal.

Clarke asked questions and the polygraph needle jumped at Valerov's responses, settled into a long, steady line, jumped again.

They allowed him to use the bathroom every few hours, Dorn standing watch in the doorway. Then they strapped him back into the chair. From time to time Dorn would leave the room, and Clarke would attempt to change the tenor of the questioning, implying that he was the one who could make things easier, could run interference with Dorn. Valerov wasn't persuaded, insulting Clarke in long streams of guttural Russian, rocking back and forth in the chair with increasing violence until Henry signaled Dorn to reenter the room.

They told him he had failed the polygraph test. They told him his lies were obvious, that it would be better for him to tell the truth. They would get it from him eventually. They questioned him again and he gave them the same answers and they left him alone for a few hours, still strapped to the chair, and then they returned to the room and told him that he had flunked another test.

We can do this forever, Clarke said, lighting a cigarette, looking at the jagged marks on the polygraph roll. We have all the time in the world.

Dorn and Valerov alone. No questions. Valerov shielding himself in a corner, hands out, trying to hold Dorn at bay. Promising that he'll talk. He'll talk if Dorn stops. Dorn under strict orders not to stop for any response from Valerov, any promise, any softening. Dorn under strict orders not to stop for anything but the sound of the bell.

Clarke found a vein, slipped the needle in, squeezed the plunger. Dorn loosened the restraints and Valerov slumped in the chair. His face mottled, bumped and swollen. Watching Dorn leave the room.

Clarke lit a cigarette, lit one for Valerov. Poured them each a drink.

We want to know why you're still lying, Clarke said. At this point it seems counterproductive.

Valerov tried to speak, fumbled over his words, stopped, took a drink. Winced when the alcohol touched the hole where a front tooth had been.

I have been telling you the truth.

Clarke shook his head. This can be so much easier, he said. You understand why we have to know. We are both professionals. If you were in my position you would need to know the same thing from me.

If I were in your position you would be dead.

Clarke stood, refilled Valerov's glass. Well then, he said. All the more reason to be honest with me.

The needle in the arm. They retightened the restraints. Valerov blinking rapidly, his eyes jumping around the room.

Stop this. Make this stop.

Valerov shaking the chair, the chair's legs banging against the floor.

Stop this. Please.

Clarke and Dorn left the bedroom, reappeared a minute later back in the office.

Dorn lit a cigarette. "He's not breaking."

"Give it time," Clarke said.

"It's been a long fucking time already."

They watched Valerov yelling and rocking the chair, writhing under the restraints. Henry and Clarke at the desks, Dorn standing by the window.

Dorn turned, looked at Clarke, at Henry, back at Valerov.

"He's not breaking."

They began to lose track of the date, asking each other what day it was, what hour of the day. Clarke and Dorn had taken their watches off that first afternoon, so as not to give Valerov any sense of time when they were in the room. Eventually, their watches had gone dead. They'd forgotten to wind them and then when they were dead they had nothing to set them by.

Henry tried not to close his eyes. He was afraid that he would sleep

and not know where he was, who he was when he came to. The horror
of Henry March waking in that room.

Valerov would not answer questions about Monarch. He maintained
that he knew nothing more than what he had already disclosed back in
Washington. That some of what he had disclosed may have been incor-
rect. He maintained that he knew nothing about further penetrations.

It was hot in the bedroom. Beastly, Dorn called it. Henry could see
the sweat soaking through Dorn's shirt and slacks while he questioned
Valerov. After a couple of hours Dorn would come into the office and
change his clothes and gulp water. Then back into the bedroom, where
dark rings appeared immediately under his arms, at the small of his back.

Clarke gave Dorn amphetamine shots to keep him awake if he was
to be up through the night with Valerov, sedatives if he needed to sleep.
After the first few days they ate very little, usually only when they had
given Valerov something to eat, and then they sat in the office and ate
and watched Valerov eating in the bedroom.

Sometimes Henry opened his eyes in the middle of the night to see
Dorn and Clarke sleeping in their chairs and Valerov in the brightly lit
bedroom, raging on amphetamines, pacing, destroying what was left
of the furniture. The silence of the scene and the bright square of the
window, the lit tableau in the dark office. Valerov had struck the mirror
sometime earlier, creating large black cracks across the shatterproof glass.
A spiderweb of lines in the frame through which they saw the room.

They sat drinking and smoking, Dorn in the chair with the straps hanging loose at his sides, Valerov unrestrained on the bed. An uneasy peace
in the room. The two men were not so far apart in their appetites, their
interests. They talked about women, about baseball. Valerov had been
following the game for years through Western newspapers and radio
broadcasts. The game as an abstraction, as box score and faceless voice.
He had hoped to see the Senators play when he'd come to Washington.
He wanted to see the actual game, the flesh-and-blood athletes he'd heard
described for so long. He knew all the numbers, the statistics. Dorn was

impressed by this. He quizzed Valerov on the Giants, on Willie Mays's batting average. He thought it was a cardinal sin that Valerov knew Mays only by statistics, by secondhand descriptions. That he had never seen the man in motion, the poetry of his movement.

You will have to take me, Valerov said. We will go and drink beer and sit in the sun.

Dorn gave a thick belly laugh, lit another cigarette, still laughing but nodding as well, as if in some way something like this was still possible.

You want to hear that I am still working for my country, Valerov said.

If that's the truth.

It is not the truth. But you want to hear it regardless.

I want to hear about Monarch.

I do not know who that is.

Now you don't know who that is.

I believe I may have been wrong, when I spoke of him before. I believe I may have had my facts wrong.

Your facts.

Yes.

Dorn shook his head, blew out a long breath.

Valerov sat quietly, looked to the mirror, the door. How many of you are here?

What do you mean?

How many of you are here?

Just me, Dorn said.

You and the doctor.

Yes.

Valerov looked up at what was left of the ceiling fan, looked at the mirror.

I want to talk to the others.

There aren't any others, Dorn said.

Valerov kept his eyes on the mirror, the cracks he had made.

Who is the liar now? he said.

41

Henry stood in front of the open mouth of the empty bus-station locker, the key in his hand. All that was left inside was a small flake of black leather, a last remnant of the ledger's skin. Anyone could have taken it. Dorn, Clarke, someone sent from back east to follow Henry. It could be anywhere now, the record of what they'd done.

He had taken the secret tapes from the south office, Clarke and his Dictaphone, Clarke and Dorn, and now he burned them in the bus-station restroom, letting the reels melt in the sink before turning on the faucet.

He couldn't find Elizabeth. She wasn't in her apartment in the Tenderloin, wasn't in her usual bars. He made his way south through the city to Hunters Point, Emma's tenement, her room on the top floor. A single mattress, a chair by the window. A small pile of books by the chair. Poetry, some of the names familiar, some unknown to him. Strangers. Laundry on a line, dresses and undergarments he recognized. The radiator banging and then hissing steam.

The door finally opened and Emma came in, bundled against the cold, seemingly unsurprised to find an uninvited guest in her room.

She offered him a drink and when he declined she poured herself one, took a long swallow to prove that it was untainted, then poured another and handed him the glass. She was still wearing her coat and scarf. She stood against the wall and they drank and she watched him in silence.

"Am I in trouble?"

Her voice broke something in the room. A moment's peace. Henry opened his eyes. He hadn't realized he had closed them. He took a bank envelope from his jacket pocket.

"I'm going to give you some money and you're going to leave," he said. "You're not going to tell me where you're going. You're not going to tell anyone."

"You look like you're in trouble," Emma said.

Henry held the envelope. Emma set down her glass, reached for it, opened the flap.

"This is a lot."

"You're going to go," Henry said, "and not stop for anything, for anyone, until you feel that you're safe."

Emma closed the flap, held the envelope at her side.

"Until I'm safe?"

He nodded.

She took a drink, looked at Henry again.

"What will that feel like?" she said.

Henry stood on the sidewalk in front of the Merchants Exchange. He set his camera on a postal box and looked through the viewfinder, adjusting the angle so he could see as much of the building as possible: the heavy stone walls, the powerful columns, a structure that had survived the last cataclysm, could survive the next. He used a short lens, which gave a vast field of vision but distorted the view, pushing the center back and bowing the edges of the frame like a fishbowl. Pedestrians passed through the glass, moving across the newly created space. When Henry was satisfied, he set the timer on the camera and stepped back into the frame.

He returned to the office to develop the film. Dorn was asleep on the sofa. Clarke sat at Henry's desk, his head tilted listlessly to one side, half awake, watching Valerov through the window.

Valerov was hunched sick in a corner of the room. He had ripped the room apart, the walls and ceiling gutted, studs and chicken wire exposed, newspaper insulation. Red finger streaks across what was left of the paint. The camera and microphone wires hanging free, fallen in tangles across the floor.

It was dark when Henry crossed the bridge into Oakland. No lights in the windows of the house. Inside, down the hallway, careful not to make a sound. Thomas was asleep on the floor beside his bed, legs straight, arms at his sides. Henry stood for a long moment, watching his son, and then bent to brush Thomas's hair from his forehead, kiss the cool skin there.

He stepped into Hannah's room. Gray moonlight through the window. One wall was covered with photographs, the entire city in black and white. Henry set the photo he had taken on her desk. No crumbled buildings, no destruction. No panic, no fear. No still-falling masonry. Just people passing on the sidewalk and the Merchants Exchange building and her father, everything secure in that moment, a day like any other.

"You're not really home." Ginnie's voice in the dark bedroom.

"No."

"When do you have to go back?"

"I should have gone already."

"Come closer so I can see you."

He took a step toward the bed and Ginnie reached over and switched on her reading lamp. A soft circle of orange light in the room. Ginnie in her blue nightgown, her hair in curlers. She sat up, watched him. He could only imagine what he looked like, the fear this struck in her. Standing folded and disheveled, his hands hanging at his sides.

"You should take a shower, change your clothes," she said. "I'll fix you something to eat."

"I have to go back."

"You should sleep for a while, Henry."

He shook his head.

"Then lie here beside me," she said. "Just for a minute."

He lay on top of the covers, still in his shoes, his coat. Ginnie lay back down and closed her eyes, took his hand.

"I'm not going to let you go," she said. "I don't care what you have to do. I'm going to keep you here beside me."

He didn't move. He could feel the black water of the bay, slowly rolling. He could feel himself drifting between names. The man who belonged on that side of the water and the man who belonged on this side.

Henry said, "You have to trust me."

"I'm trying to."

"I'm very close."

"Close to what?"

Ginnie's face was drawn, her eyes wet. He couldn't look at her eyes. He looked at her neck, her hair.

"Weir," Henry said. "I'm almost to Weir."

Ginnie took a breath, released it. Pulling from whatever reserves she had left.

He said, "It will all be over soon."

She wiped her cheeks with the back of her wrist, took Henry's hand again.

"I want you to promise that you'll come back to me."

Henry nodded.

"Please," she said.

"I will."

"You promise."

"Yes."

Ginnie studied his face, closed her eyes. She squeezed his hand a last time, then let him go.

42

Dorn and Clarke reinforced the chair, bolting it to two-by-fours which they then bolted to the floor. They strapped Valerov in and forced the water into his mouth, down his throat, massaging his neck until he swallowed. When he gagged and spat they were careful not to get any of the liquid on their skin. More water, then the blindfold, and then they cut the lights and left him, waited for the drug to take hold.

The window from the dark room into the dark room. Some of the microphones still worked, though there was nothing but the sound of Valerov's breathing, the struggle for air. They sat in the office with their headphones and cigarettes, watching the black square of glass. Dorn and Clarke passed a flask. Nothing for half an hour, an hour. Grain swimming before Henry's eyes in the darkness, tiny gray spots, like imperfections in an emulsion, underexposed film. He was beginning to wonder if they should try again when the sound began: a long, low hum, rising slowly in pitch as if reaching for something. Then Valerov's voice, just a whisper at first, tentative, a question, what sounded like a woman's name, a multistepped Russian word, soft then hard then soft.

More soft Russian, what sounded like the lines of a prayer. The rhythmic incantation. Then a silence, a long, protracted space, nothing, nothing, and then the screams, Dorn and Clarke lowering their headphones and Henry lowering the gain, the men sitting back in their chairs while Valerov shrieked, the sound white and hot, a burning point of light in the dark.

Clarke gave Valerov vitamin injections, gave him STORMY with water. They let him sit in his clothes, his mess. They left him blindfolded. They were only in the room long enough to give him more of the drug and when they left they turned out the lights.

It did not seem like he slept. There was always sound coming from the room, shouting or screaming or talking or whispering, sometimes just formless noise, buzzing and humming. Whenever there was a moment of silence, Henry would think that Valerov had finally succumbed to sleep, but it would be broken soon enough by more noise.

Dorn and Clarke slept, sometimes deeply, sometimes fitfully. Henry did not sleep. He did not know how long it had been since he'd slept. He watched the dark window, listened through the headphones. He would stay awake as long as Valerov was awake. It was just the two of them now, it was down to the two of them, so he stood by the window and listened to the man come apart.

Dorn's voice from somewhere in the office behind Henry, slurry with sleep.

"You want me to go in?"

"No," Henry said.

"When?"

"Soon."

Henry stood at the window, the red burn of his cigarette the only reflection in the glass.

"We're missing something." Dorn's voice from somewhere back in the dark. "Your book, Hank. Where's your book?"

*   *   *

The room smelled like sweat and urine, bodily waste, sour breath, gases. The heat was overwhelming. Henry turned on the overhead light. The floor was wet. The paint was peeling from what was left of the walls. An unthinkable place he had created.

Valerov didn't move. He was breathing with some difficulty. He sat slumped, head down on his bare chest, his arms tied behind the back of the chair, the blindfold a tight black strip over his eyes.

Henry lifted the blindfold. Valerov kept his eyes closed, his head down.

"My name is Henry March. I was a colleague of the man you say you knew. I was a friend of the man."

Valerov slowly opened his eyes. Squinting in the light, blinking rapidly.

"How long have I been here?" Valerov said.

"I don't know."

Valerov nodded, as if this was the answer he'd expected.

"This is your only chance to talk," Henry said. "When I leave this room you will be back in the dark. That other place. You will be here as long as it takes."

Valerov's lips were dry and cracked. He ran his tongue over his bottom lip, moving some of the dead skin away.

"That is not why I am still here."

His voice was a torn, pained thing. What was left of his voice.

"I am still here because you do not know what to do with me," he said. "I know where I am. I am in San Francisco, California. I am in the United States of America. You cannot just open the door and set me free. Not after what has happened here."

He licked his lips again, blinked at his bare feet.

"So the question now is something different," Valerov said. "It is not Monarch. It is not anything I can tell you."

Valerov looked at the wall, the door, his eyes without color, nothing but black pupil, and Henry realized that the man could no longer see, that he was still in the dark.

"The question now is one of disposal," Valerov said.

Henry turned, unlocked the bathroom. He filled a glass with water from the sink, brought it back out, held the glass to Valerov's lips.

"It's just water," he said. "Nothing else."

Valerov's mouth turned in an ugly smile. He took a drink, coughed, took a longer drink, gulping the water.

"It does not matter what it is," Valerov said.

He sucked the liquid. When he stopped coughing, he spoke again.

"I know you, Henry March. I know your paperwork. I cannot see you, but I assume you resemble your photographs. I knew your friend as well. A highly intelligent man, a sensitive man. A poet. A man with a great understanding of the world."

"What did you give him?"

"In exchange for his secrets? Your secrets? You would be disappointed. As would my colleagues back home. What did you give me for my secrets?"

"Do you know where he is?"

Valerov lifted his shoulders, winced, let them drop. "Men who betray their countries, where do they go? Rooms like this, possibly. We have rooms like this."

"And the others?"

"Further penetration. You want to know if your organization is riddled with liars. With deceivers."

"Yes."

"Of course it is. As is mine. As are they all. We are all being betrayed. We are all in danger of being heard. This is not a secret. This is not one of our secrets. You are so young, your people. You are children who do not yet understand."

Valerov stuck his tongue out. Henry brought the glass to his lips. Valerov finished the water greedily, sputtering from the overflow. When he spoke again his voice was stronger, clearer.

"My name is Grigori Sergeyevich Valerov. My father's name was Sergei Nikolayevich Valerov. My wife's name is Constantina. My daughters are Sasha and Padme. I am a citizen of the Soyuz Sovetskikh Sotsialisticheskikh Respublik. I am a member of the Kommunisticheskaya Partiya Sovetskogo Soyuza. I have nothing more to tell you, Henry March. I have told you everything."

Henry set the empty glass on the dresser.

"I ask only that you do it quickly," Valerov said. He tilted his head, his unseeing eyes rising. "A professional courtesy. Only what you would ask of me if our situation was reversed."

Into the office, Henry turning the switches on the wall, flooding the room with light. Dorn stands from the sofa, squinting. Clarke leans forward at Henry's desk.

"What did he tell you?"

"Nothing," Henry says. "There's nothing to tell."

"That's it?"

"Yes."

"Then they want him turned," Clarke says.

"I know what they want."

Clarke places his hands on Henry's desk, pushes himself up. "What do you want to do, Henry? You want to open the door? You want to let him go?"

Dorn moves slowly toward Clarke, shifting his weight from one leg to another, restarting the circulation.

"Call them," Henry says. "Call Marist. Tell them we can't do any more."

"It's already done, Henry." Clarke says. "There is no way out of here. Where is the way out?"

There is a look exchanged, Clarke and Dorn, and then Dorn is past the desks, out of the office. Henry turns to see Dorn reappear on the other side of the mirror, unstrapping Valerov, shouting at the man, knocking him to the floor.

Henry is moving again, pulling open the drawers of Dorn's desk, rummaging through the suit coat on the back of Dorn's chair.

Dorn screams at Valerov, whipping him with the straps. Valerov cowers against the wall by the blinded window, blocking his face with his hands, screaming in return.

Henry drops the coat, pulls the cushions from the sofa where Dorn had slept.

"You're looking for his gun?"

Clarke's back is to the window. He's watching Henry. Behind him, Dorn has the straps pressed to Valerov's neck. Valerov pulls at Dorn's wrists, gasping.

Clarke says, "He has it."

Henry looks past Clarke to the other room. Dorn's revolver is tucked into the back of his belt, visible beneath the open flap of his shirt.

Out of the office. He can't move fast enough, stumbling through the outer room, then through the door and into the brightness of the vestibule. Blinded, lurching. There is no sound. Sunlight in the vestibule. Dust in the air, turning. Then into the living room and there is no sound and then there is a muffled burst in the air, a plosive breath. Henry standing outside the bedroom door. The bedroom door open but not enough for Henry to see into the room. Inside, one man has shot the other. Either Dorn has shot Valerov or Valerov has shot Dorn and now whoever has the gun will turn it on Henry.

It is morning now. He can still feel the sunlight from the vestibule on his face. He can see Hannah walking down the hill to school, can see Ginnie and Thomas at the park, their faces warm from the sun. Henry's face is warm from the sun. Dust spins in the air.

There is a noise, movement from inside the room. A man stirring, coming toward the open door.

He has created this. He has created something monstrous, and it will consume him, will consume those he loves, if it has something to follow, if it has a name.

There is a noise from the other room. Henry lets the first name go, the second. Henry Gladwell, Henry March. He sees now how Weir did it. You let the names go and the man follows.

The door opens, fully. A figure in the doorway.

He realizes, now. This is how Weir did it.

This is how you disappear.

PART TWO

American Berserk

1

Summer 1972

It was the takeoffs he didn't like, the plane struggling into the air, the last gravitational grasp pulling him down into his seat, the whine of the landing gear folding into the belly of the machine, leaving the plane without lower limbs, an insane, crippling action Dickie saw as tantamount to jumping off a flight of stairs and tying your legs behind your back in midair.

He wasn't crazy about the flight itself either, but at least he could open his eyes after takeoff, loosen his fingers from the armrest, light a cigarette, have a drink if he was still drinking, which he wasn't, so there was that added to the equation. The old bird sitting next to him ordered a gin and tonic about thirty seconds after they'd reached cruising altitude, and Dickie had to make a conscious effort not to throttle her for her glass, or lick her denuded fingers for the precious liquid she spilled while positioning the drink on her tray. Instead, he picked an Antabuse out of his little plastic bottle, set the tablet on his tongue, and motioned to the stewardess for a glass of water.

One takeoff down, Moline to Vegas, with one to go, Vegas to L.A. He hadn't been on a plane since he'd started on the MAELSTROM operation, more than four years ago. An enviable period, it now seemed. Over that time he had traveled by train, or more often by bus, or most often in someone's car, almost always at night, on back roads if possible, driving just below the speed limit so as not to attract attention. Flying was for aboveground travelers, honest citizens, businessmen and vacationing families with legitimate identification they'd be willing to show at ticket counters and security checkpoints. The groups Dickie had been with had traveled earthbound, changing modes every few hundred miles, consulting Greyhound and Amtrak timetables like holy writs, *Paul's Letter to the I-5 Bus Rider*. The methods and peculiarities of fugitive movement. Time was different underground. It was slower, older, closer to the skin, an element to live in rather than an enemy to defeat.

OPERATION MAELSTROM. That was what Father Bill had called it, its official designation, though it was only now, four years later, after everything had fallen apart, that Dickie started to think of how fitting the name really was.

Father Bill was Dickie's man back east. His real name was Bill Collins, but Dickie had started calling him Father after their first couple of meetings. It was a good way to get a rise out of the man, a reference to the fact that Bill had spent six months in seminary after Yale and seriously considered the priesthood before realizing that his talents lay in other directions. So he'd married his college sweetheart and had four kids and gone to work for a government agency he refused to mention by name. The priest thing was a surprisingly personal disclosure, and Dickie had jumped on it and refused to let go, whether it bothered Bill because it was an embarrassingly candid biographical fact or a bullshit cover story being pretty much beside the point.

Bill had brought Dickie into MAELSTROM to infiltrate some of the student and antiwar groups, to get names and connections and compromising information, to work his way deeper as the groups got more serious, closer to actions other than marches and sit-ins. Eventually he would find the tiny nerve centers of the most radical groups, the planning cells, the boys and girls who crouched over workbenches packing formaldehyde bricks, hot-wiring fuses and alarm-clock detonators. He was to gain their trust, their respect, and then nudge them toward setting one of those timers, which would lead, ideally, to explosions and arrests, and the tipping of public opinion back to the side of the authorities.

During the years on MAELSTROM, Father Bill had been his only link aboveground. Dickie would call at whatever day and time they'd agreed on, once a month, once every other month, squeezed into a phone booth, vibrating from too many bennies, trying to keep his cigarette steady, the smoke from his eyes, relaying information to Bill or asking for instructions, advice. Hearing sometimes, on Bill's end of the line, the sounds of normalcy, laughter at a cocktail party in the background or the delighted after-school squeals of Bill's kids. Dickie finding himself looking forward to these five-minute conversations with an embarrassing overeagerness, the opportunity to lift his head above water for a few minutes, and then, afterward, always feeling chagrined by the disdain in Bill's voice, Bill's response to what Dickie must have sounded like on his end of the line: strung out, insomniac, very far into the weeds.

The old bird in the next seat was looking at Dickie, his hair and mustache and beard, the white octagon still on his tongue as he waited, openmouthed, for the stewardess to return with his water. Clearly not the traveling companion she'd hoped for. He hadn't done much personal grooming during the months in Iowa. His hair was still down to his shoulders, his mustache still touching his chin. He'd lost his sunglasses somewhere back in the airport at Moline, possibly while he was throwing up in the restroom stall, and he was sure that his eyes were cracked and bloodshot and betrayed his current tenuous emotional state: smack-dab in early-stage withdrawal from drinking, sure, but also from the months in his father's apartment, the day-to-day monotony at the end of life, watching the old man breaking down to nothing.

The stewardess came by with a glass and Dickie swallowed his pill. His seatmate was snoring loudly now, out just like that, some kind of narcoleptic, maybe, her mouth agape, G&T glass empty, a paperback potboiler spread-eagled on her lap. Dickie's rear end was asleep, too, so he pulled his wallet out of the back pocket of his jeans, trying to free up some space. He still had some of the cash Father Bill had given him in Iowa, along with the false driver's license and press credential, and the small collection of insane quasi-religious pamphlets that were the reason he was heading to L.A. All sorts of good things in those: half- or maybe quarter-baked accounts of government mind-control experiments, brainwashing, surreptitious drug testing, other fun stuff which Dickie wasn't really in the mood for with his stomach still doing backflips. Then there was the last little thing, Dickie's personal contraband, stashed away behind the thin sheaf of bills: his legitimate driver's license, his real ID, still a strange thing to see after years of forgeries and boosted cards. A colossal security breach to be sure, having this on him, but it wasn't his first colossal breach, probably wouldn't be his last, and he felt it was owed to him in some way, this one small reminder.

He'd found the license deep in the chaos of his father's apartment, had kept it with him during those months in Iowa, as if proximity to the information might make it true again. *Richard John Ashby*, 2/19/1947, 6′1″, 200 lbs., the name and DOB correct, the height and weight close enough, though he was heavier now, pounds added at his father's place from too many take-out burgers and Hostess Fruit Pies.

Twenty-five. Jesus. He felt a couple of decades older. Depression era, at least, in more ways than one.

He flipped the card over. His signature was on the back. His real signature. It looked like it belonged to someone else. He hadn't signed that name in years. It was strange to live another life, then to be reminded of the life you had before. Whatever that life was. It was hard for Dickie to remember. His mother was dead; now his father was dead. His sister lived in Boston with her family. He had seen her exactly once in the last five years, and that only last week, at the funeral in Iowa. She hadn't recognized him until he'd walked over and introduced himself.

He looked at his real ID, his fake ID. The real ID looked fake; the fake ID looked real. They didn't tell him that this would happen. Father Bill had never explained that once he pretended to be someone else he could never really go back.

Of course, this was how they kept you. Dickie realized this. His life was with them now. He had no one else. He had nothing but Father Bill. So when Bill showed up a year after MAELSTROM collapsed, days after Dickie had buried his father and was in some kind of numb zombie zone, with no clue what he was going to do next, and Bill improbably offered another assignment, a second chance, a plane ticket to Los Angeles, well, then, it turned out that he would do whatever Bill asked.

*   *   *

He hadn't been close with his parents or Sylvie since he'd hit puberty and discovered girls and pills. Mostly pills, to be honest, which had distanced him from his father, who lived life by the Air Force Code of Conduct, and who expected everyone else to follow the same immutable rules. His mother had tried to get through to him, Dickie could see that now, but the last thing a teenager with an amphetamine habit and a desperate need to break free wanted to hear was his mother's nagging, well-intentioned or otherwise.

So it was a surprise when he started receiving letters from his sister while he was in Vietnam. At that point they hadn't spoken in he couldn't remember how long. But it was nice to get mail, missives from a home front he couldn't really imagine, a suburban idyll of Little League games and PTA meetings and Christmas caroling door-to-door in the snow. It was like she was trying to remind him of something he'd never known and therefore never forgotten but still, somehow, missed. When he returned to the States and headed underground she kept writing. Sylvie didn't know what he was involved in, of course, didn't even know specifically where he was. In his first letter, Dickie had told her that he was bumming around the country, picking up odd jobs, and she seemed to accept that, stopped asking anything further after one or two tries. Whenever he settled in a place for any length of time he'd send her a PO box number, and a few weeks later a letter would arrive. News about Frank and the kids, the weather on the East Coast. The correspondence was heavily one-sided, as Dickie's letters back consisted of only a line or two, one of which was the new PO box number and the other a plea to keep writing. He never divulged anything. Father Bill would have appreciated that, after he'd recovered from the massive stroke caused by finding out Dickie was corresponding with a family member aboveground.

The last letter arrived right after MAELSTROM came apart. Dickie was hurriedly sweeping the area for anything he'd left behind, getting ready to disappear again, closing out the PO box, when he found the familiar monogrammed envelope. Their father was not well, Sylvie wrote. He was living alone in Davenport, in the final stages of the dementia that

had been decimating him for the last couple of years. He had rejected
any of Sylvie's help, had told her that he wanted to die alone. Sylvie refused to accept this, though, and thought that Dickie should find a way
to finish out whatever he was doing and get himself to Iowa to help their
father pass. That being her exact phrase, *Help Dad pass,* Sylvie imagining
Dickie as a crossing guard, maybe, holding Jack's elbow, leading him over
to that opposite sidewalk in the afterlife.

Under other circumstances he would have disregarded the letter, fail-
ing at one more thing in Sylvie's eyes, but who was really keeping count
at this point. In that moment, though, in the post office, getting ready
to blow out of town, the letter arrived like a Get Out of Jail Free card,
maybe literally. It was the escape route he'd been looking for.

He had arrived in Davenport on a muggy, overcast afternoon, walking out
of the Greyhound station, duffel slung over his shoulder, hair unbrushed,
teeth fuzzy, getting sideways looks from businessmen and stroller-pushing
moms, getting clutched purses, wallet checks. A visiting envoy from what
his father had called the bum-world, back before Dickie left for Vietnam,
when they saw the yowling, hirsute protesters on the nightly news.

He took side streets as soon as he could, headed down along the river
as the sun began to drop behind the humpback arches of the Centennial
Bridge. There were a couple of vagrant encampments on the edges of
the water, homeless vets still in their combat boots, squatting around
Sterno cans, passing bottles, fishing with string tied to sticks, Tom Saw-
yer–style. Dickie kept his distance, didn't feel like getting rolled during
his first hour in town. He wasn't carrying much, but he did have a handful of pills wrapped in a ball of aluminum foil, the last of his Portland
stash, and he had no interest in pushing what might be left of his luck.

His father had lived in Davenport for the better part of the last decade. Dickie had no idea why Jack had chosen this place, if it held any
meaning for him. It was possible that he'd picked it simply for its lack
of personal history. It wasn't Boston, where Sylvie and her family had
settled. It wasn't the air base in Oklahoma, where Dickie and Sylvie

grew up, where their mother had stayed after the divorce, right to her final days.

Jack's apartment was in one of the bleaker sections of town, a few blocks from the river. Liquor stores and pawnshops and the musicians' union hall, a small park with more broken glass than grass on the ground. At the end of the street was a squat brick housing project surrounded by various styles of fencing, most displaying human-size rips and holes. Jack's building was on the far side of the projects, a walk-up above a used bookstore that Dickie had never seen open for business.

The last time Dickie had been there, his mother had just died. He was eighteen and alone, suddenly, for real. Jack had been gone for a few years and Sylvie was at college in New England. Dickie didn't seem to have much in the way of prospects, as a few of his teachers had helpfully reminded him when he was in class, which wasn't often. Most of his friends were either in jail or starting to get drafted, so he figured he might as well beat Uncle Sam to the punch and enlist.

A week before deploying to Vietnam, he'd gone up to Davenport to stay with Jack, sleeping on the daybed in the living room, drinking a lot, watching the news on TV. They hadn't spoken much during that time, mostly just shared the space, trying not to rub each other the wrong way. On the day Dickie left, Jack drove him to the Greyhound station in the same white Ford Fairlane they'd had when they were all living together a decade earlier on the air base, Dickie finding chips in the dashboard plastic that he remembered from front-seat rides when he was eleven. Outside the bus station Jack had handed Dickie forty bucks and a carton of cigarettes, a gesture of such surprising thoughtfulness that Dickie had been left speechless, standing silent on the curb while Jack pulled the station wagon back out on the street.

The bookstore was closed, no surprise. The darkened front windows displayed the same sun-faded copies of *Johnny Tremain* and *The Red Badge of Courage* that Dickie remembered from his previous visit. Inside the apartment vestibule there was a thick layer of wet leaves and what looked like a few months' worth of utility bills and supermarket advertising circulars. The stairwell led up to two doors, one his father's and the other a janitor's closet, the jurisdiction of whoever kept up the building, which from the look of the place didn't seem to be anyone. He tried his father's door. Locked.

He had hoped he wouldn't have to knock. He felt that knocking would put him at a distinct disadvantage, waiting on the musty landing while his old man shuffled to the door. He just wanted to walk right in and start doing whatever needed doing, cleaning up, making his father something to eat, airing the place out. Avoiding the introductory formalities and any necessary explanation his physical appearance might require.

No such luck. Unless he was going to kick in the door, he would have to knock. Dickie swore under his breath, tapped his knuckles on the thin wood. He ran his hands through his hair, smoothed his beard.

No answer. Maybe he had arrived too late. Maybe the old man was moldering away on the daybed in the living room, or worse, in the middle of the bathroom floor, felled in mid–nature call. Seemed Dickie would have to kick the door in anyway. He took a step back and cocked his leg.

He heard shuffling from inside the apartment, tentative movement, putting his door-break fantasies on ice for the time being. A couple of painful-sounding coughs, crackling with phlegm. Then a lock tumbling, another. The doorknob turned but the door refused to give, jogged back and forth and then finally pulled in, his father's remaining strength surprising, more than a little intimidating. Then the old man's face appeared above the chain, staring out from the space between door and frame.

Jack had been forty when Dickie was born, but he had never seemed old, even when Dickie was a child and most of the other base kids had dads half Jack's age. Jack could have kicked any of their asses, and hadn't been afraid to say so. Here, though, looking out past the security chain, he seemed ancient. His cheeks were crosshatched with uneven gray stubble. His hair had gone gray, too, his military bristle thin and grown out, plastered across the crown of his head, standing at greasy attention in odd angles.

Jack didn't look at Dickie. He looked at Dickie's cowboy shirt, the garnet glass buttons down the front, on the pockets. He had once been Dickie's size, but now stood stooped and emaciated. Yellow crust flaked at the corners of his mouth, old food and spit. He looked like a POW, a man living in extreme conditions. Someone had finally captured Jack

Ashby. His eyes were alert, though, dry and clear and moving quickly, scanning the rest of the vestibule, the staircase. The door slammed shut and Dickie heard some fumbling with the chain, and then the door opened again, his father frustrated, impatient, motioning Dickie in.

The apartment was half lit, the gray day seeping through the few windows that had been left uncovered. The room was heavy with the smell of old newsprint and cigarettes, his father's acrid Lucky Strikes. Something crunched under his boots and Dickie looked down to see dry cat food scattered across the floor. He looked farther into the dark corners of the living room to see pairs of feline eyes returning his gaze, blinking warily. How many cats among the stacks of newspapers and magazines? Hard to tell in the bad light. Blink, blink. Many.

Jack took another look into the vestibule, then slammed the door shut and reaffixed the locks. He stood with his creased forehead pressed to the back of the door. Dickie knew better than to go to him, to assume the man's weight, help him to the daybed. His father had always been violently opposed to any display of weakness, even more opposed to any display of compassion. Direct assistance had never been tolerated. Dickie could remember being six or seven and learning to ride a bike outside their house on the Oklahoma base—not even falling off the bike so much as unable even to get on, missing the pedals repeatedly, collapsing in a tangle of limbs and greasy chain while Jack stood in the open garage doorway and smoked and watched. Just a hand, here, Dad, would be great, little Dickie thinking as he tried to extricate his feet from the tire spokes. Just a quick lift under the arms would be appreciated.

The man should not be standing. It was becoming clear to Dickie, the longer Jack leaned with his head pressed to the door, just what awful shape his father was actually in. The amount of effort it must have taken to rise from the daybed and make his way across the room to the door. The depth of his father's determination was still a formidable and frightening thing. How long would they stand like this? Dickie could picture the sun dropping below the rooftops out the windows, time-lapse-photography-style, the day going gray and brown, streetlights flickering on, the moon rising and falling, the sun coming up over the river, and then a sequence of days, a long string of mornings and afternoons and black nights with the two of them standing in these same spots, waiting for Jack to keel over or finally gather enough strength to start the long walk back to the daybed.

"Jesus Christ," Jack said, jolting Dickie back to planet Earth, his voice the familiar Lucky Strike rasp, but far fainter, more strained. "Get me back over there before I fall on my ass."

The most shocking thing was the old man's weight, or lack thereof. His father didn't eat, as Dickie soon discovered, couldn't keep anything down except the occasional coffee cup of vegetable broth, so watered down it was more like weak tea. He was subsisting on cigarettes and Wild Turkey, which made trips to the bathroom a nightmare, Jack discharging, often uncontrollably, a watery brown substance Dickie couldn't help but see as the last lubricant in his father's body, what was left of the liquid that kept the gears turning.

Sylvie's letter had described Jack's mental state, but Dickie was completely unprepared for the vagueness surrounding his father, a man who once functioned with diamond-edged precision, no gesture wasted, no word offered without specific intent. Now Jack lived in a glassy haze, talking to himself, to the room, conversing with ghosts, the specter of Dickie's mother, Audrey, other names Dickie didn't recognize. He would rage for hours, shouting in a shockingly strong facsimile of his old infamous bark, while at other times he turned inward, weeping into his cupped hands, skeletal shoulders shaking. When this happened, Dickie left him to his sadness, his regret, whatever it was, giving the man his space, cleaning up the kitchen or bathroom or carrying armloads of old newspapers down to the trash can on the corner.

But no matter how cloudy Jack got, he always recognized Dickie. Jack had known him the second he'd opened that door. He'd seen through the beard, the hair, the extra weight. He'd looked at Dickie without surprise, as if their eventual routine had long been established, as if the time line moving forward also stretched back somehow, and Dickie had already been there a month or two. Maybe that's what happened when you were losing your mind. Time worked both ways.

2

She went down to one knee, slowly lifting the camera to her eye, careful not to spook the kids on the post office steps. Focusing close on their hands, the dirt-smudged fingertips, the chewed nails, the passing of a half-smoked cigarette from the boy to the girl.

If they saw her and didn't run, she'd offer them a pack of cigarettes just to stay and do what they were doing, just to ignore her. She'd give them some money for food, the address of a youth shelter farther down Santa Monica Boulevard. But their awareness would change the photographs, make them self-conscious, posed, and so she kept as still as possible, trying to get a few good shots before they noticed.

She knew when she had the pictures, could already see the developed frames floating in the chemical pans back in her darkroom, so she stood and signaled to the kids. She was still close enough to their age, relatively, that they didn't immediately head for the hills. She joined them in the slim band of blue shade under the building's overhang, asked their names, gave them the cigarettes, the address for the shelter. No telling what they'd do with the information. Nothing, probably. They'd keep sleeping wherever they were sleeping, doing whatever they needed to do for food and drugs. There were so many kids on the streets now, even more than when she'd arrived. Some days it seemed like they would overrun the place, that L.A. would become a city of runaways, some kind of ragtag kid civilization, lawless and wild, no adults allowed.

"Hannah."

She turned at the shout to the faces passing on the sidewalk, in the cars waiting at the traffic light. Finally she saw Bert, grinning in his silver Mercedes, leaning across the passenger seat to the open window.

"Leave those kids alone," he shouted.

Hannah smiled, called back. "What are you doing this far east?"

"You call this east? We used to live further east than this. We used to think this was west."

"Are you lost?"

"Slumming," he said. "Pleasure, not business." He glanced back up at the changing light. "We'll talk soon. There's something I want to ask you." Bert lifted his hand in a wave, righted himself behind the wheel, gunned his engine through the intersection.

Hannah turned back to the kids, but they were already heading the other way, bedrolls strapped to their shoulders, the girl lighting one of the new cigarettes and passing it to the boy, who inhaled and passed it back, their hands staying together after the trade.

Ten years earlier she had packed what she could carry from her Berkeley dorm room and walked down to the highway, stuck out her thumb, headed south. She had no rational explanation for this. It turned out that Berkeley wasn't far enough from home. It was like an animal instinct, almost. Escape.

She knew it was a selfish thing to do. She grappled with her decision even as she headed down the interstate to L.A. But she saw no other choice. She was afraid of the life unfolding before her, trapped with her mother and brother in the house in Oakland, their narrow, fearful existence.

She had no idea what she would do once she reached Los Angeles. She had only seen the city in movies and TV shows, pictures in *Life* magazine. In their family its name was avoided like a blasphemy. Los Angeles was the last place her father had gone, the last landmark they had for him. When it was mentioned, even in passing, overheard in a newscast or a stranger's conversation, it sent a dark current through her mother's mood. So of course this was where Hannah ran, the one place she knew Ginnie would never come to find her.

It didn't take long to make friends. She made friends before she was even out of the Central Valley, hitchhiking through the mountain pass and then down into Hollywood. There were kids like her everywhere. There was always a couch or a floor to sleep on. There was always some-one who had a couple of bucks for something to eat. She tried not to overromanticize those memories. They were scary times, too, and hun-gry times, and filthy, really, Hannah cringing when she thought about some of the mattresses she slept on, the other kids she slept beside, wak-ing with rashes and bugbite eruptions, red-and-white pustules along her legs and stomach.

But she was free, and that was all that mattered. About two weeks after she'd left school she called her mother, collect from a pay phone outside a deli on Fairfax Avenue. Ginnie nearly hysterical, demanding to know where Hannah was. Hannah told Ginnie that she was in Los Angeles, she was living in Los Angeles now. There was silence on the other end of the line, and then Hannah said, I'm gone, Mom. I'm gone. You have to let me go.

Her father was the shadow over most of their arguments, the invisible spark for their anger. Hannah storming through the rooms of the house in Oakland, screaming over her shoulder, Ginnie shouting back from the hallway, the kitchen, while Thomas played with his trains on the living room floor. Hannah unsure if he was listening, if he could understand. Not caring until after the heat of battle, when the sadness set in, the guilt, and then she would sit with Thomas in his room, whispering apologies as he fell asleep.

Her father was a photographer for the government. This was what Ginnie had always told her. Who and what he photographed was never explained. When she was younger, Hannah entertained fantasies of Henry as some kind of spy, sneaking around the corridors of the Kremlin, taking surreptitious photos of plotting Communist leaders. Later, she looked at war photographs in the newspaper and wondered if he had been in those places, a witness to the gunfire, the bombs. But it seemed so incongruous with the memories she had of him, with the photographs her mother kept around the house. The plumb-straight part in his hair, his heavy-rimmed glasses. He looked like an accountant, a bureaucrat. He looked like a man who could live his entire life without coming near an explosion of any kind.

In all of their arguments, though, Henry was never brought up explicitly until the end, the night before Hannah left for Berkeley. She didn't know why she chose that moment to bring him back fully into their lives. Maybe she could sense her imminent freedom and it made her feel brave. Maybe she was just feeling reckless and cruel, wanting to wound one last time.

He's not coming back, she had shouted, standing in the kitchen doorway, glaring at her mother's back. He's dead, Mom. Jesus Christ, after all this time.

There was no response. No response was possible. Ginnie could not believe Henry was dead. She would wait until the end of the world, holding her daughter and son hostage, hoping for that knock at the door, the long-prayed-for return. But Hannah wouldn't wait any longer. She had decided this, whether she'd known it then or not.

Ginnie had stood facing the sink, her back to Hannah. She made no sound. She had simply lifted her hands from the dishpan, slicked to the wrists with soap, and pressed her fingers to the countertop tile, holding on.

3

Waking on the daybed. First smoke, first drink. Dickie picking something from his foil ball to get the synapses started. Jack already up and wandering the rooms or nowhere to be seen and Dickie stumbling into the bedroom to make sure he was still breathing, just sleeping it off in the lopsided bed, an empty Wild Turkey bottle on the pillow beside him.

Making instant coffee on the range in the kitchen. Some breakfast. Jack up now for sure, maybe standing in the corner by the table glowering at Dickie or out in the living room looking through the stacks of newspapers. Both men in their underpants, padding around in bare feet. The radio on, a news and weather station that also played a few swing numbers every hour, Artie Shaw, Lester Brown, even a few of the Benny Goodman small groups. Getting dressed, getting Jack dressed. Maybe a half hour killed right there. Getting some vegetable broth into Jack. Two coffee cups on the card table in the kitchen, one of broth, the other of Wild Turkey. Feeding the cats.

Late morning, Jack's first nap of the day. A little housekeeping, maybe, peeling the rugs off the floors and dragging them into the vestibule to beat them into dusty submission. Scrubbing the bathroom. Gathering newspapers and mail and old soup cans, whiskey bottles, tossing it all into the Dumpster behind the building. Salvaging all sorts of forgotten detritus: Jack's medals and citations from the Air Force, Dickie's old driver's license, a business card for a VA hospital with a handwritten appointment that Dickie couldn't imagine Jack had kept.

More coffee. Back to the rapidly shrinking foil ball. Sidetracked by old newspapers, basketball scores, TV listings from his time underground, Dickie hunched over the newsprint like an amnesiac excavating lost history. Jack awake and ready for lunch. The twin coffee mugs. A trip to the bathroom and the ensuing cleanup. One of Jack's outbursts, screaming obscenities at Dickie or whoever else he thought was in the room, jabbing his fists until Dickie finally grabbed him from behind and wrestled him down, holding Jack until he lay spent, limp, wheezing on the daybed.

Second nap of the day. Dickie down the stairs and out of the apartment, steering the Fairlane down to the supermarket, the liquor store, the bank if the Social Security check had arrived. Still feeling like a tourist in the aboveground world, but starting to get a few nods of acknowledgment from cashiers and clerks, despite the hair and beard. Becoming something of a regular. The time out of the apartment a breath of fresh air, literally, driving back slowly, windows down, taking slight detours to see the bridge from different angles, the river, the men standing in half circles down on the banks.

Back to the apartment and Jack up and raging or up and weeping. Trying to get a pill down Jack's throat. Getting a few down his own to calm things a bit. Jack's eyes lighting up when he sees Dickie's shopping bags, the new bottles clinking in the brown paper. Here, boy. Sit. Drinks all around. A moment of lucidity where Jack comments on a news story from the radio, something in the paper from 1969. Maybe an actual discussion, just long enough to lull Dickie into letting his guard down until Jack is after his own throat or Dickie's with a shaving razor. Dickie gathering all the sharp objects from the apartment and stashing them in the janitor's closet on the other side of the staircase landing.

Vespers. The sky purple over the river. The radio station going one hundred percent big-band ballads, sending both Jack and Dickie into a teary melancholy. Dinner for himself, a take-out burger or a sandwich with some of the cats' tuna, a couple of fruit pies. More broth for Jack. Another trip to the bathroom, Jack crying at the mess he's made, Dickie holding his father's shoulders while Jack sobs with his pants pooled at his ankles. A few more drinks, another couple of pills. Nightfall. Streetlights below, pinpricks of orange light from the housing project. Dogs barking down by the river. Dickie's thoughts of the men there, campfires and cigarette cherries in the dark. Dickie's thoughts of Portland, an explosion in an office, a Sunday morning, the man who shouldn't have been there. Jack standing in the living room, staring at the TV, a deodorant commercial, sculpting the fingers of his right hand into a mimed pistol, aiming at the screen, pulling the trigger.

Sleep, yes or no. Jack in the dark bedroom, talking or snoring. Dickie on the daybed, a last smoke, a last drink, the radio very low. Firecrackers from the street below, a chain of tiny detonations. A man at his desk, alone in a Portland office building. Dogs down by the river.

Time moves both ways.

It didn't take long for Dickie to deplete his stash, until he was poking around in the folds of the aluminum foil looking in vain for a stray tablet. After a brief, foolhardy flirtation with the idea of going cold turkey, he decided to drive up to the address on the business card he'd found and visit Jack's doctor.

The guy looked Dickie over, asked after Jack, took a few notes. Wrote a refill for Jack's medication. Dickie almost chickened out, almost walked out the door without another word, but desperation trumped shame long enough for him to ask for another prescription, just something to calm his nerves a little, maybe something else to get him up in the morning. The doc looked at Dickie again, then back down at his pad, started writing.

"When did you get back?" the doc said.

Dickie, stunned for a second, wondering what this guy knew, if something had slipped through from Portland, and then, getting a grip, realizing that the doctor meant back from Vietnam. Maybe Jack had once said something about his son overseas. Maybe the guy could just tell, looking at Dickie. Maybe it was that obvious.

"I'm not exactly sure," Dickie said.

The doc nodded, still scribbling. He tore off the sheet and handed it to Dickie without further eye contact. Sent his regards to Jack.

He returned to the apartment to find Jack playing Audrey's old records in the living room, sobbing and yelling, breaking everything within reach that he hadn't already broken. Dickie managed to get his father onto the daybed, one of the new sedatives down his throat.

When Jack was finally asleep, Dickie started cleaning. Broken bottles, broken plates, and then the records themselves, some in pieces, some simply flung into the far corners of the room. The cats still cowering behind the bookcases and the big oak hutch, furniture they probably figured Jack couldn't overturn. They obviously didn't know him as well as Dickie did.

In a corner of the living room was a box Dickie hadn't seen before. He lifted the flaps and found it full of his mother's 78s, some still in their original paper wrappers. He couldn't believe Jack still had these. His father was the least sentimental man he'd ever known. Dickie hadn't seen all of his mother's recordings in one place since the first time his father had destroyed her records, when Jack stood in their driveway on the Oklahoma base and smashed them on the street, one at a time, while the neighbors looked on and Audrey stood watching from the living room window.

His parents had met during the war, the last war, or, well, actually, the one before the one before, the one that still seemed like a *real* war, with bond drives and homecoming parades and front-porch flags snapping in the breeze. Audrey had already made her most famous recordings in Paris. She had been a darling of the Resistance, her stripped-down renditions of classic torch numbers reinterpreted under the circumstances as songs of longing for many things in addition to love: country, courage, freedom. She made a few more recordings after she came to the States with Jack, but soon they were living on air bases in towns without main streets let alone recording studios, and after Sylvie and Dickie were born she closed the book on her career, reserving her singing for lullabies and impromptu recitals for friends' birthdays.

She hadn't been forgotten, though. Every couple of years, some middle-aged guy with hair a little too long and a few days' growth of beard showed up at their house, unannounced. A writer, a college professor, a collector. Audrey tried politely to send them away, but they hadn't tracked her down to take no for an answer, so she'd invite them in, fix coffee, sit and answer questions, turn down offers to go to New York or Chicago and record something new. She always made sure whoever had come was long gone by the time Jack got home, making Dickie and Sylvie promise to keep the visits to themselves, their little secret.

At the time, Dickie couldn't understand his mother's importance to these men, what possessed them to track her down. He had fallen in with a group of air brats whose main interests included jazz and booze and raiding their parents' medicine cabinets, not necessarily in that order. Their musical tastes were decidedly modern, Ornette and Miles and Coltrane, and Audrey's records were anything but. To Dickie, they sounded like distant echoes of some lost time that he didn't particularly understand or care much about.

He had one of his mother's records with him when he started on MAELSTROM. A strange, fragile thing to take. He and Audrey weren't even on speaking terms at the time, so he couldn't really explain its inclusion in his duffel bag of bare necessities. It got as far as Ann Arbor, his first step into the student movement. He was living with Mary Margaret, a girl he'd met in an antiwar group, and during an argument one night she threw the record across their living room, shattering it against the far wall. Dickie hadn't played the thing in years, but the loss nearly brought him to his knees. It took Mary Margaret a few minutes to understand the severity of what she had done. She didn't ask him about the record, why it had stopped their argument cold. How mortal a sin she had committed. She retreated to the bedroom, leaving Dickie standing over his broken pieces of shellac.

He slid Jack's discs back into their musty sleeves, slid the sleeves underneath the big oak hutch, fighting the urge to put one on the old Decca player in the corner. He didn't want to rile Jack again, and to be honest, he wasn't sure he was ready to hear one himself. It would be a strange sound to him now. It seemed to Dickie that they were broken more often than they were played. The crack of the records fracturing was more familiar to him than the sound of his mother's voice in the songs.

It didn't take long to run out of pills again. He had another bout of cold-turkey optimism, but within a day he started to feel the clawing of withdrawal, his sinuses scratched and throbbing, his mouth dry, his body shimmering with a low-grade panic that threatened to bubble over into something more serious with each unmedicated hour.

He couldn't bring himself to go back to the hospital and beg again, so he made his way down to the river, to the men in their camp. Four bucks for a little baggie of Seconal and Benzedrine. Same price it was in Vietnam.

Some kind of commotion from the rooms below woke him on the daybed, drool-chinned and discombobulated, more than a little hungover. It sounded like someone moving around down there, and after Dickie swallowed a few uppers and checked to make sure Jack was still breathing, he pulled on some clothes and went down to the street.

The door of the used bookstore was open, the lights were on. Dickie was so used to seeing the place dark and shut tight that it seemed almost like a dream. The place was crammed floor to ceiling with shelves of hardbacks and paperbacks, old movie magazines, a locked glass display case with what appeared to be leather-bound rare editions. A graybeard crouched in the back of the store, digging through boxes. He lifted his head when Dickie stepped inside, nodded, went back to his archaeology.

Dickie perused. Something to read wouldn't be such a bad idea. He'd pretty much exhausted Jack's cache of old newspapers, felt as if he'd finally caught up on his lost years, or at least those years' *Hi and Lois* strips and Ann Landers columns. He wasn't quite sure that his attention span could currently accommodate one of those copies of *Ulysses* or *Moby-Dick,* but there was a wooden crate of comic books on the floor by the old encyclopedias, two for a dime. The price and level of intellectual commitment seemed about right.

He left with a pair from a few years back, two issues of *Detective Comics* with a pretty compelling backup feature about J'onn J'onzz, the Manhunter from Mars, a big green alien guy who was brought to earth by a mad scientist and then got stuck here when the mad scientist gave up the ghost from the shock of bringing a big green alien guy to earth.

Dickie spent the next couple of nights with the comics, reading via flashlight or the streetlights out the living room window after Jack was down for the count. There was a compelling sadness that loomed over the proceedings, J'onn stranded on Earth, trying not to be found out, using his shape-shifting powers to impersonate human beings. J'onn haunted by memories of the planet he'd left behind, shifting back and forth between his human personas and his Martian look, unsure which was the right one even when nobody else was around. Dickie could identify.

He wanted to see how things turned out for J'onn, but every time he checked, the bookstore was closed again. He had to content himself with the comics he had, rereading until the covers came loose from their staples, until his thumbs were ink black, wearing holes in the colored newsprint.

He was down at the river once a week now, more often if he'd had a particularly tough stretch of days. Sometimes he'd take a hit from a passed bottle or a joint before leaving, but he didn't say much, just sat and listened to whatever conversation he'd wandered into. Content just to be away from the apartment while Jack slept, out in the late-afternoon light with the vets, watching the water and the railroad bridge, the middle school kids walking the trestles high above on their way home, arms straight out at their sides, waving for balance.

*   *   *

If pressed, Dickie could come up with some pretty good stories about his time in Vietnam. It had come up occasionally with the student groups during MAELSTROM. Someone would ask, and Dickie would make a show of his reluctance to dredge up painful memories. Of course, this only created more interest, so when he knew he had their attention, he'd hold forth at great length—dramatic, detailed accounts of the mud and blood and horror, the living nightmare of war. His stories were the glue that sealed many a deal during those days, both proving these kids' larger points about the war and giving Dickie a well-earned legitimacy in their eyes. Someone who'd been there, who'd seen it firsthand, and had made the choice to resist.

The truth was, he hadn't seen an hour of combat. A month into basic training, the MPs busted him for possession. A few days later, a couple of guys from Naval Intelligence came to visit him in his holding cell. They'd had an eye on him, they said, both because he seemed like a fairly bright guy and because he was in with the local dopers. He seemed well liked by his fellow troops. He was a good listener. His contempt for his superiors was obvious and genuine and gave him an authenticity that was hard to fake. He was just what the NIS guys were looking for, and they were willing to make a deal. Based on Dickie's family pedigree, based on the respect that many in the mid and higher levels of the military had for his father, they offered him a choice: court-martial or playing ball for their team. Dickie chose to play.

He spent two years in Vietnam checking in to various military hospitals with vague, usually apocryphal injuries and ailments, cozying up to other patients, sussing out the users and dealers, haunting bars in some of the R&R hot spots and looking for information, i.e., who was ready to snap and shoot up his platoon or commanding officer; what the flow of narcotics was and where it was flowing from; and lastly, with this facet of his job providing some early training for his later involvement in MAEL-STROM, trying to find out if there was any contact between troops and antiwar groups back home. (The answers turning out to be, in order: too

many to name / ditto / a decent amount of heroin and hash, mostly from
the Golden Triangle; a lot of pot, mostly homegrown; a lot of uppers and
downers, from parts unknown, pills being nearly impossible to track, just
materializing, basically, in the palms of Vietnamese children in the villages, pressed into the hands of American soldiers for four bucks, U.S. /
and not much, or not enough to be overly concerned with, at least among
the white troops, who were the only guys who would really open up to
Dickie—just some books and leaflets, hand-copied Phil Ochs lyrics.)

What he hadn't considered was that whatever drug problem he had
when he entered the military was about to get ten times worse, due to
the basic pants-shitting terror he felt every second he was over there,
and the fact that his job involved an easy and steady supply of substances
that could alleviate segments of that fear and keep him functioning at
something like a reasonable level.

And, of course, there was an additional perk. It was much harder to
get shot or blown up in a bar or a hospital than out in the jungle. He
had never been much of a fighter, never had much in the way of physical
courage, or so Jack had always told him. He was better at talking and listening, turning guys in. Dickie knew it would be nothing to be proud of.
He figured it would make him feel like a fink, like a rat, and he was right.
But it had also kept him alive.

4

When Hannah first arrived in Los Angeles, she said a prayer every night, asking Thomas's forgiveness for leaving. She put herself to sleep by imagining that she was talking to him, like she used to talk to him back in Oakland, lying on his bed, whispering in the dark while he fell asleep on the floor beside her. Their long, one-sided conversations. Her plans, dreams, schemes. He was the perfect confidant. He knew everything about her, all her secrets. She could tell him anything and it would fall away into the depths, safe and secure. What he thought of what she told him she would never know, but the answering voice she imagined was forgiving and kind, wise in its way, wryly funny.

She'd had a final conversation with Thomas the night before she left for Berkeley. Not aware of what she would do a week later, but feeling a gathering sense of change, a momentous break impending. Suspecting, possibly, what she was capable of. Whispering to Thomas and hearing his reluctant approval, his understanding of why she needed to go. A completely imagined conversation, Hannah knew, but one she was able to convince herself was at least possible, was a conversation that she and the Thomas she had constructed over the years could plausibly have. Still, even after she was away she asked for forgiveness every night, unable to sleep until she heard the voice she'd given him in her head, granting it again.

*   *   *

She had a camera of her own, a birthday gift from the high school boy-friend she'd left behind. She took pictures of buildings in Hollywood, their elaborate cornices and fire escapes and rooftop signs silhouetted in the twilight. The city was sliding into something, was past its heyday, crumbling slowly. Cracked buildings and cracked kids, runaways her age or younger asking for money or dope or money for dope. Sometimes she took their pictures, but usually only in service to the buildings behind them, or in concert with them. Not portraits so much as duets. Half a face and an ear and the tall brick shoulder of the Knickerbocker Hotel. The days of those buildings maybe as numbered as the days of the kids smoking in front of them, so they seemed right together, sharing a rap-idly disappearing moment in time.

She got a job taking pictures for real estate firms. All the big property owners in Hollywood were trying to get off the sinking ship, so they needed to sell, preferably to out-of-state investors, foreigners, moneyed men who still envisioned the Hollywood of newsreel movie premieres, red carpets, popping flashbulbs. These were the ideal buyers, but her clients would settle lower on the food chain if need be, locals who planned to open pawn-shops and liquor stores and peep-show theaters, bargain-basement entre-preneurs who could see the future and wanted to be there to cash in.

The pictures she was supposed to take were dead-on frames of the buildings, front, sides, then some of the interior, the common areas, lob-bies, and elevator banks. Mug shots. But between these setups she pulled her camera from the tripod and took her own pictures, the corners and fixtures and oblique angles, planes passing rooftop radio antennas in the midafternoon sky.

This was about the time she met Bert, a film student with a day job at a B-movie factory, directing beach and biker pictures while studying Coc-teau and Fellini at night. She moved into his apartment in Echo Park and took still pictures and he took moving pictures. For a while, Ginnie sent envelopes with small amounts of cash. Hannah always intended to leave the money untouched, to send it all back one day, thereby proving her independence, but she needed the funds and usually ended up spending it within days of its arrival, feeling like a failure. Tied, still. Bound.

Eventually, she returned to Oakland for brief visits, sometimes with Bert, sometimes just with Bert's car, a day or two, a weekend. Never with much in the way of advance warning. Never on holidays. She wanted to keep the visits free of significance, as if she were any adult child returning home to catch up, visit old friends, old haunts. By then, the heated feelings between her and Ginnie had cooled, and they had relatively civil meals together, somewhat labored conversations about Hannah's work, her life, Thomas's progress, what he was learning, whom he had spoken to at the community center.

Thomas sent her postcards irregularly, a seemingly random mailing schedule that Hannah knew made strict sense in some part of his brain. Images of the bridges and the bay, downtown Oakland. The same card sometimes four or five times over the years. She wasn't sure if there was any logic to his choices, or if these were simply the options he had, the postcards in the small spinner rack at the drugstore, Thomas turning the display while Ginnie waited for a prescription to be filled.

The messages on the cards were brief, a line or two about something he'd seen or done that he'd found interesting. His childlike printing. Sometimes just his name, *Thomas,* sometimes with an exclamation point, *Thomas!,* as if he was shouting from higher up in the state, reminding her that he was still there.

After she and Bert had gone their separate ways, she found an apartment above a camera shop on Figueroa Avenue. She began frequenting the downtown movie houses, the crumbling vaudeville- and silent-era palaces, watching a bizarre spectrum of films, from the classic to the pornographic. She sat with her feet up on the seat in front of her, her camera resting on her stomach, and when a particularly interesting composition appeared she would take a picture. The on-screen images paired with the physical structure around them. Audrey Hepburn's jawline and the brocaded edge of the frayed theater curtain. John Wayne's left eye and the brim of his cowboy hat pushing the outer boundary, the top right corner of the screen.

Work begat work. She had more real estate jobs than she could handle, and her other photographs began to attract attention, first at some neighborhood coffee shops, then at a few larger spaces in Hollywood, eventually at some higher-end galleries on the west side of town.

She moved into a new space in a neighborhood a few miles north, a former roller-skating rink with a high domed roof that attracted a daily balcony crowd of cooing pigeons. She made a darkroom, a workshop, cordoned off a place to eat and sleep. It was still more space than she needed, so she turned the rest into a gallery, showing the work of some of the neighborhood artists she admired.

She left the front door to the roller rink unlocked, which she knew was foolish, but she liked coming out from the darkroom to find someone wandered in off the street looking through the gallery. A surprise in their day. Sometimes it was a runaway or a homeless man and she'd give them a few dollars or make them a sandwich to take. She was held up once by a couple of teenagers with what one of them threatened was a gun in the pocket of his sweatshirt, and they made off with a watch that was an old gift from Bert and the cash she had in her purse, which amounted to about six bucks. Much worse could have happened, she knew, but she still left the door unlocked. She wasn't willing to give up that moment when she came out into the light to find a stranger standing quietly, hands clasped behind their back, looking at the pictures on the walls.

She kept all of Thomas's postcards pinned to a large sheet of corkboard, which she hung in the living space of the studio. When she was a girl she'd had a wall of photos, too, pictures her father brought home from work, images of San Francisco meant to alleviate her fear that the city would be destroyed by a nuclear blast. She'd taken comfort in those images as she took comfort in these. Evidence that Thomas was all right, that her connection with him was still intact. At night she lay in bed and looked at the photos in the glow from one of the small skylights, illumination from the moon or the street.

Proof of life.

5

Dickie had returned from Southeast Asia with a name and a phone number, a meeting in an D.C.-area diner with Father Bill. Bill said that Dickie had come highly recommended, that his work in Vietnam had not gone unnoticed. He asked Dickie what he planned to do now that he was back in the States and Dickie told him that he didn't know. He felt deeply disoriented by his return to the States. His tolerance for everyday life had become just about nonexistent. The pleasantries and rituals of civilization seemed like a shared joke or some kind of sinister game after living in a place where moment-to-moment existence was husked down to the raw basics, to violence and survival. So when Father Bill offered him MAELSTROM, Dickie took it.

He started in Ann Arbor. At first it was mostly loose groups of hippies who met a few times a week, making signs and planning street-corner rallies, or old socialist ladies in the suburbs collecting money to send to these groups. He got in with a few publishers of leftist newspapers, journals, books, and this was closer to what he was looking for. They talked a good game about overthrow and redistribution of wealth, but it was still nearly impossible to pin them down on anything. Sometimes at the bookstores he'd make the acquaintance of guys too old to be in school, unnervingly quiet men who hung around at the edges of the movement, seemed combustible. One of them led him to the activist group with the most promise, led him to Mary Margaret, who eventually brought Dickie underground. Then to the Pacific Northwest, small actions against recruiting offices, government buildings, and then, finally, to the big action, to Portland.

The target was a nondescript industrial park, an engineering firm that designed parts of what became napalm canisters. A partially owned subsidiary of a partially owned subsidiary of. The bombing was to take place on a Sunday morning, when no one would be around. The end goal a conflagration of documents and machinery, a big blazing message that would not only make the news but knock weapons development back a few months.

They had trained and planned, and they executed well. The bomb went off beautifully, creating a fireball that ripped through rooms, feeding on furniture and paperwork, shattering windows, blowing the roof. A perfect action, except for that single, major hitch.

The office wasn't empty.

Night in Davenport. Dickie stood in front of the grocery store's refrigerated case, weighing his options with regard to prepackaged cold cuts, when he heard Father Bill's voice close behind.

Dickie assumed they'd find him eventually. Maybe they had Sylvie's mail tagged. Maybe they'd been following him since Portland. It didn't matter, really. He figured that one of the world's two foremost intelligence powers should be able to track down one of its own citizens, no matter how marginal, without too much hassle. They made a date to have lunch, as Dickie had to get back to Jack and also because he liked the idea of making Bill cool his heels for a night after coming all that way.

The restaurant was empty when Dickie arrived the next day. It was an hour or so after the lunchtime rush, if there had been a lunchtime rush. Humid and buggy outside, blissfully over-air-conditioned within. A teenage waiter was filling vases with plastic flowers. He nodded to Dickie to sit anywhere. Father Bill came in a few minutes later, dressed like he was heading out in the catamaran—polo shirt and khakis and

Top-Siders, looking maybe even more conspicuous than mountain-man Dickie with his ripped jeans and flannel shirt. Quite a pair.

They ordered and Bill drank his seltzer and Dickie drank his beer. Bill regarding him with, what? Concern? Bewilderment? Distrust? All of the above? Looking at Dickie like he was some kind of giant question mark. Finally, Bill asked what had happened in Portland, after the bomb.

"I lost them." Dickie saying this like he had any real hope it was enough of an answer, like Father Bill would nod and slap his khaki thighs and stand to pay the check. Bill, though, in reality, looking back at Dickie like this was obviously not a sufficient answer, not with all the money and time this had cost. Not to mention losing an asset like Dickie, who had gotten in so deep. This would blow other operations, wagons would be circled, paranoia would settle in among the movement groups, which in and of itself could be a good thing, could be exploited, but for now Bill's whole department was in an uproar, they had an uncontrollable thing, a wild variable. A blown operation was shut down and sealed off, cut away like a tumor, but there was always leakage, draining in frighteningly unpredictable ways.

"How many were in your group?" Bill said.

"Six."

"You lost six people."

Dickie nodded.

Bill sighed, pinched the bridge of his nose. "We were left with a body in Portland, Dickie. What remained of a body. He had a wife, a family."

"I saw the news, Bill."

"And we have nothing to show for it. Because you lost all of your friends."

Bill lifted a pack of cigarettes from his shirt pocket. He shook one out, popped it in his mouth, pushed the pack across the table to Dickie.

"I'll need the full story," Bill said.

"Fine."

"When can you come east?"

"I don't know."

"How's your father?"

"Fuck you, Bill."

"How can we do this, Dickie? We need to do this."

Dickie took a cigarette, turned in his chair, motioned for the waiter, ready to order.

"I'm free for lunch all week."

They met in various restaurants around town, Dickie telling the whole story, every detail, like a confession, until the end of their session that Friday where he got to the most important part, the explosion in Portland, what happened after the explosion, what he had done, and this he left out, turning one story into another.

It was hard to tell if Bill bought it or not. Bill was something of an inscrutable figure to Dickie. That Ivy League polish. Dickie was always disgusted with himself for caring what Bill thought, for wanting Bill's approval. That week in Davenport, he found himself acting like a petulant kid even more than usual, showing up for a couple of those lunches already half in the bag.

After their last meeting, they stepped out onto the sidewalk, shook hands awkwardly. Bill left Dickie with a new phone number, an envelope with some cash, what Dickie figured was his severance. He told Dickie to take care of himself, which Dickie answered with a snort, lighting another of Bill's cigarettes, keeping the pack.

Summer to fall to winter. Dickie bought a shovel and windshield scraper at the hardware store, cleared the walk, tried to get the Fairlane started in the cold. Jack was slipping more each day. The apartment radiators were idiosyncratic at best, so Dickie drove down at the St. Vincent de Paul, bought extra blankets, matching sweaters for Jack and himself. Bought another bunch of coats and parkas, fur-lined boots, which he left down at the riverbank when the men weren't around.

It was almost Easter, and Dickie was giving Jack his biweekly bath when the old man started coughing something fierce. Not an unusual occurrence, except this time it refused to dissipate. The coughing grew louder, wetter, Jack's whole body shaking with it, and then there was blood, suddenly, spiraling in the bath water, and Dickie looked up to Jack's face and saw a crimson-chinned vampire.

He got Jack seated on the toilet, ran out to the kitchen, called an ambulance. A dull thudding sound came from the bathroom as he gave the address to the dispatcher. Dickie strained to see around the corner of the doorway, what Jack was doing in there. Off the phone and rushing back into the bathroom to find Jack bashing his head against the edge of the sink, trying to brain himself, the room a bloody mess. Dickie grabbed his father and pulled him out into the living room, tearing off his own shirt to press against Jack's forehead, trying to stop the bleeding. Jack's eyes wide, unblinking. Baring his teeth, biting Dickie's exposed chest. Hell-bent on controlling his own exit, seemingly willing to take Dickie with him. His hands at Dickie's throat, still so goddamn strong when he needed to be. Then the sound of a siren outside, footsteps in the stairwell. A knock at the door, voices. Dickie shouting for them to kick the goddamn thing in.

The door burst open and a pair of medics rushed into the room, pulled Jack off Dickie or Dickie off Jack, hard to tell, one of the medics holding the old man while the other produced a needle, jabbed Jack in the arm. Dickie sitting on the floor, breathing hard, shirtless, bloody, wanting to beg for a needle of his own, another of those shots, Jesus Christ, please.

The morning of the funeral was bright, unseasonably warm. Sylvie and her family stayed only for the service. She didn't want to come up to the apartment and Dickie didn't really want her to see the place. She offered to take Dickie to lunch, but he declined, citing all the things he had to take care of, whatever those were.

They hugged good-bye, and Sylvie pressed a handful of cash into his hand, which just about broke his heart.

A week later, Dickie was back in the frozen-food aisle when he heard Father Bill stride up beside him. Bill offered his condolences, looked legitimately alarmed at the shape Dickie was in. The next day they had lunch, and Bill offered Dickie a new job, and a plane ticket to L.A.

Two hours before his flight he sat in the parking lot of the VA hospital, having a hell of a one-man argument. What to ask for, prescription-wise. This being an actual verbalized debate, lots of yelling, pounding the dashboard, the pulling of hair, some tears. Dickie finally feeling shaken by the last few months, few years even. More than shaken, actually, whatever the word for that would be.

Still debating during the wait in the reception area, staring at a year-old copy of *Reader's Digest*. Hard to focus, even enough to look at the cartoons. He'd finished most of his stash before leaving the apartment, having first emptied it of everything, even the cats, setting them loose down by the river, where they just stood and stared at Dickie, like, What the hell are we supposed to do now?

More than shaken. Past that. Shook.

The doctor looked at Dickie in much the same way he had the first time, maybe with a little more concern, and then brought out the white prescription pad. So easy just to let him keep writing, to forget about the plane ticket in his pocket, to go back to the apartment and occupy that same space, to let his body give way, let his mind go wherever his father's had gone.

He could still feel the bruises on his neck, the bite marks on his chest. Jack's last gift.

He told the doc to wait. Asked for something else instead. A medication he'd heard of, a pill that made you sick around alcohol.

Antabuse, the doctor said, and Dickie said, Yes, that's what I need.

I have to stop something, he said. Something has to stop.

6

"It'll be gone soon," Bert said. He took a drink, rested his forearm on the table. Hannah looked at his watch. She couldn't help looking at his watch, which was, of course, the point of the thing. It was made to be appreciated, a large, elaborate stainless-steel contraption, its band just loose enough that it slid a quarter turn whenever Bert rotated his wrist, allowing the metal to catch the light.

"A week, maybe," he said. "They're already tearing down the marquee. They've got a Dumpster in front, half full of theater seats."

The watch got Hannah thinking of the watch he had given her years ago, the one stolen during the holdup at the gallery. But Bert had bought that watch long before he'd made his first studio film, or his second or third, and it had been a department-store layaway, while this thing could make a nice down payment on a Third World country.

Bert turned his wrist again, tapped a finger along the rim of his whiskey glass. They met a couple times a year now, usually at a bar or restaurant near one of the sound stages where he was filming. After a few of their early meetings, they'd gone back to his place, and one time to hers, for old times' sake, but eventually they'd both reconciled themselves to the fact that this was a bad idea, or at least not a particularly good one, that it was better to rehash the past in public, fully clothed, without any new worries or regrets to heap onto the old.

The windows were open to the midday heat. They sat at a small high table, just inside the threshold. Every few minutes, Hannah slid her hand out through the opening, into the sun, pulling it back slowly, into the cool sleepy dusk of the bar.

"I always wanted to make something that would be shown there," Bert said. "Whenever I picture a movie I'm making as a finished thing, I imagine it shown in that theater."

"Maybe you should work the phones," Hannah said. "Is that how you say it? Call some big names. Some producing partners who want to dabble in architectural preservation."

"It's too late," Bert said. "I drive by every morning. You saw me. I've got no business on that side of town anymore except to sit in the car and watch these guys pull shit out the front door. A week and it'll be gone."

He turned his wrist again, this time to check the polished face of the watch. They'd planned to have drinks and then dinner, but Bert had greeted Hannah with the news that he could only stay an hour. His apologetic rain checks had become more frequent over the last couple of years, maybe since they'd stopped sleeping together, if Hannah wanted to be cynical. Or maybe it was simply because what they'd had was withdrawing that much further into the past.

"Did you ever take any pictures in there?" he said. "That theater? I mean any pictures that didn't have a movie playing in the middle of them?"

"Probably not."

"I feel like I'm going to lose my memory of what the place looked like. That someday I won't be able to imagine my movies in there."

"Then what?"

"I don't know. I'll have to imagine them playing somewhere else. In a shopping mall. On a TV in a motel room. I'll have to picture them smaller, fewer eyes on them. Private things."

They paid the bill and stood from their stools. Bert lit a cigarette, pulled on his sport coat.

"Have you been watching the chess match?" he said. "The American kid and the Russian?"

"No."

"I've been following it. Something to watch while I wait for the Olympics. I know you hate sports."

"I'm not sure I think of chess as a sport."

"You should see these guys play. It's a sport. You'd hate it."

They hugged good-bye, and Hannah stood at the open windows for a moment, watching until Bert turned the corner. She walked outside then, a little disoriented from the early drink, the change from the dark bar to the lighted day. Not unlike leaving a movie theater from an afternoon show, the unsettling realization that the world had continued without her, that something had been lost, possibly, while she sat in the dark, in the strange, false time of the images moving on screen.

7

Out of the Vegas airport and into the whitewashed sky. The second take-off was worse than the first, the plane straining and lurching. Dickie's seatmate this time around was a blond, long-legged coed wearing a UCLA sweatshirt. He hadn't seen one of these in he didn't know how long. A nonradicalized college student. Not a political thought in her head, he guessed.

The girl closed her eyes, took a deep breath, another, some kind of relaxation exercise, a mini-meditation. Once the plane straightened out, Dickie unfastened his teeth, blinked the dryness from his eyes.

"Flying makes you nervous?"

She shrugged.

"DC-10s have a very good safety record," Dickie said. "Their accident rate is something like point nine." He felt fairly gallant sharing this reassuring data. He was thrilled to be able to remember it. One of the kids underground had been studying aerospace engineering before joining the movement, but he'd still picked up trade journals and technical manuals, and Dickie found himself thumbing through them for lack of better reading material on some of those dead-of-night drives.

The girl opened her eyes, looked at the back of the seat in front of her. "That seems high."

"No, no," Dickie said. "Point nine is like, nothing. It's the odds of get-ting struck by lightning, eaten by a shark."

"Seems high to me."

"No, it's nothing. It's less than one." Dickie started to doubt his own premise, the whole reason he'd brought up the safety record in the first place. Was that number right? Point nine? Or was that another make of aircraft, was he getting the two confused and the DC-10 was more like a one-point-five or even a two, a 580,000-pound flying deathtrap?

"Is that number right?" the girl said. "Because I don't like that number at all."

"Excuse me for a second." Dickie shaking again, standing from his seat and maneuvering back to the bathroom. He squeezed inside, locked the door. What else did he have on him, besides the Antabuse? A small baggie of pot, which would do him no good unless he wanted to roll and light a joint right there in the bathroom. More cigarettes, what looked like half a Seconal. Not a great selection. He wondered if the girl was carrying, if they could maybe work out a trade. This seemed like a good idea for half a panicked moment, until Dickie pictured a greeting party of narcotics officers waiting for him at the Los Angeles baggage claim. He went with the Seconal.

Back in his seat with a glass of orange juice and a cigarette and a slowly enveloping pharmaceutical calm. The girl was asleep with her head pressed to the window. Dickie stared at her legs for a few minutes, the tiny blond hairs that started halfway up her thighs and disappeared under the ragged cutoffs of her denim shorts.

He took out the only thing he'd brought to read, the pamphlets Fa-ther Bill had given him in Davenport, three slim tracts, the sum total of physical intelligence he had going west. Microscopically printed, poorly proofread litanies of conspiracy theories and apocalyptic pre-dictions written by a man named Javier Buñuel, sometimes spelled Xavier Buñuel, though Dickie couldn't tell if the authorial discrepancy had some kind of deeper meaning or simply spoke to a basic confusion of identity. Or maybe they were just typos, which, judging from the incoherence of the rest of the material, seemed as plausible an explanation as any other. There was a Hollywood PO box listed for donations, but no further information about the author. It was almost hard to believe the pamphlets were legit. Javier Buñuel sounded like the kind of name Dickie would tell Father Bill he was using as an alias, just to hear the silence on the other end of the phone, the slow crunch of cocktail ice as Bill tried to gauge how much impatience and/or concern to let filter through in his response.

The gist of Buñuel's thesis was that the U.S. government, through various intelligence and law enforcement agencies, and even more various front companies and cutouts, was involved in everything from mind control to brainwashing to something called "astral projection," with these activities including, but not limited to, clandestine-drug and scientific experimentation based on the work of expatriate Nazi and Soviet scientists, illegal imprisonment, torture, and the surgical implantation of surveillance and explosive devices in otherwise innocuous household pets. Somehow, all of this was bringing about the End Times, the revelation of which Javier—or maybe Xavier—had seen in the clouds one afternoon above Dodger Stadium: a nation of burning cities, its people consumed by flames.

Father Bill had told Dickie that the pamphlets were found at a series of bank robberies in Orange County, shoved into the pockets of customers still lying on the ground with their hands over their heads when the cops arrived. What business this was of Father Bill's was a bit of a mystery. It seemed like a police issue rather than an intelligence concern, but Dickie realized that making those distinctions wasn't really in his job description.

Three pamphlets. It was no surprise that they didn't trust him with the amount of information they once had—manila folders stuffed with police and bank records, medical histories, glossy photographs, transcripts of recorded telephone conversations—all of which, once Dickie had committed the details to his then-still-reliable memory, he would toss into a wastebasket and set on fire. Those days were gone, though, after the mess of MAELSTROM, and Dickie figured he should consider himself lucky that Father Bill even trusted him with the pamphlets.

The mountains gave way to the desert, the desert to the city beyond. The ocean stretched to the horizon, glittering in the midafternoon sun. There was a facile, unearned quality to traveling this way. There was something disturbing, he felt, in the fact that someone could move around the country so fast, could be almost anywhere in just a couple of hours, arriving unannounced, with no warning to those on the ground.

He had never been to Los Angeles. Nearly everyone he had met underground talked about it, almost universally in a desultory way, as a city of sellouts and dimwits, snake-oil salesmen who made movies and TV shows to sedate Middle America. Los Angeles as one of the main reasons the movement wasn't bigger, why every person under thirty wasn't actively involved. Too busy watching *Batman*, standing in line for *Love Story*.

Dickie put the pamphlets away. The coed was stirring. She uncrossed her legs, stretched them under the seat in front of her, wiggling her toes around the straps of her discarded sandals. Heading home after a weekend in Vegas, maybe, back to her summer job, her friends, a final year before graduation. People had lives like this. Dickie could have a life like this, couldn't he? How difficult could it be? Couldn't he just toss the pamphlets into the trash and ask her name? See if she'd like to grab dinner somewhere, a movie afterward? Was *Love Story* still playing? They could go on a few dates, fool around, and eventually she'd bring him down to Yorba Linda to meet the folks and he'd propose and a year or so after the beachfront ceremony she'd be heavy with child, adorably round, glowing with good health, and they'd have a son, then a daughter, and a house down by the parents, that same cul-de-sac, and Dickie'd get a job with the father-in-law's firm, something law-related, or, no, financial, following foreign markets and betting on commodities, corn and oil and pork bellies, calendars filled with backyard barbecues and cocktail parties and season tickets to see the California Angels play in the Anaheim sun.

The nausea came quickly, a response to the drop in altitude, and Dickie was just able to get the airsick bag to his mouth before disgorging the contents of his stomach into what seemed like an impossibly insuf-

ficient space. The blond Bruin was fully awake now, watching him with
what could only be described as abject horror, a look that hadn't factored
into his reverie, but one he assumed he could grow to live with, even
adore, if its very presence at that moment didn't pretty much put the
kibosh on the whole thing.

Dickie gripped his armrest with one hand, his airsick bag with the
other. He mumbled an apology. The girl closed her eyes again, breathed
deeply, desperate to meditate him out of existence.

The landing gear bumped along the runway. The overhead PA
speaker whined to life. A stewardess blew into a microphone.

"Ladies and gentleman," she said. "Welcome to Los Angeles."

The room is on the top floor of a pink stucco building on Selma Avenue,
smack in the middle of Hollywood's dilapidated heart. A transient hotel
if you're feeling generous; a flophouse if you're not. Only the finest ac-
commodations on Father Bill's dime.

It's the end of the day, the beginning of the long West Coast sunset,
two or three hours of fading, feels like. Dickie lies on the too-small bed,
limbs hanging off all sides. He smokes a joint and looks out the window
at what he can see of the sky, clouds in cornrows of orange and gold.

The room is small, almost a perfect square, with a dresser, a mirror
above the dresser, a small wooden table and two chairs under the window. Two chairs. He wonders if every room has two chairs, what kinds
of guests the residents here expect.

There's a radio, which he's set on the windowsill, where it gets the
best reception. The radio came with the room, an unexpected amenity,
though it's fastened by a thick nylon cord to an anchor in the wall. He
could squeeze out the window and sit on the fire escape but he's very
comfortable on the bed. The radio station is seemingly free-form: a rock
song, Bowie, Jefferson Airplane, then a classical piece, maybe, an old jazz
record, popped and scratchy. Dickie can tell by the low, airless sound of
his voice that the DJ is enjoying a late-afternoon joint as well.

Apart from the radio, it's quiet in the hotel, just an occasional cough from a neighbor, the sound of the toilet flush from the bathroom next door, water in the walls.

He'd rented a car at the airport, a disgruntled Olds Cutlass that seemed like it had been drag-raced down some desert straightaway a few too many times. He'd spent the day driving around town, getting his bearings. West on Sunset, past all the strip clubs and rock clubs, the homeless kids sitting cross-legged on the sidewalks, then out through Beverly Hills and Bel Air, up the Pacific Coast Highway, cutting over the hills into the wide spread of the Valley, capital *V*, all those stucco boxes, apartment buildings and gas stations, the smog even worse up there, if that was possible. Like driving through an ashtray.

He could imagine getting lost out here, in a very permanent sense, how easy that would be. It's a time-stopped place, sun-soaked and lazy. The basin and the canyons and then the flat endless Valley suburbs and the vastness of the desert to the east. A sleepwalking city.

The DJ is playing Jackson Browne now. This after a minor-key Gershwin piano piece, Prelude No. 2.

Father Bill had told him to approach Javier Buñuel with caution, figured the guy for someone who spooked easily, might not be completely on board when it came to societal norms of interpersonal violence. But Bill had made clear that this was not an open-ended assignment, there was an *accelerated time line* here, so Dickie should be deliberate and careful but also get to work ASAP, keep out of the clubs, rock and strip, stay away from the beach, keep his head on straight, or maybe put his head on straight, as it was pretty obvious to both Bill and Dickie in those last meetings that Dickie was far from okay in even the broadest definition of the word.

Hey, Miles Davis! This actually gets Dickie up off the bed and over to the window, joint in his teeth, head bobbing. Billy Cobham pounding the shit out of those cymbals, Miles and John McLaughlin trading shouts on horn and guitar. The single, overtaxed speaker on the radio adding an extra layer of fuzz to the proceedings, like a captured transmission from some better, funkier planet.

Dickie walks the room, studying the driver's license he's been using

since he got to L.A., his photo and the alias he'd been given: *Dick Hinkle*.
Seems like maybe there's some leg pulling here by Father Bill, or the guys
in Bill's department who forge this stuff. Do they engage in leg pulling?
Another mystery. Mr. Hinkle has a realistic-looking press credential
from a fringy Bay Area weekly that Bill explained was funded by his department, though whether the editors of said weekly knew this or not
was apparently a matter of some debate. Bill figured that this was the best
way to approach Buñuel, reasoning that anybody who stands on a street
corner and spouts nonsense all day would be something of a publicity
hound, probably more than willing to talk to a reporter who could help
get his message out. Dickie can't fault the logic.

He squeezes himself out onto the windowsill, relights his joint. The
day before an approach always put him in a weird frame of mind. About
to enter someone else's world under false pretenses. A feeling that he
was stripping away another layer of what was left of himself, fighting off
waves of a strange, disassociated panic, like he was threatening to physically leave his body somehow, step off to one side and watch things from
there. Having to fight to keep himself in himself, if that made any sense.

These are stoner thoughts, Dickie's aware. He can't imagine Father
Bill having these concerns, any of Bill's golf buddies back east having
them. Of course, they didn't need to. That's what they had guys like
Dickie for.

Sometimes, back when he was underground, Dickie would look
around at the faces in the room at a meeting or strategy session and wonder if he was truly alone. If there was someone else there under the same
cover he was. He had some suspicions over the years, doubts about a few
of the older members, nothing he would call a *vibe*, exactly, more a tingle
at the side of his brain, a little insistent itch. He even followed one of his
suspects once, tailed a dreadlocked Amazon named Connie around Ta-
coma for a couple of days, but came up with zip. Wondered, of course, if
someone was tailing him, too. Such was the mind-set. This was early in
the project, this curiosity, but as he got deeper in he began to feel an increased sense of vigilance, a wariness about the people he suspected, the
threat they posed to the rest of the group. This should have been a red

flag, of course, this feeling of protectiveness for those he was supposed to be steering toward catastrophe, but things like that he usually recognized in hindsight, generally unable to see the forest for the trees.

From his perch on the windowsill he says the name aloud every few seconds or so, in time to the music, *Dick Hinkle, Dick Hinkle,* trying to get the words to fit in his mouth.

He thinks up a biography, a loose family and professional history, conjuring some names, a mother, father, sister, coworkers, ex-girlfriends. He lights another joint, switches on the dresser lamp as the sky gets dark. Keeping it close to the truth was always the rule of thumb, made it easier to remember, so Dick Hinkle was a guy who drank too much and took too many pills and had just watched his father die. Brilliant. Shouldn't be too hard to remember.

After an hour or so, he has his story straight, or as straight as it's going to get. He finishes the joint and decides to vacate the premises for a while, get some air, find somebody who can resupply his stash, realizing it might be a good idea to clear his head of Dick Hinkle's sob story before he starts to feel too bad for the guy.

Javier Buñuel paces a long spread of stone steps on Hollywood Boulevard, about a block east of the freeway cutting across town. The steps lead up to what was once an impressive and official-looking building, a bank, maybe, or some kind of government office, now security-gated and "For Sale"–signed. A good location, what with the bus stop at the corner and the heavy foot traffic on the sidewalk, a mix of office workers and prostitutes and hustlers, bewildered tourists desperately consulting maps and brochures.

Dickie watches from the front seat of the Cutlass, parked across the street. Buñuel is a large man in a small suit. Dark-complected, Mexican Indian, maybe, mestizo, with hair hanging down past his chin, wet from grease or sweat. He has a microphone wired to a small amplifier. He holds the mic in one hand and shouts at the pedestrians passing on the sidewalk a few steps below. In his other hand he holds a large wooden placard, hoisting the sign by its handle, thrusting it higher into the air to underscore a particular point. Eyes bulging, spit flying. The sign features a handwritten list of people who are supposedly ushering in the coming apocalypse: Jews, homosexuals, blasphemers, idolaters, homosexuals (again), false prophets, sexual deviants. Some creative spelling on that list, but Dickie is no walking *Webster's* himself, so who is he to judge, really.

Zero shade. Buñuel works sweating, baking in the sun on the steps. He speaks with a substantial accent and sometimes the combination of the accent and the poor-quality amp makes his rant indecipherable, just distorted noise that vaguely resembles speech. It seems possible that he's aware of this because whenever it happens he works himself into a frenzy, shouting louder and faster, reveling in the impenetrable sound.

Dickie spends the morning watching the spectacle, either from the Cutlass or a window table at the sandwich shop across the street. He guzzles coffee, smokes a pack of cigarettes, eats a rubbery sub for break-fast that contained something that may have been roast beef in a previous life. He reads through Buñuel's tracts for the umpteenth time, dozes in the hot car. A real stakeout. He feels like sending Father Bill a palm-treed postcard, *Wish You Were Here.* Don't TV detectives in these situations always have a partner to bounce jokes off of, or share bear claws with?

He'd been up early, staking out the Hollywood post office, watching as an Old Testament procession crossed the lobby: the halt, the lame, the nearly blind squinting at the wall of PO boxes and laboriously fixing their tiny keys into the locks. Each sad sack pulling out long sheaves of junk mail, bills, chain letters, hungrily scanning the envelopes for some-thing of worth, the answer to some previously sent missive. Luckless, just about all of them, turning and shuffling out the way they'd entered. Finally, the man in the seersucker suit arrived, though at first Dickie took him to be just another in the long string of jetsam that received mail at this particular PO branch. But he had the key to the magic number and pulled his mail, looking furtively in each direction. Dickie waited for Buñuel to leave and then followed him to this very street corner a few blocks away.

An ambulance roars down the boulevard and everyone on the sidewalk stops to watch. Buñuel stops and watches, too, and after the sirens fade he starts declaiming again with renewed vigor, pointing at the now-distant lights of the ambulance as if this proves something he's been saying all along.

Dickie crosses Hollywood Boulevard and sort of meanders, hands in his pockets on the sidewalk below the steps. He's not alone—there are always a few people who've stopped to listen to or ridicule Buñuel. Dickie walks past the amp, the array of tracts fanned out alongside. Spies the one he already has, but picks up some others to complete his collection. Peels some of Father Bill's cash from his roll and drops it into the coffee can where Buñuel accepts donations. The can a quarter full with bills and change, cigarette butts, wads of bubble gum, chewing tobacco, spit.

It's almost like Buñuel could hear the legal tender settling into the can, because he turns and looks at Dickie from the other end of the step, the far reaches of the microphone cord. Dickie caught for a second, deer-in-the-headlights-style before catching himself, giving a little aye-aye-Captain salute and hoofing back across Hollywood Boulevard.

He spends the remainder of the afternoon reading the new tracts, more first-person accounts of Buñuel's torture and brainwashing at the hands of shadowy government agents. What's scarier, here—the grammar, or the stories themselves? Turns out to be the latter, really, as despite the obvious nutcase quotient, this is some pretty heavy stuff. Buñuel drugged and locked into a coffin of some sort, a sensory-deprivation chamber, listening to nothing but the sound of his own screams for days. Then pulled from the coffin and hooked up to electroshock machines that wipe out his memories, his personality, and instill new memories, a new persona. Years of wandering follow, until Buñuel has a sudden revelation, all of this coming back to him, the truth, skywritten, literally, in the clouds above Dodger Stadium during an afternoon game when he was working as a janitor at the ballpark.

Shit. Dickie has to put the tracts down for a while, slide a little lower in the seat, light a joint to take the edge off the tall tales. What all of this has to do with a gang knocking over banks in Orange County is any-body's guess, but it's hard to get the image of Buñuel locked in that coffin out of his head. No sight, no sound. Dickie imagining himself in his own dark place, locked in a box with nothing but his own breath and panic.

Sundown. A red-eye explosion to the west, and then the day smol-dering to embers, cooling a little, losing its sharper edges. The postwork rush is winding down as the light fades, the streetlights along the bou-levard blinking on in random patterns. Buñuel packs his amp and sign into a small laundry cart, drags it all over to the corner, where he boards the next eastbound bus. Dickie follows along in the Olds, the bus hang-ing on Hollywood until it merges with Sunset Boulevard, the neighbor-hoods getting sketchier, the lights of the downtown buildings visible a few miles away in the brown smog haze. The bus stops and Buñuel gets off. Dickie turns onto a side street, watches Buñuel unlock a pretty serious-looking gate, relock it carefully after he's passed through, then haul his gear up a winding stone stairway to a small house at the top of the hill.

Lights in the house, windows shining, but too far up for Dickie to make out much of what's going on. He takes note of the address, takes note of his growling stomach, decides it's time for dinner and bed. Stake-out over, officially. Good night, Danno; good night, McGarrett. Shit, wait, of course, that's Hawaii, not Los Angeles, but probably, Dickie thinks, heading back on Sunset, close enough for government work.

8

They sat at a picnic table in the tree-ringed park, Ginnie with one of the Eliot volumes from Henry's shelves, Thomas with the newspaper, each section spread wide so he could see as many pages as possible. He read the paper in its entirety every morning, every article and sports score and classified advertisement. Ginnie didn't look at the news anymore; she didn't have to. Later in the day Thomas would recount it all to her, down to the smallest detail, vote counts in a Canadian election, the high temperature in Chicago the previous afternoon.

The park's grass was getting long, dotted with wildflowers, white and purple and gold. There were a few couples and young families on blankets in the shade, children chasing one another into the sun. Ginnie lit a cigarette. She had always liked smoking in hot weather, the feel of a higher heat at her lips. It was the only thing she'd ever missed about living in Washington. The close-pressed summers, the world slow and wet.

There was a man sitting on a bench on the far side of the park. Alone, reading a newspaper, smoking. Dark sunglasses, so she couldn't see his eyes, but she could feel them when the man shook his paper straight, turned the page, refolded.

She hadn't seen one of them in months, which she knew didn't prove anything. Not seeing them didn't mean they weren't there. In the first few years after Henry had gone, she'd thought they were just nervous figments of her imagination, a fear she'd caught like a virus, something Henry had left her. But over time it became apparent that they were real. Men in cars at the top of the hill; men across from Hannah's school, standing in the deli doorway, watching parents come to gather their children.

They weren't always around, as far as she could tell. A year would go by when she wouldn't see a car, or a stranger taking a long, slow stroll past the house. Then one morning she would look out the window or across the park and someone would be there, like this man in his sunglasses, turning his paper, shaking it stiff again.

Thomas came to the international pages, photographs from the war. He lifted his hands to the sides of his head, his fingers rubbing the short hair of his crew cut. Ginnie began to hum, quietly, a hymn from morning Mass, one of Thomas's favorites, a melody that usually soothed him, working its way into his brain, dampening some of the distress signals she imagined there, the flashing lights, the warning bells.

He was a man now. As tall as his father but solid, and so strong. At times she couldn't control him, his rages. She would cower in the kitchen, hating herself, this terror of her own son, crouching in a corner while Thomas threw pots and pans, plates, silverware, whatever he could grab.

His good days outnumbered his bad, though. On the good days they played games at the community center or worked in the church food pantry, where Thomas was in charge of the heavy lifting, restocking the highest shelves. The good days were blessed with all manner of surprises. Thomas repeating an overheard joke or shouting out a win in Bingo and blushing at the applause; the two of them standing in line at the grocery store and Ginnie realizing that one of the voices in the conversation behind was his, that Thomas was talking with a stranger, telling them about scheduled maintenance on a particular line, about his sister the photographer in Los Angeles.

The bad days were awful, but the good days were plentiful now. She had to remember that.

The man across the park stood to stretch, yawning like a cat. It was entirely possible that he had no interest in her or Thomas. He could be waiting for someone else, a wife, a mistress. He could be skipping work, detouring from the prescribed day.

It had been fifteen years since Roy Pritchard sat in her kitchen and told her Henry had disappeared. Roy drinking coffee at her table, another man in a car outside. They believed that Henry had suffered another breakdown, Roy had said. Possibly the entire year had been a breakdown. Roy had told her that they were still piecing together the whole story of what Henry had been doing in San Francisco. He had refused to give details, telling her that he was sparing her the particulars, but he'd tried his best to make Ginnie understand that Henry was not the man she'd thought he was, that his illness had made him into someone else.

Henry had an apartment in the city, Roy had said, and the things that transpired there went beyond criminal.

Ginnie hadn't asked Roy to elaborate. There was no need. Henry was no criminal. No matter what had happened to him, what they had driven him to, she knew his heart, his soul. She wouldn't listen to the blackening of his name.

The man on the other side of the park was gone now. His newspaper sat alone, folded on the end of the bench. Ginnie returned to the poem on the dog-eared page. Faint inky fingerprints in the margins, Henry's thumbs pressed to the paper.

A year after Henry had gone, she'd removed all of his books from the basement. She couldn't stand to see them down where he'd sat for so many months, torturing himself. She brought them up into the living room, where they could have some light, warmth on their spines. She wanted them to be part of the house. She wanted to move around them, sit across from them in the muted evenings. She wanted those books to live with her, to inhabit the space he had left behind.

She watched Thomas's hand, his finger tracing a route on a transit map in the newspaper. He'd freed himself from his own tracks over the last few years. Ginnie didn't know how or why. The trappings just fell away. One day he no longer plugged himself in to refuel. On another he left the house without looking at the sidewalk, squinting to see the rails. As if a season in the world had changed, and he no longer needed those things.

That morning in the kitchen with Roy, she had asked where he thought Henry had gone. Roy had turned his coffee cup in its saucer, stared down at the table, told her that they had no idea.

Hannah hated that Ginnie had disassembled the basement, moved her father's books. She blamed Ginnie for Henry's absence, as if the woman she believed Ginnie became after Henry disappeared, the humorless jailor, was also the woman who had driven him away. A teenager's irrational fury, Ginnie knew, but there was some truth it, what she had become. Over the years without Henry, Ginnie had felt her love for Hannah and Thomas hardening to something concerned more with survival than affection.

She was unsuccessful at that, even. Hannah went to college, and then Hannah went farther, returning once or twice a year now, arriving by bus or a boyfriend's borrowed car, staying only a few days. Hannah spent most of that time with Thomas, sitting in his room, or taking him down to the park if the weather held. Ginnie followed when they left the house, trailed them shamefully, but it was a necessary evil. She had lost her husband and daughter; she wouldn't lose her son.

She'd never told Hannah about the men watching, had never asked if Hannah ever noticed them in Los Angeles. Hannah wouldn't have believed it, would have thought it was just another instance of Ginnie's paranoia, or a ploy to scare her home. Or she wouldn't even care, possibly. Hannah liked to believe she was fearless. Maybe she was.

In the first years after Henry had gone, Ginnie had thought about traveling to Washington, demanding to speak to Paul Marist, showing up at Roy Pritchard's door, asking all of the questions she'd been too afraid or too stunned to ask that morning in the kitchen. Wanting to know everything, no matter how awful. Or calling the police, hiring a detective, using some of the money from the pension checks that came from Washington every month. She did none of this, though. Henry was gone and she could feel Hannah slipping away and she needed to stop the bleeding, the death of their family. So she narrowed their world, she closed the doors and locked the windows. She turned into the woman who at times Hannah saw so clearly. She had no other choice.

It was difficult to fight the proof. Hannah, Thomas, Henry. They had all fled in one way or another. At night, desperate for sleep, she heard the voices of Thomas's doctors from years ago, their unsparing accusations. Thomas was the antidote for this. Mass with Thomas and then, blessedly, a quiet hour at the park, an afternoon at the pantry. A surprise smile. He was all she had left, but he was enough.

The man with the sunglasses had returned to his bench, joined by a woman in a polka-dot dress. They sat hand in hand, leaning their heads close to speak. His sunglasses were on, and Ginnie wasn't sure if she could feel his eyes. It was hard to tell anymore if she was the only one still waiting.

9

Dickie drove up to a head shop in North Hollywood that he'd passed on his citywide tour, a place that caught his eye because of the hand-painted sandwich board out on the sidewalk: *Smoking Accessories, Magazines, Comix.* The air inside was damp, smelled like dust and decomposing newsprint. A heavy, bearded guy sat on a creaky stool behind the counter, visible only from the neck up behind a jumble of water pipes. The guy looked at Dickie and made him for a narc, started to struggle up from his stool. Dickie raised a hand in a sort of half-wave, don't-sweat-it gesture, walked deeper into the shop, scanning the shelves. Bongs, Zippos, beaded bracelets, death's-head belt buckles, bundles of incense.

The promised *comix* half filled a metal spinner rack in the back corner: black-and-white underground stuff, talking animals smoking joints and taking hits of acid, big-nosed cavemen chasing big-assed cavewomen. Not really Dickie's cup of tea. But there was a box on the floor filled with issues of *Justice League of America* and *Showcase* and *The Brave and the Bold* and, at the end of the box, a handful of *Detective Comics*. He opened the *Detective* issues, flipped to the final pages. More than half of them had Martian Manhunter backups.

Dickie called up to the front of the store. "How much for the comics in the box?"

"Two bucks."

"Two bucks apiece?"

"Two bucks for the box."

"You got a lid for it?"

"No lid."

Dickie carried the box up to the counter. "Are there any more of these?"

The heavy guy coughed, turned his head a second too late. He thumbed through the comics. "A dude comes by every couple of weeks with the Robert Crumb stuff, *Zap* and whatnot. He's got a big stash of old DCs he's itching to get rid of. Come back in a few days."

"My name's Dick."

"Pat."

"Sell a lot of comics, Pat?"

"The Crumb stuff. Old Marvels if I can get them."

"Sell anything else?"

"You a cop?"

"Do I look like a cop?"

"Yes, sir."

"I'm not a cop."

"Then what do you care what I sell?"

Dickie put his money on the counter. "I just want to know you'll still be in business when I come back for those comics."

Nice morning for a break-in. Dickie heads down Sunset, passing Buñuel on his steps, continuing farther east, parking the Cutlass a few streets away from the house on the hill. What he might find up there is anybody's guess. Something to tie Buñuel to the Orange County robberies, maybe. Probably too much to hope for a ski mask, a couple of handwritten notes: *Stick 'em up!*

Broad daylight, but this seems like the kind of neighborhood where a semi-overt B&E might not be a completely unusual sight. The fence down at street level is a high wrought-iron number, nothing he can cut or squeeze through, and the lock looks ridiculously complex, so it seems

Fosburying it is the only real option. He takes a quick look around, jumps, and grabs the top crossbar. Dickie thinking that he hasn't done a pull-up since basic training, many pounds ago. It isn't going to happen easily. He finally gets himself up to his elbows, pulls his fat ass over to the other side. Not a pretty sight, he's sure, or a particularly fleeting one. Taking so much time getting his weight to shift from one direction to the other that it's a wonder the cops aren't there already.

There we go, finally. Dickie flopping like a walrus over to the yellow grass on the other side. He gets back to his feet as quickly as possible, brushing off his jeans, nonchalant, everything's cool, just hanging out here on the other side of the fence, folks, nothing to see.

He climbs the stairs, almost turning his ankle a couple of times on the uneven flagstone. The house is, quite literally, perched at the top of the hill. Dickie isn't sure if it has moved toward the edge over time, or if it was built in that position for some reason, but either way it appears to be *leaning* toward street level, or, more precisely, leaning toward the steep drop that will eventually end at street level.

Another look around from the top. Some view from up here. He can see all the way back through the burnt haze over to Hollywood, the tops of the buildings there, billboard backs and radio antenna, the observatory dome and the infamous sign.

It only takes a few minutes to rake the locks on the front door, nothing too complex, just a lot of them. Dickie had learned his lockpicking skills from a kid underground who got the group into recruiting centers and research labs after-hours. Dale was his name, a good kid, and Dickie had turned out to be a good student. Dale giving Dickie his own little snake rake as a sort of graduation present, the rare gift Dickie had actually managed to hold on to, pressed into a credit-card slot in his wallet, which might, now that he thinks about it, account for some of that poor circulation in his right leg.

The last lock turns and he steps inside. No booby traps, no alarm, no dogs. There's a single large room with boxes everywhere, stacked in some places higher than the windows, none of which have any kind of covering or treatment, no curtains or blinds, so Dickie feels completely exposed, standing there on great display. He'd be visible to anyone watching from the houses in the surrounding hills, certainly anyone coming up the steps. Buñuel home for an unexpected lunch break, say, would see Dickie long before Dickie saw him. Best to look around and get out as quickly as possible.

The boxes are stuffed full with copies of Buñuel's tracts. Seems like Dickie already has the whole set, but he checks to be sure before moving to the back of the house. There are ants on the kitchenette counter, multiple trails, heading down into the sink, where they've found half a cruller, shining with glaze. Nothing but condiments in the fridge, ketchup and mustard and pickle relish. An open can of tomato soup toward the back, age indeterminate, fuzzy-rimmed, covered with a loose square of plastic wrap.

Dickie looks out the windows down the hill every few minutes, sure each time that he'll see Buñuel ascending the stairs, shaking his fists, his signs, shouting through the microphone.

He parts a beaded curtain and steps into the small bathroom. He flips the light switch, jolting the fluorescent tube over the mirror to life. More ants, marching in a long line from the drain in the sink down and across the floor and then up and over the side of the tub, disappearing behind the drawn shower curtain. There's a small linen closet with no actual linen, just more piles of tracts. No hidden cash, nothing about banks or getaway routes.

Back out through the tiny dark space between the bathroom and kitchenette, Dickie ramming his knee on a low, flimsy dresser pressed against the wall. He checks the windows again for any sign of approach. Stands in the main room with the towers of boxes, hands on his hips, scanning for something he might have missed the first time through. There's nothing he hasn't checked, except, well, the tub back in the bathroom, Dickie having sort of convinced himself that there's probably nothing to see in there, the curtain drawn for propriety's sake, knowing full well, though, that he's really more than a little chickenshit to pull back that covering, find a body, or bodies, or body parts, or whatever dark things a head case like Buñuel collects and stores in his tub behind a floral-print curtain. Those ants are heading in there for a reason.

He forces himself back into the bathroom, turns on the fluorescent again, waits for the room to fill with sickly light. Grabs one end of the curtain, takes a deep breath. Pulls, ready to scream or run or just generally freak out, throwing his arm wide, the curtain rings scraping along the rusty rod, the fabric folding back to reveal, once Dickie has opened his eyes, a bathtub full of paperback books. Hundreds of them, must be. Thin, cheaply printed novels from the looks of the volumes on top, sci-fi stories with Day-Glo covers. A few feature trippy paintings of screaming men and women with radio waves or gamma rays extending from or into their skulls. A number of others have characters cowering from advancing hordes of dark, indeterminate figures, or, on one of the covers, an army of what looks like TV G-Men, clean-cut white guys in suits and sunglasses.

Dickie digs deeper, still half sure he'll find a body, but except for another ant-mobbed cruller there's nothing but books, multiple copies of six or seven novels, some with different covers, slightly varying page counts. Twenty or thirty copies of *The Night Visitor* and *Watching, Waiting, Watching,* and *Good Morning, Dr. Lucifer.* All by the same author, someone named Robert Zelinsky, though there are no photos, no author bio on the backs of any of the books.

There's a loud thump from the other room, so Dickie kills the light and crouches down on the floor with the ants, breathing hard, waiting for Buñuel to fling open the front door and howl at the intrusion. Or maybe it'll be a gang of bank robbers, busting in and kicking through the place, spraying bullets indiscriminately.

After a few minutes of nothing, Dickie crawls out to the doorway, peers around the main room, peeks up over the lowest windowsill. He stands, finally, to see a rubber-banded bundle of mail out on the front step, a postman way down on the sidewalk already half a block away. Some arm on that guy. Dickie pokes through the mail, nothing but utility bills and advertising circulars. Buñuel probably has anything of any importance delivered to his PO box.

Back in the bathroom, Dickie takes a copy of each Zelinsky book, hoping they won't be noticed missing from the giant heap, though he knows it's possible that Buñuel counts them every night or something similarly insane. He pulls the curtain closed, double-checks that he hasn't left anything else disturbed. Takes one last look out the windows to make sure the coast is clear, and then steps out into the heated morning, relocking the front door, heading back down the steps, girding himself for another attempt at getting up and over that fence.

The afternoon goes soft, rolling over into evening. Dickie sits out on the fire escape of his hotel room with the radio and a stack of Buñuel's sci-fi books. He takes his Antabuse, wishing he had a beer, or a Jack and Coke, but you can't have everything, and the books aren't half bad. This type of stuff is not usually his thing, but Zelinsky writes hard and fast and lurid, has a way with a car chase and a shoot-out.

The novels were all published over the last ten years by various outfits, small firms, seemingly, publishers in the South and Midwest. The six were a series, starting with *The Night Visitor,* whose nameless main character starts the book as a mild-mannered accountant, a real man-in-the-gray-flannel-suit type with a wife and a couple of kids and a house in the San Fernando Valley. Most of the early part of the book is taken up by an incredibly detailed and fairly tedious meditation on his day-to-day routine, which is then, on about page 100, violently interrupted by a revelation where he recalls, with terrifying clarity, being admitted to a psychiatric hospital some years back for a nervous breakdown, where he's then secretly imprisoned and tortured at the hands of a shadowy government agency. After his revelation, he starts to suspect that he's been programmed to forget all of that, as some of the memories that return to him are memories of losing his memories, with that empty space then filled with new, artificial memories, including the relationship with the woman he's always thought of as his wife, and these two strange children he's always thought of as his kids, and his bullshit job, and et cetera. It's a fairly convoluted sequence that Dickie has to read a few times in an attempt to get straight, or at least as straight as possible.

So obviously this guy's only recourse, once he's seen the curtain, is to find the man behind it, the head government agent responsible for all of this, so he drops out of the straight life he's been living, leaves his wife and kids, his house in the suburbs, and becomes the Night Visitor, breaking into top-secret government offices and installations, appearing at the middle-of-the-night bedsides of ex-Nazi scientists and the bureaucrats who helped them secretly repatriate so they could teach the local spooks their infernal methods. These guys then conducted their dirty work in prisons and psych wards or sometimes just grabbed unsuspecting folks off the street for mind-control experiments, trying to create brainwashed assassins for the inevitable Third World War. The Night Visitor, who now calls himself Mr. _____ (Dickie unsure, exactly, of how to pronounce this tenantless underscore, either when he's reading in his head or aloud, sort of half whispering out on the fire escape . . . Mr. *Blank*?) slowly working his way up the food chain and shadow-government pay scale, piecing together the story of what had been done to him, torturing or killing those he finds and deems responsible, but always searching for the mastermind, the guy he believes ran the whole ugly plot.

Dickie takes a break every few chapters to stretch his legs, adjust the radio volume. He swallows a couple of pills to keep him up. Mary Margaret loved this kind of stuff. Dickie can't remember these exact books, but she always had some pulpy sci-fi paperback close by. She was a pragmatist, a realist, at least most of the time, but these kinds of books were her escape, entering a world where a good conspiracy theory could explain war or deprivation or even personal tragedy. She took some comfort in reading about a place where someone was always responsible, could be taken to account.

The margins of Buñuel's paperbacks are filled with notes, mostly illegible, his penmanship nearly microscopic. What Dickie can read seems to be Buñuel agreeing with passages in the books, corroborating them with personal recollections, while trying to remember, like Mr. _____, who had done this to him. Some chapters have lines or entire paragraphs blacked out, forcing Dickie to hold the pages up to the bulb in his room to try to make out what has been obscured, what was too awful to leave naked on the page.

He realizes, eventually, that the voice in which he hears the books is Buñuel's, and then he imagines he can hear Buñuel ranting from his corner a few blocks away. A physical impossibility, he's sure, even on a warm evening like this, where sound would indeed travel. A little later, as night falls, it even seems like he can hear Buñuel's voice coming from farther east on Sunset, around that last corner before downtown, the crooked little house on the hill, shrieking after counting his books in the bathtub and coming up six short . . .

Okay, so maybe the pills and the books are not the best combination, paranoia on top of paranoia, though Dickie does get the sense that this Zelinsky is a fellow traveler, no stranger to pharmaceuticals, both over- and far-below-the-counter. He takes a quick bathroom break, splashing some cold water onto his face before jumping back into the narrative. By this point in *The Night Visitor*, Mr. _____ has discovered that he's not alone, that he isn't the only experimentation subject to have escaped. So he makes it his mission to find the others, track these sleeper agents down, kidnap them, run a sort of reverse mind-control process, filling them in on what has been done to them, who they used to be. Some decide that this isn't their fight, and return to their brainwashed lives, but some are too damaged or pissed off to go back to the way things were, so they become the Night Visitor's agents, helping him find others like themselves, assembling, over the course of the books, an underground army that'll one day take down the government that created them. The big, sad irony here of course being that despite helping these others rediscover their previous lives, Mr. _____ has no such luck in remembering his own. His life before the check-in at the psych ward remains a blank. No matter what answers or secret files he discovers, he's unable to remember his old, true life, the man he was before the mind-wipe.

There's also the big question, which Mr. _____ does a good job of avoiding, of why all these other sleepers were sent off with actual covert government missions, and Mr. _____ was simply sent to a wife and kids and house in the Valley. Like maybe was he a failure of some sort, in his reprogramming? Or was his reprogramming leading to something else, something deeper? Maybe even something like he's involved in right now . . .

The books have a lot of this kind of doubling back, characters wondering what memories can or can't be trusted, who and what's been planted to push them forward on their missions versus what's real, what's actually been lived. Some of the agents suspect Mr. _____ of being just another stage of government experimentation, the underground army simply more bullshit to get them further along in their role as superspy or assassin. *Good Morning, Dr. Lucifer,* the last book in the series, even heads in a larger philosophical direction, like, maybe everything's planted, ultimately, by some kind of higher power, and then what difference does it make if covert government agencies are just tinkering around the edges?

Daybreak, the sun starting to color the sky behind the hotel. Dickie's spent the night out on the fire escape, lying on his bed, pacing his room, but always reading. A real sci-fi bender. Probably should have caught some sleep in there somewhere, but it feels too late now, his mind still racing with the pills and the books. For a second he tries to draw a direct connection, entertaining the idea that Robert Zelinsky could be a pen name for Javier Buñuel. Much of the stuff in Buñuel's tracts and performed live in his rants comes straight out of the novels. But considering the level of written and spoken English in Buñuel's work, it seems hard to imagine that they're the same guy. Dickie can, however, appreciate that this is the kind of stuff a crazy person could find and obsess on, figuring that it's truth disguised as fiction, an explanation for the voices in his head. Mr. _____'s initial revelation even comes to him at a ballpark, just like Buñuel's, though in the book it's Angel Stadium, not Dodger Stadium, which means only, Dickie guesses, that Buñuel's a National League man.

There is a bank robbery in one of the books, Mr. _____'s agents knocking over a branch to get some funds for weapons and supplies, so Dickie feels some assurance that even though most of this may not make much sense, it hasn't quite veered into wild-goose-chase territory yet either.

He should get some sleep, he knows he's little to no good when he's like this, but before cooler heads prevail he's out at a pay phone a half mile down La Brea Avenue, pumping coins, dialing the number he has for Father Bill.

"If I give you a name, can you get me a phone number?"

"This isn't *Columbo,* Dickie."

"Can you get me an address?"

"Where are you?"

"You mean, like, physically? On the corner of—"

"Where are you in the process?"

"I'm at the part where I give you a name and you give me an address."

Father Bill sighs, maybe a little too dramatically. Dickie can hear another voice in the background. Does Bill share an office? He'd never thought about this before.

"Who?" Bill asks.

"A writer named Robert Zelinsky." Dickie has *The Night Visitor* with him, the cover with a painting of a panicked government scientist making a late-night call from a phone booth, the shadowy figure of Mr. _____ appearing from out of the background gloom.

Bill said, "Out there?"

"That's my guess. Or at least he was at some point. All his books take place in L.A."

Bill sighs again, and this time Dickie's sure that it's purely for effect. "Give me a couple of days."

"What's today?" Dickie says. "Friday?"

"Yes."

"So I'll know by Monday."

"In theory, yes."

Dickie wedges the receiver into his neck, the book into his armpit to free his hands, light a cigarette. "Got plans for the weekend?"

"Dick—"

"I'm thinking golf, right? A foursome?"

"I'm hanging up now."

"Isn't that what they call it? A foursome?"

"Good-bye, Dick."

"Monday?"

"Yes," Bill says.

"You'll have the number?"

"Yes."

"Then you're wrong," Dickie says.

"About what?"

"This is just like *Columbo*."

The sleigh bells above the head-shop door jingle, cueing Pat to look up from the pieces of a water pipe he's attempting to screw back together.

"Shit, it's the cops."

Dickie lifts his sunglasses, trying to keep his hair out of his face. "Those comics come in yet?"

"You're in luck." Pat slides off his stool, makes his way back into the store, scanning the labels on a row of boxes.

Dickie drums his fingertips on the counter, leans in to look at the covers of a few old *Playboys* standing between a stack of fifties movie-monster magazines and a couple rows of paperback sci-fi novels.

By the time Pat returns with a box full with comics, Dickie has the Zelinsky book out of his back pocket, up on the counter.

"You ever heard of this guy?"

Pat wipes his forehead with the back of his wrist, gives Dickie a more-than-slightly-insulted look, like, *Who hasn't?*

"Does he live in L.A.?"

"Why do you care?"

"I've been collecting his stuff forever," Dickie says. "I figured while I was out here busting dope rings, I could make a side trip and get some of my books signed."

Pat sits, catches his breath from all the exertion. "Man, I don't know. I think he's a pretty private dude."

"So he's here."

"I didn't say that."

"I'm not trying to cause any trouble," Dickie says. "I'm just a fan, you know? If he's not into people coming around, that's cool."

Pat nods, picks up the book, flips through the pages. "I haven't heard about him in a while. For all I know, he's already shed the old mortal coil."

"You've met him?"

"Years ago. He used to come in."

"What did he buy?"

Pat shakes Dickie's box of comics. "Same worthless shit you're buying, actually." He sets the book down on the counter, slides it back toward Dickie. "Give me another day. I'll see what I can do."

10

She had a small black-and-white television in her workshop and she caught part of the chess match on the nightly news. The broadcast was from a concert hall in Reykjavik, two men sitting at a small table, the shot framed to crop out the audience. The camera was back at what Hannah thought an unusually far remove, setting the men a great way off, as if they were playing a game on the edge of something. The quality of the images was poor, weak-signaled and loaded with fuzz. A transmission from the moon.

The Russian was poised and handsome, with fantastic hair, a great, tall wave. The American, Fischer, seemed unremarkable from a distance, but when the camera pushed in, Hannah couldn't take her eyes off him. He looked like her father, the few photographs she'd seen of Henry as a young man. Lean and lanky and darkly serious, the same distracted look on his face. A rigorous intellect at work, a mind at a great distance, full of possibilities and doubt. Fischer with his hand to his forehead, staring at the board, agonizing over his next move.

She had very few concrete images of her father in memory. He'd usually managed to keep himself out of photographs. Hannah could only recall ever seeing a few, which her mother had taken almost surreptitiously. They were all from after the move to Oakland: Henry on a Christmas morning, pulling gifts from under the tree; on a summer afternoon in the driveway washing the car with Thomas. Even in these lighter moments, Henry had appeared vague, unconnected. There, but not really, not quite. This was in contrast to the memories she had of him from Arlington, before the move west. Her father teaching her to ride a bike on the sidewalk under the birch trees, or sitting on her bed, reading to her from *Quite Early One Morning*. It took more work to fix these unphotographed moments in her mind, but they seemed more real to her than the pictures. He seemed more real. He had never been fully present in Oakland.

She did still have one photograph of her father. It was the picture he'd left in her room before he'd gone. Henry standing in front of the Merchants Exchange in San Francisco, looking at the lens while foot traffic moved around him in a blur. She had never shown her mother the photograph. All through the rest of her childhood she'd kept it hidden in books in her room, changing volumes every few months to avoid discovery, the image pressed like a butterfly between pages of Laura Ingalls Wilder or *Nancy Drew*. She had considered it a secret message, something he was trying to tell her.

Fischer lost the game. He stood unceremoniously from the table and walked from the hall. End of broadcast. Hannah switched off the set. The picture of her father was in a shoe box along with some of her early snapshots, photos she'd taken as a teenager around Oakland, some of her first photos of L.A. She pulled the box down from its shelf and found the picture of Henry, cleared a space for it among the other prints on her worktable. The mystery of that image had become the driving force of her life after he'd gone. The fascination with the process and technique, how he'd done it, calculating the depth of field, setting the timer, striking the print. The mechanics involved in taking and developing a photograph. Magician's secrets. And then, once she had mastered those things, there were the larger questions about the preservation of moments, the choices of which moments to preserve, what they were being preserved against.

Parts of the earlier game were replayed on the late news, and she watched again, sitting at her worktable with a cigarette and a beer. The players' fingers hovering, hesitating over the heads of their pieces, each move a potential catastrophe, or a link in a longer chain that led to catastrophe. She watched the players' faces as they strained to see the future, the sequence of events each move would set in motion before their fingers made contact.

She dialed the telephone number up in Oakland, sat watching the screen with the receiver cradled between her ear and shoulder. She listened to the ring, imagined the sound in the house, echoing in her room, Thomas's, Ginnie's, the bell struck again and again in the wall phone in the kitchen, loud and insistent and alone.

11

"Shit, Pat, a phone number *and* an address." Dickie smiled at the paper rectangle Pat handed him, a subscription card from an old *TV Guide* with the information scribbled into the empty spaces.

Pat scratched his beard, adjusted his weight on the head of the stool. "You should call before you try the address. Get permission to approach. The guy's definitely kind of infamous for not wanting to be bothered."

Dickie nodded. "I owe you."

"And this isn't from me," Pat said. "You know, if anybody asks."

Dickie lowered his sunglasses, stepped back toward the door. "We never had this conversation."

He took the Cutlass west on Sunset Boulevard, heading toward the ocean, catching glimpses of water beyond the low hills, the road switchbacking for the last mile or so in progressively sharper curves, then out, finally, onto the Pacific Coast Highway, roaring north, the sky going pink, the water reflecting the last of the day's sun in warm yellow streaks.

The address was on the ocean side of the road, just past Malibu. A weathered beach house on wooden stilts, the tide crashing on the rocks below, soaking the lower slats of salt-licked clapboard. Dickie rolled past, parked a few houses away. He walked back along the access road, finishing his cigarette, watching surfers beyond the shallows climbing onto their boards and paddling out toward the waves.

He knocked at the front door, waited. Tried the knob. Went around to a narrow wooden walkway that stretched to the back of the house. He stepped out, looking over the shaky railing to the crashing water below. There was another door at the end of the walkway, but he held off on knocking. Maybe this wasn't the best idea. If Buñuel's tracts had been found at the robberies, and Zelinsky's books were the source for the tracts, it stood to reason that Zelinsky might be, what, involved in some capacity? One of the culprits? Or just an unwitting influence? Dickie watched the water, let the concern flow, then ebb like one of those waves out yonder. It was too late to call for backup. Also, there was no backup. He knocked on the door.

No answer. The sun was dropping fast. He cupped a hand, peered into a salt-coated window. He turned the knob, which gave, the door opening without much resistance.

The room was still, underlit. The windows that weren't covered with thick curtains had been fogged by years of weather. Dickie took off his sunglasses, folded them into his shirt pocket. Bookcases of various sizes and styles hugged the walls, filled layers deep with academic texts, novels, note pads. There were more books in teetering piles by the overstuffed couch on the far side of the room. A doorway led into a dark hall, back to the rest of the house.

He moved in slowly. The coffee table and the windowsill behind the couch were lined with pill bottles, both prescription grade and some bearing labels of a more ambiguous type, vitamins and powders, ointments and balms. Multicolored crystals were interspersed between the bottles, the glass catching what little light made it into the room and refracting it in weak rainbow rays across the ceiling. There was a heavy medicinal smell, sickly-sweet, mixed with cigarette smoke. A couple of overflowing ashtrays sat on the coffee table, ringed with crystals in what seemed to be a deliberate arrangement.

Dickie noticed a change in the smell, an increase in that medicinal odor. He turned to find a large man in a stained undershirt and pajama pants standing in the hall doorway. The man leaned on a metal crutch with one hand, held a shotgun in the other, its single barrel leveled at Dickie's forehead.

Dickie raised his hands. "The door was open."

"No, it wasn't."

"Well," Dickie said. "It was unlocked."

The man was sweating something fierce, his unshaven jowls shiny. One of his pant legs was cut away, revealing a bloated and bandaged foot, yellow toes looking ready to pop.

"Are you Robert Zelinsky?"

"Who wants to know?"

If the first response wasn't a denial, Dickie had learned, you usually had your man. That's why he'd always been so quick to deny. "My name's Dick Hinkle."

"I don't know who that is."

Zelinsky breathed through his mouth with some difficulty. He was in his sixties, Dickie guessed, though he could be older, it was hard to tell. Age wasn't his defining characteristic. Sickness was. He was profoundly unwell.

"I'm a friend of a man named Javier Buñuel," Dickie said.

"A friend?"

"A caseworker. Javier's one of my clients."

"You're a shrink?"

"Catholic Charities."

Zelinsky gave Dickie the once-over. "This is what the Pope is sending around now?"

Dickie looked at Zelinsky's bad leg. "You want to sit? You can still keep the gun on me."

Zelinsky blew sweat from his upper lip, worked his tongue around his mouth, considering. "Give me the first two lines of the Nicene Creed," he said.

Dickie stood in the middle of the room, trying not to make any sudden moves, drawing a pretty big blank, not able to remember much from those Sunday school classes a decade and a half back.

"Then how about some Saint Augustine?" Zelinsky said.

Dickie shook his head.

"Catholic Charities, my ass," Zelinsky said. "Though that's a good one. One of the better ones I've heard." He finally got into gear, limping across the room, keeping the shotgun trained on Dickie. His move at the couch was less an act of sitting than simply letting gravity win the ongoing fight, a weight drop into the cushions. He used the end of the crutch to lift his bad leg up onto the coffee table.

Zelinsky widened, then narrowed one eye. Dickie wasn't sure what he was doing. Realized, finally, that Zelinsky was sighting him through the notch on the end of the shotgun. Comforting.

"You mind if I sit?" Dickie said. "At least lower my hands?"

Zelinsky cleared his throat. "You look like a smoker. Save me a trip off the couch, will you?"

Dickie pulled out his cigarettes, lit two, handed one across the coffee table. Zelinsky nodded at an ottoman. Dickie sat, resting his hands on his thighs. Zelinsky fit the cigarette between his lips, took a short pull, coughed.

"How do you really know Buñuel?"

Dickie was picking something up here. Hard to pinpoint exactly—something in Zelinsky's manner, a discipline and formality beneath the ruined exterior. A military background, possibly. Dickie switched gears, recalibrated to a more deferential tone, the way he'd spoken to neighbors on the air base when he was a kid, the fathers and husbands, Jack's fellow officers.

"I've listened to him speak," Dickie said. "I've read his work."

"You've read his work? That couldn't have taken long."

"It led me to your work."

"But not to my house."

"That was a favor from a friend."

"Not a friend of mine, obviously. Though it doesn't make much difference. You would have found me eventually." He set the stock of the shotgun into the crotch of his pants, reached for a pill bottle on the coffee table. "I used to be able to spot it earlier. But I've been wrong before. The ghosts they send sometimes look like you, like the other kids. Like Buñuel." He unscrewed the top of the bottle and shook out a couple of tablets. Looked at the label, popped the pills into his mouth and chewed.

"The ghosts used to be obvious," Zelisnky said. "Real Brylcreemed Brahmins, Ivy Leaguers. G-Men. Easy to spot. They basically introduced themselves. But then they got smart about it. Started coming dressed as traveling salesmen, Jehovah's Witnesses, kids like you. I can still tell the difference, though. You're no ghost."

Zelinsky leaned forward again, selected another bottle from his array. He unscrewed the top and shook a few tablets into his palm. Glanced up at Dickie.

"What do you need?"

"What do you mean?"

"I know my own kind, son." He nodded to a brown paper bag sitting on a pile of books. "I got a kid who comes by every week. Sells me whatever I want. He's a walking pharmacy."

Dickie reached into the bag, his fingertips brushing pills and tablets, a couple of glass vials. He felt around for a familiar shape. Something to bring him down a bit after the whole shotgun thing wouldn't be completely unappreciated.

"You thought Buñuel knew something you knew," Zelinsky said.

Dickie held a pill between his teeth, swallowed, nodded, more than willing to let Zelinsky lead here.

"And he does," Zelinsky said. "You just can't understand his method of articulation. Not yet."

"But then I found that his stories were from you."

"Everyone who finds me through Javier thinks that. But the opposite is true. Javier told me his story and I put it in a book." Zelinsky fixed his cigarette into what appeared to be his preferred position, hanging from his bottom lip while he spoke. "Javier was the first, but then others came. They told me their stories and I put those in the books."

The sun was below the waterline now, dimming the room to an auburn murk. Zelinsky leaned to his side, switched on a reading lamp, illuminating little but his leg, the bloated foot at the end.

"The books are signals," Zelinsky said. "Coded messages. Those who speak the code find me, eventually, like you have. They tell me their stories and I write another book. Then that signal goes out into the world and someone else knocks at the door."

"And then what?"

"Then you find that you're not alone. That there are others like you."

Zelinsky finished his cigarette, stubbed it out, motioned for another. Dickie lit one, passed it across the coffee table.

"What was it?" Zelinsky said. "Nightmares or a vision?"

Most of the characters in Zelinsky's books had their revelations through horrific recurring dreams, so Dickie decided to go that route. "Nightmares," he said.

Zelinsky nodded. "That's the most common way of discovery. In dreams. Memories that won't stay suppressed. But every once in a while someone has a rip in their day where they can see everything."

He slid the end of the crutch off the coffee table, planted it in the carpet, pushed, rocked, trying to catapult himself off the couch. Dickie wasn't sure of the protocol, if he should offer a hand or let the man do his thing. He opted for the latter, deferring to the buried military bearing, thinking of Jack's refusals of assistance.

Zelinsky finally got himself up with a groan, stepped around the coffee table, back behind Dickie, looking for something on the bookshelves.

"I'll hear your story, but not tonight. I'm in no shape tonight." He lifted his face, peering onto higher shelves, reading spines in the bad light. "Where are you staying?"

"Hollywood."

"Near Javier?"

"Yes, sir."

"Good. Stay near Javier. I'll find you."

Zelinsky checked another shelf. "Those fuckers take everything." He turned to look at Dickie. Something had shifted again. Whatever trust Zelinsky had been willing to grant had evaporated.

"I'd check your pockets," he said, "but what good would that do? If you're a ghost, then ghosts don't have pockets, do they?"

Dickie kept an eye on the shotgun Zelinsky had left over at the couch, fairly sure he could beat the guy in a footrace if need be.

"They sit where you're sitting and tell me they've read the books," Zelinsky said. "They listen to me ramble. Then they make their threats. Awful things, worse than anything I could make up. Power-meter readers, Avon ladies. Every one of them dropping their masks to reveal red eyes, sharpened fangs."

Zelinsky turned back to the shelves. "They're afraid of what I'm assembling. They're afraid of people who remember. Someday they won't just come to steal. Someday they'll be here for more. I'm ready for it. If you like the shotgun, you should see my bedroom. When that last ghost comes and I make him for what he is, we'll have the Gunfight at the O.K. Corral."

Zelinsky found what he was looking for, turned and handed Dickie a well-thumbed paperback. *Johnny Tremain.*

"When was the last time you read this?" Zelinsky asked.

"I couldn't say."

"Dick Hinkle." Zelinsky said the name slowly, relishing the preposterous sound. "Take this and whatever else you need from the bag. And then you should be going."

Dickie stood, walked to the door.

"*Watch, O Lord,*" Zelinsky said, "*with those who wake, or watch, or weep tonight, and give Your angels and saints charge over those who sleep.*" He leaned back against the bookcase, the crutch no longer enough to hold his weight.

Dickie opened the door. Moonless outside.

"Saint Augustine," Zelinsky said. "Might be worth remembering."

12

She worked around the photo of her father for the better part of a week, keeping it in the center of the table while she made prints of her runaway images. She would forget about the photo for a while and then feel the anachronistic shock of seeing Henry in 1950s San Francisco, his suit and hat, the clothing and bearing of the ghostly figures crossing behind and in front. His look versus the kids in the modern photos on the table around him. Not that different, maybe. People on the street, unable to find a way home.

She watched coverage of the chess match every night it was on. There was a delay when Fischer demanded that the proceedings be moved out of the main hall and into a closet-size room in the back of the facility usually reserved for table tennis. There was another delay when the Russians had Spassky's chair dismantled, his clothes swept, his morning orange juice tested, sure that his suddenly somnolent play was the work of CIA poisoning.

Fischer had now banned all filming, so the news reports relied on still photos, drawings from artists in attendance, renderings that looked like a cross between political cartoons and courtroom sketches. There were detailed animations illustrating each move, along with expert commentary from former grand masters. Hannah tended to watch without sound. She was interested only in the real-life images, the few still photographs that had been smuggled out, shots of Fischer and Spassky hunched over their table. The rest was irrelevant to her. She had never played a game of chess in her life and didn't believe she probably ever would. The establishing shots of the Icelandic landscape at the beginning of the broadcasts were beautiful but beside the point. They could be playing anywhere, as long as it was remote, inaccessible. She cared only for the interior of that room, the men it contained.

Images of Spassky now showed him sweating like a man who had indeed been poisoned. The match had been moved back to the main hall, but Spassky hadn't played well since the game in the back room. He had been outmaneuvered and he looked like he knew it. He realized the mistake he had made. He could see the catastrophe at the end of the chain.

She built a frame at her worktable, cut a mat, and brought the photo of her father out to the gallery. For the past month she'd been displaying the work of another photographer, images of drag performers at underground cabarets throughout the city. She hammered a nail into an empty wall and hung the picture of Henry. She stood back, surprised at how odd she felt, shaky and short of breath, as if she'd just told a long-held secret.

The next day, with the front doors open again, she came out of her studio whenever she heard a visitor. She stood just outside the doors, one canvas sneaker on the sidewalk, smoking, watching out of the corner of her eye as whoever had come in looked at the cabaret photos, working their way across the exhibit, finally coming to the lone island of her father almost twenty years ago, the black frame against the rest of the empty white wall. She watched for a reaction, not sure what she was expecting, what she was hoping to see. Some recognition of the enormity of the image, the freighted history it carried. She watched her visitors press their faces closer to the shot, and then, invariably, moving away, back to the other photos, or out the door entirely, nodding quickly in her direction before stepping back out onto the sidewalk and away down the street.

13

Dickie sat in the Cutlass watching Buñuel and reading *Johnny Tremain*. This had been the routine for the last few days, since his visit to Zelinsky. He still owed Father Bill a phone call, but didn't quite feel like admitting he might have hit a dead end so early in the operation. Instead, he read the newspapers for anything new about the Orange County heists, tried to think up a story for if Zelinsky actually came for him, though it was hard to imagine the man even leaving his house. The story would need to be in line with Zelinsky's books, but with a new wrinkle or two, enough to pique the man's interest, draw him in a little further until Dickie could suss out what, if any, connection there was between the writer and the preacher and some dudes knocking over banks in high-end beach communities.

Dickie decided that he'd be one of the kids in the mental hospitals so prevalent in the books. Committed, maybe, by his hard-ass military father for recreational drug use that the old man saw as nothing less than a major mental defect. Seemed reasonable that could have happened at some point. And then young Dickie was shuttled from the hospital proper to a shadow wing, where he was drugged, tortured, mind-wiped. Sent down, maybe, to Vietnam, where he could be their eyes and ears, could rat out other kids who'd been snatched and sent southeast by other, less covert but equally nefarious government agencies.

Another day done. No sign of Zelinsky. No sign either from Buñuel
that Zelinsky had clued him in to Dickie's presence. Maybe it was time
to go with Plan B, whatever that was. When Buñuel had packed up and
headed out on the eastbound bus, Dickie decided to get some exercise,
some not-so-fresh air to help him think. He left the Cutlass and started
the walk back to the hotel.

It was dark by the time he approached the electronics store on the
corner, just the light from the TVs in the window brightening the sidewalk in front of the glass. More war footage, he assumed, helicopters
banking low over rice paddies and villages, tracers streaking through
the air.

Closer to the TVs, he could see that it wasn't the war. They were
showing a vehicular accident, a rusted four-door beater and a police car
on what looked like a fairly desolate stretch of road. Great Plains–ish.
Wheat fields filling the screen. The beater nose down in a ditch, the police car right-angled across the road, its front end crumpled. Glass everywhere. The asphalt slick with gasoline.

Another shot of the beater. The front and back windshields shattered.
Bullet holes in the doors. Cops walking the scene, talking among themselves. Someone taking pictures. A few fire trucks sitting, lights turning
idly. A team of paramedics down in the ditch, pulling bodies from the car.

Photographs on-screen then, and Dickie stopped, staring at the familiar shots from the "Wanted" posters they'd been so proud of, the kid
on the left's name escaping Dickie at the moment, vanished from his
memory banks because the photo on the right was a face he knew by
heart.

Mary Margaret. The photo on the right was Mary Margaret. And
then her name was up on the screen, along with a question mark under
the photo of the nameless kid on the left. A headline under their faces,
END TO FUGITIVES' RUN.

Dickie had to make an effort to close his mouth, not say her name
out loud because there were other people around him now, watching
the broadcast, what he thought might be a gathering crowd, but he
turned and it was only one figure; no, two; and then someone coming

up behind him as well, Dickie unable to see faces in the dark, in the TV screen backlighting. He could only see that there were no faces, that the figures had something stretched over their heads, distorting their eyes and mouths, and one was raising something in its hand, a baseball bat, a Louisville Slugger, he could make out the familiar branded seal on the barrel just before it cocked back, eye level, just before the figure jabbed the barrel forward and Dickie felt a sunburst of pain between his eyes, his sight flickering to nothing but the TV screen, the afterimage on the backs of his eyelids, Mary Margaret's face in the glow.

14

She had dreams of Saturday mornings, that first spring in Oakland, crossing the Bay Bridge with her father in their station wagon. In her dreams she could hear the records she left playing in her workshop when she finally lay down to sleep, a vinyl stack three-quarters of an inch high, as much as the changer could hold. Skip James, Leadbelly, Blind Willie Johnson. Hymns of longing and regret.

Driving on the lower deck, the new morning sun appearing behind the wide steel supports. Her father telling her something while he watched the road, the car's mirrors, always cautious, his voice buried just beneath the lyrics of the blues records that crossed into this abeyant space. Her father stopping the car at Yerba Buena Island, turning around on the gravel access road, sitting and watching the bridge. Hannah unwilling to go any farther, an irrational childhood fear, refusing to enter the city on the other side of the water.

On the ride back in the dreams, she is always alone in the passenger seat. There is no one driving; the steering wheel turns on its own. The music has ended by this time, the stack of records exhausted. Just the rhythmic whirl of the turntable spinning, filtering into her dream. Hannah heading home, watching out the windows to catch sight of the dead-man holes pocking the walls on the other side of the tracks. The dream fading, coming apart like a cloud. Hannah straining to keep it for a moment longer, looking for movement, a man's shape ducking into one of the holes where he will be safe. Trying to hold on long enough for a glimpse of a familiar figure, here and then gone.

She stepped outside the rink for a late-morning smoke break, wandered down the block, the summer smog hanging in the dry heat, the sky beach-colored, as if the air was full of sand.

There were two young men in the gallery when she returned. Mexican, one tall, one short. They stood a few paces apart, looking at the cabaret images, whispering to each other in English and Spanish, their fingers reaching out occasionally, touching, hooking, then releasing when one or the other moved a little farther down the wall. The taller man looked not unlike one of the subjects in the photographs, a drag queen in a platinum wig and sequined gown, a cigarette burning in one hand, standing majestically, fearlessly, poised and glamorous in a way that seemed to elude most actual Hollywood starlets.

Hannah was about to introduce herself, ask the taller man if he was indeed the subject of the photo, when he stopped in front of the picture of Henry, alone on its wall. His hands lowered slowly to his sides. He stared at the photo. His friend came up beside him and whispered something. The taller man turned to Hannah.

"Where did you get this?"

Something in the man's tone was so loaded that Hannah stopped herself from the immediate, obvious answer. She didn't want to expose any more than she already had by placing the photo out in the gallery.

"I've had it for years," she said. "In my collection."

The taller man turned back to the photo, spoke to his friend. "I know this man. This man worked for my father."

"When?" Hannah asked. She tried not to sound too eager, wasn't sure if she succeeded.

"I was a teenager," he said.

The taller man looked to be in his early twenties, Hannah guessed, so not that long ago.

"Are you sure?"

The taller man nodded at the picture. "I wouldn't forget him."

"What work did he do?" the friend asked.

"Things my father was not willing to do."

"Where?" Hannah's voice was shaking. She could hear the vibrato, tried to steady it.

"Down the coast. Not far from San Vicente." The taller man looked at Hannah again. "You don't remember where you got the photograph?"

She shook her head.

The taller man spoke to his friend. *"Este es el hombre que me pagó para largarme."*

"I'm sorry, I don't—" Hannah took a step toward the men, realized her arms were crossed protectively over her chest. She forced them into the pockets of her jeans. "My Spanish isn't that good."

The taller man looked at her, irritated. She was intruding on a personal conversation.

"Do you remember his name?" Hannah asked.

"He didn't have a name," the taller man said. "We called him *La Escoba*, because he cleaned up my father's messes. Sometimes we called him *El Fantasma Güero*."

Hannah shook her head. "I don't know what that means."

"Ghost," the shorter man said, turning back to the photo. "The white ghost."

15

Nothing. Black only. Then tiny explosions, little white flowers of light in the dark. Pain approaches from some far place, filling his head, his lower back, his knees, growing quickly. He has been given painkillers and they are wearing off. He knows the feeling well. He cannot move his hands or feet. When he breathes his breath comes back to him hot and rank, the expelled air returning from somewhere close. He remembers Zelinsky's books and Buñuel's tracts and knows that he is in a closed container, he is in a coffin. He has been buried alive.

No, he is sitting. He can feel the bend in his hips, his knees. His feet are bare and cold and they are not touching anything, there is no floor, but he is sitting. He is not in a coffin. He has to try not to panic. There is nothing to focus on but the rapidly growing pain, so he focuses on that, the white flowers bursting. There is pain and that is his, that is something he knows, something that belongs to him, the feel of his body. He has to focus on that.

There is movement in the air. He can feel it on his feet, his wrists. His wrists are behind him, bound around something. The back of a chair. He has to try not to panic. He is in a chair, his feet tied and twisted so that they do not touch the floor, giving him the sense of floating, of falling.

His eyes are open but he sees nothing. His breath comes back to him and he makes a sound, a low, quiet *uhhhhh,* just to hear his own voice. His voice goes nowhere. The sound stays close. There is something over his head, covering his face. He sucks air in sharply through his mouth and tastes rough fabric. He holds the fabric in his teeth.

He has been hooded like a bird.

This is what they did to him in the hospital. He remembers the hood and the chair.

No, wait, that is something he made up. That was a story he created, a story to tell.

My name is Dick Hinkle. Richard Hinkle. No, wait, that was a story they created, something they made up. His name is Ashby. Richard John Ashby. His father's name is Jack.

Was Jack. His father's name was Jack.

He is in withdrawal. He knows this feeling. He needs something for the panic and something for the pain. Something to help him hold on to this little kernel of clear thinking. If he could stop shaking and stop hurting then the kernel would expand and he would know what to do, he could work through the options.

He remembers the hood, the chair. This is what they did to him in the hospital.

Mary Margaret crosses a beam of warm orange sunlight, schools of dust motes swimming, following her movement. The hair on her arms shines as she passes through the beam, the holes in her old undershirt flashing, circles of freckled pink skin beneath, on her shoulder, her lower back. The first light coming to her apartment slowly, at oblique angles, entering to the side of a wooden shutter bent open like an elbow.

Her apartment. His apartment. Dickie had lived there for three months by that morning, a strange and unexpected domesticity, his toothbrush standing crossed with hers in a cup at the edge of the bathroom sink, his mother's record among the Hendrix and Joplin in the wooden citrus crate in the living room.

Dust in the air. An apartment of books, records, open windows. Motes changing direction as she moves in the kitchen, the light bending around her body, wrapping her in a quick embrace and then releasing her, snapping back to its original stalwart beam. The dust regathers, settling, drifting in the light, charged slightly, atoms waiting for her to cross again.

He comes sleepily to the edge of the kitchen, stopping at the border between wood and tile floor, his toes pressing the seam. He watches Mary Margaret crossing back and forth, making coffee, unaware of his presence. Dickie imagining, for just a moment, an alternate universe, a different life. Staying quiet so as not to disturb her, wanting to remain unnoticed, to hold this other place as long as possible. Breathing slowly, his toes pressing into the rough gap in the floor between rooms.

It is hard to tell when he is sleeping and when he is awake and when he has simply passed out. It is all dark. He must be awake because he can feel the pain in his head and the ache in his wrists and ankles. He can suck in air and taste the fabric between his teeth. He must be awake because he remembers the dream, Mary Margaret moving in the kitchen. He must be awake because he remembers the news report, the car crash, the bullet holes in the door, the covered bodies on the ground. Mary Margaret and Dale. The boy's name was Dale. How could he have forgotten. Dale with his lockpicks, his snake rakes.

He needs to stay in this space, out of the dreams. He needs to stay in the dark, fight the pain and nausea, the shaking withdrawal, the fear. Fight the memories that are not his, that are things he created. Taste the fabric between his teeth. Feel his own hot breath on his face. Think of Mary Margaret. Feel her skin against his. Hear her voice in his ear.

Your name is Ashby, Richard John Ashby. Your mother's name was Audrey. Your father's name was Jack.

The first voice he hears outside of his head is a woman's, but it does not belong to Mary Margaret. It is lower in pitch, flatter in tone. It comes from behind him, a few feet away from where his hands are bound.

"What do you need?"

The junkie's greeting. How many times has he heard this. He can feel his own sweat now, he is aware of it for the first time, cold and slick on his forearms, soaking his shirt. Withdrawal sweat. He is shaking so much that his chair is creaking, another noise he is suddenly aware of.

"What do you need?" the woman asks again, and Dickie licks his lips and clears his throat and tells her, his voice hoarse and close in the hood. And then he is alone in the room and then she is back, or someone else is there, and his right arm is loosened, hanging useless and numb from restraint, then straightened and tied off and then the needle prick in the vein and then the blessed wash, the cleansing warmth, sweeping him away.

When he had finally learned to ride the bike, when he had stopped toppling off while Jack watched, smoking, from the garage, nobody could get him off it. He rode the streets of the air base, past the pavement and through the scrub brush and dirt to the high chain-link fence, watching fighter planes refueling, taking off, and landing in the distance on the other side.

He was riding home one afternoon when he saw a man leaving their house, another of the tousled collectors who came attempting to lure his mother back out into the world. The man stood in the driveway, holding his clutch of 78s between his knees while he lit a cigarette. Dickie stopped his bike. His father would be home soon. If Jack saw this guy he would beat the shit out of him on the front lawn. It had happened before. The MPs would come and pull Jack off and haul the beatnik down the street and out through the gates and come back and stand with Jack on the lawn and chuckle while Jack cracked a beer, fumed. Dickie sat on his bike at the end of the driveway and thought about telling this guy to hurry up with his cigarette and hightail it off the base. Instead he sat and watched, and when the man finally started moving again, Dickie said, "Why do you care?"

The man stopped, the cigarette burning between his lips. He loosened the leather strap from around the 78s, paged through them carefully, reading the labels as each sleeve passed through his fingers. He stopped on one, lifted it from the small stack, held it out. Dickie took the record, read the label, a song of his mother's he'd heard a thousand times, a song his father put on the record player when he'd had too much to drink, when he was feeling maudlin or romantic. Dickie looked back up but the man was already walking down the street toward the front gate, unhurried, trailing smoke over his shoulder.

It would be years before Dickie understood. Playing the record, alone in Mary Margaret's apartment, hearing his mother's voice without her in the room. Just the hope and sadness, the fragile beauty of the sound.

Another voice in the dark. A man's this time, small and pinched, slightly nasal.

"Do you know who we are?"

"Yes," Dickie says. His throat is sore. His voice sounds weak within the hood.

"We know who you are," the voice says. "You're a ghost. Richard Hinkle."

"That's not my name."

"Your license says Richard Hinkle."

"My name is Ashby. Richard Ashby."

"Who sent you?"

"You know who sent me."

"Specifically."

"I can't give you a name. A real name."

"Why not?"

"I don't know any real names."

"You have two names and they have none." The sound of chair legs scraping on the floor, the man's weight shifting. "What were you trying to do?" the man says. "Following Buñuel, going to Zelinsky."

"I was trying to find you."

"Find us."

"Talk to you."

"Talk to us about what?"

It is hard to breathe within the hood. Dickie feels as if he can't get enough air, that he is breathing fabric. The drugs are wearing off again. The hood is close, tight.

"Can you take the hood off?"

"No."

"Take it off. Please." There is no more oxygen in the hood. He's just breathing his own bad air. "Can you take it off?"

No answer.

"Please."

No answer.

"Please." Dickie's throat raw, his voice loud and painful in the hood, a frightening sound, sending his panic higher.

"Why?" the voice asks.

"Because it reminds me of the hospital."

"The hospital."

"Please." Dickie's face is wet. He wants to scream but he is afraid of what the sound of a scream in the hood will do to him.

"Which hospital?" the voice asks.

"I can't."

"You can't what?"

"I can't talk."

"You're talking."

"I can't breathe, please."

"You're breathing."

"Not with the fucking hood. Take off the fucking hood."

"What do you need?"

"Please."

The sound of another chair scraping. Someone else in the room. The girl?

"The same?" the voice asks. "The same as what you got before?"

"The hood, please."

"What do you need?"

"The hood."

Both chairs scraping and movement in the room and for a second Dickie thinks they are going to take off the hood, but then there is the sound of a door opening, hinges groaning, and then the door closes and he is alone. There are no other sounds except his panicked breathing, then his chair legs banging on the floor as he rocks back and forth, trying to tip himself, trying to smash the chair. Then nothing, no noise except the sound of his screams in the dark.

Early in MAELSTROM, he had called Father Bill from a pay phone outside of Ann Arbor, freaked over a protest at the university that had ended in a shouting match with a group of Young Republicans, spilling over into confrontations in various parking lots, skirmishes in back alleys. It was nothing Dickie hadn't been involved in before, except this time when he was trying to break things up, pull his guys away, there was this YR with thick black glasses screaming at Dickie about the beauty of killing commie gooks. Dickie tried to ignore him, shot him a few warning looks, like *back off, no, really,* but the kid kept screaming, *commie gooks commie gooks,* his spit spraying Dickie in the face, and then suddenly Dickie was on him, he had this kid on the ground and was hammering his glasses into his face, the frames cracking and the lenses breaking, Dickie pounding away until he was pulled off by the guys he was pulling away just a second ago, the rest of the fight having ceased in the face of the ferocity of this assault, Dickie dragged out of the parking lot and this YR kid lying on the pavement crying and holding his hands over his eyes.

Later, in the phone booth, Dickie on the line with Father Bill, confessing, expecting Bill to respond with weary disappointment, to pull Dickie out, abort mission, and Dickie deserving this, he knew, for believing his own bullshit, for buying into his own cover to the point where there was now a kid with God-knew-what kind of damage to his eyes, and Father Bill taking a silent moment, processing, Dickie hearing only his own scared breathing in the phone's receiver, and then Father Bill telling him that there was nothing better for establishing bona fides than forgetting your own cover to the point where you can't be questioned, to where your motives are unassailable.

That's good work, Dickie, Father Bill had said. They can't touch you now.

"You're calmer." The man's voice in the room.

"What did you give me?"

"I'll bet you can make an educated guess. You seem well versed."

Maybe he had slept. Maybe he is sleeping now. It's hard to tell. The panic has subsided, though. He is warm, he is calm.

The voice says, "Can we talk now?"

Dickie nods.

"What did they send you to do?"

"Find you," Dickie says. "Infiltrate."

"Infiltrate."

"That's the term."

"So far, so good." The voice laughs. It's an ugly sound, dented, a little cruel.

Dickie can smell the cigarettes as soon as they're removed from the pack. The sulfur whiff as the match is struck, the tobacco burning. The voice sucks in, exhales. Smoke clings to the cloth of the hood.

"But you changed course," the voice says.

"Yes."

"Did you change course?"

"Yes."

"Why?"

"I read his books."

"Zelinsky's books."

"I read the preacher's tracts and those led me to the books."

"Your masters didn't give you the books?"

"No."

"Interesting." The voice sucks, blows smoke. "You read the books and what?"

"I'd always thought it was a dream. Or a fantasy. Something not real."

"What?"

"The hospital."

"You had dreams?"

"Yes."

"You had moments, where, what?"

"I'd be back there."

"But you thought they were nothing."

"I thought they were nothing or that they were drugs or—"

"You thought you were crazy."

"Yes."

"What hospital?"

"I need you take take off the hood."

"We don't have to do anything."

"I know. I'm asking you."

The voice sucks, blows smoke. "We'll see."

"Please."

"We'll see." Chair legs scraping. The man stands, his voice rising in height. "Were you working alone?"

"Yes," Dickie says.

"Are you sure?"

"Yes."

Footsteps, more than one pair, coming toward him. More movement, grabbing Dickie's arm.

"What are you giving me?"

"Sleep," the voice says.

"What are you giving me?"

"Sleep, sleep."

It seems like one of the restaurants back in Davenport, an Italian place where he and Father Bill had lunch a couple of times, but it can't be, it has to be a dream or something, the weather out the front window is all fucked, even for Iowa, rain, then bright sun, then rain. Dickie is ravenous, attacking a bowl of tortellini, half a loaf of bread. Father Bill sits

on the other side of the table, sipping his seltzer, watching Dickie eat.
A waiter stands back by the door to the kitchen. When Dickie looks he
sees that the waiter is holding one of Javier Buñuel's signs, the long list
of the damned.

"You gave them your name," Father Bill says. "Your real name."

"Yes."

"That's what I like to see. That level of commitment."

"I know."

"All in."

Dickie takes another mouthful of pasta. "They're not just a bank
crew, are they?"

"We have our suspicions."

"Meaning what?"

"If I knew that," Father Bill says, "you wouldn't be here."

"Here?" Dickie lifts his face from his bowl, looks around the restaurant.

"What was that you said about a hospital?" Father Bill asks. "You
mentioned a hospital and they bit. If they were just a bank crew that line
would have landed with a thud."

Dickie sets down his fork, wipes his mouth with a napkin. He pulls
The Night Visitor out of his back pocket, sets it on the table. "Do you
know these books?"

Father Bill looks at the cover.

Dickie says, "The author said he heard Buñuel's story, other victims'
stories, and incorporated them into the books."

Father Bill picks up the book, flips pages.

"It's about a guy named Mr. _____," Dickie says, "and his band of
Merry—"

"Schizophrenics?"

"You know the books."

"I didn't say that."

"Maybe he heard their stories," Dickie says. "This group. Put them
into the books."

"This man in the room with you," Father Bill says. "You think he's
Mr. _____?"

"Is that how you pronounce it?"

Bill studies the cover, looks pensive. "What are their stories?" Bill says "stories" with an additional affect. Stories meaning fiction. Stories meaning delusions.

"I don't know," Dickie says.

"Well." Bill sets down the book, looks past Dickie, out the restaurant windows. "Then that's why you're here."

He opens his eyes into brightness. He has to squint. His pupils are sensitive from the time under the hood, but he tries to force them wide, absorb the light. He is hungry for it.

He breathes deeply. The hood is gone. The room comes slowly into focus. A large cement box, walls chipped, flaking skins of old paint. A damp space, humid, lit with two rows of fluorescents in protective cages, fastened to the low ceiling.

He is alone in the center of the room. There are two empty chairs a few feet in front of him. There is something on the wall behind the empty chairs. Something large, a rectangle with long alternating bars of black and white, a gray square in the bottom corner, rows of small white stars.

His eyes focusing, slowly. It is a flag hanging in front of him, an inverted American flag, black and white and gray, a reversed image, a colorless twin.

He cannot see behind him. He suddenly needs to make sure there is no one else in the room, no one watching, but he can't turn his head that far. His hands and ankles are tied. A leather belt encircles his stomach and the back of the chair. He is wearing the same clothes they caught him in, jeans and a western shirt. He has soiled himself, he can tell by the feel and the smell. He has no idea how many times it has happened, how long he has been sitting in it. His feet are bare and cold.

A door opens from somewhere behind him and he tries to turn his neck but he can't swivel far enough. Someone enters the room. Footsteps on the cement floor. He notices a drain in the floor for the first time, directly under his chair. The footsteps get closer, and then a man is there, passing Dickie, sitting in one of the chairs opposite. The man is Dickie's age, short and slight, with a full brown mustache but a hairline that starts up at the top of his head. He is wearing a checkered shirt tucked tightly into stiff-looking jeans. Everything about him seems small and hard, precise. Hands like paws. Front teeth protruding slightly from his closed lips.

A girl passes by. Dickie hadn't heard her enter, and then he sees why: bare feet stick out of the bottoms of her jeans. She sits next to the ratlike man. She is probably six inches taller than he is. Blond, fresh-faced, with that serene, half-glazed look common to cult members, religious casualties. Like the light in her eyes has, maybe, a dimmer switch.

He has seen their faces now, so he knows a decision has been made. He's either leaving the room with them, eventually, or he's not leaving the room.

The man lights a cigarette, passes his pack and matches to the girl. She sets them in her lap. They both watch Dickie.

"My name is Walter," the man says. "That is my real name, my only name." The familiar, reedy voice. "You are Richard Benjamin Hinkle of San Francisco, California."

"That's not my name." Dickie's voice is little more than a dry whisper.

"It is for now." Walter glances at the girl and she stands and walks past Dickie, reappears a moment later with a paper cup. She holds it to Dickie's scabbed lips. Cool water. He almost chokes, coughing and sputtering but refusing to stop until he has drained the cup.

The girl sits again, places the cup in her lap beside the cigarettes and matches.

"We've never caught a ghost before," Walter says. He tilts his head to the side as he smokes, studying Dickie. "Tell us your story, Richard Hinkle. Tell us your ghost story."

"Can I have more water?"

Walter nods and the girl stands again, filling the cup from somewhere on the other side of the room, returning to hold it to Dickie's mouth. She lights a cigarette and takes a drag and then holds it for Dickie. He inhales deeply. He looks up at the girl, nods, grateful, embarrassed, suddenly, of his smell and mess.

She leaves him the cigarette to hold in his lips while he speaks. He tells them of his time in Vietnam, in the underground. The same establishing of credibility that worked with the student groups. Except this time he tells them everything, about Father Bill, about the explosion in Portland, about Jack in his Davenport apartment. The truth is all he has. No one is looking for him here, no one is going to rescue him. He can see that these two will only believe him if he gives them everything, if he holds nothing back. All in.

When he is finished, Walter and the girl stand, and the girl brings Dickie another cup of water, a few pills that she places on his outstretched tongue. And then they are gone, the door closing behind them, and Dickie is alone in the room again, with the lights and the drain and the colorless flag.

A tall black kid was untying him when he woke, pulling the last of the straps from Dickie's wrists. Dickie's arms hung heavily at his sides. Everything logy, slow to respond. Whatever they'd given him made him feel like a big, dumb animal.

The kid was a few years younger than Walter, in his early twenties, so thin as to seem almost emaciated. He looked like one of the runaways Dickie had seen on Hollywood Boulevard, crossing below the stairs of Javier Buñuel's perch carrying bedrolls and ratty backpacks. Everything skinny except for the full Afro sitting on top of his head like a space helmet. He was surprisingly strong, though. He got Dickie up and over to a corner of the room. There was a hole in the floor where Dickie could relieve himself.

Nothing much else on this side of the room. Just the hole, a water spigot set into the wall, a big iron door, now closed. The kid helped Dickie out of his soiled clothes, left the room, came back in with a hose, which he attached to the water spigot. Dickie washed himself. The kid stood at the door, looking down at his tennis shoes, chewing a fingernail. When Dickie was finished, the kid left the room again, returned with an outfit of green hospital scrubs for Dickie to put on. Nothing for his feet. While Dickie was getting dressed, the kid left again, came back with a plate of black beans and rice, a lump of boiled carrots. Dickie sat against the wall and devoured the food, grabbing clumsily with his fingers, choking, too much too soon. He asked for some water and the kid nodded to the spigot.

He splashed water on his face, drank from his cupped hands. Looked around the room, studying the walls, searching for a hole, a deep crack, something they could be watching him through. Not sure why it mattered, but he wanted to know where they were, where their eyes were hiding.

The kid was gone. Dickie's plate was gone, the iron door was closed. The lights buzzed overhead. He crawled to a corner, as far as he could from the chair where he'd been bound. He lay down, closed his eyes, slept.

"My name is Sarah. That is my real name, my only name."

Dickie opened his eyes. The blond girl was there, Walter's sidekick. Dickie was lying on the floor, cheek pressed to the damp cement, so everything appeared sideways. He felt slightly more alert, was able to get to his knees, turn the room back to its upright state. He was still untied, and alone in the room with her, so he figured there was some mechanism in place if he were to make a move, someone watching, aiming something at him. Or maybe she was tougher than she looked, maybe she'd have him back on the floor in no time flat if he tried anything. Either way, he accepted the food she'd brought, the water, the pills, the cigarette.

She was wearing a loose summer dress, its straps hugging her pale shoulders. Her feet were still bare.

The chair with the straps had been removed from the room. They sat in the remaining two chairs, and she talked while he ate, telling him her story, starting with her childhood, her abusive parents, working up through her teenage years, the boy-and-drug experiments, through to a year of junior college, a suicide attempt, hospitalization. She presented it all without shame or guilt or remorse. It had the dry, confessional ring of a rehab monologue, the rap Dickie'd heard from many of the kids in the army hospitals in Vietnam. Dickie smoked, watched the gnawed cuticles of her fingernails as she gestured and spoke. He had heard this story before. It was recounted, almost verbatim, by a character in one of Zelinsky's books.

She left him, and while he was alone he slept, or walked the room, looking for holes in the walls. Wondering who was watching, Sarah or Walter or the other kid. The overhead lights burned all the time.

When she returned they sat in the chairs and Dickie ate and listened to more of her story, the experiments in the hospital, the torture, the sensory deprivation, the drugs. He remembered it all from Zelinsky's book. They had sucked out her identity, her name and personality, leaving a clean white space. Then she was given a new name, with new memories, a loving childhood, a spotless adolescence, this new person squeezed into her brain, one drop at a time, until she was full with it, and then she went out into the world and lived that life.

She came and went. Each time, she picked her story up exactly where she'd left off. Dickie wasn't sure how long she'd been talking, over how many hours or days. He tried to get his head out of the room, think past the walls, the current moment. Didn't have much success. He was here, that was all. Whatever they were giving him now was not as powerful a sedative as before, but it still kept him cloudy and slow. He considered not taking what was offered, but figured that they'd find out soon enough, simply inject him with what they wanted him to have. That and the memory of withdrawal kept him swallowing the pills Sarah held out for him.

She came and went. She gave him back the copy of *Johnny Tremain* that Zelinsky had given him. She told him about the new, false life she'd lived. Her job, her fiancé, a failed pregnancy. The moment, on the drive home from her gynecologist, when she realized what had been done to her and began to piece together her old, true life.

When she was finished telling her story, she stopped coming. Dickie waited, read his copy of *Johnny Tremain*. Alone for hours, maybe another day.

When she returned, it was with Walter.

"Your story panned out," Walter said. "The explosion in Portland, the dead man." He lit a cigarette. "But what does this give me, really? You didn't tell me anything I couldn't have read in a newspaper."

"So you read the newspaper."

"Don't fuck with me."

Dickie motioned for a cigarette. Sarah looked to Walter and when he nodded she lit one, handed it to Dickie.

"There was a police shooting," Dickie said. "Somewhere in the plains, I think. It was on the news when you found me."

Walter worked his lower lip against the bristles of his mustache, nodded.

"A young woman and a young man were killed," Dickie said. "Radicals from the Portland explosion."

"Yes."

"How long has it been?"

"Nice try."

"Not long?"

"No."

"I knew them," Dickie said.

"They don't have the boy's name."

"They don't, yet?"

"No."

"I do." Dickie sat, an attempt to give Walter a slight height advantage. "I'll give you the name and you have someone make a call. Let the cops check it out."

Walter worked his mustache, finally reached into the front pocket of his jeans, came away with a handful of pills, shook out a few he was looking for.

"Take these."

"I'd rather not."

"Take them."

Dickie reached forward, took the pills, dumped them into his mouth, swallowed. He was dizzy immediately, the room starting to spin, gathering speed.

"The name," Walter said.

Dickie gripped the sides of the chair, feeling like he might lift off at any second, spiral out across the room. He managed to get Dale's name out before his blood pressure shot through the top of his head, the room going dark, Dickie flying, untethered, off into space.

Strapped to a chair in the black room, a metal helmet tight on his head, needles passing through bone, squeezing memories, squeezing the new person into his skull, the soft tissue within.

Richard Benjamin Hinkle of San Francisco, California. A newspaper reporter, a burnout, a dropout, an addict and alcoholic.

An orphan.

No, this is Sarah's dream, Zelinsky's dream. This is Dick Hinkle's dream. This is not his dream.

This is his dream:

"You look good," Father Bill says. "You're losing weight."

"I'm hungry all the time," Dickie says, mouth full.

"That's good. Staying hungry is good."

The restaurant is empty. The waiter with Buñuel's sign is gone. It's still raining, then sunny, then rainy. Dickie cannot eat his pasta fast enough. He is terrified that someone will take it before he finishes.

Dickie says, "Your real name isn't Bill, is it?"

"Isn't it?"

"What about the seminary? The wife and kids?"

Bill sits back in his seat. "Let's not make this personal." He pushes a basket of bread across the table to Dickie. "How crazy are these kids, scale of one to ten?"

Dickie swallows, wipes his mouth. "Twelve?"

"Crazy is dangerous," Bill says. "Crazy is unpredictable."

"But it doesn't mean they're lying."

Bill places an index finger on the handle of his unused fork, shifts it a quarter inch, lining it up beside the knife, the spoon.

Dickie says, "Are they lying?"

Bill looks over his shoulder, ready for the check, maybe. He turns back to the table, pulls his chair in tight, sits looking over his silverware, the position of his plates.

"We have a saying," he says. "My people. The listeners. The worriers. It's what keeps us going, keeps us scared." He turns his salad plate, just a hair, lets it sit. "Our motivational motto. Do you know what it is?"

Dickie shakes his head.

Bill touches his plate again, looks at the position of the knife, the fork, hesitating, unconvinced.

"Just three little words," Bill says. *"You never know."*

16

Ginnie started painting again after Hannah left. Rediscovering the impulse surprised her, as if everything that had been removed from her life had revealed it again, a long-lost friend.

She built small wooden frames, purchased paint and lengths of canvas from the art supply store near the park. At night, after Thomas was asleep, she worked on the living room floor, under the shelves of Henry's books.

Cutting the canvas, stretching it across the frame, pulling it taut. Muscle memory she had assumed was lost. Holding the carpet tacks between her teeth while she hammered the canvas to the frame. Her fingertips running across the pebbled fabric. The smell of the wood, the hardware. She'd forgotten how much she loved the feel of tacks in her mouth. Memories of her father working in the barn when she was a girl, hammering loose boards, his lips bristling with nails.

She talked to Henry while she worked. She always had, in Chicago, in Arlington. She painted while he read in a chair on the other side of the canvas. She saw no reason to stop their conversation just because he was no longer in the room.

She painted large shapes, blocks and lines of color. When she was younger she had brooded over canvases, believing that the blank space should only be defiled if it could be improved upon. She had no such qualms now. She painted to feel the ache in her shoulders after a few hours at the easel, to feel the wring in her lower back. The sensual nature of her body's fatigue after work. Lying in the tub, the hot water untangling her muscles, her fingers bleeding green and yellow swirls across the surface of the bath.

Once, during one of their more heated arguments, Hannah had accused Ginnie of being dead inside, and Ginnie had immediately thought of painting. This part of her that Hannah didn't know. She had still been able to feel it, a small warmth in her chest, in her fingertips. It was all that had sustained her in the hours after the argument. Ginnie convincing herself that it wasn't true, that she couldn't be dead inside if she still had this desire somewhere within.

"At night I split apart," Thomas says. "Parts of me fly all over the world, even farther. In the morning I only have a few minutes to get them all back before I wake up."

Ginnie squares the edges of a new frame, pulls a nail from her mouth, sets the tip into the soft wood. "What if you wake up too soon?"

Thomas watches the head of her hammer as it strikes the nail, strikes again. "Then part of me would be missing," he says.

Someone on the other side of the food pantry makes a joke and someone else laughs and Thomas laughs, too. Ginnie stops what she's doing to watch him, wondering if he is responding to the humor or simply mimicking the sound.

He listens closely to people, he absorbs their words and phrases but also their inflections and quirks of delivery. Repeating what he has heard days or weeks later. I believe Richard Nixon is one of the three most intelligent presidents in American history, he says, and Marion at the pantry asks who he thinks the others are. Thomas looks off to where the wall meets the ceiling, makes some of the bleeping noises that arrive when he comes up empty, like a computer realizing a gap in its programming.

That night after dinner he consults the encyclopedia, and the next day at the pantry he finds Marion. Abraham Lincoln and Franklin Delano Roosevelt, he says. Possibly John Adams, whose son John Quincy Adams was the sixth president of the United States but who is not on this list.

She had trouble with her heart. There were days when she was too weak to get up off the couch. Her chest weighted like it was made of stone and Marion or the boy from the pharmacy delivering her medication. Thomas in the kitchen making his own lunch. Eating at the table just out of her line of sight and then bringing her a bowl of soup, still warm.

Marion once gave her a pamphlet for a group home in Oak Center, a place where young men like Thomas shared apartments, worked part-time jobs. Ginnie thanked Marion for the pamphlet and then didn't speak to her for a week. Feeling accused again, judged, like she was back with the doctors in Arlington.

She knew that she had no idea what he was capable of, what he could do on his own. She wanted to believe that she kept him close for his own protection, but she knew that was no longer true. She was keeping him close because of her own fear. She was more afraid of the world than he was, possibly. Thomas offering to walk to the pharmacy and Ginnie calling Marion, calling the delivery boy instead.

She kept the pamphlet in the drawer of Henry's old desk in the basement. Photographs of men Thomas's age, working the checkout at a supermarket, clearing a table in a restaurant. A phone number on the front, *New Resident Applications*. The pamphlet waiting for the day when Ginnie would be weak enough to throw it away, or strong enough to carry it back aboveground.

She saw the man in the parked car glance over the top of his newspaper, saw him see her at the front window of the house and then look down, quickly, and before she knew exactly what she was doing she was out the door and across the lawn, striding up the middle of the street toward the gray sedan.

She wasn't sure what had come over her. She'd had enough possibly. All of this sneaking around.

The man in the car noticed her too late, fumbled with his paper, his keys, but she was already there, trying to suppress her surprise at the face she recognized. He frowned, folded his paper, rolled down the window.

"Wouldn't you rather come inside, Roy?" she said.

In the kitchen, she made coffee, poured two cups. Roy took a seat at the table. Thomas stood in the doorway, watching.

"This is Mr. Pritchard," Ginnie said. "He's come to see us a few times. You might not remember him."

"I remember him."

Ginnie placed the cups on a tray. "What do you remember?"

Thomas stared for another moment. "He took my picture when I was a baby." He turned and disappeared into the living room.

"He seems to be doing well," Roy said.

"Yes."

"He looks like Henry."

Ginnie carried the tray to the table. "You could just come to the front door and knock."

"I know. I'm sorry."

She took a breath. "Has something happened?"

Roy poured milk into his cup, stirred. "No."

"Would you tell me if it had?"

He lifted his spoon from the coffee, tapped it dry on the edge of his cup. "How's Hannah?"

"I haven't seen her in six months," Ginnie said.

"I'm sorry to hear that."

"It's not as bad as it could be. It's been a year before. Longer than a year." She looked at Roy. "Have you been down there?"

Roy shook his head.

"You're not watching her?"

"Not as far as I know. There isn't any reason to."

"Is there any reason to watch us?"

"I don't know."

"I see you, I see the others, and it gives me hope," she said. "When you stop coming, I'll know he's really gone."

"I'm not here to mislead you, Ginnie."

She stood from the table, carried her cup to the sink. "Do you remember that day in Arlington, when you brought Henry home? I was standing at the door, watching him come up the walkway in the snow, his coat open, his hat crooked. I thought, I had the thought, that this was the worst moment. That this feeling, the fear and helplessness, watching him come to the door, I thought that this was as bad as it could ever get. I could see, right then, a life without him, and I didn't know how I could do it. I couldn't imagine that life."

"I'm sorry, Ginnie."

"Yes." She turned on the hot water, let it lift the ring of coffee grounds up and over the rim, down across her fingers to the drain. "You've said that."

Where was he? She woke every morning with this question on her lips. Years of mornings, middle-of-the-night awakenings, abrupt resurfacings after dozing naps. Opening her eyes some days and needing time, an eternal-seeming moment to remember who *he* was. The loneliness divorced from any specific missed presence. No one could understand this. Widows she knew at church, at the community center, who spoke as if she was one of them. She wasn't one of them. She was something else.

Where was he? Someone used to share this space, this house, this bed. Someone used to recite verse to her while she closed her eyes. His face beside hers on the pillow, his breath in her ear. The last thing she heard, floating toward sleep.

She was in the kitchen making lunch when she felt something grab in her chest, some phantom hand. She made a noise, then swallowed it, not wanting to scare Thomas. She could hear the TV in the living room, joking celebrity banter on *The Hollywood Squares.* The kitchen started to spin, slowly, like a carousel starting up. She held the edge of the sink. She knew what was happening and she did not want to fall and scare Thomas, so she sank to her knees, still clutching the countertop. She pressed her forehead against the cabinet door. She could smell the jugs of ammonia and bleach she kept under the sink. She was having trouble breathing. She had lost all strength in her left arm, all feeling. Her hand slipped from the edge of the sink, dropped to the floor. The pain acute now, sharp and frightening. She held on with her other hand, kept her head pressed to the cabinet.

One more day. If she could just have one more day, she could find a place for Thomas, make sure he was safe. But it was too late, there was only this moment kneeling at the sink, the TV sound from the other room, the pain filling her body and her refusal to make a noise, her determination to allow him at least another few minutes without fear, without knowing. Let him watch his show. The rest would come soon enough.

If she had one more day, she could call Hannah. Take your brother. Hold him close. He is yours now.

Goddamn you, Henry. The curse slipped in. She had been holding it back for years. An ugly, dark thing, living within her. How dare you leave me here, leave us here. Waiting for nothing.

She felt her hand slip from the counter, her body spreading across the floor. The pain was so great. She forced her eyes open. This would not be what she saw, at the end. The lime-green linoleum. The fear and bitterness and disappointment. This would not be what she saw. She would see that morning in the park, the sun shining, the green grass, Thomas at a picnic table with his newspaper, the light in his hair. Ginnie humming and then Thomas finishing the verse of the hymn she'd started. No matter what else was taken from her, there were years of mornings like this. This was what she would see. The last moment would be beautiful.

Sunlight and her precious boy.

17

Summer 1972

His story checked out. Dale's name was the puzzle piece the cops were missing. Looks like we set the pigs on the right trail, Walter said, leading Dickie out of his room, what Dickie had come to think of as his room. The large cement box. Dale's name was in the newspaper, and now the feds were tracing things back to the explosion in Portland.

Congratulations, Walter said. You got your bust after all.

They had him now. They could drug him, dump him, make a phone call, and Dickie would be nabbed for the Portland bombing. Where would Father Bill be then? On the golf course, out on his back patio with a drink. In his office, burning paperwork.

They had him now.

He is given new clothes, which look a lot like his old clothes. A western shirt and faded jeans, a beat-up pair of boots. He is led through the warren of rooms where they live. An abandoned bomb shelter, big enough for a large family to weather a nuclear storm for some time. Concrete walls. No windows, of course. One stairway up, kept behind a locked door at the end of a short hall.

He is shown into the skinny kid's room, which he will share. The kid's name is Julian. That is his real name, his only name. There is a cot against the wall where Julian sleeps. Julian brings in a sleeping bag for Dickie, which he sets on the floor. They eat in a small storeroom which has a card table, folding metal chairs. Another inverted flag hangs on the wall, covering shelves lined with canned goods, tinned meats, dried fruit, a full complement of Zelinsky's novels.

Walter has a room, Sarah has a room. There is a small bathroom. Every few days Walter or Sarah or Julian exits through the locked door, climbs the staircase to the outside. They return a few hours later with more canned food, plastic jugs of drinking water, newspapers from the past week.

He doesn't see any weapons. He doesn't see any money. Newspaper clippings from the robberies are taped to a wall in the storeroom. No one mentions the clippings. There is no radio or television; probably no reception this far down. Julian reads Spider-Man comics, the same issues over and over from a small pile he keeps in their bedroom. Sarah strums a third-hand guitar, hums tunelessly. She has an undernourished, xylophone-ribbed cat, another escapee, a test subject sprung by an animal liberation group. The cat, he is told, was part of an experiment in the mind control of domestic animals, brainwashing household pets to spy on their owners. Some even had transmitter chips implanted into their brains so they could record what they saw and heard.

Not this one, Julian says, stroking the cat's back. This one's clean. We checked.

Walter is often behind closed doors, in his room, in the storeroom. Sometimes Sarah joins him, sometimes Julian. Dickie is not privy to these conversations, whatever plans are being made. Sarah and Julian share nothing, but their moments alone with Walter rekindle their fervor, the larger ideology, what seems to be a revenge fantasy writ large, holding to account those responsible for what was done to them.

Julian tells Dickie his story at night, when they are lying in their room in the dark. His previous, false life, and then his true life. A teenage runaway, sent to juvenile hall, where he was tortured, mind-wiped. Dickie knows the story from one of Zelinsky's books.

Everyone calls him Hinkle. He tells them that this is not his name, but eventually he stops protesting, accepts it, answers to it.

The room where Dickie was questioned is the largest in the shelter. Its door is kept locked. He passes by frequently because he has found the holes in the walls where he can see inside, into the dark empty space where he was kept.

One night, sitting at the table in the storeroom, he tells Sarah and Julian his story. The history he had rehearsed as Dick Hinkle, that had come back to him in dreams, the story about the mental hospital, the shadow wing, the drugs, the experiments. He tells them that he can't remember if he was in the hospital before or after the war, if there was an earlier stay, when he was a teenager, maybe, sent there by his father. He was a troubled kid. He'd started drinking early, taking pills. There was a lot of fighting in his house, his father shouting, his mother shouting, his father raising a hand. Dickie was no angel. Maybe he'd been sent away for a while, shipped somewhere to straighten out.

He doesn't know when it happened, he tells them. When he was infected with this false life. He just knows that this isn't right, this isn't who he is. He just knows that there's something else.

Every time his story runs off the rails he worries that they'll see through it, pick up on the missed connections, the dangling threads, but whenever he looks up from the table, lost and frustrated, Julian is looking back at him, nodding, holding his hands out, letting them rise and drop, telling Dickie, gently, to slow down.

They are always clean. Sarah's hair smells of coconut shampoo; Julian's face is freshly shaved. Dickie doesn't know where the showering and grooming take place. Somewhere up above. Every couple of days Julian lets Dickie back into the room with the drain, and Dickie washes himself with the hose and a bar of soap. The two folding chairs are gone, but the chair Dickie had been bound to remains. It sits in the middle of the room over the drain, straps hanging slack at its sides, waiting.

They all have a tattoo of the word *Sons* written in script across the inside of their right wrists, taken, Dickie guesses, from the Sons of Liberty, the secret resistance group in *Johnny Tremain*. Not a great idea, distinguishing-feature-wise, but it doesn't seem, from the way any of them talk, that they plan to be taken alive.

Sarah and Julian sometimes mention an *action* in vague, excited terms. Marching out to do battle, setting this whole place to burn behind them. When Dickie asks what this action is, when it will occur, they only smile, shake their heads. Patience, they say. Patience.

He tells his story many times. They want to hear it repeated. He is shocked by the level of detail he has conjured, frightened by this thing he's made. Sitting at the table in the storeroom, trying to get his hands and legs to stop trembling. Ashamed, embarrassed of what happened to him, what he says happened to him. Unable to speak further, to get enough air. He can feel the earth pressing into the walls, down onto the ceiling. His fingers up, trying to cover his face.

He can't breathe. Sarah leans forward, holds a couple of pills to his lips, places a hand on his back. Julian puts a hand on his arm. For a second Dickie is afraid that they have seen through his story, that they are going to take him back to that room. But they don't move, and he doesn't move. He simply sits shaking with their hands on him, with the earth pressing down, no story left to tell.

He wakes to find the shelter empty. There is no sign of Sarah or Julian. Walter's door is locked, the room with the drain is locked. The door at the end of the hall is open, though. He can see the stairway leading up. He sits at the table in the storeroom for much of the morning, drinking coffee, smoking, waiting. Listening for Walter to return, impressed that Dickie didn't take advantage of the open door. Some kind of test passed.

It's the sunlight that finally draws him from the room. A thin slice of white light, resting on the bottom step beyond the open door. Dickie leans into the stairwell, looks up. A pair of closed blast doors at the top, a slender gap between them, letting in the light. He climbs, places his hands against one of the doors, pushes. The stairwell floods with sun. He stands on the top step, the light and heat on his face, the air in his mouth, a drowning man breaking the surface, gasping.

He is on a hillside covered with long, dry grass. Acres of open land, nothing but a few eucalyptus trees on the horizon. A sharp taste in the air. Salt. The ocean is not far.

He turns to see a large house at the top of the slope. A facsimile of a Spanish villa, stucco walls and an orange tile roof. Wooden shutters on the windows, some open. Flower boxes beneath the sills, either empty or full of vegetative corpses.

The hill is not steep but the ground is rutted and uneven and he has not walked very far in a while. By the time he reaches the back patio he has to lean against a low wall to catch his breath. He can hear birds chirping in the distance. A faraway engine; a plane, maybe.

The patio doors are open, so he steps inside.

The room is cool and dark, and Dickie waits again for his eyes to adjust. A living room, with leather couches and armchairs, a glass coffee table, a large television. Art on the walls, landscapes, seascapes. Framed photographs on the top of the TV, faces coated with a film of dust. A man and a woman and two adolescent boys, a young, blond family, at a birthday party, at the beach, posed for a professional portrait, the husband and wife side by side, smiling, their hands on the shoulders of the children standing in front. One of the photos taken on the patio Dickie just came through, their backs to the doors of this room.

He walks up a few steps to the kitchen. There is a large dining room, a small bathroom. Everything is in its place but everything is untouched. The water in the toilet has been undisturbed for so long that it has made a thin green ring around the top of the bowl.

There is a driveway out the front window, empty, though a dark oil spot stains the cement, still wet, glistening in the sun. There's a gate at the end of the driveway, and a high wall that surrounds the property, blocking any view of the outside, any view in.

Dickie climbs the stairs to a long hallway. The first door is open to a master bedroom, dresser drawers hanging, bed unmade. Ransacked, looks like, in contrast to the stillness of the rest of the house. A struggle, maybe. A hurried departure. The master bathroom has been used. It is humid in the room, the mirror is partially fogged, the sink and vanity top wet. There's water on the floor of the walk-in shower. There are toothbrushes by the sink, bristles damp. Back out in the bedroom, there's a television on top of one of the jumbled dressers. Dickie sets his palm against the side of the set, feels the warmth of recent use.

He follows the hallway toward what he can sense is life in the house, movement in the dead space. Past a couple of guest rooms to an open door at the end of the hall. The boys' bedroom. Bunk beds against the wall, a pair of small desks, overoccupied bookshelves. Posters on the walls, sports cars and ballplayers. A plastic racetrack on the carpet, half assembled, with a line of waiting toy cars.

Sarah is sitting on the floor in an orange sundress, cross-legged, bare-foot, her back to Dickie, her hair still wet from the shower. She has a book in her lap, a pirate story, and she is reading it aloud, softly, pausing before turning each page to allow time for the brightly painted illustrations to be fully appreciated. Dickie looks farther in to see who Sarah is reading to, but she's alone in the room.

She turns a page, stops reading. "You can use the shower if you like," she says. "In the big bedroom. There are toothbrushes under the sink."

"Where's Walter?"

She gestures to the window, another view of the driveway, though this time Dickie can see over the wall, an empty stretch of road. "Getting supplies, gas for the generator."

"Where are the people who lived in this house?"

Sarah stands, crosses to the bookshelf, sliding the pirate story back between the other spines.

"You can come up here whenever you like," she says. "You have that right, now. We're not supposed to loiter, but I do, Julian does. I've seen him down in the living room, in the dining room. He's seen me, too, I'm sure. Sitting up here." She finds a book on the shelf, pulls it free. "Do you have any children, Hinkle?"

"No."

"Did you? In your false life?"

Dickie shakes his head.

"I wanted that baby so much," she says. "It wasn't real. I know it wasn't real. But it all seemed so beautiful sometimes."

Her dress is loose, low-cut, and there is something on her chest, a small mark revealed when the fabric gaps as she moves. She sees Dickie looking and steps closer, pulls the dress down to reveal the skin over her heart. Backward letters, small and black. A name in reverse. *Sarah*.

She turns and looks in the mirror hanging above one of the desks. "Julian did them," she says. "The tattoos on our wrists, and these. So we'll never forget. So they can't be taken from us again."

Dickie waited at the table in the storeroom, drinking the last of the coffee, working his way through another of the Zelinsky novels, more than a little worried that he was going to come across one about a guy sitting at a table in a bomb shelter storeroom, waiting, drinking coffee.

"Hinkle."

Dickie turned. Walter stood in the doorway, holding a long canvas duffel bag. The fabric strained with the weight of whatever was inside, the contents clanking when the bag shifted.

Out into the bright noontime to a wood-paneled station wagon parked in the driveway. Walter and Julian lifted a false floor from beneath the middle bench, secured the duffel within.

They headed east, a quick glimpse of the ocean disappearing behind another rising hill. Their house looked to be the only one in the area. Walter drove with Sarah beside him, Dickie and Julian in the back. They rode for the better part of an hour, through grassy hills, then marshes, flatlands. Finally, the outskirts of a city, Santa Ana, maybe, if Dickie remembered his Orange County maps correctly.

They stayed on the margins, wide streets and low-slung stucco houses, laundry strung between porch railings, drying in the motionless air. Climbing a ramp to the freeway, gaining speed as they continued east. Dickie watched what he could see of Walter's eyes from the backseat, Walter checking the rearview mirror, the side mirrors, then back out the windshield, a continuous, unbroken circuit.

Sarah played with the radio, settling on a station for a few seconds, a couple bars of music or half a commercial before turning the dial again.

Julian smoked and read through a small stack of maps, street-level sche-
matics for an urban area with the name of the city cut out, small rectan-
gular holes in the pages. No one spoke. Just the sound of the radio in the
car, Sarah singing quietly to the hook of an old song she recognized, an
appliance-store jingle.

They stopped for gas on the edge of the desert. Walter pumped and
Sarah went into the station and Dickie got out, stretched his legs. Julian
stayed in the car, looking at his maps.

Walter chewed a toothpick while he gripped the pump handle.
"When was the last time you fired a gun?"

Dickie watched his own reflection, distorted in the lenses of Walter's
sunglasses. "During the war."

"At anybody?"

Dickie shook his head.

Sarah came out of the station with a brown paper grocery bag. They
drove for another hour, past the last signs of civilization save the road
itself, and then they were off the road, Walter turning the wheel at some
marker Dickie didn't catch, out into the brown expanse, sand flying
from the tires, engulfing them in a miniature dust storm. Walter rolled
up his windows, lit a cigarette, hit the gas. The engine noise in the car
was terrific. Visibility out the windshield was near zero, as far as Dickie
could tell. Walter steered the wagon toward the one thing that could be
glimpsed through the dust, the purple silhouettes of mountains in the
distance. Sarah turned off the radio, set her head back, closed her eyes.
Julian paged through the folded squares of his maps, seemingly oblivious
to anything else.

Finally Walter cut the engine, let the wagon roll, the car burning
through the last of its speed. The dust and sand settled around them,
covering the windows. Walter popped the door latch, pushed it open.
Sarah followed him out. Julian refolded his maps, slid them into the
pocket behind the driver's seat, opened his door. Dickie, alone in the car,
realized that he'd been gripping his knees so tightly that it felt like he'd
left bruises. He unlatched his door but couldn't get it to budge. He finally
kicked it open, stepped outside.

They were in a vast, empty space. Nothing but sand, scattered cacti, scrub brush. There was no sign of the road, just the trail they'd created. The mountains looked even farther away than they had when Dickie had last seen them.

The sand was still falling, clinging to Dickie's beard, the hair on his arms.

Sarah lowered the back gate of the wagon, hopped up to sit, emptied the contents of the grocery bag beside her: bottles of soda and handfuls of candy bars. Walter and Julian removed the false floor, lifted out the duffel bag. They pulled out a picnic blanket, spread it across the ground, then unloaded the weapons, a pair of single-barrel shotguns modified to pistol grips and a couple of small-caliber handguns. Julian checked out the guns while Walter drank a soda, ate a candy bar at the back of the wagon. He brought a drink and a bag of M&M's over to Julian. Sarah motioned to Dickie and he joined her at the back of the car, made his choices of what was left.

Walter pulled a brace of broomsticks from the duffel, a stack of large paper targets, human-shaped. He walked out a few hundred feet, drove the broomsticks into the ground in a long line, fastened the targets to the sticks. Julian handed out foam earplugs. Sarah opened a box of ammunition, began loading one of the pistols. Walter returned and asked Dickie which he preferred. Dickie chose a pistol. Sarah slid over and showed him how to load the clip, check the safety. Walter and Julian fitted shells into the shotguns.

Just the muffled blasts with the earplugs in, a noise Dickie always associated with World War II submarine movies, the sound of depth charges underwater. He stood at the end of the firing row, trying to keep his arm straight, his head steady, all the things that Jack taught him in a not dissimilar landscape, the scrubby wasteland a half hour from the Oklahoma base, shooting at soup cans balanced on fence posts. Jack's hand under Dickie's elbow, his body pressed close behind, his voice from just above Dickie's left ear. *Steady, steady.* The quick muzzle flash, then the long, languid trail of gray smoke streaming from the barrel. *Steady, steady.* Everything slow, the world halted around them. The soup cans glinting in the sun, labels peeled down to the ribbed tin flesh. *Steady.* The bang and flash and smoke, the jolt in the arm. Jack's hand at his elbow. The smell of the gun, like the burn of some distant fire.

"You grew up shooting," Walter said. "I can tell." He had come up behind Dickie, stood looking out at the pockmarked targets. "You shoot like a kid. That's good. The army teaches you all sorts of bullshit about firing a weapon. Overtrains you. A kid with a gun, though."

When it was too dark to shoot they sat on the back gate of the station wagon and ate a dinner of candy bars and soda in the light from the dome lamps. Sarah went around to the front of the car, took a small shortwave radio from the glove box. Julian produced a baggie of pills and she joined him out past the light of the station wagon, disappearing into the darkness. Dickie could hear the radio come to staticky life, the smear of noise and voices as the tuner moved across the dial.

Walter opened another candy bar, peeled the wrapper, took a bite.

"Why banks?" Dickie said.

"Easy money."

"Money for what?"

Walter looked at the chocolate on his fingers. "It's still too early, Hinkle. You don't need to know anything yet."

Dickie walked out through the halo of the car's light into the darkness of the desert. The sky was pinpricked with stars, but there was no moon, so the station wagon seemed to float in its own glow the farther he went. He followed the faint static sound until he found Sarah and Julian sitting in the dust, sharing a cigarette, the radio in Sarah's lap, illuminating their faces from below.

She looked up and smiled when she saw him. Dickie sat down.

Sarah passed him the baggie and Dickie felt around inside for a familiar shape. Julian was checking his watch in the meager light. After a while he said, "Ready, ready," and Sarah turned up the volume on the shortwave. They sat listening to the white noise for a while, and then Dickie heard something else, a high screech coming through the static, getting louder, breaking apart into what sounded like a telegraph, a flurry of high-pitched electronic tones.

A woman's voice, then, German-accented, saying, "Ready? Ready?"

"It's Olga," Julian said.

Sarah smiled. The woman recited a long string of numbers, then repeated the sequence. Hard to tell if this was a live broadcast or a recording. The sound quality was bad, swimming in all that static. Sarah and Julian watched the radio, enraptured, as the woman spoke.

Dickie listened to the voice, looked up at the stars, back to the glow of the station wagon, Walter's dark figure sitting on the back gate. The pills were kicking in, and his nerves began to settle, the lingering jumpiness from the gunfire, the claustrophobia of the earplugs.

"*Six, nine, six,*" the woman said. "*Six, nine, six, eight, three, three, five. Finis.*"

There was another blast of the telegraph tones and then the static wave retook the frequency.

Sarah lowered the volume. "We call her Olga. There's Olga and there's Gretchen, a few others. There's a man sometimes, and once we heard a little boy. Julian thinks they're a lost family."

"Sarah thinks they're aliens," Julian said. He stood and stretched, uncomfortable, maybe, with sharing whatever moment this was with Dickie.

"I'd like to find a way to send a message back," Sarah said. "Whoever they are. Just so they know that someone can hear them. Julian's working on it, a radio we can use to broadcast back to their location."

A door of the station wagon slammed shut and they all turned. Walter had closed the back gate, was walking around to the driver's side. Dickie stood and gave Sarah a hand, pulled her to her feet. She turned the radio off and they all walked back toward the car.

18

She worked in her studio. She took the picture of Henry down from its wall, regretting her decision to display it, feeling that she had left her memory of him exposed, endangered. When the photographer of the cabaret photos came to pick up his work, Hannah asked him about the subjects, hoping for more about the man who'd come into the gallery. He told her that he didn't know anything about the performers, that everything he knew was in the photographs.

I know this man. This man worked for my father.

She was not sure what to do with this information. She wasn't even sure that it *was* information, that it was anything more than mistaken identity or muddled memory. She buried it in work, but it surfaced again, late at night, while she watched the chess match on TV. Fischer's hands and face on the screen and Hannah looking at her father in the Merchants Exchange photograph. The white ghost.

There was no response from Oakland. She called every night, and then began to call again in the mornings, but there was nothing, just the faraway sound of the unanswered ring.

The coastal drive was prettier, but the route up the heart of the state was faster, so she pushed Bert's car north through the garlic ranches and cattle farms and flat acres of brittle yellow grass; hot, dry country that seemed more desert than the desert itself. She stopped only for gas and coffee. The panic had set in as soon as she'd made the decision to go, and now she couldn't get there fast enough, regretted turning down Bert's offer of a plane ticket and asking instead only for one of his cars.

It was late afternoon when she arrived. The familiar house on the hill. A few of the surrounding houses were still occupied by the same neighbors, though much of the area had long gone to seed, gotten harder, poorer, sending most of the families they'd known, what was left of those families, fleeing to the suburbs.

Hannah parked in the driveway behind the station wagon, looked at the lawn, the weeds towering above the unkempt grass. Patches of dandelion, goldenrod, a few soda and beer bottles half buried in the overgrowth at the edges. The unkempt bushes like great shaggy beasts squatting at the front of the house. The bay windows covered by the same curtains Ginnie kept closed tight against the afternoon sun, what she'd always worried were prying eyes.

Hannah felt sick. She feared who would answer a knock on the door, the Ginnie and Thomas that lived in this house. One of them ill, possibly. Both of them ill. Hannah's neglect made glaringly physical, something she had to walk through, broken glass and candy wrappers, flattening a path through the grass to the door.

There was no answer from the doorbell, so she worked her way through the bushes, stood at the windows with her hands cupped to the filthy glass, trying to peer through thin gaps in the curtains, looking for movement, changes in the shadows. She kept turning back to her mother's car, which looked decidedly inert, like it hadn't been driven in months.

"Hannah?"

There was an old woman standing at the edge of the lawn, indistinct, turned into a dark silhouette by the setting sun over her shoulder. Hannah shaded her eyes, stumbled out from the bushes, approached from a lower angle.

"Hannah, honey, is that you?"

The woman was wearing a terry cloth housecoat and soiled white slippers. She was unhealthily thin, her arms and legs little more than sticks wrapped in paperweight skin, the veins in her calves swollen and bruise-purple.

"It's Mrs. Sullivan. Doris Sullivan, from across the street. I haven't seen you in I don't know how long, Hannah."

Hannah hadn't recognized her, still didn't recognize her. This woman on the edge of the lawn was a sepulchral version of the poised and refined woman Hannah had known. A childhood ghost.

Doris said, "You've come for the house?"

"I'm sorry?"

"I'm afraid selling it will be easier said than done. This is no longer the neighborhood it once was."

Selling it. Hannah looked at the station wagon, the weeds growing up through the driveway at the base of the tires. Looked back at the house.

Doris's hand went to the collar of her robe. "Oh, Hannah, I'm so sorry. How foolish of me. You didn't know."

Hannah placed a hand on the dusty hood of the station wagon, giving the car some of her weight.

"When?" she said.

"Some months ago," Doris said. "We'd called the police because Dick saw someone snooping around the house. They went in and found her. She had passed. I wasn't able to do much. Dick hasn't been well for some time, and we've been in and out of the hospital. I told them that she had a daughter, but I couldn't remember where. San Diego?"

"Los Angeles."

Doris nodded, remembering, the nod ending but the movement continuing, a Parkinsonian echo. "They may not have known how to find you."

Hannah could feel the drive's coffee rising, burning into her chest, her throat.

"Where's Thomas?"

Doris licked her bottom lip, released the collar of her robe, letting her hands drop to her sides. That little tremor, that little nod.

"Oh, honey, I thought he was with you."

There was a spare key under one of the stones in the backyard. Hannah had hidden it there as a teenager for nights when she had lost her own key out on some adventure, though in the few instances when she'd used it, she'd let herself in only to find Ginnie sitting at the table in the dark dining room, smoking, waiting.

The house was cold. There was a damp, musty odor coming from the kitchen. She stepped inside, water pooling around her shoes.

There was a leak under the sink that had spread across the floor, rotting sections of the linoleum, the bottoms of the cabinets. Maybe a quarter inch of standing water. Dishes in the sink, the baby-blue decorative plate patterns Hannah had grown up with. Dishes on the counters, cups, open boxes of cereal. Bugs everywhere, crawling down the sides of the cabinets, drowning themselves on the floor in a mindless frenzy to find what food was left.

It was dark in the house, but she was afraid to touch a light switch with all the water. She sloshed into the dining room, the table piled high with newspapers, unopened mail, advertising circulars. Every chair covered, most of the floor. Invoices, bank letters, medical bills.

Back into the bedrooms, more of the mess, more clothes, more food. Every one of her mother's dresses had been pulled from her closet and laid across the floor in her bedroom. Every piece of jewelry laid out in the hall, as if a trail to somewhere, or a remembrance. Thomas. This would make sense to Thomas. His room was the worst of all. The open cans of food and the bugs and the smell. Hannah retreated, closing the door behind her. And then her room, untouched, relatively, except for an imprint on the bedspread, a body at rest, long, wide. Hannah sat on the edge of the bed, lay down inside the hole Thomas had left.

*   *   *

She filed a missing persons report, almost a year too late. She described Thomas and the police officer wrote *history of mental illness* on the report. The officer asked questions, an incredulous tone in his voice, unable to believe the level of Hannah's neglect. She hadn't known that her mother was dead, that her brother was missing. She looked over the high front counter to the officers' desks beyond. They all had framed photos of wives, kids, mothers. They kept their families close.

The church had handled the burial. She visited the graveyard, the small stone at the head of the plot, a cross and Ginnie's name inscribed. Hannah brought nothing. Flowers seemed obscene. She came with only a useless apology, whispered to the dirt, too late.

The police told her to go back to L.A. and wait. Because of his postcards, she knew that Thomas had her address, and he might try to contact her there. She returned Bert's car when she was sure he wouldn't be home. The idea of explaining what she had let happen, and what Bert would think of her, rightfully, was too much.

She was an orphan now. She had been an orphan for some time and just hadn't known it.

In her mother's bedroom she'd found a few paintings. She'd forgotten that her mother painted. Hand-stretched canvases, slashed and speckled with color. Beautiful things. She'd only ever thought of her mother's painting as a weapon to use during their arguments, evidence that Ginnie had given up.

She didn't speak to anyone. She didn't call Bert. She kept Ginnie's paintings against a wall in her studio. She felt that she needed to work there with the canvases, to acknowledge them, at least, their existence.

She tried to picture Thomas, where he could be, and every possibility was worse than the last. Everything she could imagine was a horror.

She hung a new show in the gallery. She watched the chess match. She stayed close, listened for the phone, jumped out of her skin when she heard someone outside the front door. She went running at night, not far, not long, just enough to get herself outside and moving. She ran with a loose-limbed gait, no grace, no rhythm. Pain in her knees and a burning wheeze in her lungs. She was smoking too much, drinking too much. Crying while she ran, sometimes, tears streaking laterally into her ears from the speed and the wind.

Whenever she saw a homeless man she slowed to look at his face. There were so many, sleeping in doorways, on benches, pushing shopping carts clattering with scavenged tin cans. But none of them was Thomas, none of them had the face she was looking for.

She didn't run far, or for very long. She didn't want to be away from the studio. She stayed by the phone, by the door, waiting for a call, a knock, a sudden appearance. A lost voice calling her name.

19

They sat in the station wagon a few blocks from the bank. Just after lunchtime; a bleached, high-sunned afternoon. There was a decent amount of foot traffic on the sidewalks, office workers returning from restaurants, taco stands, ice cream carts, alone and in couples and trios, dyspeptic and heavy-lidded. Walter said this was the best time for a job, right after lunch, when everyone was sleepy, slow, stupid.

On the drive in from the bomb shelter, Walter had briefed Dickie on the bank's layout, the positions of the two guards, the manager, the vault. He and Julian had watched the location for weeks. Julian and Sarah were already out in the city, looking for a truck or a van, which they'd steal and park near the bank. Walter and Dickie would join them at the entrance, hitting the doors just as one of the guards was reopening after lunch.

Walter shook a few pills out of a baggie into Dickie's palm, into his own. He handed Dickie a mask. Dickie shoved it into his jacket pocket, shoved his pistol in alongside. They unlatched their doors and stepped out. Walter looked around, sunlight glinting on the metal frames of his sunglasses, flashing off the lenses. A white plumber's van sat around the corner from the bank. Dickie could see Sarah and Julian in the front seat.

And then they were moving, Walter first, Dickie following, walking fast, heads down, Walter's shotgun revealed and then hidden again beneath the flapping skirts of his black duster.

The pills began to kick in. The world sharpened: the building entrances, the cars, pedestrians in the crosswalk. An incredible clarity. Everything had a defined edge, separate and distinct from everything around it. Every sound separate, able to be plucked out, examined. Dickie could zero in, focus on whatever he chose. Details of faces, minutiae, shaving nicks and old acne scars and bubbles of spit on chins. His muscles relaxed, his hands, his knees. He and Walter crossed the street, calm, focused, moving though the slow-motion world.

They joined Sarah and Julian at the front doors of the bank. Julian in the same black duster Walter wore, his shotgun at his side. No one batted an eyelash at their approach. Walter had been right. If you moved deliberately, with purpose, you could cross a city street carrying just about anything.

They pulled their masks from their coats and jackets, characters from a long-forgotten TV cartoon that Walter had searched for in junk shops. A panda, a pig, a cat, a dog. A detail Dickie had read first in one of Zelinsky's novels.

Walter in his panda mask was the first through the door, shotgun pointed straight ahead. Julian the pig followed. Sarah the cat, Dickie the dog. There were three customers at the counter, three tellers, the two guards, the manager behind a desk by the windows. Dickie could see everything, even in the stuffy confines of the mask. Could hear everything, smell everything. His own smoky breath. He was amazed at how long it took anyone to notice the guns. This is a robbery. No one even had to say the magic words. Julian chained the front doors together. Dickie took aim at the closer of the two guards, a thin, wiry man, Jack's age. What would have been Jack's age. A woman at the counter screamed. Walter spoke for the first time, his shotgun leveled at the younger guard's forehead.

Everyone on your hands and knees on the ground.

The assumption was that the alarm would be triggered within seconds of their entrance. There was nothing they could do about the alarm. They'd be in and out before it could be a factor.

They took the guards' revolvers from their holsters. Julian jumped over the counter and instructed the tellers to fill his bag. Sarah kept her pistol trained on the kneeling customers. Dickie watched the door, the older guard.

Walter steered the younger guard and the manager back toward the vault. The manager fumbled with his keys and Walter prodded him in the back with the shotgun. Dickie glanced at the clock on the wall behind the counter. Just minutes, that was all that had gone by. So fast, everything so fast.

Stay down. Sarah shouting, thrusting her pistol at one of the women on the floor. Her cat mask wide-eyed, wide-grinned.

Walter was in the vault with the manager and the younger guard. Julian worked his way down the line of tellers, tossed a full bag over the top of the partition. It landed on the floor by Sarah's shoes. She kicked it back toward Dickie. Dickie crouched to pick it up, keeping his gun on the older guard.

Something flashed out the front windows. Dickie glanced. Just the sun off the hood of a passing car. More passing cars, people on the street. A woman and a young boy walking by, hand in hand, oblivious to what was transpiring on the other side of the glass. That day out there; this day in here.

Dickie looked back and the older guard was watching him from the floor. Dickie could see the fear on the man's face, the revulsion, the indignity. Staring at the smiling dog mask. Dickie fought the urge to shout something, to tell the man to look away.

Walter was out of the vault, carrying a full duffel. He'd left the manager and younger guard locked inside. Julian came around the counter to take the bag. Sarah moved from customer to customer, shouting at them to turn their heads while she pushed copies of Javier Buñuel's tracts into their pockets and purses.

Walter and Julian were at the door, unwinding the chain. Dickie looked at the clock. Another couple of minutes had passed. Nothing. This was like nothing.

Movement on the floor. The older guard was getting to his feet. He stared into the eyes of Dickie's mask as he stood. Defiant. Shamed into

defiance. The guard turned to Walter and Julian at the door, their backs
to him. Dickie pointed his gun at the guard. The guard had a gun, too,
somehow, a small pistol in his right hand. They'd pulled the revolver
from his holster but he'd had this on him somewhere, hidden. An old
pro. Julian was having trouble with the chain at the door. The guard
lifted his gun. Dickie shouted, but his voice died in the mask. The guard
took aim at Walter's back. Dickie shouted again, pulled the trigger. The
guard's knee disappeared. He folded, clutched. Everyone turned. The
guard rolled on the floor, grasping and moaning, a red explosion on
the tile beneath his leg.

Walter turned, looked at Dickie, looked down at the guard. Walked
back into the room and stood over the crippled old man. The dead eyes
of the panda mask, looking down, showing nothing, but Dickie could
see Walter's contempt in the cocked slant in his posture. He pointed his
shotgun, fired.

Out on the street, the roomful of screams behind them, into the open
air and the noise of the city, distant sirens, Julian and Sarah peeling off to
the plumber's van with the bags, Dickie following Walter, watching the
back of his duster as they crossed the streets to the station wagon.

Walter started the car, pulled the jug of gasoline out of the backseat,
doused the interior. He put the car in gear and they pushed it out into
the street, got it going as Walter lit a match, tossed it in through the open
window. The plumber's van came around the corner and Dickie and
Walter jumped into the back, the van turning, and they watched out the
back windows, the flaming wagon like a Viking funeral boat sailing into
midday traffic, and everything—the burning car, the onlookers' faces,
their eyeballs and fingers—pointing in one direction as the Sons of Liberty go, are gone, into the other.

20

Spring 1971

They'd driven from the office park, the explosion still ringing in their ears, Mary Margaret and Dickie in a small sedan, Dale and the rest of the crew packed into a VW bus. A serpentine route away from Portland until they reached the woods, the cabin deep within. When they were sure they weren't being followed, they ditched the cars and ran the rest of the way through the trees, jubilant and adrenalized, trying to contain themselves until they were all inside, the doors and windows closed, and then there was a celebratory release, shouting and cheering, hugging, kissing, beer passed, joints lit. There was nothing like seeing something blown up. They were now at war. They thought this was what war was like.

One of the kids found a news station on the radio, and they all circled around, waiting for a live bulletin to interrupt the somnolent Sunday-morning broadcast, a "This Just In" that would reshape the public conversation. An engineering facility bombed, records destroyed, secret ties to the military complex exposed.

Dickie stood in the living room doorway with Mary Margaret. She took his hand, fingers squeezing, pressure and warmth, anticipation.

The bulletin came, finally. Shushing in the rooms, throughout the small cabin. They all crowded around the speaker, expectant smiles spreading wide.

Dickie remembers the exact words from the newsman: *There is a casualty.* The jubilation drained from the room, water let out of a bath-tub. An unidentified male, the newsman said. The authorities are wait-ing to confirm his identity, to notify his family before any other details can be given.

One of the girls was the first to cry out, *No, No,* an insistence directed at the radio, and then others followed, yelling, sobbing, or simply stand-ing in shock, their hands on their heads, on their mouths.

Some of the guys started to yell for Dickie. This had been his idea, and they wanted to know what he had to say for himself. He left Mary Margaret, steered Dale into the bedroom, shut the door behind them. They were both breathing hard. They were holding hands somehow, like little kids in trouble. Dale asked Dickie if he'd known, and Dickie told him the truth: he'd had no idea anyone would be at the office. And then he told Dale that he had to get everyone out, get everyone away. Dickie could promise them an hour, at most. Dale asked what Dickie was talk-ing about and Dickie said, *I'm not who you think I am.*

He moved through the rooms like a sleepwalker while Dale shouted instructions, everyone packing what they could carry, some of them screaming at Dickie, calling him a fink, a rat, a Judas. Someone took a swing, cuffing Dickie in the ear before Dale pulled the guy away.

Through all the commotion, he found Mary Margaret by the front door on the other side of the room. Her eyes down, her arms at her sides. She looked like she was going to be sick. Dickie couldn't think of what to say, any kind of explanation. Out of words for the first time he could remember. He could still feel her hand in his from the moment before, when they'd stood in the doorway listening to the news.

He was shoved to the side then, by a couple of guys carrying boxes. When he stumbled upright again and looked toward the door she was gone.

21

Summer 1972

"Your name is Richard John Ashby. That is your true name, your only name."

Walter stood before the inverted flag in the storeroom. Sarah sat with the cat on her lap, the low light softening her features, the beatific expression.

"All other names are gone from you," Walter said. "All other lives. There is only this name, this life."

Julian sat with his needle and ink, moving the point along the inside of Dickie's wrist.

Dickie didn't know how long it had been since he'd had a drink. He hadn't taken the Antabuse since Hollywood and he could feel it gone from his system, the void left behind. He wanted a drink or a pill. The first thing he would do when his hand was free would be to dig into his pockets for a pill.

"There is only this truth, one truth, absolute," Walter said. "You no longer have to guess, or wonder, or believe. You no longer have to remember. You only have to know."

The guard had looked at Dickie and Dickie had let him stand, let him turn and point his gun. There was the guard on the floor of the bank and the engineer in Portland on the floor of his office. There was Dale in the seat of the crashed car. There was Mary Margaret.

The cat jumped down from Sarah's lap, slunk around the corner, out of the room.

Dickie felt like he could kill someone for a drink, a way to sleep.

Julian lifted the needle, the last drop of ink clinging to the point, thick as syrup. The hot sting on the reddened skin of Dickie's wrist.

"There is only this," Walter said.

Sons.

He followed Walter across the dark yard to the house. The night was cool and damp. The tattoo on his wrist still burned, and the change in temperature felt soothing on his skin.

Walter switched on a lamp in the living room. He had been carrying something covered in brown butcher's paper, and now he unwrapped what looked like a leather-bound accounting ledger. Dark, soft from age, its covers gouged and stained.

"This is something you must read alone," Walter said. "That we have all read alone." He passed the ledger to Dickie. "This is the Old Testament. You deserve to know where you came from."

Dickie's first instinct, after Walter had gone, was to run, to take this thing or leave this thing and go out the front door, down to the gate, jump the fence, running until he found civilization again, streetlights and stoplights, gas stations, restaurants, people on sidewalks. But that was crazy, that was impossible. There was nowhere to run, unless he continued past the wall and across the highway, down the slope to the sand and water. That was the only place, if he went out far enough, deep enough, his body sinking, his head, his mouth, his nose. Another hood pulled over his face. That was the only place he could go if he didn't want to run anymore.

The first few pages of the ledger recounted some kind of road trip in minute detail. Towns, distances driven, amounts paid for food and lodging. Then there were pages of what seemed like photographic instructions, or maybe a log of techniques—apertures, shutter and film speeds.

Dickie kept turning. He found columns of a man's name written again and again, first in what seemed like a natural signature, then modified, repeatedly, the height and slant of the letters, signature after signature, working toward the simple, elusive feel of a name resting comfortably on the page.

Dickie knew what this was. He'd done the same thing himself. Getting a new name on paper, in his fingertips, his hand, his body. Assuming a new identity. In the first few pages of the ledger, this man was becoming someone else.

Henry Gladwell Henry Gladwell Henry Gladwell Henry Gladwell.

More pages, bureaucratic bookkeeping: a requisition list, apartment floor plans, neat columns of expenses and reimbursements. But further into the ledger a kind of personal shorthand took over, maybe a code of some sort. The things that Henry Gladwell didn't understand, or that he was learning, were written out, only to be abbreviated later, once he had internalized them. Chemical names and measurements, milligrams and micrograms, dosages, onset times. Dates and names, or parts of names, fragments, descriptions of men, approximate heights and weights, ethnicity, occupation, demeanor.

Dickie recognized nearly all the drug names, could picture the doses. This was an area of personal expertise.

Clyde from Buffalo. Ernest from El Paso. Lonnie from San Francisco. Each man given a page, sometimes more than one. Prosaic details, physical descriptions, scraps of conversation, and then a chemical name and dosage and onset time and then, finally, the shorthand description of nightmare after nightmare.

15 July 1956. 18 July 1956. Subject Negro male, late thirties. Subject Caucasian male, approx. early fifties. What was done to these men. The things that were done. Dickie read, his hands wet, his heart stuttering an irregular rhythm. It felt like he was choking, the horror of the ledger compounded with the horror of the day, sitting in his stomach, his throat.

Subject transient. Subject alcoholic. Subject known schizophrenic.

There were appearances by others. A doctor called C. A monster called D who tortured the men for hours, attempting to gain information that was never recorded, at least not into the ledger. Henry Gladwell had not been interested in that information, only the methods of its extraction.

Subject has forgotten name. Subject has forgotten biography. Subject given different name and biography. Subject answering to new name consistently. Subject able to answer questions about new biography, elaborate on details.

D entered the room. D entered the room.

Dickie was sitting on the sofa with the ledger closed on his lap when he realized Walter had returned, had been back for some time, maybe, standing in the dark doorway.

Dickie cleared his throat. "Where did you get this?"

"Robert Zelinsky is one of the men in that book."

"Where did he get it?"

"Does it matter? It exists. It is here. It can be exposed, brought into the light."

"It could be fake," Dickie said. "It could be fiction."

"Are you fake, Richard?" Walter looked around the room. "Is this? Are we?"

"No one would know what to make of this."

"Not without proof, no. Not without corroboration."

"You have proof?"

"We have the means of acquiring it."

In Walter's hand was another ledger, newer, but otherwise nearly identical to the first.

"This is the New Testament," Walter said. "This is where I record the stories of the children of that first book. My story, Sarah's, Julian's, yours. There are others. Some alone, some in groups like ours. Up the coast, inland, out in the mountains. A group right across the Canadian border. We've been outfitting these groups, weapons bought with the bank money. A redistribution of wealth."

Walter stepped into the room. "There is a hospital up north. Many of our brothers and sisters are children of that facility. Some of the doctors are still there. The same rooms, maybe the same machines. We won't know until we get there."

"And then what?"

"Then we make so much blood and noise that we will be impossible to ignore."

Dickie opened the ledger again, turned to the pages covered with *Henry Gladwell,* the name chanted, repeated in columns.

Walter said, "The man who wrote that book, who kept those notes, was named Henry March. That was his true name."

"Where is he?"

"I don't know."

"But you've been looking for him."

"Since the day I first read the book."

"And?"

"There is a woman living in Los Angeles," Walter said. "A photographer. Her name is Hannah March."

"His wife?"

"His daughter."

"How do you know?"

"We have eyes. We have as many eyes as they do. Some of us are not in groups. Some of us are out in the world, watching."

"You think she knows where her father is."

Walter shrugged. "We'll have to find out."

"You want to take her."

"Yes."

"Just like that. Off the street."

"Yes."

"A hood and some drugs and that room."

"It's what we know."

Dickie stood. He was still holding the ledger, his fingertips pressed into the soft leather. He turned to the window, the blackness at the front of the house. Somewhere out there was the wall and the slope and the water.

"Let me do it," Dickie said.

"What?"

"If something goes wrong with her, you'll never get to him."

"Nothing will go wrong."

"If we get caught dragging her off the street—"

"We won't get caught. We haven't gotten caught."

"Not yet."

Dickie watched their reflections in the window, Walter chewing his bottom lip, pulling loose a thin sliver of skin.

"This is what I do," Dickie said.

Walter's eyes were on the ledger in Dickie's hand, then up to Dickie's eyes in the window.

"You don't trust me," Dickie said.

Walter shook his head. "We are brothers. I would be dead if it wasn't for you."

Dickie turned, looked at Walter. "Then let me go."

22

The lock on the door to his flophouse room was gone. The Zelinsky books, his pills, his cash. The Sons had taken it all before they'd caught him, or a neighbor at the hotel had taken it. Dickie wasn't sure it mattered. He wanted to lie down but he couldn't lie down. Someone would find him. The room was empty, but its smell was still there, maybe his smell, what he'd smelled like before. Something familiar. He wanted to stay in the room. This room was the last safe place he'd been.

He walked past an all-night newsstand and tried to stop himself from looking at the headlines. He didn't want to see a name, a face. It was there, though. He looked and it was there. The white, aged face that had looked up from the floor of the bank, the guard lifting his hands, feebly, shaking them at the wrists, trying to erase something. Walter standing over him in the mask, with the gun.

Walter had insisted Dickie take a pistol with him, ammunition. Dickie found a paper bag on the street and shoved the weapon inside, dug a hole under a freeway overpass, hands pulling at the dirt, burying his treasure.

At a bar on Highland Avenue he sidled up to an old woman sitting alone, talked with her so she'd buy him drinks. He could feel the alcohol filling the space the Antabuse had left behind. When the woman got up to use the bathroom, he reached into her purse, took the cash folded within, left the bar and found another, began drinking again.

An hour before dawn, he made his way out onto the street, the phone booth at the corner. The glass was smeared with handprints, streaks of bodily fluids. A sepia carpet of cigarette butts covered the floor. He smoked while he dialed the number, adding his own ash to the layers below.

There was a teenager waiting for the light to change on the opposite curb, a black kid in a hooded sweatshirt, a skateboard under his arm, bobbing his head to some interior sound track. Sliding his feet, turning them at the ankles and scuffling across the sidewalk, one pace, two, then standing, then dancing again to something only he could hear.

"Bill."

"Dickie? Where the hell have you been?"

"I need to know if a name means anything to you."

"What?"

"I need to give you a name."

"Dickie, you sound drunk."

"Henry March," Dickie said.

"Dickie—"

"Did you hear me?"

"Henry March," Bill said.

The light changed and the dancing kid crossed the empty street, walking normally, then bobbing and shuffling in quick bursts.

Bill said, "I don't know who that is."

"Are you lying to me?"

"Why would I lie to you?"

"About any of this?"

"Dickie, you don't sound well."

The kid hopped up onto the curb as the light changed back. Bobbing, his eyes closed, listening, then his eyes open, locked on Dickie for a second before he shuffled away.

We have eyes, Walter had said. We have as many eyes as they do.

Dickie could barely hear his own whisper in the receiver.

"Bill, I am not well."

He could hear another voice on Bill's end of the call, muffled, distant. Someone else in Bill's office, or a cross connection, another listener somewhere, a ghost in the line.

"We know about the robbery in Irvine," Bill said. "The robbery and the murder. They're looking for four suspects."

Dickie let the last of his cigarette fall from his fingers, explode into powder on the floor.

Bill said, "How many of them are there in this group?"

Dickie licked his lips, nauseous, dizzy. He looked at the handprints on the phone booth glass, waited for that kid to pop out at any second, bobbing, shuffling, watching.

Bill said, "Dickie, there used to be three."

He uses the last of his change to get on a bus, heading north, then east across the city, the morning sun topping the hills, throwing light across the dry yellow slopes, the gray freeways cutting between. He rides longer than he needs to, changing buses, sitting with his head against the window, keeping an eye on everyone who gets aboard.

He couldn't find the Cutlass. Either the Cutlass was stolen or towed or the Sons took the Cutlass or he just can't remember where he'd parked it.

He has an address on the northeast side of the city. He has a photograph of a woman about his own age. She's tall, thin. Her face is partially concealed by a camera as she takes a picture of a couple of runaways smoking against the outside wall of a post office.

He gets off on a long boulevard just shy of Pasadena, an east–west storefront strip crammed with liquor stores, clothing shops, Mexican restaurants. Late morning, the sun high and bright. His eyes and mouth are dry. He reaffixes his sunglasses. He needs a drink.

The address is a building kitty-corner from where he's standing, what looks like a small gymnasium, maybe, a green concrete box with a high domed roof. He has no plan. He did not spend the previous night getting a new name into his mouth, a new history into his head. He does not currently have that capacity, despite what he told Walter.

He could still run. He is out in the world and maybe they are watching him but he could still try to run, screaming in the daylight. But that would mean leaving this woman. It would mean letting the Sons take this woman, knowing what they will do to her.

Dickie touches the edge of the photo with a lit match, watches it curl and burn, the flame licking down to the tips of his fingers.

He needs a drink. If he has a drink, or two, he can pull himself together. There's a bar across the street. There's always a bar. Looks like a Mexican pool hall. There's always a bar and there's always someone inside to talk to, to flatter and charm, someone whose desperation for company matches his own desperation for a drink. An even exchange, maybe. Almost even.

He steps into the crosswalk. He sees the car but there is nothing he can do. He is hungover and lumbering and single-mindedly eyeing that bar. The car swings around the corner, nailing Dickie in the hip, spinning him, then hitting his opposite knee for good measure. Dickie rolls up onto the hood and then off the side, dropping hard to the asphalt, the car slowing, briefly, then speeding off down the boulevard, burning rubber as it goes.

Traffic stops. Dickie is curled on the street, rolling a little with the pain and shock. There's a man standing over him, speaking in Spanish. Dickie hears *hospital* and *ambulancia* and tries to shake his head but the pain in his neck stops that effort, so he croaks out a few words, *No hospital*, shit, Jesus, that's the last thing he needs. He really just wants to lie here, on the street, in the sun. Feels like he could sleep, actually. But then the man grabs him under the arms and someone else has his ankles and they lift him with considerable effort, carrying him across the street and depositing him on a bus-stop bench.

Dickie curls up, sucking air at the pain in his ribs, then grimacing at the pain caused by sucking air. His knee is throbbing, feels volleyball size. The high green wall of the gym, March's daughter's place, looms over the back of the bench. The man who was speaking has his hand on

Dickie's shoulder, and Dickie nods, letting him off the hook, free to go about the rest of his day.

He's alone again on the bench, eyes closed. He can hear people come and go, waiting for the bus. Can hear traffic on the boulevard, engines idling at the light, radios through open windows. He keeps his eyes shut tight, his body curled as closely as he can. He sleeps, finally, submits to sleep, fearful of what he will find there, but unable to keep his eyes open any longer.

PART THREE

Gerontion

1

There's no such thing as a quick piss anymore. A painless piss. Instead, there's a broken, lurching stream that strikes the water in the bowl, the rim of the toilet, the surrounding tile floor. Instead, there's a rising burn in the space just behind his balls, the *perineum,* a word he learned from his urologist, radiating into his ass and down his legs, hardening to a serious ache, weakening his knees. Just enough time to shake and flush and wipe up the splattered piss before he has to steady himself by holding the edge of the vanity, fingertips pushing into the marble in time with the dull throb in the lower half of his body.

He used to take grim satisfaction at the urinals of the golf club, the line of men making similar groans, the pitiful sound of their familiar Morse-code streams. He could feel that he was part of a natural aging process, humiliating but unavoidable, the depreciation of equipment. There was comfort there, but now he has passed them all, he is so far beyond, leaning against the sink in his own bathroom, breathing hard, sweating from the top of his head, hot pokers in his balls, his ass, his perineum.

He won't go back to his doctor. He knows what the offered steps will be, the course of treatment. He is familiar with the course of treatment, what it did to Elaine. He's unwilling to go down that road again.

There's an old man in the mirror, creased and pink and bald. It's three o'clock on Saturday and his eyes are already red-rimmed with booze. He steadies himself with both hands on the vanity, knuckles white with wispy hair. He feels like the mountains in which the house sits. He has gone white and hard like them, old and still.

The house is quiet. Just the sound of the TV in the living room. Normally he would hear Jayne moving through the rooms, gathering laundry, vacuuming, humming a hymn from last Sunday's service. But she's gone for the week, down to Savannah, shopping and sightseeing with some girlfriends, so he is alone in the house.

The game has started again, flashing hot across the big screen in the living room. He bites his lip and settles back onto the edge of the leather chair. He forgot to refill his bourbon. His glass is nothing but ice and piss-yellow water. The team is down by six. The coaches and bench players mill on the sidelines, looking mystified. They've lost the thread. They took their eyes from the field for a moment and it was a different game when they looked back. It can happen so quickly, he knows this, and it's nothing more than sloppy coaching, poor leadership. You can never take your eyes off the field.

The TV was a concession on Jayne's part when they built the house. An incongruous mass, squatting fat and loud in the living room among the clean, spare lines, the bright color screen pushing against the lean austerity of the rest of the house, the white walls and exposed beams, Jayne's gray paintings of Shaker women at work. She knew she could have whatever she wanted when it came to designing the house, the checkbook would be open, the criticism would be muted, as long as he had something to watch college football on Saturday afternoons.

The night before, he'd sat out on the back porch with some men from the club, not friends, necessarily, men from the club, retired business execs and town councilmen, fellow golfers. Drinking, flinging bullshit, a few getting drunk quickly and then getting loud, roaring into the night. He'd joined in at times, laughing when appropriate, but mostly he'd sat in Jayne's rocking chair watching the town in the valley far below, listening to the wind. The last men left late, almost two in the morning by the clock on the stove, and he'd emptied the ashtrays and dishes of mixed nuts, washed the tumblers, poured himself a final bourbon, walking through the empty house, touching railings, replacing chairs at the dining room table, straightening the pictures on the walls.

He doesn't sleep well when Jayne is gone. He reads until his eyes burn, a maritime novel set during the Spanish-American War, and then he turns out the light and lies in bed in the dark and listens to the wind rushing through the gap in the mountains. The sound of fast water, the sound of trains. He looks out the window, the small lights of the town below, and he feels what he knows is fear, what would be fear if he submitted to it, if he softened or loosened, a wild, shrieking thing that would consume him long before morning. So he does not soften, he does not relent, he lies in the dark with his teeth clenched until sleep overtakes him or he labors out of bed and pours another drink, walking through the house in the moonlight, in the light of the little bulbs Jayne installed in some of the lower outlets so they could find their way through the house in the dark.

He'd risen with the sun. It was a clear, bright day, cold for this early in the season. He took the dog for a walk, a great hairy beast of a golden retriever, cross-eyed and overbred, Jayne's dog from her previous marriage, living here like some kind of stepchild, his responsibility during the Savannah week. The dog shat and pissed, a great enviable stream against the dead leaves at the side of the road. The house smelled like booze when they returned, secret spills from the night before, some of those assholes dribbling covertly on the upholstery, on the rugs, not saying a goddamn word about it. Not their house or their wife, not their problem. He opened a few windows, let some air in. The mist was climbing the mountain. The dog collapsed in a heap in a corner of the kitchen, waiting for Jayne to return so it could be underfoot, its favorite place to be.

The doorbell rings. When they built the house, he'd had the contractors install an ultrasound sensor at the top of the driveway so the bell would ring whenever someone was on their way down to the house. An expensive toy. Tripped by wild turkeys, mostly, an occasional bear. The sound of the bell stirs the dog from its fitful sleep but it settles back quickly enough, twitching and shimmying.

The fog is climbing, has reached the railing of the back porch. He can feel the damp chill it brings, the stillness. It straddles the roof, descends again, covering the windows.

Another time-out, another piss, this one jerkier than the last, stop-start, stop-start, and burning twice as hot. He can picture it, a glowing white mass in his perineum, an ancient thing, dumb and primal, something he's carried for years that has finally grown to maturity. The same creature they found in Elaine's stomach, in her colon, the same spreading child, rabid and pure, that devoured his first wife, ten years ago now. It feels strange to think of her at times like this, to miss her so intensely while he's leaning over the toilet, but that is what he thinks about, Elaine coughing sputum in a dry hospital room. He remarried, they all remarried, but nothing would ever be the same, he knew that, something was lost for good, and now, finally, the thing has returned to take him.

The doorbell rings. A small clutch of turkeys, four brown waddlers working their way down the driveway through the mist. The dog pushes its nose to the window and barks, fogging the glass. He claps his hands to move the dog away, to stop the stupid animal from putting its face through the window. The turkeys couldn't care less, they continue down the driveway and around the side of the garage, out of sight.

The second quarter of the game peters out, the players standing on the field in loose configurations, watching the clock dribble down to zero. They're just waiting to lose now, waiting to board the bus or the plane or whatever they ride these days and go back to their dorms and girlfriends and keg parties. They've given up on the crowd, the viewing audience at home, and he knows now what he has sensed for a few seasons, that this is not his team, this is not the team he's been following since his retirement, the years in the mountains. These are just kids in familiar uniforms going through the motions. His team disappeared some time ago, left the field when he wasn't looking, faded into the Carolina countryside.

He opens the door to the garage, flips on the light. He had planned to wait until the end of the game, but now there seems to be no point. He has already written the letters. Two sealed envelopes sit on the dashboard of the car. One for his son, one for Jayne. He'd written them last

night, after the golfers had gone, after his slow tour of the house, night-
cap in hand. He'd composed the letter to his son first, sealed it, addressed
it. They'd had their differences, their estrangements, but he was proud of
the man Steven had become, whether Steven knew it or not. A good husband, a good father. He knew Elaine would have been proud. He didn't
know if Steven would understand, but he owed his son a letter, an explanation. What Steven did with it would be up to him.

To Jayne, he owed apologies. He'd written half a page of them before
he realized that he'd started off writing to Elaine, a slip of the pen, the
bourbon addling his addled mind. He tore the letter up and flushed it
down the toilet. He didn't want Jayne to find the pieces after the fact,
didn't want to add another needless injury to the decade's worth he'd
already heaped on her. He started again, careful this time, *Dear Jayne.*

He pushes the dog into the house, steps back into the garage, closing
the door behind him. Here is the rubber tubing, here are the pills, here is
the shotgun. It is important to have options. Here is the CB radio he will
use to call the police. It will take them a while to get up the mountain,
just enough time for the pills or the tubing, more than enough for the
shotgun. He fiddles with the dials and holds the microphone, listens to
the crackling static moving down the airwaves.

Someone answers and he says, "I have reason to believe that my
neighbor is dead in his garage." He gives the address and turns off the
mic. No need for Jayne to find his mess.

Earlier in the morning he'd thought he'd settled on the pills, quiet and
cowardly, but now he is feeling the pressure of the call to the police, can
imagine sirens already screaming up the mountain, cops and paramedics
on a brisk Saturday afternoon trying to beat their personal best response
times. The shotgun. He sits in the front seat of the car, places the stock
between his knees. The fog pushes gently at the windows of the garage
door, drifting in and away, making little visible clearings on the driveway.
Last night he'd backed the car in so that today he could look out the ga-
rage-door windows while he sat with whatever choice he'd made, pharmaceuticals, exhaust, twelve gauge. A turkey wanders through a clearing
in the fog. Fitting last sight.

He places the barrel on his mouth, taste of metal and oil, not entirely unpleasant. He yawns for some absurd reason. Tired old man. The doorbell rings again. He remembers the TV in the living room, still on. Leave it, something to keep the dog company until the police arrive. He imagines sirens climbing the hill, taking the curves, getting closer by the second. Do it, already. He pictures the mess, quickly, how many times has he seen it before, brains and blood, but that's somebody's job, it's covered in the homeowners' insurance, he's already checked. Money earmarked for cremation, ashes to be spread near Elaine's grave, one final selfish wish, no way of knowing if Jayne will honor it.

Enough already. Do it, old man. He turns the key in the ignition. The engine thunders to life, unbelievably loud in the sealed garage. It's not enough. He flips on the radio, an orchestra wailing now, full volume, any noise to fill the space, to give him the balls to do what needs to be done. The fog clearing here and there through the windows, blowing around the driveway. Enough, already. Be sorry one final time and then do it.

The fog swings away from the windows to reveal a man standing in the driveway. The man is not a cop, not a paramedic. He looks like a door-to-door salesman, gray hat and trench coat, and he's peering into the garage, gloves cupping his face so he can see through the glass. Their eyes meet and the man smiles, a quick flash of teeth. The man disappears from sight and then the garage door lifts and the man steps inside, stomping his shoes on the cement floor.

"Jimmy Dorn," the man yells, loud enough to be heard with the car windows up and the radio on. He smiles even wider. "Jesus Christ. Looks like I almost missed you."

They sit in the living room in front of the muted TV. The dog ambles in, lies down. Jimmy had poured himself another drink, bourbon and new ice, something to steady his shaking hands, and when he turned the man was standing there holding out the telephone. Jimmy calls the police and tells them he'd made a mistake, he'd forgotten to take his medication and had called in his own death, premature, but now he's taken his pills and a friend is over, everything's under control. They know him in town, he and Jayne, he gives money to the cops every year, the Police Benevolent Fund. Harmless old man.

He hangs up the phone and they sit across from each other in the living room, the third quarter beginning silently on the TV between them.

"You must be the new-model asshole," he says.

The man smiles. He's sitting on the couch, self-satisfied, happy with the circumstances of his arrival. "This is some place," the man says. "Isolated."

"We like it that way."

"So quiet my ears are ringing."

"They should have sent someone I could talk to."

"We would have sent one of your contemporaries, but they're all dead. Either that or wasting away in homes, diapered and drooling. You're it, Jimmy. The last of the Mohicans."

"They give you names anymore?"

"Bud. Bud Squires." The man looks like he's withholding massive laughter, like he could erupt at any moment. "That's some hill. My rental car almost gave up the ghost on the climb."

"I should have built further up."

"It's just nice to be away from the office. I rarely venture out. I'm a systems man, plans and planning."

"What does that mean?"

"Numbers, mostly," Squires says. "Budgets. I add things up and move them around, launch equations into the ether. Six months later I read about the end result in the newspaper. Page twelve or thirteen, second section. Wire report, no byline. The kind of story that's designed to be skimmed over on your way to the comics. The kind that makes you say, 'Where the fuck is that country, anyway? Does that place even exist?'"

"But you were sent."

"I'm here in a very unofficial capacity." Squires shakes his head. "Jimmy Dorn. You're one of those countries on page thirteen. Does that place even exist?"

Jimmy takes a long swallow of his drink, pushes the dog from his feet.

"A while back, I was transferred to the Black Line Squad," Squires says.

"That's what we called it. A demotion. The last stop, probably, before getting fired. There were five of us in an office with Folgers coffee cans full of black markers, redacting documents. Squeak, squeak, squeak. Drawing lines through official correspondence, unofficial correspondence, memoranda for the record. Paperwork going back ten, twenty years. Ask me how many times I drew a line through the name Jimmy Dorn."

"I've got a short window to bullshit," Jimmy says. "The police will be here soon."

"You called them off."

"They'll come anyway. Old man talking about his own death. What else do they have to do?"

"You want to hurry me along."

"You're the systems man."

"I came all this way." Squires looks hurt. A whine threatens to overtake his voice. "Driving for hours down into the boondocks and then here, finally, up the mountain."

"You came to hear stories?" Jimmy says. "What? You came to blackmail?"

"I can't believe this. Your quiet life. Dead in the car. Last of the great white hunters."

"They're coming now. I can hear them. Sirens climbing the hill."

"Hurry me along."

"I want you out of my house."

"Now. You've decided this."

"Yes."

"Sit down with a drink, dog at your feet, and now you want me out of your house."

"Yes."

"Should have left you in that car, spread out across the back windshield. What's it say in those letters? One to the wife. One to the son."

"Talk fast."

"Real tearjerkers. Let me open one. Early Christmas present."

"Out."

"He's up, folks. He's out of his chair."

"I want you out."

"No dice, Pops."

"Shotgun's still loaded."

"No dice."

"They make you bulletproof now?" Jimmy says. "Plans and planning? The Black Line Squad?"

Squires stands and that's all it takes, the height and breadth, the young man in the old man's room.

"I'm the new-model asshole," Squires says. He walks to the end table, the television clicker by the ashtray. "Now, do you mind if we turn off the goddamn TV and get down to brass tacks?"

"You can't imagine the boredom," Squires says. "I'm not a history buff. I live in a region of northern Virginia lousy with preserved battlegrounds, registered buildings. Before I quit smoking I had to sneak out of my house on weekends, sit in my car and inhale. I'd watch the tourists tramp through the fields, these paunchy dads with Confederate infantry hats and period maps, oblivious to their hapless families trailing along behind. Falling to their knees to dig in the dirt for musket balls and shrapnel. I had no interest. History made no sense to me. Disconnected events. The documents I scribbled on never added up to anything. They were random samplings. Random saplings." He smiles at his turn of phrase, pleased with the clever surprise.

"About a year ago I was given another assignment," Squires says. "I was back in the good graces, liquidating documents. Sometimes, black lines aren't enough. The paperwork I was destroying was very specific. It pertained to a project from long ago. That project and its ensuing subprojects. I couldn't help, on the way to the incinerator, looking at the files. Natural curiosity. And then this particular job became less boring. Things started to piece together. There was a thread. And there was a name that kept popping up, a familiar character, the star of my old Black Line days. The great redacted Jimmy Dorn."

Squires remained standing after Jimmy sat back in the chair. He has taken the place of the television, Squires; he is the room's sole source of entertainment. The police never arrived.

"I do more reading than burning. Weeks and months. I enter the office early in the morning and leave late at night. I stop talking to my family. I spend my time at home sitting, staring, thinking about what I've read. I quit smoking, or, rather, I forget to smoke and the habit follows. I'm piecing together that story, Jimmy, memo by memo, I'm deciphering poor penmanship and faded ink, I'm translating the typewritten correspondence of what appears to have been an entire fleet of dyslexic secretaries. But a story is forming and it is well worth the effort."

Jimmy can feel another piss coming on, a bonus piss, one he never thought he'd take. He shifts in his seat, pushing the feeling away.

"I follow the story through to the end," Squires says. "The end of the documentation, at least. Last folder into the fire. I'm a little overwhelmed. I have trouble sleeping, which I'll go out on a limb and assume is a shared trait between us. And I'm far from an idealist, Jimmy. I'm not a blind patriot. I do not spend weekends on my hands and knees pawing in the dirt for lumps of bloody lead. So when a decision was made to reestablish contact, I volunteered. I demanded. I wanted to be the one to stand face-to-face with Jimmy Dorn."

"This was over long ago," Jimmy says.

Squires takes a drink. "I wouldn't be here if that was true."

Late afternoon. The fog pressing at the windows again. Jimmy has poured two more drinks. They sit at the dining room table, the long wooden slab. Squires has a folder he's produced from somewhere, the folds of his coat. Papers on the tabletop, memos and correspondence, unaltered, free of black ink. Jimmy looks at the names on the bottoms of memos, signatures and initials, and faces come back to him easily. He's surprised how quickly they return. What has he been doing up here in the mountains? Waiting.

"How do you know he's alive?" Jimmy says.

"We don't."

"But there is a man already out there, looking."

"Yes."

"Your man?"

"No."

"Who does he belong to?"

"I couldn't say with any certainty. He's just the hound. We have the hound, and now we need the hunter."

Jimmy stands from the table, throws a log into the fireplace, sets it alight. He prefers this to the house's lazy central heating. He chopped this wood himself, and he can remember each piece he tosses in, the individual battles against knots and knobs.

"I can get you a ticket to Los Angeles," Squires says. "First class, tonight. Change in Atlanta, change in Dallas. Arrive first thing in the morning."

"I'll handle it."

"No."

"I'll call you a cab to take you back to town," Jimmy says. "Rent another car. Leave yours."

"No."

"I handle it or I stay right here, watching football."

Squires bites his lip. He seems to be getting drunk fast. Wouldn't have survived half an hour here last night with the golfers.

"How will I contact you?" Squires says.

"I'll contact you."

Squires produces a small note pad, tears off a blank sheet of paper. "Here are my phone numbers. Home and work."

Jimmy takes the paper, tosses it into the fireplace. "Find another one. A pay phone, nowhere near your office. I'll call your home number once and you'll give me the new number. We'll go from there."

Jimmy calls a cab and they wait, drinking silently at the table. When the driveway bell rings, he walks Squires to the door.

"There's a legacy, Jimmy," Squires says. "I guarantee that you have not been forgotten. I can tell you about a location in West Germany. I can tell you about a location in the Philippines. I promise you that the men in those rooms know your name."

"Give me your keys."

Another ring when Squires tops the driveway. Jimmy watches the cab start back down the hill, disappear into the fog. He moves to the dining room table, looks across the memos and dispatches, touching the raised ink on the pages.

Henry March. Jimmy has thought of the man every day for how many years now? The loosest of ends. He scans the newspaper headlines every morning for an old story that has been exhumed. He holds his breath when Jayne calls him into the living room to see a news story on TV. This man and what he knew. His disappearance had turned Jimmy into a dirty secret. Jimmy imagining his son or Jayne reading about the days in San Francisco. Imagining Elaine, if she were alive. No one would understand. No one understood what their lives and families cost, what they necessitated. Everything here is free. In this country, they spit on soldiers returning from war.

He gathers the papers into the folder and then tosses it into the fire. Everything but a couple of photographs, a few addresses. He sits at the table and composes two new letters, one for Jayne, one for Steven. They come easier this time, the apologies. He goes into the bathroom, stop-start, stop-start, thinks of Elaine, remembers sitting by her hospital bed, the aquamarine light, her hand in his, just cold bones and skin. He walks through the house, touching railings, straightening the pictures on the walls. Returns to the dining room. He'll let the fire burn down, it'll keep the dog warm. He fills a bowl with kibble and another with water. Washes and dries the bourbon glasses, puts them away in the cupboard. Pulls on his coat, gloves, hat, shoes. Quite a process. He goes out into the garage, pushing the dog back into the house. The original letters on the dashboard are gone. Squires must have taken them. Jimmy sets the new letters on a shelf where they'll be seen. Puts the shotgun, the rubber tubing, the pills all in the trunk, then drives out toward the top of the hill, the garage door closing behind him.

2

Hannah sat across the worktable and watched him eat, macaroni and cheese from a box that she'd cooked on the hot plate. He ate like he was starving, gripping the fork in his fist, shoveling bright yellow pasta. He wouldn't look at her. He kept his eyes on the food, embarrassed of the way he was eating, possibly, but unable to stop. She let her own plate sit untouched, knowing he would need it when he finished his own. One hand around his fork, the other around the beer can she'd set next to his plate. A territorial animal. A haunted man. Alcohol, drugs, probably; something else.

He finished his pasta. I'm so sorry, he said, shaking his head, and she stood and walked around the table and cleared his plate and set hers before him and he said, Thank you, I'm sorry, yes.

Digging in again.

She had found him on the bus-stop bench outside the gallery. It was going on into evening, and she'd stepped outside for a cigarette, some air. She'd been working all day, cleaning, waiting. The phone had only rung once, at about noon, and she'd run to the receiver to hear the voice on the other end of the line asking after someone in Spanish, another wrong number.

The man on the bench was not one of the usual faces, the wandering souls who stumbled into her gallery, who hovered over the bus-stop trash can looking for food scraps. He was not one of the men she gave sandwiches to, or cigarettes, or an occasional beer if she had one on hand. He was about her age, tall, heavy but not yet fat, bearded and maned like a lion. He was not particularly dirty. His clothes were in decent shape. His hair looked semirecently washed. He had a bruise shining at the corner of his mouth, a cut on his forehead. He was grabbing his right knee in his sleep. A bloody hole in his jeans there. His body twitching, his arms and legs hanging over the ends of the bench.

When she first saw him, she'd thought he was Thomas. She had been expecting to find Thomas on a bench like this, Thomas sitting in a park, sleeping in a doorway. He was about Thomas's size. She could imagine Thomas bearded, his hair long from neglect. She'd known almost immediately that it wasn't him, but now she couldn't shake what remained of that feeling, some kind of connection to this man.

The streetlights on the boulevard came to life. An older Mexican woman with a purse in each hand stood at the stop and got on the bus when it came. Hannah finished her cigarette and walked around to the front of the bench, watching the man's face while he slept. She crouched down, put a hand on his shoulder, said, Hey, Hey.

He ate his macaroni and cheese, drank his beer. He looked exhausted and scared. She asked him what his name was and when he said Dickie Ashby she told him that he didn't sound so sure. He apologized, said that it had been a long day, one that had included getting hit, pretty hard, by a car. She smiled, nodded, not wanting to push him further.

His ribs on his left side, his knee. The bruise at his mouth, the cut on his forehead. She had iodine and bandages in her bathroom for dealing with the slices and punctures that came while cutting mattes, hammering frames. He sat on the closed toilet and she stood over him, pressing alcohol-soaked gauze to the cuts. Bruises on his elbows, the palms of his hands. He had a tattoo on the inside of his wrist that looked fresh, that said *Sons*. He smoked while she worked, a cigarette from the flattened pack in his back pocket.

She said, We should really get you to a hospital, and he'd responded quickly, assuring her that he'd be fine. There was no serious injury. A bruised rib, maybe, something out of whack in his knee.

She wanted to look at the knee but he couldn't roll his jeans high enough, so she told him to stand and take them off. Knowing this would have been inconceivable in a previous time, what now seemed like another life, before the drive to Oakland. She hadn't found Thomas, but she had found this man. A month ago she would have given him a sandwich or a cigarette, but that was no longer enough.

She put a hand under his arm and helped him stand. He looked at the opposite wall as he unbuckled his belt. Hannah slid his jeans past his undershorts, to his ankles, gently, helping him step out and then sit again. His hands shaking as he brought the cigarette back to his lips.

He stood at the open medicine cabinet, overwhelmed.

"People come to parties and leave things," she said. "I keep the more interesting-looking ones around, thinking there might be something to shoot. To photograph."

He studied the faded labels, removed a bottle, replaced it. Finally selected a tall, thin plastic tube, shook a small constellation of pills into the palm of his hand.

"What are those?" she said.

"Painkillers."

"What hurts?"

"Everything."

She poured him a glass of water at the sink, watched him toss the pills back, the water. He closed his eyes, swallowed.

*   *   *

They sat talking at the worktable. The pills had calmed him. She told him her name again, reintroduced herself. She'd told him when he'd first woken, out on the bench, but she wasn't sure he'd heard, or processed, his eyes moving quickly out there, passing over her face and then over her shoulder, looking for something, hunted. He looked at the new beer can she'd set in front of him and said, I don't know why you'd do this, and she said, I don't know either, and then she'd smiled and he'd smiled, still looking down at his hands.

He wasn't from anywhere. He had grown up on air bases, the longest stretch in Oklahoma, but he wasn't really from anywhere. He'd been drafted but had suffered an injury during basic training and spent the rest of his time in Army hospitals. He'd bummed around after that, he'd said. Ended up in Davenport, Iowa, caring for his ailing father. His father was dead. His mother was dead. He had a sister on the East Coast he had lost touch with. He'd come to Los Angeles to find an old friend but had run out of leads and money and then he'd been hit by a car crossing the boulevard.

Should I call anyone? she asked. Should anyone know you're here?

He thought about this for a moment, and then said no, that there wasn't anyone to call.

He lay on the old sofa in her work space. The sofa was large, but he was larger. His hands dragged on the floor, his feet crested the top of the far arm. He took another couple of pills and closed his eyes and she turned out the light.

She couldn't sleep. It wasn't due to fear. She did not feel threatened by him. She didn't know if she should, but she didn't. She felt something else. It was the strangeness of the situation keeping her awake, prickling her skin. Standing out in the gallery, in her bedroom, feeling him on the other side of the thin walls. This strange man in her private space.

Leadbelly, Son House, Blind Willie Johnson. He coughed once and she went to the doorway and asked if the music was keeping him awake. Speaking into the dark room. There was no answer, just the sound of his breathing.

He'd tried to sound detached when he'd spoken about his family, reciting his biography for her as a series of facts, names, dates, but the emotion was there, in his voice, his eyes. It had made her want to tell him about Ginnie, about Thomas, her nightmarish trip through the house in Oakland. She'd had to fight the urge to unburden herself to this stranger. She didn't think she could talk about it the way he had told her about Oklahoma, about Iowa. He was someone who had learned to live with regret. This seemed like an acquired skill, and she wanted to know what he knew, how he did it.

She works at her table and he looks through her photographs, newer prints, the files of older photos she keeps. He swallows her pills, holding the bottles close to his face, squinting at the labels. He combs through her shelf of records, browses her books. He sleeps on the sofa and she turns down the music to listen to him breathe while she works.

She has known addicts, has lived with a few. Not Bert—Bert never used, never drank much. Bert was addicted to work, and her, for a while, but movies were his real obsession, and when she figured that out she knew it was time to go. But she recognizes the behavior, the compulsion that draws this man to the medicine cabinet at regular intervals, pulls him to the refrigerator for a new beer before the old one is finished.

She should call the rehab house at the end of the boulevard. She should call a hospital. He pulls a book from the shelf and says something and has to repeat himself before she notices that he has spoken, turning from her work to look across the room. Not used to another voice in this space in the middle of the day. She is used to being alone.

Dickie. A child's name. Something someone his size should have outgrown long ago. It fits him, though, perfectly, somehow.

He finds a passage from a book he likes and reads it aloud for her. He looks at her runaway photos, studying them like he's searching for a specific face. He tells her stories about growing up, about his mother, a forgotten singer. They order food, Chinese, Thai, Indian. When the delivery boy arrives Dickie always finds his way to a distant spot, standing behind something, sitting, hidden from whoever is waiting at the front door.

He sleeps on the old couch and after a few days she is able to sleep soundly, too, waking in the morning to the sound of a cough or the toilet flushing and remembering then that this is not a strange dream, that he is out there, on the other side of the wall, his bare feet on the cement floor.

She changed his bandages in the morning, at night. He had a long cut under his shoulder blades, and at night he took off his shirt and sat on the toilet or the edge of the bathtub and she pressed rubbing alcohol into the torn skin.

He wrapped his wrist with a bandage, covering the tattoo. She wasn't sure there was an injury there. He hadn't said anything about pain in his wrist.

Everything was strange but nothing felt strange. He took a bath every night, after they ate their delivered dinner. The bathroom was just a corner of the living space that she'd had run with plumbing and cordoned off with a few large white sheets hung with twine from the high ceiling. Diaphanous walls, semi-opaque. She wasn't used to seeing anyone on the other side of the sheets and she couldn't stop staring. His shadow undressing gingerly, stepping into the big metal tub she'd filled with hot water. Sucking air through his teeth at the heat on his skin, the hurt places. The sheets billowing, slightly, as he moved. Lowering himself until all she could see was the shape of his head and his arms and shoulders along the sides of the tub.

Everything was strange but nothing felt strange. She thought back to the days before she'd driven to Oakland, before she'd found this man on the bus-stop bench, and that was what felt strange, that other life.

She heard him exhale deeply from the bathtub, heard the water moving, watched the dark shape on the other side of the sheets.

Nothing felt strange.

*   *   *

She needed to get some groceries and he said that he'd be fine, so she walked to the market and then to the department store by the freeway and picked up some clothes that seemed his size, jeans and checkered western shirts, a package of socks, undershorts, a sweater she thought he might need. She didn't even consider how reckless this was until she was on her way back, evening falling. How irresponsible, leaving him alone in her home. What he could steal, what he could deface. She didn't consider it and then felt guilty when she did, first for the thought and then for its lateness in coming. What she would find when she opened the door.

The gallery was dark when she entered. She moved through the rooms, turning on lights. Everything was as she'd left it. She stood in the middle of the workroom and set down her bags and finally said his name.

There was a noise from the gallery and she stepped back through the doorway, her concern growing to fear, hands balled into fists. He was there, standing in a far corner, watching the front door. She'd walked right past him in the dark. He had a broken wine bottle in one hand, was brandishing it, that was the word, and watching the door, looking wild, stripped of whatever defenses he had left.

She talked him out of the corner, got him to set the bottle on the floor. His boots crunching on the broken glass as he stepped into the center of the room. Keeping her voice low, like calming a feral animal. She got him to the couch and went into the bathroom and shook a few pills into her hand.

She sat with him until she could feel that the drugs were working, his body untangling, growing heavy beside her, and then she stood and swept the glass from the gallery floor, mopped up the wine. He sat on the couch, watching her, breathing slowly again, his hands on his knees.

He said moments still came back to him from the war, some of the things he'd seen and done. She said that she'd thought he'd spent most of his war time in the hospital and he said yes, like that fact wasn't a contradiction. She was not sure he was telling the truth and not sure that it mattered. Standing in a corner with a fistful of jagged glass. She wasn't sure that level of fear required a verifiable explanation.

She put on some records and he took some more pills and lay back on the couch. She switched off the light and turned from the room and he asked her to stay. His voice in the dark. She walked back into the room and found the stool at her worktable by memory and touch, sat listening to the music from the other room. Sometime later she got up to leave, sure he was asleep. She crossed out of the room, turned on the bulb in the hallway, and then she heard his voice again, awake and clear but calm, settled.

Thank you, he said, and she nodded in the light.

The phone rang and it was Bert. It had been a few weeks since she'd brought back the car and he wanted to make sure everything was all right up in Oakland. She said that it was, not believing she was capable of such a lie even as she said the words. You're okay? he asked, and she said, Yes. Everything is fine.

There was a patio up on the flat part of the roof where she'd arranged a ring of plastic lawn chairs beneath a web work of white Christmas lights. In and around the ring were some potted cacti, a few marigolds and day lilies she always forgot to water. Openings ended up here some nights, the quiet comedown after a show, a small group, Hannah and the artists and significant others, friends, gallerists, looking at the lights in the hills to the south, streetlights and house lights and porch lights in the distant trees.

A ladder at the back of the work space led up to the roof hatch, and she insisted that he climb first, though she had no idea how brave this demand was, what she could really do if his knee balked and he fell back onto her. Up on the roof, they sat and smoked and drank a bottle of wine, lit by the Christmas lights and the streetlight on the corner. Looking at the skeletal shapes on the neighboring rooftops, silhouettes of TV antennas, telephone wires, the latticed metal bone work at the back of a billboard. He told her more about his mother. It seemed like he was hoping, due to Hannah's musical taste, that she'd heard some of his mother's records, but she didn't believe she had, didn't think she should lie about it. After a while he talked more about his father, that last year in Davenport. The anointing of the sick parent, a filial sacrament she hadn't realized was a responsibility until it was too late.

She climbed back down into the studio to get more wine. On her way back up she became worried suddenly that she'd come upon him with half a bottle in his hand again, or standing out at the edge of the roof, removing his back foot, stepping out into space. The level of relief surprised her, seeing him still there, in his chair, quiet, looking out into the trees. She had to stand at the top of the ladder and breathe for a moment, compose herself. She told him about her mother, her father, her brother. Before she knew what she was saying she was saying it. Moving slowly, back and forth in time, recounting as memories came to her, fragments, imaginings. And then, finally, about the house in Oakland, what she'd found, what the police had said. How she was waiting for her brother. How she hadn't told anyone. How there wasn't anyone to tell.

He didn't say a word, but it still seemed like a conversation. The relief hit her again. He didn't have any judgment or platitudes, he just listened, and she felt lighter, slightly, like she had given some of this to him, and maybe that was a fair trade, maybe that was how he saw it, sitting there, listening, that this was something he could take for her in return.

They watched the chess games together at night, in folding chairs in front of the TV. The match had stretched to the end of the month, then over into the beginning of the next. Hannah kept the sound off and played records instead. Dickie was talking more, commenting on the chess or the music. He was starting to sound normal again, what she assumed was normal, what maybe he'd sounded like before she'd found him.

She had her camera in her lap, was lifting it occasionally, taking pictures of the TV, the edges of the screen and the cinderblock wall behind it, knowing she'd be unhappy with the results, the jittery cathode glow, and then she turned and looked at Dickie and asked if she could take a picture of him.

"Doing what?"

"Sitting there," she said.

"Watching TV?"

"Sure."

"Not the most interesting subject."

"We won't know until we see the picture."

He stood and he was smiling but she could tell this had made him uncomfortable.

"Never mind," she said.

"I'm sorry."

"Forget it. It's not a big deal."

He walked over to the bathroom. She heard the toilet, the pop of a pill-bottle cap, water in the sink. She felt like she should put the camera away before he came back, like she was holding a weapon of some sort.

"I know that seemed strange," he said.

"Plenty of people don't want their picture taken."

"Right."

"Happens all the time."

"Afraid you'll steal my soul."

"No, you're not."

He smiled awkwardly, standing by his chair.

"You don't have to explain," she said.

"I feel like I do."

"You don't."

She left the camera in her lap. After a while he sat again. She said good night when the broadcast was over, went back to her room, leaving him there with the late news, not entirely sure why she felt so banged up, so wounded by this.

"This is the picture."

She turned from the worktable. Dickie was sitting on the sofa with a box of prints. She knew what he was looking at before he turned it for her to confirm. Her father outside the Merchants Exchange in San Francisco.

"I feel strange having told you about that," she said.

"Why?"

"Like it has some meaning."

"Of course it does."

"Apart from the memory. I think its only meaning is in the memory."

"That's not what you said the other night."

"It's what I'm saying now."

She leaned over on the stool and extended a finger to hook the handle of her coffee mug. She always left her coffee on the floor when she was working, to keep the liquid away from the photos on her table. She hooked the handle and straightened herself and took a sip, lowered the mug back to the floor. She could see that he was still looking at the photo.

"A guy came into the gallery a while back," she said. "I had that hanging with another exhibition. Just sitting on its own wall. He said he knew the man in the photograph. That the man worked for his father. Recently."

"A guy from where?"

"Mexico. San Vicente, he said, I think."

"You think."

"San Vicente."

"This was before you went up to Oakland?"

"Yes."

"Worked for his father doing what?"

"I don't know."

Hannah bent again, reaching for the coffee mug, her index finger hooked, feeling in the air for the handle.

Dickie was still looking at the photograph. "What else did he say?"

"Nothing."

"What else did you ask?"

"Nothing."

"You think it's a coincidence."

"I don't know."

"Or a mistake."

"I don't know what I think. Yes. I think it's nothing. I think it's a mistake."

Hannah gave up on the coffee, straightened, arching her lower back, popping something into place that shifted when she was on her stool too long.

"San Vicente isn't that far," he said.

She let this sit. Not pretending she hadn't heard, but letting the sentence fall, gravity's pull, hoping the words would do something, combust, disappear when they hit the floor.

"What does that mean?" she said.

"You're thinking that if you go, you change everything."

"Yes."

"There's nothing there, it was a mistake, but now everything has changed."

"I'm waiting for my brother."

Dickie's eyes lifted from the photo to Thomas's postcards on the wall.

"How far?" she said. "San Vicente."

"Half a day, maybe," Dickie said. "Maybe a day."

"That close."

Dickie nodded. His eyes moved from the postcards to Hannah.

"I don't want to spend my life," she said.

"I know."

"This is something that would never end."

She leaned from the stool again, bending deep, searching with her hooked finger. Came away with nothing. She straightened, put her hands on her worktable. Let that thing in her back sit out of place, a dull throb, a disk shifted a fraction of an inch.

"I'm waiting for Thomas," she said. "The police told me to wait."

Dickie watched her for another moment. He looked at the photo one more time before slipping it back into the box.

Spassky didn't appear for the final game of the match. The previous day's contest had been adjourned without a winner, but now Spassky had sent a message from his hotel before the game's resumption, forfeiting the championship. There was footage of the anticlimax from a camera some-one in the audience had hidden in a bag. A shot of the stage, the table and two chairs, one empty. The forfeiture was announced over a loud-speaker. There was stunned silence, then applause from the audience in the hall. Fischer remained in his chair, sitting back, his long legs splayed out at odd angles, his chin resting in his hand, looking at the pieces on the board, still set from the previous day's game. The broadcast cut to shots of the jubilant crowd outside the building, then a cheering group watching the match at a rec center in New York, newscasters shouting into microphones, gap-toothed kids waving at the camera. Then back to Fischer, still sitting in his chair. His unwillingness or inability to exit. It was the most compelling moment of the whole match, waiting for Fischer to leave the room. Would he or wouldn't he. Hannah leaned forward in her seat, bending toward the television. Fischer's hand at his chin, at his forehead, while the crowds cheered. She understood what he was doing. The game had changed but he was still playing. He was still calculating the moves, straining to see the future. Following the chain, the sequence of potential actions. What would lead to the safe path amid all the other possibilities that simply led to the end.

She was talking about Thomas. The match had been over for a while, the TV was off, and she wasn't sure why she'd started talking, what Dickie had asked that she was responding to. She was talking about the last time she saw him, over a year ago now. She'd walked in through the front door of the house in Oakland and Thomas was sitting on the living room floor with a fingertip pressed to a railway map. And she'd thought, Oh God, this is how it will be forever. Thomas as a young man, Thomas as an adult, as an old man. Sitting on floors with his fingers in maps. She'd wanted to turn and run from the whole thing, again. She'd never felt so scared and ashamed and then he'd looked up at her and said, *Hello, sis,* just like that, just like any younger brother would say it, jaunty and a little playful, smart-alecky, *Hello, sis,* and Hannah had stood there, open-mouthed, as if he'd started reciting the Bill of Rights or *War and Peace,* but no, this was even more shocking, recognizing her as she'd come in the door, acknowledging her with what seemed like a little joke. This was the most incredible thing she could imagine coming from him, greeting someone when they entered a room.

She was telling all of this to Dickie and then she wasn't saying anything, there was something in her throat, some kind of hard blockage, and she swallowed and choked and then she was sobbing, she couldn't get a handle on it, it was out of her grip, flooding the room, covering her, covering everything. She could hear herself moaning, making some god-awful sound she'd never heard before, a primal wail, shuddering and sucking air, and she stood because Dickie stood, she wanted him to stay away, she didn't know what was happening to her, it felt like she was losing control of her body, and she backed out of the room, through the kitchen and into her bedroom, kneeling beside the bed, shuddering and sobbing and terrified of this thing that was coming out of her.

She could barely hear him. He was saying her name. He was beside her and she was pushing him away but he was stronger now, he'd gotten stronger, and he lifted her up onto the bed and she curled against the wall, holding her legs in tight, pressing her forehead to the cinder blocks. Still shaking, that sound still releasing from her. His hands were on her shoulders and she could feel the bed sag with his added weight. Could feel his body pressed to hers, his arms around her, one hand on her hands, one hand between her forehead and the wall. Breathing slowly, deeply, his chest rising and falling and how that must hurt, how that must feel in his ribs, guiding her body to take air with him, keeping her head from the cinder blocks, his weight wrapped around her, his voice close in her ear.

Just breathe.

They were out of coffee and milk and she needed to get out of the building, onto the street, go somewhere. He didn't want her to go. At first she thought he was worried because of her display the previous night, her breakdown, but then she could tell there was something else, an external concern. He wouldn't say what, he just didn't think it was a good idea. It was getting late, it would be dark soon. But she needed to get out, so he insisted on going with her.

They walked up the boulevard, past garages and gas stations, a couple of small markets. Dickie walked close, his hands pushed deep into the pockets of the new cardigan, a burgundy knit that looked nice with his beard. She could see his eyes moving, scanning the path in front of them, the cars passing at their side. She had a sudden impulse to hook her arm through his but then she thought that this was a fairly crazy idea. She kept her hands in her own pockets. The grocery store was at the end of the boulevard, maybe half a mile away, and they walked slowly, favoring his bad knee.

The light changed against them, so they waited at the corner. Headlights on now; taillights smearing in the drizzle that had begun to fall. Dickie's eyes moving this way and that. She wanted to say something about the night before but didn't know what to say. It didn't seem like he was expecting anything, any show of gratitude. There was something comforting about him, despite the circumstances of his arrival, despite the pills, the incident with the wine bottle. She knew that this was beyond all logic. He'd told her that he'd done things that still came back to haunt him and yet she still had no fear. There was no explanation for this. She didn't know what this was.

She heard it first, a low buzzing, what sounded like a woman's voice, electronically filtered, and then they turned as someone joined them at the curb. A teenager in a hooded sweatshirt, pressing a small radio to his ear. He was singing under his breath, swaying, dancing a little.

Dickie's hand was at her elbow, then down around her wrist, tightening slowly.

The boy was really dancing, it was something to see, popping out quick explosions of moves and then still again, then in motion, then still, staring straight ahead the whole time, watching the crossing signal on the opposite corner, the radio to his ear, singing along in a whispery falsetto.

Ready, ready? Six, nine, six, eight, three, four, five.

Dickie pulled her arm, jarring her out of her stance, and then they were heading back down the sidewalk the way they'd come, Dickie almost dragging her until she could catch up to his hurrying limp. He looked back over his shoulder every few seconds, his eyes like when she'd found him in the gallery, fear-filled and wide.

Hannah said, "What the hell?"

The boy was still back at the corner. The light changed, but he didn't cross, just stood where he was, watching them. Dickie yanked Hannah again, pulling her along, jogging now, their boots splashing in the quickly forming puddles.

Back inside the gallery, he checked one more time, the sidewalk, the cars parked at the curb, and then he locked the front doors. They were both wet. He stood with his back to her, water dripping from his beard, staring at the seam where the two doors met, his mind racing, she could tell, struggling with a choice, which way to go.

"What did you see?" she said.

He leaned forward, a hand on each door. He spoke, finally, and she didn't know if he didn't face her because he was afraid to face her or because he wanted to face the doors, if he was standing between her and something outside.

He said, "I have something to tell you and I need you to hear me out, no matter what."

She didn't want him to go any further. She thought that if she didn't respond they could just stay like this, motionless in this space, perched but not yet falling.

He set his forehead against the doors, dripping rain, breathing hard.

She didn't want to hear anything. She didn't want to know.

She said, "Tell me."

3

Into the blare and shine of the airport terminal. Moving sidewalks, careening baggage carts, directional signage a cryptographer couldn't decipher. Jimmy squints at arrows, stops to swivel at intersections. At each stage of the trip he has been asked if he needs assistance, if he requires a wheelchair, help finding his seat, an elbow to hold on his way to the lavatory. If he would like an attendant to contact someone in his destination city so they can be waiting at the gate when he arrives.

He rents another car, drives past the airport sprawl, out through Santa Fe. Night in the desert. Into a little two-lane town, stopping at the first bar he sees. *Hutch's Blue Room.* He orders a drink, another, standing instead of sitting, trying to get some circulation back into his legs after the flights, letting the pain fall, slowly, from his crotch to his feet.

He checks into a motel, cash, one night, using Squires's name. The room is the room, stale carpeting and mesa-print wallpaper, a pair of double beds, cool to the touch. There are only a few hours until morning but he leaves the beds undisturbed, sits at the desk with the miniature bottles of whiskey he hoarded from the flight and the Gideon's Bible he found in the bedside table.

Elaine became religious in her final months. It was something Jimmy couldn't agree with, but he held his tongue. She was a smart woman, but desperate. She needed to believe this wasn't all there was, that her life wasn't being cut short so much as she was moving on early. So Jimmy kept his mouth shut, sat silently in the hospital room while the priest placed the Eucharist on her dry tongue.

Jayne was born-again, had found Jesus ten years before she'd met Jimmy, in the exact moment between the swing and connection of her first husband's fist with her left cheekbone. She saw everything in that moment, she said, her life before and her life to come, her mistakes and her possibilities, and by the time his fist shattered the bone she was already gone, at least in spirit, already packed and away, starting her new life. The first night they went to dinner she told Jimmy her whole story, and then she asked if he was ready to accept Jesus Christ as his personal savior. Jimmy looked across the table at this woman, twenty years his junior, one eye drooping slightly, but the clarity in her face when she asked the question, that quiet certainty, was something he thought he could find comfort in, so Jimmy said, Yeah, sure, why not, I've accepted everything else to this point.

On vacations Jayne brought books, handbags full of romance novels, but if there was a Bible in the hotel room she'd read it before bed. They'd drive out to the coast, little beach towns and tourist traps, wherever she wanted to go. Jimmy didn't care, was happy to make the reservations and follow along. She was always moving, even in the house, room to room, cleaning, arranging, settling rarely, for meals, a phone call, but then back up and over to the laundry room, downstairs to change the bedding in the guest rooms even though they weren't expecting guests. She made the trip down the mountain almost every day, weather permitting, shopping or lunch with friends or meeting with her Bible study group. It was easy for Jimmy to see that she was still trying to outdistance something, but at least now she was running from one safe point to another. At the end of the night, when she was finally motionless in bed, Jayne's face would compose into that calm look of certainty, that belief in something greater, and if that was the last thing Jimmy saw before he closed his eyes then he didn't have so much trouble getting to sleep.

He sat in the motel room, waiting out the night. The bottles and the

Bible. He didn't believe what Jayne believed, but he hoped the arithmetic of the situation was enough, her faith canceling his doubt.

He had an envelope of cash he'd taken with him from the house. Jayne wouldn't notice it was gone, not right away. He'd invested his pension well, was the recipient of off-hours phone tips, calls from men he'd worked with who still needed to go to an office every day and had moved to the private sector. Men still terrified of the man Jimmy hadn't been in a decade. He took no pride in it. It was no way to make money, talking on the phone, writing checks, opening mail. Any idiot with a pulse and a few well-connected acquaintances could do it.

He opened another bottle. He thought of Henry March in a room like this, waiting. March in some in-between place. March the mystery, how a man could disappear so completely. Jimmy had come out of that room, past that monstrosity of a door, and March was nowhere to be found. His ledger nowhere to be found. Clarke in hysterics. They'd been livid back east, and terrified. They didn't trust Jimmy with much after that. He still got calls, but it was mostly strong-arm stuff, intimidation work, nothing like the apartments on Telegraph Hill. Excommunicated. Henry March's escape was seen as his fault. Many times he'd thought about going to the house in Oakland and beating something out of the wife, the retarded son. But March wouldn't have told them anything. He would understand that knowing nothing would keep them safe.

There was a hound on the trail and Jimmy had been sent to hunt the hound but then who would be sent to hunt Jimmy? He was little more than another loose end, he knew this, despite all of Squires's bullshit. There would be another engine in the system soon, waiting for Jimmy to do his job before taking Jimmy out. Or maybe they knew more than they let on, Squires and his superiors. Maybe they had talked to Jimmy's doctors, seen his test results. Maybe they knew that Jimmy had brought his own hunter with him.

He greeted first light with a final drink, the Bible still closed on the desk. He made a couple of phone calls back east to some of those old acquaintances, looking for an address north of Santa Fe. He left the room as he'd found it. Stopped at a pawnshop on the way out of town for a pistol, thirty bucks cash, a battered silver L that had been much used, easy in his hand, a thing with its own weight of memory, that carried its own dark history.

The house was in an unfinished subdivision below a smooth rise of bare hills. Only a few completed hacienda-style homes among the other un-broken lots. Cactus and manicured sand in the front yards, foreign cars in the driveways. Jimmy heard coughing from behind the house, let him-self through a side gate onto a back patio dense with vegetation. A small fountain burbled somewhere unseen. Jimmy moved through the growth to the center of the patio, the man on his knees there, his hands deep in soil, repotting.

"Doctor," Jimmy said. "You look well."

Clarke stopped digging, stared at the plant in front of him. After a mo-ment he stood and turned. He was still a handsome man, tanned and fit. His hair was white now. A clipped white mustache sat on his upper lip.

"Nice place," Jimmy said. "Quiet. Are we alone?"

"My wife is away for the weekend."

"First? Second?"

"I've been married a few times."

"I'll bet."

Clarke's hands hung at his sides, dirty to the knuckles. He reached for a towel on the edge of the fountain, wiped the earth from his fingers.

"You weren't hard to find," Jimmy said.

"I stopped hiding years ago. I realized it wouldn't make any differ-ence. Anyone can be found."

"Not quite anyone."

Clarke refolded the towel, lifted a cigarette pack from his shirt pocket.

"When was the last time you spoke to Henry March?" Jimmy said.

"I speak with him every day." Clarke shook a cigarette from his pack. "Don't you? I plead with him for a few more years of silence, to allow me to finish out my days undisturbed. You look sick, Jimmy."

"Is that a professional diagnosis?"

"What do you have?"

Jimmy looked back over his shoulder, past the distant roofs of the rest of the subdivision, the purple hills beyond.

"Let's go inside," Clarke said. "Have a drink."

"It's early."

"Since when?"

Jimmy turned back to him. "You keep a gun in the house, Chip?"

Clarke lit his cigarette, hands shaking.

"We'll stay out here for now," Jimmy said. "When was the last time you spoke to the flesh-and-blood Henry March?"

"You know when."

"Nothing since?"

Clarke shook his head.

"Spoken to anyone else?"

"No."

"A lot of years," Jimmy said. "A long time to keep quiet."

"I've never told anyone, Jimmy."

"No?"

Clarke shook his head.

"One of those wives?"

"No."

"Somebody else?" Jimmy said. "Middle of the night. Another secret."

"I've never told anyone."

Clarke pulled anxiously on his cigarette. Jimmy watched, wanting one for the first time in years. He hadn't smoked since Elaine's doctor had given them the test results, as if Jimmy quitting could somehow change her diagnosis. As if there was a balance to things, a zero-sum accounting.

"I expected this years ago," Clarke said. "You coming, someone coming. I've watched it all on TV. The protests, the marches. My son went to New York for that concert in the field. Do you remember, one of the johns talked about rolling around in the mud? We gave him STORMY. The man sat naked on the bed, talked about it for hours. Then I turned on the television and saw a hundred thousand people rolling around in the mud. My son in there with them, somewhere."

Jimmy looked back past the garden, the nearest house maybe a hundred yards away.

Clarke put the cigarette to his lips, took a shaky pull, lowered his hand again. "We let something loose into the world," he said. "I expected you years ago."

"You want to go inside now?"

Clarke looked at the surrounding plants, the pot he was working in when Jimmy arrived. "I'd rather stay out here. This is where I'm most at peace."

Jimmy put his hands into the pockets of his coat. The rental-car keys there, his sunglasses, the cold metal L.

"I've never said anything, Jimmy." Clarke's eyes were wet. "I've been quiet."

"I believe you, Chip."

"I've been quiet."

Jimmy nodded. He watched Clarke's hand tremble as he lifted his cigarette, Clarke's lips reaching, desperate for it.

Jimmy's hand tightened in the pocket of his coat. Everyone he saw, he was seeing for the last time.

4

Dickie had told her everything. She'd wanted to leave and he had told her that she couldn't, that the Sons would find her, so she'd climbed up onto the roof to get away from him. He could hear her up there, pacing, the boards creaking in the high ceiling.

He took a couple of sedatives, drained a bottle of wine, knowing that it would be a long time before he swallowed another pill, another drink. He turned on all the lights in her work space, sat with her photos, her brother's postcards, the picture of her father. A final impression of Henry March, Henry Gladwell, the man fading, the photo fading, black and white and gray.

At one point he thought he saw Mary Margaret sitting on the sofa at the other end of the work space. At one point he thought he saw the security guard from the bank. This could be the sedatives. This could be the alcohol. This could just be what he carried with him now, the company he would keep.

In a shoe box he found the pictures that Henry March had taken when Hannah was a girl. She'd told him about these, photos of San Francisco meant to alleviate her fear of nuclear war. Dickie could see the first stirrings of her work in them, shots of buildings standing solid against the sky, or fixed among the uncertainties of human motion, blurred pedestrians passing. She had her father's eye, his interest in the periphery, the movement at the edges of a frame.

He had told Hannah everything except how he felt that he under-stood her father now, his ledger. What happened when you took an accounting of your sins, a book filled with the names of the dead and damaged. Dickie could have his own ledger. He could account for his own names. He could commit to paper what he had done. They weren't so different, he and Henry March. He wondered what he would find in Mexico. What happened to men like them.

You could still run.

This was Father Bill's voice, coming from the couch behind him. Dickie doesn't turn, he just listens. This could be the sedatives. This could be a dream, though he doesn't think it's a dream. It could just be Bill because Bill is who he talks to, Bill's voice is the voice he hears now when he's alone in a room.

You know how to run, Bill says. You could get out of this. Cut your losses.

Dickie lights a cigarette. There's not much left to cut.

You'd be surprised, Bill says. There's always more. But you want to find this man.

Yes.

And if it's him?

Then they can have him.

This group? These killers?

Yes.

You'll trade him for her? She won't go along with it.

Dickie places the photo of Henry March in the center of the table, surrounded by the photos March had taken, the city twenty years in the past. Making him solid again, a man in a time and place, surrounded, vis-ible. Willing March's image not to fade entirely, not just yet.

But then, Bill says, I suppose she doesn't have to know.

Everyone had lied. Dickie, her father, Ginnie, who could not have shared a bed, shared a life with that man without knowing something.

That man. Hannah thought of Henry as someone else now, a stranger moving through her memories. She stood on the roof of her studio, watching plane lights blink across the blue-black sky. Everyone had lied.

Your father shaves in the morning, leaning over the bathroom sink. The mirror fogging from the hot water pouring from the tap. His glasses sit on the edge of the basin, their lenses clouded with steam. His face appears in the mirror, pulling the razor down across his cheek, creating a pink trail in the cloud of white foam.

Your father dresses in his bedroom, shirt, slacks, socks, shoes. Looping his tie in the mirror. A man's secret, the intricate sleight-of-hand that leads to a tight knot at the throat. Combing his still-wet hair. The chemical-sweet smell of aftershave and hair tonic. Humidity from the shower and sink, warm weight in the air.

Your father eats his breakfast at the dining room table. He takes a lunch your mother packed in a small brown paper bag. He kisses your mother, your brother. He kisses you, just above the left ear, his aftershave and cigarette smell strong for a close moment and then gone as he walks down the short hallway, out the front door.

How could she reconcile her memory of her father with this life she'd been told he'd led? These things he may have done, may have been a part of. This man in the morning; this man in the station wagon beside her, driving along the lower deck of the Bay Bridge. This man in the photo outside the Merchants Exchange, staring into the camera lens, saying good-bye.

She'd gone up on the roof because she needed to get away from Dickie, from what he'd told her. He wouldn't let her walk back out onto the street, but she had to go somewhere, so she climbed and was relieved when he didn't follow.

The things he said her father had done. The things he, Dickie, said that he'd done. A man dead in a bank in Irvine; a man dead in an office in Portland. A woman he'd been involved with, a girlfriend, dead in a car, shot by the police. He'd told her these things to establish his legitimacy, she guessed, so she would think of him as a reputable source.

She could climb onto the adjoining roof and make her way down to the fire escape at the far end. She could go to the police. She could run. She could call Bert. She thought about Dickie's descriptions of the mem-

bers of this group he'd been with and tried to remember having seen any
of them on the street, around the gallery, in one of her countless photos
of kids and buildings throughout the city.

Or maybe no one had lied. Maybe Dickie was crazy, maybe he had
escaped from an institution somewhere, had just happened to wash up
on the bus-stop bench. A drug addict, an alcoholic. She'd taken him in
and confided things and he'd turned them back on her, warped and distorted. He was playing through some dark fantasy that now included her
and her history, her secrets.

He'd described her father's handwriting and that could be a coincidence, a lucky guess, but she remembered the ledger from their cross-
country drive, the nights in the motel rooms and her father recording
all sorts of minutiae about his camera and film and shutter speeds, apertures and light. It was the first time she'd ever seen those terms and she'd
never forgotten how they looked on the page.

Dickie had listed the towns and cities they'd visited on their trip in
exact order. Charleston, Lexington, Louisville. He knew the names of
the roadside motels where they'd stayed, every one, and she knew them,
too. He had an astonishing memory and she'd never forgotten.

He'd said the Apple Tree Lodge in Carmi, Illinois, six dollars, and when
he spoke she saw her father writing the same words in his book in that
motel room and she knew that her life was not what she'd thought it was.

She climbed back down the ladder as the sun rose. A few lights on in her
studio, in the gallery. It was so quiet that at first she thought he was gone,
but then she smelled coffee coming from the kitchen.

"I found half a can in the back of a cabinet," he said. He held up the
coffee container. He had to prove everything now. He was standing at
the counter, wearing the same clothes as the night before, the burgundy
cardigan. His hair had dried to a high frizz. The teakettle was on the hot
plate, the heating coil turning pink, then red.

She took off her jacket and draped it over the stool by her worktable.

"I can't go," she said.

"You can't stay."

"What if Thomas comes?"

"You won't be here. If you stay, they'll take you."

"This group."

"Yes."

"This is insane."

"Yes."

"This is how they teach you to talk?" she said. "Under questioning? Yes, yes, yes, yes." She grabbed her cigarettes from the edge of the counter. She'd been dying for one all night but hadn't been willing to come back down just for that.

"What if you're lying to me now?" she said. "What if you take me right to them? Isn't that possible?"

"It is."

"How do I know you won't do that?"

"You don't."

The teakettle began to whistle. Dickie turned off the hot plate, lifted the kettle, poured the steaming water into a mug on the counter.

"How long do we have?" she said. "Until they lose patience with you. Until they come."

He lifted the mug, crossed to her. "I don't know. Not long."

After a moment she took the mug, held it with both hands, absorbing its warmth.

"What if it's him, down there?" she said. "Then you give him to these people? Knowing what they want to do?"

He didn't say anything. He was still standing a few feet in front of her, arms at his sides.

"And if it isn't true," she said, "then you finish your job and go on to the next one?"

He didn't say anything.

"And what if there's no answer?" she said. She wanted to throw her coffee at him. "What if there's nothing there?"

He looked down at her hands, his.

"What if there isn't," he said. "Yes. I don't know."

5

They took everything worth taking. Notes, drafts of books he was working on, interview transcripts. His pills sometimes, his crystals. Sometimes not taken, just moved. He'd come out of the bathroom and things would be different. This thing here, that thing there. Letting him know what they were capable of.

They never touched the guns, the ammunition. They left the bedroom alone. This did not seem strange to him. When the time came, they wanted a fair fight. They would not kill an unarmed man. That was something they left to others, that they had left to him, originally.

He sees the Chinese man in the liquor store reach for the telephone on the wall and so he raises his gun, fires.

He was looking for a particular notebook but of course it was not where he'd left it. The notebook in which he'd written Walter's story when Walter first told him. He read through that notebook often, as Walter's story was similar to his own in many ways, and it helped lift his memories from the dirt where they were buried. He read Walter's story and more of his own fell into place. But the notebook was not on the high shelf in the living room where he was certain that he'd last left it.

It was like they knew what he'd want, what he'd be looking for, before he knew himself.

He sees the Chinese man in the liquor store reach for the telephone on the wall. He has not fired a gun since the war. Ten years, longer. He raises the gun and fires and the Chinese man falls back, disappears behind the counter.

The war. This is something he remembers. The seasick ocean journey. The Belgian forest. Blood and smoke and screams in the trees.

He moves paper while he looks for the lost notebook. Towers of manuscript, books, letters, notes. Tall, dry, brittle. He carries what he can lift and pushes the rest into position with the foot of his crutch.

He had written stories before the war, before the forest, sent them to publishers, magazine editors. Received letters back a few months later. Thank you but no. Sometimes not even that polite. Outer-space stories, journeys to the moon, Martian invasions. Things he knew nothing about, things he had written because he didn't know what else to write. Then he had gone to war and the forest and come back and what had he done? What had he done?

Sometimes pieces fell away, back into the dirt, and he fought to remember. Reading others' stories helped. If he could find the notebook, Walter's story, that would help him dig, reclaim.

He watched the Chinese man fall. He stood in the middle of the liquor store until he heard sirens. He didn't know how long he remained there. Sirens jarred him out of his sleep-mind. He slid the gun into the pocket of his coat and walked out of the liquor store into the rain. He was careful not to run. He did not want to draw attention. There were a few people out on the street, other Chinese who had heard the gun. He was out in the rain but he was not getting wet, he could not feel the rain on his face, and then he remembered the mask and took it off. A grinning panda, a child's mask. The sirens were getting closer. He walked out of Chinatown. Somewhere he lost the mask and the gun. He couldn't remember what he had done with them, only that they were there and then they were gone.

He stacks the paper into towers and then moves the towers, building walls, leaving a single winding trail from the front door to the bedroom. Soon he won't need any of this. It has served its purpose. It brought the others to him: Javier, Walter, Sarah. How many others? Scores over the years. It brought them to him but now they are ready, they are his rage, focused, and they no longer need him.

Sometimes the missing things in his house are simply put somewhere else and sometimes they're actually taken. He cannot find the notebook with Walter's story. Walter's story would help him remember his own. He could remember some, but he wanted to remember it all.

Standing in the high weeds across from the apartment. The apartment sat on top of a mechanics' garage and he didn't know the city but he had found his way back by walking every street he could find, looking for that garage. Not sure how long it had taken him to get back. Standing in the high weeds on the embankment across the street. Lights glittering on the dark water behind him, down the hill. Lights in the apartment windows above. Curtains moving.

He wrote stories but the stories were no good and then he went to war, into the forest, and he came back from the war and what had he done?

He takes another pill for his foot. He pours himself a drink. Pushing the paper towers with the base of his crutch. Building walls. Living room, kitchen, bathroom.

A man finally came out of the front door of the apartment. The man was tall and thin, wore glasses and a gray overcoat. He followed the man with glasses through the city. When the man got into a car, he got into a car, pushing its driver out to the pavement. He followed the man across the water to a house on a hill. He watched the man enter the house. He saw a woman in the front window, a girl. They appeared to be arguing.

He followed the man back and forth from the apartment to the house on the hill to a motel in the city. The man was the only thing he knew. He did not remember how he ate, where he slept. He only remembered following the man.

The man's name was Henry March. He stood on the house's doorstep one morning when no one was there and held the man's mail in his hands.

Night on the ocean. He turns on the lamps in the living room, watches the light focus through the crystals. Feels the healing rays on his foot, bringing the dead stump back to life. He wants to be able to stand on both feet, like a man, when they come.

He returned from the war and what had he done? Sometimes it felt as if the answer was right beside him, but whenever he turned it was gone.

He followed Henry March to a bus station and March put something in a locker and paid for the key and when March was gone he pried the locker open and took out a leather-bound ledger filled with black ink.

Here is his lighter, right where he left it. Here are his cigarettes. Here is a newspaper, recent, with a picture above the fold. His delivery boy brought this. The picture is a security-camera photograph of a bank robbery. Blurry figures as seen from above, standing with guns drawn. The figures are wearing animal masks. He knows this not from the picture, which is too blurred, but from the artist's sketches that accompany the article. Illustrations of smiling cartoon characters. Panda, pig, cat, dog. Familiar faces.

He's read interviews with writers who talked about seeing their books turned into movies, watching their creations projected up on the big screen, but that is nothing compared to this.

He read Henry March's ledger. It was a book in code but it made perfect sense to him. He could see the words behind the words. He read the ledger and his head opened and he remembered. He remembered the interior of that apartment and the girl and the men and the liquor store in Chinatown. He remembered the mask. He couldn't remember how he had gotten there, what had come before. He could only remember what they had done to him, not what they had taken away.

By the time he had finished reading the ledger Henry March had disappeared. All of the men had disappeared. The girls. No one came in or out of the apartment. He stood in the weeds and watched, but no one came.

He created a new life, a false life, out of what remained. He found his way down to Los Angeles. He started writing again, but this time he knew what he was writing about. Others found him through his writing. They'd all had revelations, moments packed with remembered truth, and he envied them those moments. He'd had no such thing. Over the years some memories had come back, in dreams, sometimes, but he knew not to trust dreams. When he slept his defenses were down and they could talk to him then, tell him lies. He knew not to trust dreams.

He had gone to Denver. There was an address in the ledger. At the address there was a house and inside the house was a woman and two girls. Twins. There was a name in the ledger and that name matched the name on the mail on the doorstep in Denver. The name meant nothing to him at the time but he knew that it would, someday. He knew that the people inside the house meant something to him but he could not remember what and after what he had done in the apartment on the hill and in the liquor store in Chinatown he had no right to enter the house. He walked away and never returned. He pulled that page from the ledger and burned it, his only defacing of the book.

He came back from the war and what had he done?

Pushing paper towers, careful to leave enough space for the front door to open, for someone to enter the maze.

The woman's name had come to him in a newspaper article. She was a photographer, showing some of her work in a gallery in town. This was before the foot had gone bad, and so he'd gone to the gallery and looked at her photographs. He had recognized some of the faces in her pictures, street kids who had told him their stories. He saw her standing at the far end of the room, smiling and talking to a group of admirers. He had seen her before, long ago, when she was a girl. He had seen her in the front window of the house on the hill, arguing. Henry March's house. Her name was in the paper; it was stenciled onto the front window of the gallery, as if she wanted to be found.

What Walter was planning. What they had planned together. The hospital in the north. He could already see the flames on his TV. He could already see the news broadcasts. How many hostages, how many dead. He could see the headlines, transcripts of investigations, high-level hearings. The truth pushed into the faces of the sheep reading their morning papers, forcing them to see what they were a party to, what their lives, their houses and dreams really cost. He wishes he could be there when it happens, at the hospital, that he could stand in the rubble among the bodies, but he knows he will never leave this house again. He must content himself with his own final action. The last ghost will come and they will have their battle. So he must stay vigilant. He must be ready.

Some writers talked about movies, about TV shows, as if this meant anything, as if it could compare to this.

He came back from the war and what had he done? Such a simple question. He'd asked it so many times. What had he done?

He had sold telephones. He had sold telephones.

He reached for his notebook, his pen. He needed to write this down before he forgot it, before it was taken from him again, but his notebook was not where he'd left it. He moved as quickly as the dead limb would allow, crashing into furniture, lamps. Pill bottles toppling, crystals falling, breaking their beams of light. Breathing hard, his heart grinding like it was going to sputter and fail. Not yet. Don't go yet. After all this time, the waiting, the planning. He sits on the carpet, trying to catch his breath, slow his heart. Feeling the numbness in his arm dissolve. Not yet. The notebook is there on the floor, right beside where he fell. He picks it up, opens to a blank page. Pen tip on paper, a tiny dot of blue ink. What he had remembered. He had come back from the war and what had he done?

It was gone. He dropped the notebook, the pen. All this paper surrounding him, so tall, so dry. Moths in the air, flitting from tower to tower, dust falling from their wings.

He let his head fall back against the bookcase.

They took everything worth taking.

6

Jimmy wouldn't do the radiation or the pills. Elaine had done the radiation, doctors in goggles behind leaded glass, Elaine alone in a chair on the other side, bombarded with atomic rays. Her skin burned, her hair shed. Her body still warm as Jimmy carried her back to her hospital room. The orderlies were there, offering, it was their job, but Jimmy was going to lift his own goddamn wife into her bed. Elaine pleading to stay uncovered even though it was the middle of winter, the room bone cold, Jimmy's teeth chattering. Elaine's cheeks and breasts burned, her insides burned. Jimmy holding a glass of ice water to her forehead, her wrists. Elaine saying, I don't think they're going to get it this way, I don't think they're going to burn it out of me. Jimmy telling her not to talk, to save her strength. Holding the glass to her cheeks, her ankles. Elaine saying, I think it's tougher than this.

The pills were no better. Elaine's roommate had been taking the pills. A woman about their age, already a widow, her husband dead from a heart attack a few years earlier. An easy exit. This woman given paper cups of capsules and tablets, gagging while she tried to swallow. Lurching out of bed to vomit in the toilet, or the sickness coming on her so suddenly that she couldn't stand fast enough and simply threw up on herself, on her bedclothes. Spitting, crying while the nurses cleaned her up, carried her from the bed while they changed the sheets. The woman reduced to this, something to be lifted and wiped.

The pills were no better than the radiation. When he'd been presented with the options, Jimmy had told his doctor that he wasn't interested in either.

In Los Angeles he rented another car, a massive Lincoln, a grandchild of the car he'd driven in San Francisco, maybe. He called Squires's number from a pay phone and got another number from Squires and hung up and waited. Called the new number. Squires sounded like he couldn't believe the call, that this was really happening. Jimmy asked what new information he had and Squires said that there was nothing yet, just what he'd already passed along. Squires asked about his trip, where he'd gone, where he was now. Jimmy hung up the phone with Squires in midsentence.

He sat in a motel room with the photographs Squires had given him. Pictures of a big guy with long hair and an unruly beard. Looked like a burnout, looked like a bum. Shots taken from a distance, the bum coming in and out of a drugstore with booze bottles in brown paper bags. This was their guy, or somebody's guy, the hound who was already on the trail. He looked about right. He looked like one of the fuckups they used back when Jimmy was working, guys who would do just about anything for money or booze or dope, the chance to feel like one of the boys.

Squires had given him three addresses. The first was Henry March's old address in Oakland. March's wife was still there, supposedly, along with his son. This would be a dead end. Jimmy wasn't sure why Squires had given him the address. He already knew the address. Jimmy sitting down the block from that house years ago, watching Hank March taking a walk, holding his unsteady son's hand.

The second address was March's daughter, now in Los Angeles. This was closer to what he needed. This was more of a possibility. She'd estranged herself from her mother, apparently, and this might mean something, the reason for the split, something she might know.

The third address was a house on the beach, a science-fiction writer who Squires had stressed should be seen first. Squires had said that he didn't know the relevance of this man to what they were doing, only that he was relevant in some way. The writer's name meant nothing to Jimmy. Back at the Atlanta airport, waiting for his flight, he'd looked at the paperback spines on the newsstand shelves but had come up empty.

It wasn't much, but it was enough. He could work with it. His old self was coming back. He could feel it in his arms, his hands. Strength returning. Getting off the mountain, out of those fucking airports. Driving in the Lincoln with the windows down. West Coast air. Shaking off the rust.

He lost two days to his sickness. Two days, three days, it was hard to tell. Facedown on the floor in the motel bathroom. Sitting on the toilet. Unable to stand for the hot spears in his groin, his ass. Stripped to his undershirt and shorts, his sweat chilling on the cold floor. Two days, three days. Drinking water from the toilet like a dog.

There was a small window high on the wall, facing the alley behind the motel. Bums came into the alley, rummaging in the trash. Men laughing at night, drinking, breaking glass. Hacking coughs and curses in Spanish. From his angle on the floor, Jimmy watched the window, listened in the dark.

He stayed in the bathroom. Sometimes he turned his body to look out into the other room, the beds still undisturbed. He had to fight the urge to crawl to a bed, burrow inside. He knew that if he got in he would never get out. He would die in that room. But he would not die in the bathroom. He knew this, somehow, he was sure of it. As long as he remained prone on the floor this would pass. This was a warning, a glimpse into the future. What he had to look forward to.

He slept intermittently. He had learned over the past few months how to sleep through pain. He had come to accept it, a constant companion. He put himself to sleep knowing it would be there when he woke and was proven right when it was waiting for him in the morning. This was comforting, somehow. There was some small measure of vindication involved.

On the second day, the third day, he smelled hot dogs cooking through the window from somewhere down the street and he wanted a hot dog, hungered for a dog with the works and then he knew he would get up from the floor, would stand again, would walk, reenter the world. Before long he was in line waiting for his hot dog, was standing by a picnic table in the parking lot devouring the thing, his teeth slashing, the meat bursting from its skin. Knowing he'd throw all this up in a matter of hours, minutes maybe, but unwilling to moderate at this point, not after what he'd been through over the last few days, not after getting a look at where he was headed.

The waves tumbled onto the beach, spitting froth. Jimmy sat in the Lincoln and watched the house, the water, waiting for night.

Jayne would be home by now. She would have found the notes, would have called Steven, and he and the kids would have flown down, everyone looking for Dad, for Grandpa. It would have made the local news, maybe. Search-and-rescue teams trawling the gullies and creeks.

Full dark. Jimmy got out of the car, crossed the road. There was a wooden footbridge that ran back along the side of the house. He was now at the point where simply walking was painful. This was called progression. This was called metastasis.

The windows of the beach house were dark, curtains drawn, though there seemed to be a light in there somewhere, seeping through. Jimmy realized he already had the gun in his hand. Must have taken it out as soon as he'd left the car. Old habits.

The door was unlocked. Jimmy turned the knob, pushed it open. Tight hinges, like there was someone behind it pushing back. No, it wasn't the hinges, there was a bunch of shit in the way. Through the light from the road Jimmy could see what looked like walls of paper, books, notebooks. Slowly sliding, little avalanches, blocking the door. He shoved it all the way open, stepped inside.

His eyes adjusted, slowly. Paper everywhere, piled nearly to the ceiling. A path or a tunnel carved through it, leading farther into the house.

A flashlight. Maybe a flashlight would have been a good idea. Stupid old man.

There was light coming from the other end of the tunnel. Jimmy went farther in. The tunnel turned, turned again.

Someone coughed. Jimmy knew that cough. Jimmy woke with a cough like that every morning. An old man's cough, impossible to stifle. Expelling dust. Jimmy turned a corner. Paper walls. Another corner. Another and a man was there, ten feet away, standing in the tunnel, backlit from the room behind. A fat man on crutches, his face unshaven and soaked with sweat. The man looked at Jimmy and something tumbled into place inside him. Fear now, flickering in his eyes.

Something clicked inside Jimmy, too. This man.

Jimmy said, "I know you."

The man backed into the room, just a single lamp on in there but so bright compared to the dark house. Jimmy blinded, walking forward with his eyes almost closed, the gun pointed out in front and thinking, I know this man. Strip away the age and sickness and this man is familiar to me.

"My name is Robert Zelinsky." Jimmy heard the voice from somewhere in the room. Still so goddamn bright. He tried staring at the black metal of the gun to focus his eyes. Pointing in the direction of the man's voice.

"My name is Robert Zelinsky," the man said. "My name is Lawrence Tarhammer."

Jimmy's eyes were working again. The man was standing against the back wall of the lighted room. The bed had been pushed to the side, a dresser, a desk, piles of paper, everything shoved to the walls except eight or ten kerosene tanks set in two rows across the room. Jimmy standing in the middle of the rows, this man standing at the other end holding a shotgun.

"My name is Daniel Davis," the man said. "Denver Dan Davis. That is my true name, my only name." His shotgun aimed at the kerosene tank closest to his bandaged foot.

Jimmy turned back through the door, into the tunnel, heard the shotgun fire, then nothing, no explosion, a missed shot, lucky, lucky, stumbling back through the darkness, the paper walls collapsing, threatening to bury him, Jimmy pushing through the paper, another shot, then nothing, still lucky, Jesus, out the front door onto the footbridge, running, limping, the pain beyond pain, making it to the end of the footbridge, out on the road, no headlights, the pavement hard under his steps, the pain everything, and then there was another shot and the explosions chained through the house, ripping through the walls and roof, lighting the night orange and yellow and red. Jimmy fell forward, off the side of the road toward the Lincoln, rolling, explosion after explosion, the night lit to midday, Jimmy covering his head, the sound of the house collapsing, the stilts giving way, the footbridge, a wooden groan and crash on the rocks, and then just the sound of fire and a ringing in Jimmy's ears.

He opened his eyes and the sky was mostly dark again, just gray smoke and the light of the fire behind him. Something in the air, falling. Looked like confetti. Landing on his eyes, in his open mouth. A slow rain. Weightless paper scraps twirling in the air.

PART FOUR

Blue Line

1

Coming back, calling, waking slowly, thoughts returning, smells, sounds returning, coming back, touch, the feel of air on his face, in his nose, his mouth, his eyes still closed, calling, gathering pieces of himself, coming back, waking slowly, then Thomas's eyes open, Thomas awake.

Just before dawn, dark shapes in the gray room. The other bed, the shared dresser. Outline of the window; slow, rippling flashes in the glass, occasional headlights from cars or the train. Grain swimming in his sight like television static, soft and silent as snow.

Thomas sets his feet on the floor, pressing his toes into the wood, the balls, the heels, feeling the solidity beneath him, the earth two stories below. The ragged end of a prayer or verse circling in his head. Trying to catch it by its tail, pull it back so he can see its entire body, the long bright string of words, his lips moving in the dark.

Prayer of Richard. Hezekiah's Prayer. Prayer for the Sick.

The rusty squeal of far-off train brakes navigating a turn. He stands at the window that later in the day will look out onto the brown brick of the neighboring building but now simply looks out into more gray. Cold morning, the second in a row. He squints at the clock, trying to make out the time in the dark. Alarms are set for five-fifteen, seven days, but he is always up early.

Dressing quietly. Ducking to see himself in the mirror. Patience with his thick fingers as they attempt to maneuver his shirt's buttons through their eyelets. Patience with the ponderousness of his movements. Breathing deeply, fully, as he has been taught.

In the bathroom, someone flushing in one of the stalls behind him, another early riser, Geoffrey or Gregg or Lavar, one of the newer men who still can't sleep, haunting the hallway all night, pacing down to the bathroom and then turning and walking to the window and the fire escape at the other end. The movements of these men a comforting thing to Thomas, their eyes open while he slept and splintered, while pieces of him scattered in the night.

Philippians 4:13. Matthew 8:8. Lord, I do not deserve to have you come under my roof, but just say the word and my servant will be healed.

Breakfast in the dining hall, other men coming in, stifling yawns, lighting cigarettes, sitting at the long tables with coffee and eggs and bacon, hash browns, buttered toast. Smoking and talking, low-toned conversations, just a word or two on each end, then long spaces of silence. Checking watches, the clock on the wall above the bulletin board. Checking Bibles, checking watches.

Everyone into the Fellowship Hall at 6 A.M., filling the rows of folding chairs. More cigarettes, smoke swirling lazily in the overhead lights. Some men already wearing their orange jackets, checking and rechecking their pockets for Bibles, cigarettes, change, the small paper cards with the address and phone number of the ministry barracks. Always checking, rechecking. No one here used to constancy or routine. No one here used to things being where they thought they'd put them.

Reverend Lee's aftershave enters the hall a half second before Reverend Lee. Six-oh-five, precisely. Routine is crucial, precision is crucial. Out beyond the boundaries of routine and precision are chaos, temptation, anger. The men have all been taught this and they know it to be true. They have lived beyond those boundaries.

Reverend Lee steps to the podium. His gray slacks, his white dress shirt, his black tie. Shirtsleeves rolled to his elbows, shoes shined and gleaming. He checks his watch. Even Reverend Lee reduced to checking from time to time. Even Reverend Lee still feeling the pull of that other place.

Reverend Lee looks out over the assembled and says, Let us pray. The men stand and bow their heads. There is the prayer and a short sermon and then any necessary announcements. Lists of duties, names of new arrivals, a weather report. Things to be aware of. Construction on certain lines, problems in certain cars. At the end of the meeting Reverend Lee steps from the podium and takes the hands of the men in the front row and those men reach back and everyone clasps hands, reaching over empty seats, across the center aisle, heads down, eyes closed.

Prayer for the Work Day. Prayer for Peace. Happy are we who are called to His supper.

They leave the Fellowship Hall and wait outside to board the bus. Early light now, noise from the street. The bus's exhaust mixing with cigarette smoke. The bus is a repurposed school bus, painted black with white hand lettering: *Outreach Christian Fellowship. Rev. Lee Metzger, Pastor.*

Out onto Division Street, and then from train station to train station, dropping a man at each. Thomas's view from the back of the bus is of the men shoulder to shoulder, *Outreach Christian Fellowship* in large white letters across the backs of their orange jackets. The ranks thinning gradually, spaces opening in the seats as the bus makes its way around the city.

Thomas gets off at Clark and Lake. His territory is the handful of stations at the far reaches of the Blue Line, just past the city limits. There is some overlap, one or two stations where Thomas could see another orange jacket walking the aisle a few cars down. There was no contact between the men if it could be avoided, nothing but the briefest acknowledgment, a nod through the windows at the ends of the cars. As a rule, the men worked alone. Reverend Lee did not want them to be seen as a gang or a cult. *Bible Riders* was the term people in the city used for them. It was meant to get a rise out of the men, but Reverend Lee told them it was nothing to get upset about. If the shoe fits, he said.

Down the stairs to the subway platform. The cold-air sewage smell of the station, garbage from overflowing trash cans. The bright metal smell of the rails. Thomas feels the wind of the train from the tunnel and hears the oncoming rush and then finally sees it. It is the most beautiful thing. He has always found it beautiful. A train is a prayer moving through a city. The engineer's voice squawks through speakers in the ceiling. Doors open on the left.

He had been approached on a train. They all had. There was a rightness to the symmetry of the process. They came from trains; they returned to trains. For Thomas, it was at the Kimball station by a man named Kimble, who disappeared not long after, one of the men who worked the Ministry for years and then went out one morning and didn't come back. Returned to the places past the walls of discipline and routine.

How many people on this train, do you think, share the name of the station? This is what Kimble had first said to him. Sitting beside Thomas, close, their knees touching, their thighs. Probably just me, Kimble had said. With the same name. I am probably alone in this regard.

Let me pray with you.

Thomas walks down the aisle of the first car. He slides open the door at the end and steps through. A second in the unprotected passage, then into the next car. He walks forward against the momentum of the train. Screech of the wheels grinding through a curve. Keeping his feet firmly pressed to the floor, redistributing his weight automatically in counterbalance to the sway and jerk, the thousand tiny movements of the train. Hands in his pockets. A small act of vanity, this ability to walk the cars without touching a pole or seat back.

You've been crying, Kimble had said, which surprised Thomas, because he hadn't cried in days. He'd done nothing but cry when he left Oakland, but by the time he'd reached Chicago he had stopped, as if there were nothing left, as if he was dried out. So he thought this was remarkable, how Kimble knew. It would be weeks of riding on his own before he could see what Kimble saw. What he'd looked like in that moment, on that train. Weeks of riding before he would learn that nothing was hidden if you had the strength to see.

You've been crying. Let me pray with you.

He averaged two or three a day. This was initial contact only. Most of this contact was ignored or rebuffed. Spat upon, hissed at, pushed away. Maybe one man a week he gave a card to would actually call. One man who would find the card in his pocket at some terrible hour and maybe find the dimes still taped to the card and find a pay phone and call the number and talk to whoever was assigned to the hot line. Maybe one man a month would actually come down to the barracks. Maybe one in three of these would stay. The odds are not good, Reverend Lee would say. The odds are great. The odds are exceptional.

Kimble hadn't asked who Thomas was, how he had ended up riding the train. It was as if those things didn't matter, as if they were so far beside the point that they were not even worth mentioning. It was early evening, rush hour, and Thomas had been riding for days. The other passengers forcing themselves not to see him. Not looking at Thomas and not looking at the space beside him. The empty seat a shared, shameful act among the other passengers. Then Kimble sat, without hesitation, their legs touching at one and then two distinct places. The raw, burned smell of cigarettes on Kimble's breath. His head bowed and his cowboy's growl low but clear enough that it was easy to hear through the rest of the noise, the conversations and radios and rattling progression of the train along the tracks.

We believe in one God, the Father, the Almighty, maker of Heaven and Earth. Of all that is seen and unseen.

He had come to Chicago because it was the only other place he knew. His mother had told him stories about how she and his father and Hannah had lived there before he was born. Hannah lived in Los Angeles, he could have gone to her, but he didn't know that place. To him there was Oakland, there was Chicago. He had maps and he thought that he might know the way.

He'd lived in the house with her for a while, after she passed. Her body on the kitchen floor. He arranged her arms and legs so she was lying comfortably. Placed a blanket over her at night. Stared into her eyes, but there was nothing there. This was the shell. He lived in the house and then he knew he had to leave, that if he didn't then someone would come and get him, and so he took what money he could find and rode a bus east. Days and nights, through mountains and farms, towns, cities. He remembered a trip like this from when he was a boy, sitting beside his sister in the station wagon, watching out the windows, the world moving in time.

He was tattered and dirty. He had been crying since Oakland. People kept their distance. When he reached Chicago he walked into the cement and noise, and then he saw the train overhead, the rusty trestles, the cars shaking by. His father had told him about this, years ago. Riding the train. Thomas sat and rode alone until Kimble found him.

It had taken Thomas weeks of riding to finally approach someone. Kimble had told him it would be hard. There was nothing easy about it. Those he needed to approach would be those he didn't want to approach. Those he was fearful of. Those clenched with rage. Those whose anguish came off their bodies like waves of heat. Those actually shaking with fear. Men speaking to themselves, whispering, moaning into the palms of their hands. Men smelling of sweat and other bodily fluids. Smoke and neglect. Terror.

Men on crowded trains with empty seats beside them.

The first few times he couldn't look the men in the face. He looked at their hands as he spoke. The calluses and cracked knuckles, the mighty rivers of vein. Thomas speaking so loudly that every other head in the car turned to see what was happening. But he learned to lower his voice, and he got enough courage to lift his face, to look these men in the eye. What he saw was great and terrible, just as Kimble had told him. After he'd looked at the first face, he was unable to look away.

Let me pray with you. Let me read you this passage. Let me give you this card with a phone number you can call. Let me give you change for the call. My name is Thomas. I am going to sit here in this seat beside you.

They did not approach women. There was a sister ministry farther down on Division Street that worked with women. They did not approach children, though there were plenty of children riding the trains alone, running from something. Children were the responsibility of the city. They would be pulled from the trains into foster homes, group homes. Out of one fire and into another. We'll see them when they're older, Reverend Lee said. Be patient, though it is difficult, though you see the fear and suffering. Be patient. You'll encounter them on the same trains when they're men.

He has lunch on a bench on the Jefferson Park platform, a bag of pork rinds, a bottle of Filbert's grape soda. Licking salt and grease from his fingers as he watches the traffic on the expressway below. He keeps his Bible on the bench beside him, unopened. That morning's prayer or verse still in his head, regaining volume now that he is outside the noise of the train. The buildings of the city far in one direction, the plains stretching away in the other. Blue sky, clouds piled high like towers. The train cars that stop at the station shedding steam in the cold air.

When he was a child, he'd believed he was a boy made of metal, with an engine for a heart, a computer brain full of schedules and routes. He'd moved along tracks that he'd constructed, or that he had found, left behind by others like him. Something had changed, though, he knew this. He had changed. The metal skin was a suit for a child and he could no longer fit inside. It still called to him, though. When he was sad or angry, or when he thought about his mother, when he missed her, he could feel the pull of the wires. He could still see the tracks stretching before him on sidewalks, along the barracks floor. In those moments he had to remind himself that he was no longer that child. There were no clear tracks to follow anymore, no metal skin for protection. But sometimes he still ached for the machine.

Early afternoon. Light through the grimy windows of the train. Forced-air heat. Seats nearly empty. Thomas walks the aisles, crosses between cars, sits for a time, watching the city blurring past. Telephone poles and wires, television antennae on rooftops. Montrose, Irving Park, Addison. Belmont, next stop. Doors closing on the left.

He had followed Kimble off the train. Thomas was one of the few who'd come directly onto the bus, into the barracks. He had dinner in the dining hall, went up to the bathroom to take a shower. When he came out of the water a towel and toothbrush and clean clothes were waiting for him on the edge of one of the sinks. He became Kimble's roommate. That was another rule: If you brought a man off the train, or a man called with a card you had given him, he came to live with you. He was your responsibility until he could stand on his own, until he was issued an orange jacket.

It took Kimble three nights to tell his story. Both men in their beds, Kimble smoking, the glowing red tip of his cigarette the only light in the room, pulsing like a radio tower. Kimble spoke slowly, deliberately. Where were we? he said at the beginning of each night, right after lights-out, lying flat on his back in the dark, the tiny red glow floating a few inches above his voice. His story a polished, oft-told thing. Kimble out beyond the limits, his old life, then Kimble on the train, approached by a Rider, then Kimble calling the number, coming to the barracks. Lighting a new cigarette from the dying end of the old. Telling his story until the first blush of sun out the window and then the alarm ringing, alarms ringing in rooms all down the hall, and Kimble saying, To be continued, rolling himself upright, placing his bare feet on the floor, toes, balls, heels, showing Thomas how to find his footing for another day.

More passengers on the train now, the end of the workday. Thomas walks, watches the faces and the prayer in his head. It is in the last car that Thomas sees him. A black man, middle-aged, sitting with his knees up, elbows on his knees, his hands open, head resting in his long fingers. The car crowded, but the seat beside this man empty.

The man's clothes are grease-stained and worn. A workman's jumpsuit. His eyes are closed. He is taking slow, shaky breaths, trying to get through some ferocious moment. Thomas checks his Bible, his watch. Begins to move through the car.

The apprenticeship with Kimble lasted a month. Thomas riding with him, plain-clothed, sitting inconspicuous, watching the man work. Having lunch together on a bench on the new Jefferson Park platform, then back on the train, Thomas watching, gradually realizing that he was hoping Kimble wouldn't make any contact, hoping that no one would take Kimble's cards, no one would stand with Kimble when he stood, for that would mean Thomas had been replaced. Kimble bringing this up one day while they ate lunch on the Jeff Park bench. Kimble already knowing this was something in Thomas's head. Telling Thomas that this was normal, this was what they all felt at first. That it was something to be embraced. You want to be replaced, Kimble had said. Being replaced is a joyous thing. It means someone else has heard. It means another man who realizes he is not alone.

There was no ceremony in the receiving of the jacket. Thomas didn't know what he had expected, some kind of formal presentation, but one morning it was simply hanging on the doorknob when he left their room. No one said anything. No one acknowledged anything. He dressed and ate breakfast and put on his jacket and sat with the other men in the Fellowship Hall and listened to Reverend Lee and then boarded the bus. When they reached Clark and Lake, Kimble nodded to Thomas and Thomas exited the bus alone. It wasn't until he'd got enough courage and looked the first man in the eye that it all made sense. It wasn't until that man had looked up at Thomas, until Thomas had sat. In that moment he realized the ceremony. The jacket was just a jacket.

Getting dark now. Thomas works his way to the back of the car, the black man sitting alone. The man's eyes closed, his mouth open, limbs pulled in like a mantis. Thomas squeezes past the man's upraised knees, sits in the empty seat. Other passengers looking and then looking away. You do not need to open your eyes, Thomas says. You do not need to uncover your face. Thomas's head down, his voice low through the noise of the train. The train's brakes screeching then silent then screeching. Let me pray with you. The other man's mouth closing, his jaw clenching. Let me be with you through this. Thomas speaking the words he had woken with, the prayer he'd found in his head that morning. The other man's knees lowering, his leg touching Thomas's in one place, in two.

The holy moment.

2

Raw light at dawn, white and blue, a clean chill in the air. Hannah stood at the pasture gate, her hands on the rough wood, fingertips finding the cracks and splits. She wore an old sweatshirt, the hood back so she could feel the air on her neck, her ears.

The motel had once been a ranch of some kind. It still had some of the wide tractor trails, the sheds and animal pens. There had been horses out there once, maybe, in the pasture, gray figures stepping through the early light. But it was a windswept, lifeless place now. The scrub brush and tumbleweed had reclaimed the land beyond the half-rotted fence. The ranch overcome when the desert returned.

There were birds on the fence posts farther down the line, crows smoothing their wings, beaks darting, feathers rippling from the contact. This felt like a far country. It hadn't felt that way the night before, the day's drive still in her mind, the manageable space between two points. But this morning, in this light, she felt that she'd woken in a very distant place.

They had taken buses west from her studio, changing lines every mile or so, Dickie insisting that they keep to the most populous areas of the city, streets with crowds, buses with standing room only. Safety in numbers, Hannah supposed, though she didn't feel safe. It was evening by the time they reached Bert's house. Dickie waited outside while she spoke to

Bert, telling him about her impromptu trip, assuring him that everything was fine. Bert offered her some cash which she immediately refused and then thought better of, accepting the small, thick roll along with the car keys. There was someone else in the house, she knew. She could hear music from upstairs, the bedrooms. Bert asked again if she needed help, but she'd already backed out the front door, started down the long driveway to where Dickie stood waiting.

She'd called the photographer who'd taken the cabaret pictures. He'd given her the address of a small bar in the shadow of the Silver Lake Reservoir where the cabaret appeared one night a week. Dickie stayed outside, keeping watch, while she went in. The room was still the daytime bar, with a handful of locals half haunched on stools, but it was beginning to transform. A few young men carried garment racks filled with gowns, others hauled lights and sound equipment through the front doorway. There was no door in the doorway, just a black curtain the men had to brush aside with no small degree of annoyance as they carried speakers inside, a mixing board, a cardboard box filled with colored gels for the lights.

The young Mexican was in the bar, directing traffic. The other men called him Gael. He recognized Hannah when she walked through the curtain. He stiffened a bit, watching her while he gave instructions to a man carrying a bag of multicolored boas.

It is the ghost catcher, he said. He nodded to the bar and when she declined he motioned to the bartender, who made him a drink, something dark with ice.

She told him she wanted to find the man from the photograph he'd seen in her gallery. She'd always been fascinated by the picture, couldn't get the thought out of her head that he might really exist. She was hoping to make her own photograph of him, all these years later.

Gael laughed. I don't think anyone makes pictures of the white ghost, he said. But he took a drink and gave her the information she asked for, the location of his father's ranch, what little else he knew about *El Fantasma Güero*. He believed the man lived in one of the surrounding southern coastal towns, though he had no idea which one. The ghost always just appeared when Gael's father needed him, standing at the gate to the ranch with his suitcase and tripod. Gael believed that he rode the bus up to the ranch. There was only one bus, which stopped a couple of miles south of his family's home, and this was probably where the ghost disembarked, walking the rest of the way along the side of the dirt road.

"They met in my father's office in the main house," Gael said. "Wednesdays, always the middle of the week, in the afternoon. That was the routine. My father is a man of routines. I suppose the ghost received instructions then, if there was something that needed handling. If not, I don't know what they talked about. Maybe they just had a drink. My father's confidant, possibly. His confessor."

Another young man stopped and asked a question and Gael pointed toward the back of the bar.

Gael looked at the camera hanging from Hannah's shoulder, and Hannah asked if she could take his picture. He threw up his hands theatrically, said that he wasn't dressed. Then his smile faded and he nodded, his hands returning to his drink. He looked away, out into the changing bar, a practiced pose of chilled indifference. Hannah waited, watching his profile in the frame, his jawline and dark eyes, the neon beer signs in the background, red and yellow and green. She waited until he turned back, confused, impatient, looking at her, into the lens, and then she pressed her finger, releasing the shutter.

Before they had left her studio, Dickie had told her to throw away the rest of the pills. She'd flushed them, a bottle at a time, tablets plopping into the toilet water. He'd told her that it might be rough for a while, but she just had to make sure he didn't find anything else to take.

On their way out of the city, he had stopped under a freeway overpass in Hollywood, knelt in the dirt there and dug something free, a brown paper bag, folded tight. She had been relieved when he'd opened the bag and she saw that it contained a gun, not pills, though she knew this meant that she was very far down the rabbit hole indeed.

She'd watched him as he drove Bert's car. He had changed since that final night at her studio, as if telling his story had resurrected some long-dead side of him. He spoke and acted with a quiet determination now, a clear focus. His body had changed. He moved simply, purposefully. It was not any kind of drug or fluke or instinct. This was training, this was experience.

They'd pulled over a few times so he could throw up by the side of the road, or just retch and heave, groan and spit. Each time he climbed back into the car, pale, shaky, and each time he shook his head when she started to speak. He stopped one other time, at a small pharmacy in Tijuana, and she was about to argue when he gave her a list of a few things they'd need, nonpharmaceutical.

The motel was the last stop before the coastal towns Gael had spoken of. It had come out of nowhere the night before, appearing in the headlights as they made their way in the dark. Nothing else around for miles. There was one other car in the dirt lot, a pickup with blue-and-white Jaliscan plates, but the windows of the motel rooms were dark. A husband and wife ran the motel. The wife checked them in, wrote down the name Dickie gave and took the money and handed him a key. Her husband puttered in the room behind the counter. They seemed like farmers to Hannah, as if maybe they had owned this land in its previous life and had simply adapted to the new terrain.

They had shared the single motel room bed, sleeping stiffly. Hannah had woken to a rooster crowing somewhere in the distance. She'd risen and sat on a wooden bench that hung from chains fixed to a corner wall. She had found a book in Bert's car, a paperback western with a painted cover of a cowboy on horseback, a town's main street behind him, the hotel and general store, a group of worried-looking men outside the saloon doors, all pointing at something approaching from off the cover. Hannah couldn't tell if the rider was readying himself to defend the town or if he'd just robbed it blind and was on his way out. The sky above was a mad swirl of fire, orange and yellow and white.

She didn't know if this was something Bert was considering turning into a movie or if he was reading it for pleasure or if it belonged to someone else, left behind beneath the passenger seat. She'd sat on the bench in the motel room and tried to read but the light was bad, so she'd set the book down and put on her shoes and a sweatshirt and left the room, walking out to the fence, the last barrier against what was out in the desert, what the desert contained.

She watched the sky color slowly and imagined it red and orange and white, swirling with fire, the sky from the Wild West cover. She imagined the thing in the desert rushing out through the fence and through her and the buildings behind, sweeping the land clean, leaving nothing but dirt, dust, ash.

She'd wanted to take Dickie's picture while he slept. A violent act, the first that had come to mind. After she'd woken, she'd stood over him, her toes on the cold tile, pointing the camera. She'd wanted to take something from him for what he had done, for bringing her to this place. But she'd known this was not quite right. She'd lowered the camera, walked to the bench, picked up the book. She wasn't really sure who was to blame.

The rooster crowed again, finally on time. She watched the last bird leave its fence post, lifting into the air, and then she turned back to the motel, the truck in the lot, Bert's car parked at the other end. Dickie was there, had been there for she didn't know how long. He was sitting on a stool outside their door, watching her, smoking, the cowboy paperback open on his knee.

3

A night of blowing paper dust out his nose, plaster dust, soot. Coughing up something that looked like schoolroom paste. His clothes smelled like kerosene, so he threw them into the Dumpster behind the motel. He still had his gun, all his limbs and digits. He'd turned his ankle when he'd fallen on the road but other than that he couldn't say he was anything less than damned lucky. He used every tissue and towel and roll of toilet paper in the motel room, blowing his nose, coughing it out. Finally had to pull the sheets off the second bed, use those.

Denver Dan the Telephone Man. Jesus Christ.

Jimmy stood in a phone booth down the street from the motel and dialed, ready to tell Squires that their first lead had almost gotten him killed. He thought better of it, though, and hung up the phone before the second ring. This wasn't really any of Squires's business. It wasn't any of their business. Squires, Paul Marist, whoever else might be sitting in an office somewhere back east. It never had been. Jimmy realized this now. He rolled up the paper with Squires's number and shoved it into the phone's coin slot, watched it disappear.

He tracked down the address for Henry March's daughter, a corner building in a Mexican neighborhood at the northern edge of the city. Jimmy sat in the Lincoln and watched the place for the better part of an afternoon. He was just about to throw in the towel when she appeared, with none other than the bum from Squires's photos, driving a more-than-gently-used Mercedes, baby blue.

She was about the same age as Jimmy's son, looked nervous in a way that didn't quite fit her, as if the worry was something new that she was still grappling with. Jimmy followed them to a bar a few neighborhoods south. The March girl went inside and the bum sat around the corner in the Mercedes keeping watch. The explosion at the beach house had been in the news and Jimmy didn't know if this meant anything to the bum, if Denver Dan meant anything, if that was the reason for the jitters and the lookout act. The bar had a curtain in lieu of a door and when someone came in or out, Jimmy could see the girl inside, talking to a tall Mexican. A while later Jimmy followed her and the bum back to her place, sat down the street for a while, but there was no further movement and he was exhausted, his ass and ankle aching, his ears still ringing, so he went back to the motel, hoping somebody had changed the towels and sheets.

He lost two more days to the sickness. Two days, three days, shivering on the bathroom floor. This time he began to hallucinate, shapes and figures forming in the dark. Women in the room with him when he reached up and turned on the light. The two whores from the apartment on Telegraph Hill all those years before. The skinny white girl standing in the shower and the junkie Negro sitting on the john, both staring, watching him shake on the tile.

He turned and saw Henry March standing in the corner, wearing his headphones, holding his camera and ledger. March's face impossible to read, the fluorescent light filling the lenses of his glasses, obscuring his eyes, whatever expression might be back there.

Where's your book, Hank? Jimmy whispering in the bathroom. Where's your book?

Jimmy thought of Jayne. Stories in the newspapers, on TV. A dark moment returned, exposed by Henry March. What was written in his ledger. Jimmy thought of Elaine, the memory of Elaine, hearing those things, seeing those things. Those rooms on Telegraph Hill. He thought of Steven, his grandchildren. This is how he would be remembered, what his name would come to mean.

One fist, then the other. He pushed his knuckles into the tile until his head and chest lifted from the floor. His body like lead. He grabbed the toilet rim and pulled. Grabbed the edge of the sink. Watch this, girls. Watch this, Hank. Hearing a noise in the room and not knowing where it was coming from and then realizing it was coming from him. A prehistoric growl. The pain just fucking unreal. Pulling himself to his knees, his feet. His face in the mirror, the reflection of the bathroom, his private audience, watching. Blood on his knuckles, blood in his eye. Eyes in the mirror, teeth in the mirror. Watch this, Hank.

The roar rising, filling the room.

When he came back to the bright autumn world the March girl and the bum were gone. The Mercedes was nowhere to be seen. There was no movement at her place. Jimmy let himself in. A photographer's studio and gallery. A small living space. Boxes and binders of pictures and negatives, more than he had time to go through. A wall of postcards that had been sent by her retarded brother.

It took him too long to get the name of the Mexican that March's daughter had been talking to at the bar. He had to squeeze the bartender a bit. Took him too long to find the Mexican's apartment. He spent too much time inside the apartment, waiting for the guy to come home and then dealing with him when he did, but this he couldn't help. He was amazed by how much strength he still had when he got going, how much his body remembered. He fed off the fear in the room, wanted to sink his teeth into it. The room white and hot, Jimmy pushing hard, the Mexican pleading. He was taking too long but it felt good to feel strong again. Jimmy pushing hard until the Mexican told him what he wanted to know. Not enough, though, not enough.

Jimmy pushing hard.

4

They drove to the last town before the coast. Dickie had traded Bert's Mercedes for the motel owners' pickup while the couple was out working in the chicken yard. Two criminal acts, suddenly, that Hannah had been a party to. He had pulled her down into this so quickly. She could see how it happened now. One move, another, and then there was no way of going back.

Dickie steered the truck along the town's crowded streets. There were people everywhere, drinking, singing, pushing into bars. Mexicans and tourists, some Americans. Strings of colored lights hanging low across the alleyways. The traffic moved slowly, cars and buses and flatbed trucks, horns honking when the revelers passed.

They found a hostel in the center of town. Four floors, with more partiers sitting in the long rows of open windows, drinking, laughing, shouting down to those on the street below. They paid for a room on the top floor. Many of the doors in the hallways were open, young men and women passing through with drinks in their hands. Dickie kept Hannah moving, into their room at the end of the hall.

A single mattress on the floor, a water basin and a pitcher on a table, an open window with a sheet hanging for a curtain. Dickie stood in the window for a few moments; too long, Hannah thought, before he finally pulled the sheet closed. One light, a single bare-bulbed lamp on an empty fruit crate by the mattress. Dickie emptied the bag from the Tijuana pharmacy. Scissors and hair dye, an electric razor. She sat on the crate and Dickie cut her hair, his hands moving at the nape of her neck, brushing the tops of her ears. She bent over the basin and he worked the dye through. They sat smoking, waiting for the color to set, and then she leaned over the basin again and he stood behind her, poured cool water from the pitcher, rinsing the dye clear, squeezing it loose with his hands. A brunette now, in the mirror, with what looked like a guerrilla cut, the kind of uneven chop she saw in news photographs of overseas extremists, women who left bombs in cafés and busy marketplaces.

Dickie took off his shirt and sat on the crate and she cut his hair, wrestling with the thick tangles, pushing his head one way and then another in an attempt to keep things symmetrical. She finally dropped the scissors and took after him with the electric razor. How many years is this? she said, and he made a sour face. The beard was next, one hand on his chest to steady herself, moving the buzzing machine up his cheeks in long, slow strokes.

When she was finished he stood in front of her in the mirror and they looked at the strange reflections. Lean distillations, reductions of their former selves. Her hands hung at her sides, still tingling from the work and the razor.

Hannah saw a last lock of hair on the crest of his clavicle, the bare skin there. He said something that she didn't quite hear. Her hands hot and buzzing. She leaned forward into his shoulder and blew.

Once it was dark and they'd changed clothes, he sent her down the back staircase, told her to exit through the alley behind the hostel. Get onto the main street and stay in the crowds. Don't look back. There was a parking lot they'd passed on the edge of town and she was to go there and wait. If he didn't arrive within an hour he told her to come back to the town center, find an American, ask to be taken to the police. Tell them everything.

He followed Hannah to the back door, watched while she made her way to the end of the alley, toward the crowd on the street beyond. He looked back over his shoulder one last time, then started after her.

The street was full and loud, cheers and songs and firecracker explosions like gunfire. Gunfire, possibly. He struggled to keep Hannah in view, her new profile, while watching other faces in the crowd. Looking for Walter or Julian or Sarah. He knew that they must be there, somewhere, that they must have followed this far. This was the only chance of losing them, even temporarily, before they reached the coastal towns. A new haircut, a shave, a separation.

Men held drinks out to him, women grabbed at his arms. He pushed through, watching Hannah, looking for Walter, looking for the man he'd seen back in Los Angeles, the old bald man watching them at the cabaret bar and then back at Hannah's studio. Someone from Zelinsky or Father Bill, he didn't know which. He wasn't sure that it mattered anymore.

A rousing cheer from the crowd and then the sounds of brass and guitar, a man's high voice, a mariachi band moving through. The crowd parted to make way, cutting Dickie off from his view of Hannah, seeing and then losing her again. Dickie trying to stay calm, moving forward, restraining himself from the impulse to pull or shove, careful not to draw attention. The band appeared, crossed directly in front of Dickie, the trumpet blasts filling his chest, Dickie losing Hannah and then seeing her again for a moment before she was swallowed by the crowd.

She walked with her hands deep in her sweatshirt pockets, her head down, moving through the crush of bodies, bumping shoulders, hips. She tried to think of herself as someone else, with a new face, a new name. Imagining that if she believed it then it would be true, and they would look right through her, she could pass free to the other side.

Horn honks. The sound of a band somewhere behind her. Hannah bumping elbows, chests. At every touch feeling sure that there would be a shout, a hand on her shoulder, at her throat, pulling her away into the dark.

*　　　*　　　*

He walked twice around the perimeter of the parking lot. There was a single light high on a wooden pole in the center but the edges of the lot were dark. Full of cars, many with U.S. plates. He didn't see her and didn't see her and then something hit his arm, a small stone. He turned and another hit him in the chest and there she was, a few rows away, crouching between cars, watching him, shaking, rocks in her hand.

PART FIVE

Half-World

1

The bum and the March girl had given themselves pretty good witness-protection jobs. Jimmy had almost lost them. The bum looked like a new man, younger, harder, more defined without all that hair. Not unlike the dodgers and deserters already in the coastal towns, kids with military-issue cuts, eyes dark from lack of sleep, too many drugs, fear.

The bum had traded the Mercedes for a pickup, so Jimmy traded the Lincoln, did it the old way, getting out at a stop sign and walking to the green Ford in front of him, sticking his gun in the window. *Vámanos.*

There was a string of towns along the water, with no significant differences between them that Jimmy could see. Noisy, loose, dusty. Bars, tchotchke shops, maybe a movie theater. Churches, more bars. The main streets empty during the day but nearly solid with bodies at night. It seemed a transient place, without memory or history, wiped clean by the ocean wind every morning.

He could be here. Here or somewhere close. This was a place Henry March could live unnoticed.

Jimmy had first seen the station wagon when he crossed the border. Two men and a girl inside, following the bum's Mercedes and then the pickup. They'd gotten turned around in the first town, when the bum and the March girl changed appearance, and so now they were following Jimmy instead.

Jimmy trailed the pickup, careful to keep enough distance so that the station wagon would stay lost. In the third town he placed the bum and the March girl and when night fell he headed back to the outskirts, parked the Ford, waited.

He'd bought a bottle of something to help dull the pain. The liquid was thin and clear but foul-smelling. The man at the liquor store spoke a little English, said that the expat kids drank it to get rid of hangovers and VD. Jimmy pulled the bottle from the glove box, covered his nose with his wrist, drank. It tasted like it smelled. He put his gun on the seat, lay back, waited.

There was a streetlight about a hundred feet from the car, bright, throwing shadows across the road, into the vacant lot on the other side. He closed his eyes and when he opened them sometime later there were two figures standing beside the car, guns pointed in at him through the open window. Young men, one black and tall, the other white and short and balding, with a mustache that hung down over his mouth.

Jimmy stayed prone on the seat, one hand open in surrender, the other still folded under the back of his head, his fingers now tingling and swollen with sleep.

He said, "Squires send you?"

No answer. He could see another figure out at the edge of the light, pacing. The girl, long-haired and thin.

The mustached kid said, "You're after Richard Ashby."

"Is that his name?"

"He said they would send someone."

"He was right."

The muscles in their faces jumped as they watched Jimmy, the bones in their gun hands twitching. He couldn't see their eyes but figured they were on something high decibel.

The kid licked the bottom of his mustache. "The girl he's with."

"What about her?"

"You can have Ashby."

"We're making a deal here?"

"We can shoot you right now."

"My guess is you already would've done that."

Jimmy waited, watched them twitch, fingers on their triggers.

"The girl doesn't mean anything to me," he said. "Whatever you do with her is none of my business."

The kid licked his mustache, nodded. "There it is, then."

"There it is," Jimmy said.

He needed to shift on the seat, relieve some of the pressure in his groin, but he resisted the urge. The kids watched him and finally the taller kid sniffed hard. Jimmy wasn't sure if this was a signal to the short kid or if he just didn't want to reach up to wipe his nose but at the sound they backed away from the car, shrinking in Jimmy's line of sight and then gone, just the sound of their shoes on the gravel road. Jimmy pulled himself up by the steering wheel and picked up his gun and watched the three kids jump across the grassy ditch and up into the empty lot. He shook his sleeping hand, trying to get some feeling back, then got out of the car, leaving the door open behind him, crossing the road and stepping down one side of the ditch, up the other, and then out across the lot, the kids maybe halfway to the road on the other side, stopping to light cigarettes with their backs still to Jimmy, his left hand still dead. The kids walking again, Jimmy gaining ground, watching their backs as he followed. He was breathing hard already but still gaining, backlit by the harsh white streetlight. His shadow grew, stretching out across the lot and when the head of his shadow passed underfoot of the kids the girl saw it and turned and Jimmy fired, hitting the short kid in the back and then the tall kid turned and fired wildly into the light and Jimmy fired again and hit him in the chest, banking on the guess that the girl was unarmed or slow to her weapon and he was right and so he shot her in the chest, now no more than twenty feet away. Couldn't be more exposed in the floodlit empty lot, so he shot them each one more time on the ground, the crack of the gun echoing in the cold air.

Their station wagon was parked on the far road. He opened the back-packs they'd left, found a bunch of Denver Dan's science-fiction books, some ammunition, baggies of pills. Was about to toss it all back into the car when he came across a brown paper bundle, something wrapped inside. He spun it loose and Henry March's ledger fell into his hands.

He stood for a moment, holding the book. He didn't open it. He didn't need to open it. He'd seen it so often in his dreams. What this book contained. What these kids knew. What the bum knew, maybe. What March's daughter knew.

Sixteen years of nightmares. He was shaking. He'd lost most of the strength in his arms and hands. He couldn't remember the last time he'd felt fear like this. All because of a little book. This thing's existence. This man's existence. What had he been doing, all this time up on the mountain? Not waiting. Hiding.

Jimmy dropped the ledger back into the car. He pulled a couple of sweatshirts from the seat and tied them together. Unscrewed the gas cap, fed one of the sweatshirt's arms down into the tank. He found a lighter in the glove box and held the flame under the far end of the sweatshirt until it caught. Sixteen years. He stood and watched the flame until he was sure it was strong enough to travel and then he crossed the lot again, past the three kids lying in the grass.

2

They entered one of the coastal towns that Gael had told Hannah was on the bus route. She counted on a calendar in her head, how much time had passed since she'd last known the date. It was Tuesday; tomorrow would be Wednesday, the day Gael had told her that the white ghost rode up to his father's ranch.

Dickie didn't want to stay at another hostel, they were too open and crowded, so they drove the streets away from the town center, into long rows of stucco houses, close-set, electrical wires running between them along the low roofs. Some of the houses with dogs chained in the front lots, some with kids playing. Everything beige and orange and brown. Hannah saw a sign in a window that said *Cuarto*, a Spanish word she knew, so she told Dickie to stop the car. A young woman answered the door. There was an older woman working in the kitchen beyond and three children, a boy and two girls. The woman spoke some English, for which Hannah was grateful.

When she started back toward Dickie there was an unfamiliar car there, a green Plymouth hatchback, and it took Hannah a moment to remember that they had abandoned the pickup, that this was their current vehicle.

She got back into the car, closed the door.

"They'd rather rent it for a month," she said. "A week, at least."

"Tell her we'll pay for a week."

Hannah didn't say anything and then Dickie said, "What is it?"

"I don't want to bring something to them."

"We won't."

"You don't know that."

"We won't be here long enough." He took his eyes from the mirror, watched her until she turned to him.

"Give her the money," he said. "Trust me."

They lay in bed, whispering. There was a light behind the house and it shone through the curtains, leaving dim strips of white across the floor, the bed. They could hear one of the women out in the kitchen, the older woman probably, Inés. Clatter of pots on the stove. The others were asleep, Inés's daughter Esmeralda and Esmeralda's children, Ramón and Eva and Luz.

"If it's him," Dickie said, "he'll recognize you."

"He hasn't seen me in sixteen years."

"You're his daughter."

"So I stay here, with the women and children."

"Hannah, please."

It was the first time since they'd left Los Angeles that he'd said her name. They'd come up with other names and had used them checking in to the motel, the hostel, but they'd never said them aloud. They'd spoken to each other for days without names.

"If it's him?" she said.

"Then I'll take you to him."

"And then what?"

"That's up to you."

They were up before the sun and Dickie left out the back, crossing the small dirt lot toward the neighbor's yard. Hannah went out into the kitchen and found Inés washing dishes, looking out the window over the sink, watching Dickie climb her fence.

She had breakfast with the children at the kitchen table. Fresh tortillas with beans and eggs and chorizo. Inés didn't look at Hannah. She worked at the stove, the sink, chopping vegetables on the counter. Esmeralda came into the kitchen with a glass of milk in her hand and a textbook under one arm, kissed the children, checked the progress on their plates, left again to study in the front room.

Hannah sat on the bed with the book she'd found in Bert's car. The photograph of her father was there. She'd brought it with her and kept it in the pages of the western. She tried to imagine Dickie moving through the town, riding the bus, looking for an older iteration of the man in the picture. That morning while he was getting dressed, he'd looked at her in the mirror over the dresser and said that he was sorry. She'd asked him what he was sorry for and he'd simply lifted his hands, as if that was the answer to the question. Everything.

The children were playing in the backyard. Hannah parted the curtains, watched for a while. Then she got her camera and went through the back door into the bright morning sun. The girls were kicking a soccer ball and Ramón was riding a purple tricycle. Inés sat on the steps, smoking a cigarette, pushing ash from her apron. Hannah sat beside her and after a while she asked if she could take pictures of the children. Inés nodded and Hannah stood and moved along the fence line, snapping the shutter, and then the children noticed and started mugging for the camera, stretching their mouths with their fingers and sticking out their tongues. Hannah moved in, got down on her knees, encouraging them. Ramón came over and wanted to hold the camera, so she helped him with its weight and he turned it on his grandmother and said, *¡Diga whiskey!* and Inés frowned and waved him off. The girls posed on the tricycle. Hannah stepped away to light her own cigarette, her back to the fence. The children waved and called to her in singsong and she smiled and gestured to the cigarette, patience, patience, but then Luz ran out and grabbed her by the leg, so Hannah stubbed the cigarette on the bottom of her shoe and allowed herself to be pulled back into the yard, into the laughter and ringing of the tricycle bell.

3

The streets were nearly empty and so he walked exposed toward the center of town. A warm morning after all that cold. He kept looking back at Inés and Esmeralda's house until he turned a corner and it disappeared from sight. He'd given Hannah the gun, for all the good it would do. He tried not to think about her needing to use it. He would be gone a day, or most of a day, and these would be the riskiest hours of the whole thing.

He found an open *carnicería*. The butcher was hacking at something on the counter above the display case. When Dickie entered the butcher glanced up. His face was flushed with exertion, like he'd already been working for hours.

"*Buenos días.*"

"English?" Dickie said.

"Yes."

"What can you tell me about the bus that goes north from here?"

"What do you want to know?"

"Where does it pick up?"

"In the plaza across the street."

"When?"

The man checked a clock on the wall behind Dickie. "Sometime in the next hour."

"When does it come back?"

"It makes a circle." The butcher drew one in the air with a red-stained finger. "It carries through the towns and then up to the ranchos in the north, dropping off workers. It comes through again at the end of the day, picking up workers, then back down to the towns for the night."

Dickie nodded at a carton of cigarettes on the counter and the butcher wiped his hands on his apron, handed a pack over, took the money Dickie held out.

The butcher said, "You have a job up there?"

Dickie lit a cigarette, nodded.

"You can take the bus or if you want to pay more for a faster ride there are trucks that will take you."

"Who rides the bus?"

"Whoever can't afford the trucks. Maids in the ranch houses, men who work in the fields, who do odd jobs."

"Americans?"

The butcher smiled. "We are all Americans."

"North Americans?"

"Some."

"Are they here long?"

"A few weeks. Then they are gone and someone else comes and works for a few weeks." The butcher scratched at his chin with his forearm, his hands stretched away from his face. "They are running from your war."

The butcher resumed hacking. There was a table by the window, so Dickie sat and watched the plaza on the other side of the street. A church stood at the far end, its doors open, a few elderly women hobbling inside for morning Mass. There was a small tile fountain in the center of the plaza. It looked like it had been dry for some time. Wires had been strung between the stucco buildings on either side, a few faded fiesta decorations hanging limp in the early heat.

There were a few men in straw hats sitting on the edge of the fountain. Another came. Another. And then an American, Dickie's age, maybe a little younger. Same haircut, same build. More Mexicans, a couple of women carrying large canvas bags. An older man, walking slowly, shielding his face against the sun. Dickie sat forward but when the man turned

Dickie could see that he was Mexican as well. Another American kid arrived, curly-haired, a backpack slung over one shoulder.

Earlier that morning, as he'd dressed in the bedroom, he'd apologized to Hannah. He knew that she'd assume it was for all that had happened, and he'd had to stop himself from saying more. He was sorry for the lie, another lie, that is what he'd meant. She wouldn't meet her father. She couldn't. Walter and the Sons were here, somewhere, the bald man was here, and Dickie was going to lead them all, he was the Pied Piper, running south, heading straight to the ghost. He would trade Henry March for Hannah. He was sorry, but it wasn't even a choice.

Dickie checked the clock and stepped out of the *carnicería*, walked across the street to the plaza and the fountain. He sat beside one of the women with the bags, drawing quick looks from the other American kids, sizing him up. Dickie kept his eyes on the street, smoked his cigarette.

Another older man entered the plaza, holding an empty shopping bag that folded in the breeze. He walked to the fountain and leaned in, pulling coins from the dry tile and setting them into his bag. The others made room for him as he shuffled along the edge. When he'd circled the fountain he twisted the bag closed and walked off toward the other end of the plaza.

There was a squeak of breaks and a long pneumatic sigh and then the bus appeared. Everyone stood. The bus looked like an American school bus that had been painted pink. There were faces in the windows and Dickie looked for an old white man. He waited in line and stepped up onto the bus and handed his money to the driver. The seats about half full. Another look at the faces before him. He found an empty seat toward the back and sat against the window. The bus started again, rolled away from the plaza.

The white ghost came aboard in the next town over. He was tall and thin, carried a cardboard suitcase in one hand, a battered camera tripod in the other. The legs of the tripod were bound tight with twine. He pressed its feet to the floor as he walked down the aisle to an open seat. He wore a loose shirt and linen pants, both almost white. A straw hat, the brim low and straight across his forehead. His face was roughened and

browned by the sun, cracked to long wrinkles at the corners of his eyes.
He wore glasses with dark lenses clipped onto the frames.

Dickie had no doubt it was Henry March, what was left of Henry
March. He recognized him from Hannah's photograph, despite the toll
of years and sun.

March made no show of it but he had seen every face in every seat
before him, quickly, even Dickie's before Dickie could look away. Dickie
knew men whose eyes moved that way. His own eyes moved that way.

March sat in an empty seat in the middle of the bus and the rest of the
passengers from the plaza got on and the bus started again. They moved
through the last coastal town and picked up a few more riders, then turned
north on the dirt road, the bus bumping along, up through the low hills that
ringed the towns, then into flat, barren country. The harvest was over for the
year. The work on the ranchos at this point probably maintenance, cleanup,
preparation. Men smoked on the bus, leaned across the aisle to share cigarettes or talk. March faced forward, or out the window, and when he turned
toward the glass Dickie could see him in the narrow strait between seat
backs. He thought of whispering the name up the thin passageway to the
face at the other end to see what reaction those words would provoke.

There were small wooden signs every few miles, signaling dirt roads
that led back to the ranchos. At each sign, the bus pulled over and let off
a rider or two, Dickie watching the man or woman walking down a path
through the brown stumps of a harvested field in the bus's wake of dust.
At the third stop March stood and walked to the front of the bus, got
off alone. Dickie watched him through the back window, March walking
with his suitcase and tripod toward a large ranch house in the distance.

Finally, only the curly-haired American and Dickie remained on
the bus. The driver approached another wooden sign, slowing, and the
American kid stood, looked at Dickie in the seat behind him, asked for
a cigarette. Then he gestured out the window to the rancho across the
field and asked if Dickie was looking for work. Dickie said that he just
needed to get out of the town for a while and the kid nodded like he
understood. He thanked Dickie for the smoke and walked to the front,
waiting for the bus to stop and open its doors.

4

He followed them to a residential area north of town. They stopped in front of a house with a sign in the window and Jimmy watched from the next street down. The March girl spoke with someone at the door and then she went back to the hatchback and talked with Ashby and then got out again with a backpack and went inside the house. Ashby drove away, probably to dump the car. Jimmy waited and a while later Ashby returned on foot, looking over his shoulder before quickly entering the house.

Jimmy spent most of the day in the Ford, moving streets every few hours, watching the house. The windows of the car were streaked with bird shit and dead bugs. He'd started drinking the firewater early and by nightfall he'd finished off the bottle and the next thing he knew he was waking to the sun pouring through the windshield, his body splayed across the front seat, bladder and head pounding. Stupid old fool. He got out of the car in a panic and pissed in the weeds. Pure alcohol, smelled like. Felt like liquid glass. He hitched up his pants and crouched, watching the house two streets over. There was no movement. His watch had gone dead but by the sun it looked to be midmorning. He got the gun from the car and shoved it into his waistband and walked, sweating from the top of his sunburned head, his mouth dry, legs stiff and slow.

There were some kids playing in the backyard and then he saw

the March girl standing by the fence, taking pictures of them. No sign
of Ashby. He watched for a while longer and when there was still no
sign he walked down to the house, knocked on the front door. An old
woman answered, smelling of a fresh cigarette. Jimmy told her he was
a police officer, an American. He knew jackshit in the way of Spanish.
Americano, he said, which he then thought might be a drink. I'm here to
see the woman, he said. The American woman. I have news about her
friend. Her *amigo.* Christ, he sounded like a fucking comedy routine.

A younger woman appeared in the hallway, looking concerned, and
then the March girl was there. She made him immediately, turning and
disappearing around the corner, so Jimmy pushed past the old woman
into the front room, following the March girl deeper into the house.
Down the hallway, to a room at the end. He entered in time to see her
legs waggling through an open window. He turned back down the hall,
the old woman yelling at him in Spanish, Jimmy pushing her aside,
marching into the warm yellow kitchen and then out the door into the
bright back lot.

Three kids, two girls and a boy, riding a tricycle in the dirt. The boy
steering, the girls holding on to his shoulders. Other houses and back
lots crammed in close. A fierce-looking pit bull chained to a metal stake
on the other side of the fence. The March girl stood at the end of the
lot. She wouldn't try to climb. Slow as he was, he'd get to her before she
made it. The children stopped riding and looked up at the commotion.
One of the girls rang the metal bell strapped to the handlebars. Jimmy
looked up and the March girl was moving toward him. He wasn't sure
what she was doing and then she stopped in front of the kids, blocking
them somewhat. She yelled to them and they moved away. Jimmy tried
to smile, took a step forward. Held his hands out, empty. Said, Honey, I
just want to talk.

There was a roar and the March girl yelled and something blistered
open in Jimmy's left leg, the meat just above his knee. He fell forward into
the March girl and she assumed his weight reflexively and then backed
away, letting him fall. Jimmy turned his head to see the old woman standing in the kitchen doorway holding a battered rifle, smoke leaking from

the barrel. He looked down at his leg. Not a direct hit, but direct enough, knocking out a chunk of his thigh. He felt nothing. This was shock or this was his leg numb already from the sickness.

Faces in the windows of the neighboring houses. Dogs barking at the gunshot. There was a man in the next lot, unchaining the pit bull and dragging the animal toward the gate, pointing the dog at Jimmy. Jimmy pulled his gun from his waistband and pointed it at the old woman but the rifle she was holding looked single-shot, so he turned it back on the man with the dog on the other side of the fence. The March girl had gathered the children and was moving them back inside the house. Black spots swimming in Jimmy's eyes. He tried to stand, fell, tried to stand again. Upright at last. He kept the gun trained on the man with the dog and walked through the gate into the neighboring lot. Into the house there, through the kitchen, the front room, out onto the street. Dizzy, the sun too bright. His legs working, though, so he made his way toward the Ford. Listening for he didn't know what. A siren, men shouting. Oh, this was fucking rich. They'd love this story back at the station. Jimmy shot by an old woman with a rifle that looked like it had been at the Alamo. Hobbling toward the car. No feeling below his belt, his legs moving purely by instinct. Left, right, left. Even a baby could do it. They'd love this back at the station, this would get some real guffaws at his expense. He'd left the March girl back there. He'd made a very loud noise. This was not the way things were done. He was trailing blood along the street and listening for whatever might be coming. The Ford was very far away. He fell to his knees and knew that the pain should be tremendous but there was nothing. Tried to get up but could not. He would not stay on his knees, though, he had never been on his knees for anyone and he wouldn't start now, so he unfolded all the way down, lying on his belly in the street. Arms out, the gun still in his hand. Dust in his mouth, the aftertaste of the firewater.

They'd love this back at the station but he'd be damned if they'd ever see him on his knees.

5

The bus drove back through the towns. Dickie sat alone, looked for the bald man, for Walter. Even if the change in appearance had worked and Dickie had lost them for a night, they'd have recovered, would be gaining ground.

They pulled over for a few hours so the driver could sleep in his seat. Dickie fought the impulse to get another car, go back to Hannah. He fought the impulse to find a drink. He sat in the shade outside the bus and watched the few faces that passed, hummed a tune in his head, one of the records Hannah had played back in L.A., a wordless blues that had seeped into his dreams.

In the afternoon, they started again. The bus passed low stands of manzanita, sandy tracts of pitchfork cactus, an open field where there was some police action, men staring at bodies in the grass. They drove through the third town and Dickie looked at the rooftops of the houses beyond the main street, trying to discern which one belonged to Inés and Esmeralda.

They stopped for gas at a station by the plaza and Dickie asked the driver how long they'd be staying. It wouldn't take much time to run back to the house to check on Hannah, but the driver said he was just filling the tank and then they would leave again. He didn't seem to care why Dickie had been riding his bus all day.

The plaza was empty except for birds. At the far end Dickie could see the old man with the shopping bag walking down the steps of the church. The driver finished and gave a short whistle to Dickie and they got back onto the bus.

They made the reverse circuit, most of the same riders getting on at the stops by the rancho road, sitting heavily in their seats, their faces streaked with sweat. A few of the men passed bottles of beer across the aisle. The sun was low, disappearing behind the far hills. Henry March got back on the bus, carrying his suitcase and tripod. He looked over the riders' faces again, quickly, before taking his seat.

It was dark by the time March got off at the plaza in the center of his town. Dickie waited for the bus to continue on a few streets before he stood and walked to the front and told the driver to let him off. The streets were getting full again, night crowds spilling out of the bars. A mariachi band was playing in a far corner of the plaza. The brass echoed off the surrounding walls, receding as Dickie moved past. A few blocks later, he found March on a quiet road of mostly abandoned storefronts, walking with his head down, in and out of the streetlight glow. Dickie stood back and watched March stop and unlock a door and enter. The door closed behind him. Dickie waited another few minutes and thought of Hannah again and started down the street, keeping out of the lights.

The door March had entered was a thick metal slab in a wall without windows. But the door just prior was open and the space was lit. Dickie stepped inside. It was a gallery, with framed pictures hanging on the cinderblock walls. A work light was blazing in the far corner, flooding the room. The room so bright that the windows facing the street now looked black. Dickie blind to whatever moved outside.

He walked forward and looked at the pictures. Images of faces, mostly Mexican men and women, workers like the people on the bus, looking straight ahead, or just slightly to one side, with a similar oblique gaze, almost always intent, questioning, as if they were attempting to make sense of what they were seeing. The faces close to the lens, but seemingly without any knowledge of the camera. No vanity or ego. Private things.

He turned. The pictures mounted on the wall behind him were the same as those behind the subjects in the pictures he'd been staring at. To the side of the image he'd been studying there was a small hole. He covered it with his thumb. There were other holes along the wall, between the picture frames, all at different heights. He stood between the two pictures in front of him with his thumb over the first discovered hole. It seemed that if he took a step to either side he would fall into something, through something.

There was no noise but there was a presence and Dickie looked to the front of the gallery and Henry March was standing in the doorway. He was without his hat, and his white hair was combed back from his forehead. The sunglass clips were off his glasses. His voice was deep and even and quiet. A ghost's voice.

"Someone sent you."

Dickie nodded.

"Who?"

"I don't know."

Dickie couldn't see the man's eyes. Even without the sunglass clips, March's lenses held the glare from the work light.

"I'm looking for a man named Henry March," Dickie said. He didn't know if the man still thought of himself by that name, if the name still meant anything to him. Dickie knew how possible it was to forget. Names, connections, memories. These were things they were supposed to leave behind.

He could see no change in the man with the name now in the room. March stood perfectly still except for a slight movement in his right hand, his thumb and forefinger rubbing together. A tic, maybe, or the neuron misfirings of age.

Dickie said, "People are coming for his daughter to get to him. They might already be here. Her name is Hannah. I don't know how long I can keep her safe."

The movement of March's thumb against his forefinger. Dickie realized he still had his own finger pressed to the hole in the wall. He let his arm drop slowly to his side.

"If I'm speaking to the wrong man," Dickie said, "then I apologize for bringing you trouble. If you're the wrong man then they'll just continue on after his daughter. And that's none of your concern."

Dickie watched March for some sign or recognition, some spark of memory. The man made no movement except for his thumb, his finger.

This was what happened. Dickie understood. This was what happened to men like them. Everything cut away. Even color cut away. The white ghost in this place. Dickie here, someday. A man in a room looking through holes in the walls.

Dickie walked toward the door. When he was a few feet away March stepped to one side to let him pass.

"I came here," Dickie said, "because I was told that you have a reputation for cleaning things up."

Dickie crossed into the doorway, their bodies close, and the ghost spoke again.

"And his son?"

Dickie stopped.

The ghost said, "This man's son?"

Dickie shook his head. "I don't know."

"His wife?"

"She's gone," Dickie said. He passed over the threshold, back onto the street. "I'm sorry. She's already gone."

6

1 bookcase
1 lot of electrical small parts including microphones, etc.
2 cameras, mounted
1 camera, loose
1 tripod
2 buckets paint, black
1 folding card table
2 sealed-beam work lights with clips
2 extension cords
Assorted cans of meat, vegetables, fruit
1 chair
1 electric hot plate
1 ceramic coffeepot
1 lamp
1 cot with sleeping bag
1 cardboard suitcase, with film
1 recorder, with headphones
1 man, standing, listening
The ghost, alone in his room.

*   *   *

There was a name now, in the air around him. He sat on the edge of his cot in the darkness and the name buzzed like a fly, circling. He swatted at it with an open hand but it was insistent, its small noise growing larger, the only sound he could hear.

In the beginning he had come to this country, working his way south, changing towns, rooms within towns every few months. A room in _____ with crying children on the other side of the thin wall. A room in _____ with a sheet in the window to block the sun and keep out the birds. He stayed off the streets as much as possible. When he was on the streets, he watched for Americans, white faces.

He had some money. He learned the language. He paid a woman in _____ to sit with him three times a week and go through books, line by line. He went to the towns' small, shabby cinemas. He practiced his Spanish in the dark, speaking along with the faces on screen, watching the same films two or three times a week. He grew to know Mexican cinema of all stripes, the actors and actresses, the names of the directors and cinematographers. He found the *novelas* some of the films were based on and picked his way through the grammar, the familiar plots, hoarding words. Alone in his rooms, he read the *novelas* aloud to hear his voice carrying the sound.

He did not read the newspapers. He wanted to know of nothing beyond the spaces he moved within. He kept a small radio and there was a station that arrived when the weather was warm that played film music most of the night. He was constantly wanting for sleep. It took him months to get used to the diet, the oversweet drinks. He took to rolling his own cigarettes because the Mexican cigarettes were unpalatable. The coffee was good, though, dark and rich. The coffee made up for the cigarettes. He grew accustomed to taking it with milk. Moving rooms, moving towns. He finally visited a dentist in _____ about the pain in his teeth and the man pulled the rotten bone from his mouth and set metal in its place. An infection set in and he was delirious for days, his face throbbing like a guitar string. He found himself at the house of the woman who taught him Spanish and she brought him inside and bent him over the sink in her bathroom and placed towels soaked in tequila in his mouth until his fever had subsided. He was left with the taste of metal in his gums, on his tongue. This faded but never left him entirely. The new teeth buzzed sometimes, in parts of certain towns. Coming into a radio field, perhaps, some kind of invisible current.

There were other Americans in the towns, criminals, artists, alcoholic businessmen fleeing their losses or their wives. In later years, young men began to appear, avoiding war, unkempt, bearded, believing that hair made a disguise, false names made a disguise. Not understanding the difference between hiding and disappearing.

Spiders in his room the size of a child's fist.

He bought a camera and lenses and a tripod. Films of various quality. He found work as a photographer and then as something else, developing a reputation as a man who could settle delicate matters. He traveled to the ranchos in the north or the villas by the sea and took photographs at lavish first communions or *quinceañeras,* and afterward the father of the girl would take him aside, into an office or bedroom and ask him to deal with something, destroy something, speak with someone discreetly. Criminals and whores, young women with babies. Paying them when possible, bus fare to leave town, sending them somewhere they couldn't cause trouble for the wealthy father of the child in their arms.

El Güero Fotógrafo. A name he disliked because he thought it would draw more attention than his skin alone. Or sometimes he was called *La Escoba,* which he was assured was not an insult, just a statement of fact. Or sometimes the ghost, the white ghost, a name given to him by the curious, timorous children of his wealthy patrons.

The fly buzzed in the dark room, growing louder, more insistent.

He traveled on foot or by bus if he was going a great distance. Up to the ranchos for a wedding or an anniversary. Sometimes accepting his patrons' hospitality and spending the night in a back room while the guests drank and danced in the fields. Laughter and song and fireworks in the night. He would be up with the sun and back down to the towns to deal with an indiscretion or a gambling debt or a bad investment, letting the men in question know that this was the final payment, that any further compensation would not come in pesos.

There were times when men would not accept money or threats. There were other ways of dealing with these situations and this was something he knew how to do, this was a skill he had acquired. Distancing himself from the moment. The action taking place in front of him but seeming very far away. This is who he was. He was a man who could do these things.

He had no history prior to Mexico. Every morning when he woke he cleared his mind of any memory, any name that might be waiting there.

The money was not as important to him as the accumulation of favors, respect, fear. This created something of a protective ring, a thin perimeter of men who were powerful in these small worlds and who needed and feared him and so would alert him to any danger coming his way.

After many years he settled in the string of coastal towns at the end of the peninsula. Dry places, despite the closeness of the sea. Everything was dust. He stood waiting to cross the main town street and the buses and pickup trucks passed by flinging dust. He could taste it on his tongue, feel it in his eyelashes. The furniture in his room sat under a thin film of it. Every night he took apart his camera and lenses and brushed the dust loose. His hand on the windowsill in the evening comes away powder white.

In _____ he came across a pair of storefronts on the south side of the street. The larger of the two had wide plate-glass windows at the front where he could see the entirety of the sun's daylong arc, the slow progression of light across the town. The smaller storefront had a thick metal door, an old, impenetrable-looking thing, green with calcium, striped with rust. There was a sink and a toilet at the back of the room. There were no windows. The man who sold him the rooms told him that the larger one had been a barbershop at some point in the past and that the other, the room with the door, had once secured something valuable, though he didn't know what.

So this was where he lived, in the smaller room with the door, without windows. A card table, a lamp, a hot plate, a sleeping bag on a cot. A monk's cell.

He stood and waited for the bus on the rancho road. Holding his suitcase of camera and lenses, his tripod. The motes of dust in the evening air moving like a flock, rising and falling, turning in unison to disappear, and for seconds it seems that the air is clear but then they turn again together and catch the last of the sun and it is like a thousand little golden doors closing.

He went to work in the larger storefront, sweeping out the dirt and trash that had accumulated over the years of its dereliction. He purchased some tools, drilled small holes in the cinder block between the two rooms, just below eye level.

Every couple of hours he took a break from his work and stood out on the sidewalk and smoked. There was an open lot behind the empty storefronts on the other side of the street, and in between the buildings he could see boys playing *fútbol,* running and kicking between the short groves of weeds and grass. A moment of banished history returned to him, as those moments sometimes did. Fugitive memories returning because of the bend of sunlight along the edge of a wall, the smell of American cigarettes, a stray line of verse. He watched the boys playing and inhaled his own smoke and thought of a boy kicking a ball in an alleyway long ago.

He lay on the cot at sundown and waited for sleep. Hours sometimes; sometimes it never came. He watched the last light withdraw from the room, disappearing through the tiny eyelet in the door.

He purchased other cameras, hung wooden blocks on the wall, mounted the cameras on the blocks, the lenses focused through the pinholes into the other room. There he hung framed pictures near the holes, images of weddings and *quinceañeras,* family gatherings in late afternoon light, a stretch of ripe cotton field bursting in the blurred distance. He drilled a small hole in the cement floor of the gallery and placed a tiny microphone inside.

When he was finished, he switched on the work light he'd set in the corner, propped the door open to the street, left the storefront space alone. He sat in his room on the other side of the wall and listened to shuffling steps, muffled voices. Spanish, Portuguese, English. He sat with the cords and buttons for the shutters of the cameras. The cameras clicking against the wall, the sound smothered by the cinder block before it could enter the other space. A voice every few hours, maybe; sometimes nothing for days at a time. Voices at night on occasion, the work light burning continually, drawing visitors, while he sat on the other side with the cords and buttons, shutters clicking in the dark.

He wasn't interested in photographing people who knew they were being photographed. There was some sacred space that disappeared when they were aware. A posed picture was a lifeless thing.

He developed the film in the back of his room. A line of glossy images strung across the ceiling. In the night their wetness gleamed in the light of his cigarette or the flashlight he used when he was reading *novelas*. When the prints were ready he made simple wooden frames and hung the pictures alongside the earlier photos in the gallery, slowly filling the walls. Occasionally the subjects of the photos returned, stood looking at the earlier photos of their own faces. This was what he waited for on the other side, clicking his shutters blindly. To capture an image of someone capturing an image, and the realization that would come, the play of features on their face, the understanding that something had been taken.

The fly in the room buzzed. He sat powerless before it. He couldn't let something like this stay with him, but the buzzing in the room had grown so insistent, the things the young man had said, the name, so he allowed this moment to fill his head, and with it came other moments. He saw himself lying in a motel room, smoking, staring up at the ceiling in the dark. There were others sleeping in the room. Their names flashed before him, their faces, and he tried to swat them away, swinging his hands around his head. Driving on the lower deck of a bridge and the girl on the seat beside him. Hiding behind a curtain in a living room while the boy trudges through the house, laughing, searching for him. The smell of the woman in their bed, the sweat at her neck, his hand finding hers in the dark.

There was a book. He remembered now. He could see the pages clearly, the handwriting, the ink pressed into the paper. He could see a secret history, dates and times and lists of chemicals. Accountings and reconciliations, as if mathematics could justify what they had done.

He saw a diagram drawn by his own hand of a door, the metal case filled with gears and tumblers and the long bolts that transfigured it, that made the door into something else.

He was surrounded now, a host of flies, their drone rising to a single note.

The things he had loosed into the world and the faces of his wife and son and daughter. He sat on his cot and wept into his hands. Music from films in his head. Names returning to him. *El Güero Fotógrafo. La Escoba. El Fantasma.* Another name, and then another, deeper name. The name returned to him by the young man. Brought back and held before him, shimmering in the air.

His face in his hands. Dust in his throat, in his mouth. Dust on his lips as he speaks the name aloud in the room.

He redrew the schematic from memory. There were men in the town that he hired for certain work and he showed them the schematic and they acquired the necessary hardware, the long metal they would cut into tumblers and bolts. He told them that there wasn't much time and they worked quickly, removing the great green door from its moorings and altering its body in such a way that it became the door from the schematic. Before they set it back into place he told them to reverse it, so that the metal arm which locked it was facing the interior of the room. He showed them one more drawing, a spring mechanism that would dislodge the metal arm once it was pulled. The door would become a wall then, irreversible. When they were finished the men looked at the door and one of them said, *Con esto, se puede permanecerse en este salón para siempre.* He paid the men and burned the drawings in his room, watching the paper fold and crumble, rise as smoke.

He didn't know who was coming, but he could imagine another figure, reemerging, a great beast who would never have forgotten what they had done, who they had once been.

He said the name again, the name the young man had returned to him, said it aloud to get the feel in his bones, in his hands. He repeated it, alone in his room, chanting until there was no other name, until the ghost became flesh again, and then he was ready to leave the room and walk into the daylight of the town.

7

He'd come to after passing out in the street and when he'd opened his eyes the man with the dog was almost upon him. Other neighbors gathering. Jimmy clambered to his feet and held them all off with the gun, limped to the Ford. Found a roach-ridden hostel in the fourth town, what seemed like an endless drive from where he'd been shot. He spent a feverish few days in the shade-drawn room, where he wrapped the leg wound and lay down foolishly, thinking that something would pass and then realizing finally that nothing would ever pass again and standing from the bed and moving slowly across the floor.

There was an unrecognizable face in the mirror. He'd lost blood and weight. His eyes were recessed and hard. There was no feeling in the leg. He could move it, he could walk, but it was nothing more than a post he dragged behind. He poked at it with a finger and felt nothing. Pressed the tip of his pocketknife into the skin and muscle and felt nothing. One limb gone. He pissed and felt nothing and knew that this was worse than the pain, that there was no stage after this. He cleaned himself up as best he could and left his room and walked into the bright day of the town without a plan, without thought of a plan. He sat on the edge of the small concrete fountain in the plaza with the birds and the other old men and tried to eat once and threw up the handful of sunflower seeds into the dry basin behind him and so only drank, slowly, another bottle of the clear, foul liquid that moved through him and cauterized. His sunburned head itched and peeled. A woman walked by selling straw hats and he bought one, grateful for the shade on his face. An old man came by with a shopping bag and picked through the dry fountain, lifting coins from the cement, avoiding Jimmy's sickness which baked in the sun. Jimmy took the change he had remaining in his pocket and set it beside him on the edge of the fountain but the old man ignored the coins, twisting his bag closed, walking away across the plaza. A bus came and people got on and later in the day it returned and people got off. It grew dark and Jimmy slept sitting with his hat and in the morning when he opened his eyes someone had left additional coins beside him. He saw Jayne and Steven and the grandkids walking though the empty plaza. He saw Elaine and she was a young woman when she first stepped up off the street but she aged and sickened as she passed the fountain and at the other end of the plaza she was bald and burned and fell to the tiles and lay there in the sun and he was unable to stand and carry her away. He saw Denver Dan and Clarke and the whores and then he saw Henry March on the other side of the street and so he got to his feet and followed.

Away from the center of town to a long street, empty storefronts on one side, an open lot on the other. Henry March walked along the storefronts, his skin pale and his body old and slight as a ghost. He finally stopped at an open door and stepped inside. Jimmy felt like he had been walking forever. There was a rip in the brim of his hat and the sunlight streamed through. He walked with a hand shading his eyes under the hat and came to a storefront with pictures hung on the walls but there was no one inside and he continued on to the next doorway, which led to a dark cinderblock room. Henry March stood at the far end with his back to Jimmy, facing a sink, cupping water in his hands, lowering his face to the water. Jimmy had never coveted something as deeply as he coveted that water, the feel of his face in March's hands, the coolness on his skin, his eyes. He stepped into the room. He said, Hello, Hank, and March straightened his back and let his hands fall from his face and said, Hello, Jimmy.

March turned from the wall and looked at Jimmy and Jimmy lifted the gun out of his loose waistband and said, I don't have much time. I still have other people to see.

March said, I know.

Jimmy turned back to the bright rectangle of the open door and squinted into the light and could see kids in the open lot across the street kicking a soccer ball. He said, I've had dreams of this for years. This moment. Have you had dreams of this?

March said, Yes.

Jimmy watched the kids in the lot. I never pictured it like this, though, he said. A place like this.

He turned to the door. It looked like something dredged up from the bottom of the sea, claimed from a shipwreck, stern and weathered. He put his free hand on the door and said, Look at this fucking thing, pushing with all his remaining strength to get it closed. The only light in the room a thin white beam coming through the eyelet. March still standing on the other side of the room, facing Jimmy, his hands at his sides, water dripping. Jimmy wanted to get to that sink, wanted to feel Henry March's wet fingertips on his own burned skin. He looked at the back of the door, the mechanisms and bolts there, and smiled and said, I remember this, and he grasped the lever with his free hand and pushed it down, slamming it into place, pleased with the strength it took, the strength he still had, the door's tumblers turning and locking and then Jimmy said, Oh, Hank, as the lever came away in his hand.

8

Inés had shot the bald man, and Hannah had run from the house to the church in the plaza, waiting inside, frantic, trying not to scream or call out in some way that would give voice to what had happened. Everything in her alive and terrified. When the bus came and Dickie wasn't there she used the last of the money Bert had given her and paid for rides from one town to another, working her way north. Climbing into each car or pickup and wondering if the driver was someone who had been waiting for her. She thought back to the house and the family there and the bald man moving through their rooms like a bull. She had run without thinking and had left the gun behind in the bedroom and she prayed that one of the women found it before the children.

Up into Tijuana and across the border and feeling no sense of child-like safety at returning to her home country. Refusing to sleep. Drinking coffee and taking some of the small white pills the truck drivers offered, weighing the risk of the pills against the risk of sleep, making those kinds of calculations now. Up through San Diego and into Los Angeles, finishing her journey on a bus that let her off at the bench in front of her studio.

No one there, just mail, but nothing from Thomas. She went to the bank and stood in line and waited for the doors to burst open, animal masks waving guns. This was the way she saw the world now. She withdrew all of the money she had left and bought a bus ticket north. She did not contact Bert. She did not want to bring this thing to anyone else. She rode the bus and thought of Dickie riding a bus along the rancho road in Mexico. She wondered if he had come upon the ghost, and who that man had been.

At the house in Oakland, she dragged rugs out into the thin October light, wringing them dry, hanging them over the lower boughs of the oak tree in the backyard. She knew she could be found here, that whoever was after her would think to look in this place, but she could be found anywhere, they had proven that, and there was still a possibility that Thomas was nearby. In that way it didn't seem like a risk, coming home. There was no safe place anymore.

She mopped the kitchen and dining room floors, threw out the trash, swept the bugs into teeming garbage bags. Got on her hands and knees and scrubbed until it was a habitable space again. She lay with a pillow and a blanket on the floor of Thomas's bedroom. The sounds of traffic and laughter from the street, a radio playing, a blues singer she couldn't hear clearly enough to identify. Her body stiff and heavy, whispering to her brother in the dark until she slid beyond.

She took Thomas's maps and timetables from his room and crossed the bridge and rode the trains. She carried the most recent photograph of him that she could find in the house and asked passengers, conductors taking smoke breaks. At night she continued cleaning the house, eventually making her way to the basement. The leak from the kitchen had found its way down, soaking her father's empty desk. The smell of rotting wood, mildew. Hannah pulled his chair over to the high window on the cement wall. She climbed on top and banged the latch with the heel of her hand, breathed deeply of the night air. She'd snuck down here as a teenager to smoke. Another place she knew her mother wouldn't follow. Standing on the chair at the window, her nose pressed to the sill, the ancient smell of her father's cigarettes, captured history. The scent was still there now, Henry's smoke deep within the wood.

At night she lay on the floor of Thomas's room and read the books of poetry from her father's shelves. The poems themselves, the narrow islands of black ink on the white page, and then her father's handwriting surrounding the poems, filling the gutters and margins. Books within books. She read the poems without him and then she read the poems with him, allowing him to lead her around them, through them, within.

She rode the trains and saw the bald man everywhere. She saw Dickie everywhere, caught herself calling out to him a few times. She didn't see Thomas, didn't see anyone who looked like Thomas from any angle. She walked the streets toward the water and then up the steep incline because Dickie had told her that one of the entries in her father's ledger had read *Telegraph Hill*.

At the top she looked out across the Embarcadero to the dead prison and the bay and then turned and looked at the faces of the buildings on the hill. They were mostly new, recently built condominiums, pricey water views. The cement of the sidewalk was new. Someone had scribbled a name and a date into one of the squares with the end of a stick or a finger.

She waited, trying to feel something, ghosts, standing on the street until the shadows got too long and the light too low. Then she walked back down through the city and rode the train, scanning faces, asking questions, her brother's picture in her hands.

9

Dickie searched the coastal towns, looking for signs, a trail leading to where he would find her safe. He could not afford to sleep and so he bought pills from some of the American kids, and after a few days he couldn't come down, so he bought other pills, finally sleeping fitfully in the last car he would ever steal.

He made his way back to Los Angeles, to her studio. Hard to tell if she had been there. He hoped that she had gone to the man they'd borrowed the car from. Bart. Bert. He hoped that she'd gone to the police. He looked through the newspapers that had been delivered while they were gone and read the story about the mansion in Orange County that had gone up in flames, the bomb shelter in the yard that had been flooded with gas and set alight, that was still burning, sending a continuous plume of gray smoke into the sky over the sea, a long tower of ash ever rising.

At night he lay on the couch in her dark workroom and listened to her records, waiting for someone to come through the door.

Mail slid onto the gallery floor in the mornings. Nothing until there was a postcard, the same as many of the postcards fixed to her wall, a black-and-white photograph of an Oakland streetcar. Her brother's handwriting, which Dickie had grown to recognize. Much the same message as Thomas had written on all the others, but the date and the postmark were different and so Dickie set off north and east, hitchhiking because he needed to save the last of his money for pills. Los Angeles to Reno, Nevada. Reno to Salt Lake City. Salt Lake City to Laramie, Wyoming. Stepping out of an eighteen-wheeler in Chicago on the first day of winter, knowing nothing but the zip code on the postmark and the trains.

Days of riding. Nights. Changing lines, one end of the city to the other. He was offered money sometimes, from businessmen or housekeepers or high school kids, money which he refused and then began to accept. He needed to eat, to stay awake. He thought of Father Bill, thought of arriving at Bill's leafy suburban home and killing the man at his dining room table. He thought of Walter and Julian and Sarah and didn't know what he wished, his fantasies changing by the hour. The three of them knee-deep in the gasoline-filled shelter when they set it alight. The three of them out in the world, in the fresh air, free. He didn't know what he wished.

His beard had returned, his hair. He rode the Green Line, the Brown Line, the Red. He rode the Blue. He sat in a seat at the far end of a car and could no longer see, could no longer remember what he was looking for. His hands had been clenched into fists for so long that when he opened them there was a thin line of blood where his nails had bitten the skin. He wiped the blood on his jeans and lifted his hands again and set his face there, unable to catch his breath. Sinking his teeth into the heels of his hands to stop whatever noise was coming from his mouth. Hoping the other passengers couldn't hear him, see him. Shaking in his seat and making that noise and crying with shame.

There was a presence, close, the smell of cold air clinging to the skin of a jacket. There was weight there, someone sitting in the empty seat beside him. Dickie unable to lift his face from his hands, to stop the noise he was making. A shift in the weight. He felt a face move closer, warm breath on his hands, his cheeks. You do not need to open your eyes. You do not need to uncover your face. The voice low and close within the surrounding noise of the train. Let me be with you through this. Let me pray with you. Dickie shaking, making that terrible noise. The man's body beside his own.

Their legs touching at one place, at two.

CODA

In the gallery a man is touching her arm, complimenting the work. The woman beside the man smiles, nodding in agreement. The space is full, the crowd spilling out the doors and onto the sidewalk. Some sit on the bus stop bench with their drinks. The music comes from the record player in the other room and it is a woman singing in French, torch songs, war songs, and it is a sound she always imagines calling out of the open doors into the night.

Bert is standing by the refreshment table holding the baby and Hannah catches his eye and he smiles.

There was a postcard that morning from her brother in Chicago. A photograph of the river that cuts through the city, train tracks crossing the water. She wants to see him, wants proof that he is healthy and safe, but she does not want to force herself into his life. He has a new life now, one he created on his own. She has the postcard folded in the front pocket of her jeans. She always writes back, invites him to come when he's ready, to see her city, to meet his niece.

Some laughter from outside, more people squeezing into the gallery. She watches the door. She always watches the door when this record plays.

That morning while sweeping she found a small shard of glass in the corner of the gallery. She couldn't remember anything breaking in that room and then she remembered the wine bottle, the jagged glass held like a weapon. How long ago? Her hands on Dickie's shoulders, moving him back across the room to the couch on the other side.

How many times she has swept this room since that night, and yet today, a single sliver of glass, no longer than her thumbnail.

The song ends and one of Bert's friends steps to the record player in the work space. She expects to hear a different record, something loud and modern, but when the music returns it is the woman singing in French again, the sound filling the room, just below the laughter and conversation.

A man touches her arm and compliments the work on the walls.

She watches the door. She always watches the door.

AUTHOR'S NOTE

MKULTRA, the CIA's human experimentation project, was active from the 1950s through at least the late 1960s, and included clandestine safe houses in New York City and San Francisco, as well as tests on unwitting subjects in prisons and mental institutions.

In January 1973, all official project records were destroyed.

This novel, though inspired by fact, is a work of fiction.

ACKNOWLEDGMENTS

I am indebted to many writers and historians whose work informed and inspired this book:

Philip Agee's *CIA Diary*; *A Very Private Woman*, Nina Burleigh's biography of Mary Meyer; Alex Constantine's *Psychic Dictatorship in the U.S.A.*; *The Fifties* and *The Coldest Winter* by David Halberstam; *A Look Over My Shoulder* by Richard Helms and William Hood; *James Jesus Angleton*, Michael Holzer's masterful biography of the Agency's longtime head of counterintelligence; Ronald Kessler's *Inside the CIA*; *Cold Warrior* by Tom Mangold; *The CIA and the Cult of Intelligence* by Victor Marchetti and John Marks; *The Search for 'The Manchurian Candidate'* by John Marks, the seminal work on Project MKULTRA; David C. Martin's *Wilderness of Mirrors*; *The Man Who Kept the Secrets*, Thomas Powers's biography of CIA Director Richard Helms; *In the Care of Devils* by Sylvia Press; John Ranelegh's *The Agency*; *The Very Best Men* by Evan Thomas; Timothy Weiner's *Legacy of Ashes*; *Inside CIA's Private World*, edited by H. Bradford Westerfield; and *Molehunt*, David Wise's account of James Angleton's obsession with possible Soviet penetration within the CIA.

There was also much to be found in the files and Congressional Reports of the Church Committee and Rockefeller Commission, as well as in the archives at Stanford University.

ABOUT THE AUTHOR

Scott O'Connor was born in Syracuse, New York. He is the author of the novella *Among Wolves* and the novel *Untouchable,* for which he was awarded the 2011 Barnes & Noble Discover Award for fiction. He lives with his family in Los Angeles.